T0367492

FACE VALUE

DONNY R. CRAWLEY

ARCHWAY
PUBLISHING

Archway Publishing books may be ordered through booksellers or by contacting:

Archway Publishing
1663 Liberty Drive
Bloomington, IN 47403
www.archwaypublishing.com
1 (888) 242-5904

ISBN: 978-1-4808-7225-7 (sc)
ISBN: 978-1-4808-7226-4 (hc)
ISBN: 978-1-4808-7224-0 (e)

Library of Congress Control Number: 2019903429

Print information available on the last page.

Archway Publishing rev. date: 03/21/2019

This body of work is dedicated to the creative spirit and beautiful souls that I have surrounded myself with to elevate consciousness and be truly present in the moments that are the now. To allow those moments to shape me, guide me and ultimately elevate me to higher plateaus of peace and true happiness. I am forever grateful to those souls for their patience, words, encouragement, love and faith in me to simply be me and perhaps speak words that would possibly become difference making to those who wished to listen. 2 of those souls that have blessed me are my sons Justin and Mitchell for which I have immense love for and will always be grateful to be their father. This body of work is dedicated to all of my family for always being the lighthouse that is seen and sought during any storm to guide me home. This body of work is dedicated to my love Erica who always encouraged the words to be spoken, written, received and experienced. My twin flame has and continues to inspire me in all facets of life that allow me to cultivate, water and grow my garden that is whole, balanced, radiant and loved!

HIS mom and dad argued a lot while Jessie was growing up and when he looked back shortly following his life altering moment he wondered why the argument's that they would have did not disturb him more.

He guessed the way that every other family had a routine that they had become accustomed to, The Harrell Family had theirs.

His father telling his mom when to be home, what to make for dinner and what to think or not think had become natural.

When his mother did not listen he would punish her the way he would punish Jessie when he did not listen. These actions became as natural and routine to him as tradition or religion are to others.

Born Jessie Glenn Harrell March 22nd 1970, only son to James and Kelley Harrell who have been married for 6 years and living in Arlington Texas current day 1983.

They live in a very good neighborhood. The kind of neighborhood that has all nice cars in the driveways, the grass is always green, cut and edged around the sidewalk.

The kind of neighborhood that knows the names of the neighbors and their children. The kind of neighborhood that if you did not live here you found yourself from time to time driving through it to admire it and its residents.

Everything here is so right, down to earth and The American Dream,,,,,,,,

On the outside.

PART
ONE

1

JESSIE and his father were very close growing up and Jessie really looked up to him.

James taught his son how to read, how to balance himself when riding a bike and helped him with things he could not reach or understand. The ironic thing is that James is also teaching his son how to be a monster.

James is teaching his son prejudice, control, anger and hate without even knowing it.

Arlington has a lot of country side, it was not a small city by any means just undeveloped. New track home communities, shopping centers and a large mall complete with every clothing company, Spencer gifts and a movie theatre. There is a lot of open space and fields surrounding Madison Junior High School where Jessie is currently enrolled.

Jessie is sitting in 7th period math reviewing problems from the previous day. He sits staring into his notebook unable to understand the problem. On a 345 mile trip to Hoboken New Jersey The Winkleman Family averaged 57 m.p.h. so how long did it take them?

This really frustrated him because he truly wanted to understand what the class was reviewing and simply did not. Looking towards the window's in the classroom he could see and smell the rain falling down outside the window.

Jessie loved thunderstorms and found them to be fascinating . The rain was, in a sense, a purifier. The earth, he thought, was filled with dirt, garbage, debris and here comes the rain to cleanse its surface and purify its soul

Removing the problem he did not understand from his thoughts. He then cast his imagination, to picture himself, running through those fields chasing lightning. He saw himself running patch to patch arriving just seconds after the lightning had finished its deed moving on to the next

The bell rang awakening Jessie from his adventure . He and his friend Kevin Anderson, who lived in the neighborhood, would go into the field about a mile past the large weeping willow that the older kids in his school would gather to smoke cigarettes.

Jessie took from his bag 3 of the baseball cards that his grandfather had given him for his collection.

He produced a: 1979 Ozzie Smith, a 1979 Rollie Fingers and a 1980 Keith Hernandez.

Jessie was going to use his cards to trade with Kevin for a 7 inch dual bladed hunting knife that he found buried in his Fathers closet.

The knife was as fascinating to Jessie as the rain that poured onto Arlington that afternoon.

The knife was like a key to Jessie.

A key that could open things. Thing's you could use to see the inside of from the outside and Jessie was going to use this new treasure to open things, just like a key. He returned home at about 5:15. No one was home so he opened the refrigerator and made some chocolate milk before going into the living room to watch some television

He heard a car pull into the driveway and when he saw that it was his mother he quickly turned off the television picked up his books from off of the floor and opened the book to that same problem that had troubled him 3 hours earlier.

His mom came in the front door and said nothing. She threw her keys onto the kitchen table and headed to her bedroom.

She returned from her bedroom with a change of clothes and a deep breath before finding Jessie at the table to give him a hug and a kiss.

She then sat beside him and simply stated "My day was hell". Jessie asked "Will you help me with my math?" and she replied "I will honey, but after dinner okay, right now i just need to relax before getting dinner started" and then continued complaining in detail about her day.

Kelly Harrell was a customer service representative for one of the large clothing stores in The Arlington Mall. I guess that listening to everyone else's problems day in and day out would bring even the happiest person down to earth but she was not happy to begin with.

When Jessie was younger it seemed as though she was happy but as he got older he began to see a mold. A very well rehearsed laugh and smile.

To what extent or depth that she was unhappy he did not know but he was becoming more and more receptive to it the older he was becoming.

That night after dinner his homework was finished, He still did not understand that same problem in math but it was finished and had the correct answer."Thank you Mom!" he said

He left the room and went to the front yard with a sharpening stone and began sharpening and admiring his new friend. From the porch he could see the light on in the garage from underneath the door and through the decorative small windows that lined the front.

The garage was where his father James spent the majority of his time when he was home.

Kelly had fallen asleep on the couch watching an episode of Matt Houston and was still there when Jessie was approached and told by his father to go to bed at 9:30 p.m.. He was unable to sleep right away and it was only a little after 10:00 so he went down the stairs to the kitchen to eat some cereal before going back to bed.

When he approached the bottom stair the house was flickering with light. He then realized that it was coming from the television still on inside the living room but the sound was turned down.

He walked towards the living room and as he approached he saw his mother lying with her clothes that she was wearing earlier partially on her but what was strange to him was that she was still sleeping. He would take one more step and stop immediately freezing right in his step towards the living room when he saw his father in there knelt down on one knee beside her. He was kissing and touching her partially clothed sleeping body but he could not see Jessie.

Jessie started to take steps back more toward the darkness of the remaining part of the house and each step that he took backwards he could not help but think or ask himself if he ever touched him like that when he was sleeping.

He saw her stomach move as he was kissing her harder and then she spoke very much under her breath " James, I hate it when you get like this ". " Please stop I just want to go to sleep ".

He then stood and planted his knee on the other side of her stomach and used both of his hands to keep hers down.

She then said the word "no!" 3 times with the 3rd being more forceful in tone and body movement but never did she shout or raise her voice.

Jessie remained standing there in that darkness thinking that all families were different maybe other families acted this way as well. " Should I say something? " he asked himself still frozen

It seemed play-full and again no different than how he directed her other actions so many times before.Jessie knew about sex and this was again just another form of his father's will is what he kept saying to himself when suddenly she broke free and ran past the kitchen, not seeing him, and up the stairs.

He was again frozen there and then watched his father slowly stand up, wipe his mouth, calmly run his hands though his hair he then took one deep breath. Jessie, from the darkness where he stood, watched a smile appear on his face as he approached the foot of the stairs and then proceeded up them towards the bedroom where his mother had gone.

2

UNABLE to open the locked bedroom door he, in one swift kick, took the door from its hinges.

She had locked herself in the bathroom and you could hear her weeping and crying in unstable breaths through the door.

Throughout the course of their marriage James had taken and dominated many things from Kelly. He had taken her self respect, her self esteem, her liberties and ideals.

He demanded many things of his wife and expected them to be given without question or exception.

Kelly had very much loved her husband and was always overwhelmed with the idea of a perfect family. James was everything she had dreamed of when they first met. He was cordial and romantic. She had never met anyone with his drive or confidence and she found him intoxicating.

They were married and then had Jessie. He did provide for her and their son very well. Financially that is.

James had a good deal of money. More than she had ever seen or knew when they met and it only grew through his drive. His drive had paid for the 2 very nice cars in the driveway, the beautiful 2 story house they live in and the trust fund that he had set up for Jessie.

James had another side of him that became apparent not long after their marriage. Those few and far between incident's that were not so far from her own upbringing.

James, standing outside the door, began to speak to his vulnerable wife.

"You are my wife Kelly", "Till death do us part" You are to honor, to love and to obey!". "When I want love, you will not keep it from me Kelly "!! Lowering his voice to almost a whisper his last statement was "Open this fucking door right now."

Kelly opened the door knowing that had she not, the love he would take from her that night would have been far more physical and violent and not to mention waking Jessie.

What she did not know was that Jessie was awake and had seen.

James raped his wife that night and thought nothing of it. None of the times that he had taken her love, had he found it wrong. He simply thought that he was a man and she was his wife therefore everything of hers was for the taking.

Jessie's role at Madison Junior High was an average one, the one thing that he did have going for him was his fathers money.

Jessie was not active in school sports so he was not considered to be athletic. He had some trouble in his classes so he did not excel academically, but he was not a trouble maker or a rebel either.

He did not pick fist fights or smoke cigarettes and maintained a C-B average throughout his entire time at Madison.

He made plans with his friends Saturday evening to see Poltergeist at The Parkway Theatres, where the greater population of his 7th grade class would be found on a Friday evening.

Billy Howe was the only on that had a date that evening but his date Sheila, ran into a bunch of her friends on the way to the theatre and told them they should all hook up after afterwards.

The movie let out and every one of them talked in the parking lot about wanting to have their own homes taken over by spirits from the afterlife. Sheila was talking with her friends, while the others re-enacted parts of the movie, about going with us into the fields that were closer to their house track.

Billy got his older brother to buy a 12 pack of Budweiser and Jessie had taken a bottle of Cooks champagne from his parents bar and left in the fields on the way to the movie.

They all sat in the fields drinking and talking but the highlight of that evening was now all about one of Sheila's friends named Amber.

Amber went to his school but he had never talked to her before. She was a tall girl with long brown hair to the middle of her back and big brown eyes.

He loved the way she smiled and how easy it was to talk to her. This was the very first time he had ever experienced such a self conscious need to be liked by someone.

Jessie got home about 11:15 a few minutes past his curfew but all of the lights were off so everyone must have been asleep. He went to sit down in his father's recliner that his mother had bought him on Father's Day 2 years ago. This was the most comfortable spot in the living room. He grabbed the remote and turned on the television changing the channel to M.T.V. where there was a segment being done on Metallica performing in Oakland, California. He went to bed around 1:45 but still thinking about his meeting with Amber.

Jessie woke up on Sunday morning with the smell of breakfast filling the house but he could hear his father outside mowing the lawn which was a sad reminder that this was his job to do and his father would be sure to remind of that as soon as he saw him.

Walking into the kitchen he could hear the sound of a football game that was on in the living room. He walked past the table made eye contact with his mom but said nothing and picked up the phone connected to the wall. He continued to walk pulling the phone cord out till he was in the room next to the living room. Jessie was calling Billy to see if they could everyone from last night together for a football game back at Madison once he was done helping his dad with the lawn.

Before hanging up the phone and dragging out the phone conversation he finally got to the real reason for the call. He wanted to ask Billy to ask Sheila, his date last night, what Amber thought about Jessie and let him know today when they met up at the school.

He listened to Billy laugh and make fun of him for what felt like another 10 minutes before agreeing to it.

"Good morning. " he said to his mom when he returned to the kitchen to hang the phone back up. "What is for breakfast?" he asked as he approached the sink to look out the atrium window to view the backyard and see if he could tell if his dad had only done the front yard.

"Egg's, bacon, hash browns and fruit " she replied before adding " now go outside and help your father. " OK " he replied and headed towards the door. Before reaching the door Jessie's mom asked " Ask Sheila if Who said anything about who"? Jessie turned to display a smile but said nothing and turned back around and proceeded through the door towards the front yard where his father was still mowing the lawn.

Jessie grabbed the weed eater, the rake and the edger from the garage and carried them to the front. James was almost finished with the front when he saw Jessie and turned off the mower.

"Nice of you to get up "he started " it is your responsibility to mow the lawn, not mine, correct"? " Yes " he replied providing the shortest answer because no matter what he had said he was wrong and would be reprimanded for it.

"You are given an allowance for little responsibility, all you have to do is mow the lawn Jess ", " that is all you have to do " " so get over here and finish your god damn responsibility". He finished, picking up the back end of the mower and thrusting it back to the ground causing it to bounce. He then walked away passing Jessie with a fast enough pace that it sent a breeze rushing by him where he stood.

Jessie finished the other ½ of the lawn his father had not and was putting the mower away when his mom yelled to him that breakfast was ready and to come on inside and eat.

They all sat at the dinner table. The table was wood, circular in shape and had a center leaf in it to accommodate the food she had made. The room was so bright from all the kitchen and patio door blinds being open filling the entire area with natural light. You could not help but look forward to eating Saturday or Sunday morning breakfast at The Harrell house. James or Kelly would cook each weekend and this too became another one of their traditions. This morning his mom had prepared yet another amazing tasting and looking meal. The table was set to perfection as if there was a photographer coming to shoot the home for red book or Better Home's and Garden's.

The placemats, the napkin rings, the silver and plate-ware. Then you get to the meal. She had cooked the bacon, eggs and hash browns, toast and fruit as stated but there was an art to how she presented the table for them each weekend as if to paint her portrait so it never left and always reminded her of what she had vividly seen in her mind again and again growing up of what the perfect family would do and say to each other around this table each weekend.

The phone rang during breakfast. " Hello.", James answered . " Is Jessie there?" a boy on the other line asked ? " Jessie, it is for you" his father said handing him the receiver. It was Billy calling back as promised to tell him that Sheila did speak to Amber and she told him that if he wanted to do something she would be at home but would meet him somewhere if he wanted.

Jessie finished the brief conversation and when hanging up the phone he had felt the sense of excitement rushing through his body that was equivalent to how he would feel each night before Christmas when he was growing up.

Jessie turned back towards the table where everyone was seated and still eating. His father met his eyes and before Jessie had said anything James stated " You have chores to do and choice to make ." " Dad please. " he started before James interrupted " we discussed this outside already now you either go and finish your chores or you will spend not only this weekend but a few more in your room".

"Oh Jim let him go, it is with a girl" Kelly declared but in a school girl tone that was low and was accompanied with a crack of a smile coming from the corner of her mouth as she made eye contact with Jessie.

"Kelly", James returned with what was almost a humorous tone, like he was going to start laughing all while buttering another piece of toast and not making eye contact with either of them at the table. " Let us not forget who it is that is the decision maker in this home" " So,he continued, is there anything else on the matter that you would care to comment on" " No" she stated making eye contact with him as he looked up beginning to bite into the toast he had meticuliously just prepared. " Jessie go on outside then and finish your chores " James stated ending the conversation.

Jessie rose from the table, carried his plate to the sink and exited the silent kitchen until that silence was broken by the sound of the door shutting behind him as he left the house towards the garage.

Kelly rose then as well to begin clearing the table when she was met by James who stood in front of her as she turned to place the items into the fridge and trash. Their eyes staring into one another while silence still filled the air " he could have finished " she started to say and before any more of that sentence was completed the sound of a ruler hitting a desk as his hand left her face and her body met the floor. " Don't you ever, he said leaning over her with his voice agitated but not loud, question my judgment or contradict me in front of him or anyone else ever again" " Do you understand me " he said leaving her violated body lying half cocked on the kitchen floor trying everything in her power to control and overcome her tears.

3

JAMES caught up with Jessie in the garage as he was filling the mower with gasoline to complete the remainder of the lawn.

"How much more do have to do, on your chores"? He asked Jessie.

Jessie went through the items remaining " well where is it that you are in such a hurry to get to that you cannot wait until your responsibilities to me and this home and fulfilled." James inquired standing over him with his arms crossed.

"I met a girl " he said " A Girl His father said, his voice elevated" " A girl " Jessie repeated again.

"I met her last night after the movies and she wanted to see if I could meet her today and I am not trying to get out of my chores " He finished with his voice elevating a little

"I will do them, but can I go see her today and do the rest of what I have to do when I get back, I won't be gone long"?

"Jessie, his father started again now standing stoic in his posture, " if a man dropped everything he was doing every time a woman wanted to see him or if the men in this country, that built this country reacted the way you are right now where do you think this country would be"?

He then leaned over with his hands on his thighs nearing Jessie so close that he could see every blood vessel and speck of color in his father's eyes. " Men, son have built, sailed and discovered the land in which you and I stand on today " he said now straightening his back and standing up right. He took a deep breath and a step forward before he continued on. " Men are the decision makers son ". " I am the decision maker in this home and one day Jess you too will become the decision maker in your home and you are not to let a woman or any one for that matter stand in the way of your decisions or dreams. Can you understand what I am saying to you son"?

He asked turning to face him again and placing each hand on each side of his shoulders." Of course " Jessie replied not wanting any further confrontation or conversation regarding the matter. " Finish the back yard and I will finish the rest for you so you can go " James said removing his hands and turning away. " are you sure ?" Jess asked surprised. " Yes. " His father had said adding "you think about what I said" as Jessie started to run towards the backyard with the weed eater and cord " Think about what I said " his father yelled as Jessie was already around the side of the house but heard him as did his mother in the kitchen cleaning the items that had spilled and broken on the floor. What was it that he had said to him she thought and asked her-self. What is he telling Jessie?

Jessie finished the backyard quickly then called to start on the address or location of where to meet Amber. While Sheila and Billy worked on that he showered and then proceeded to try on everything in his closet,,,,,,,,twice. He received a call from Billy with the address which was her home but Billy asked " Are you still going to come and play football"? " Of course he replied " Lying, all he wanted to do was go and see her. He decided on a pair of levis and a Iron Maiden t shirt and then left the house for hers.

The conversation with his father was running though his mind but he still could not get to her house fast enough. He kept repeating her address in his mind 1654 Rosalie, 1654 Rosalie and then began to fantasize about them being along because as he arrived and walked up the driveway he had noticed that there were no cars in the driveway.

Amber opened the door smiling and made a whimsical comment like " Won't you come in " "Don't mind if I do " he replied. Entering the Clevinger home the first thing that Jessie had noticed was the hallway filled with family portraits. They were very proud of what appeared to be their only child and her face was very much a part of the homes décor.

The home had all of the ambiance of a cabin in the mountains. Full of oak tables, oak beams, fireplace mantle and plants throughout. There were 2 cocker spaniels he noticed through the sliding door.

"What are their names " he asked " The big one is Mammoth, he is a boy and the other is Zion, she is a girl" she stated proudly, holding each hand clasped tightly to her chest endearingly. " Do you like animals "? She asked him

"I have a natural attraction to them" he said jokingly. " Mammoth and Zion are 2 of my parents favorite vacation spots" she offered " Have you and your family ever been to either of them"? She continued " No " he answered hoping that she would further explain and continue to conversation. She was great at this he thought, she was so comfortable, confident and in control. " We go skiing in Mammoth every winter if possible " " and Zion he added quizingly " well Zion we do more in the summer for hiking and this is located in Utah" she offered.

Jessie could not help but again just feel comfortable with her. They talked and watched t.v. for a about an hour when she said " you should probably get going, my mom and dad will be home in a little bit and they do not like it when I have people here if they are not here".

She risked getting into trouble for him he thought. She liked him and he liked her which made the trip over here and any additional words his father had for him about coming worth it,,,,definitely.

She began to walk him out the front the door and towards the end of the drive way when Jessie asked hopefull " Can I have your phone number to call you so I no longer have to have Sheila do it"?

"O.K. " she replied then added with a serious look " you cannot call after 9:00."

"I won't " he promised with a smile " I will call you tonight, O.K."?

"I will be waiting" she said smiling with a higher pitched voice, her thumbs in her back pocket and swaying so softly left to right causing her hair to also move back and forth from her neck and face.

Gripping firmly on the piece of paper she had written her phone number he began his journey home.

It was 4:38 when he arrived at home and his father was still in the garage. The garage door was open so he caught him as he was walking past to go into the house.

Jessie not saying anything still walking heard his father say to him " Billy had called and wanted to know why you did not show up with the others today".

"What did you or mom tell him"? He asked.

"You can thank me later, I did not say anything about you running off like you had never seen a girl before" His father returned.

Jessie continued to move towards the front door with his head down but stated " Thanks dad " for the sake of the brief conversation.

"Next time Jessie, have her meet you half way at least, do not go running to her every time she calls" James was saying to him as he watched Jessie continue to approach the door with a look of attempted escape.

"Be a man is all I am saying son, be a man " he continued until Jessie stopped now and began to look up as if the conversation was going to continue regardless if he was participating in it or not but then his father ended with " Your mom is almost finished with dinner so go on inside wash your hands,o.k."

Jessie ended with "o.k." and went inside the house. He loved how the house smelled when she cooked " what is for dinner? " he called out as he walked towards the kitchen where his mom was bouncing back and forth between the stove and sink. " We are doing Chicken Fried Steak, mashers, green beans and a salad " she said looking at him with anticipation regarding his time with his new friend.

"You hungry?" she asked deciding not to jump right into the questions she really wanted the answers to but settled on at least one before sending him to wash up.

"What is her name? " is all she asked and let him take it from there

"Amber " is all that he did share at that moment and walked towards the restroom to wash his hands.

The majority of the dinner conversation revolved around Jessie. They discussed his homework, grades and his rapport with his teachers.

"I do not think I need to remind you of the significance of each semester and how it will impact your future now do, I Mr. Harrell"? His father asked in a tone that was each combative and concerned.

He was always concerned with Jessie's school activities more so now with the attention his father was getting due to the success of his company. The growing success of his architecture firm which he was head of was also making him more prominent in the Arlington community so Jessie understood the constant attention on him. His actions would ultimately reflect on everyone seated at the dinner table.

Following dinner Jessie offered to do the dishes which mad his mom happy. He liked doing things for her and he really felt that she deserved it.

After finishing the dishes Jess went to his room to prepare for Monday by getting his clothes ready. He checked to see if his complexion was clear,,,,well clear enough. He then sat in dilemma if he should or should not call her and when he considered what his father had spent the day telling him he decided against it.

Waking up Monday morning even before his Father had come in to make sure he was up was a great way to start the morning, he thought to himself.

Clothes laid out ready to put on, homework is done, wide awake and full of excitement, Jessie felt so positive today, so responsible and in control of his life. James had left for work. It was 2 minutes till 7:00a.m. Jessie left his bedroom and went to the kitchen and poured his very first ever cup of coffee from the pot his father had left behind.

He turned on the television in the kitchen to break up the silence in the house and just before hitting the power button he heard, what he thought or sounded like, someone throwing up. Huh he thought, laughing it off and considering it to be a delirious side effect of the unusual mood he was in.

He hit the power button and watched a few minutes of the morning news and drinking his first cup of coffee. He shut off the lights, t.v. and locked the door departing for school 35 minutes early and feeling very mature.

The noise he had laughed off earlier was his mother Kelly. She was usually gone before Jessie but was not feeling well at all and was in the bathroom in fact throwing up. She waited a few hours but her discomfort failed to cease so she called her physician.

Dr. Jason Talbot Helms had been her physician since Jessie was born and treated her for many accidents she and Jessie had there-after. He always fit her in at the most convenient times. She was in fact the ideal patient: Accident prone and always paid in cash.

"Kelly " he said entering the room with all of the bravado of an entertainer taking the stage. " what can I do for you this afternoon"? " I understand that you are not feeling well" still showing every tooth in his mouth, he reached to her. " Come, let us make you better, yes ".

Kelly laughing to herself how funny he is with his European accent.

Kelly truly enjoyed the Dr's company, even under what the circumstances may be, she felt like a woman again well for an hour anyway. It was the only fantasy that she really had. He was handsome, gave her attention and made her feel important which when compared to feeling necessary it was worth paying for, she thought.

He performed his usual routine on Kelley and they conversed over issues such as Jessie, Jessie's grades, her work and her husband which when asked was quickly danced over.

"I do not understand Jason I am not aware of a virus or flu going around".

"I am eating right", she explained.

"I don't know I woke up this morning and it just hit me."

"I feel terrible, I honestly have not felt this bad since I was pregnant with Jessie!!!!!!

Within seconds of hearing those words leave her mouth, she,

without question and beyond any doubt, knew within herself what those test results he was running would determine.

"YOU'RE FUCKING PREGANT".

Thinking all at once of the many times James was relentless with his punishment during her first pregnancy. Maybe this could be the answer to all of her prayers she asked herself.

Maybe learning of this baby he could repent and find redemption for all that he did and be a better father to this one.

"Kelly."

"Hello in there, are you alright my dear. "? The Dr was asking.

"Yes, sorry, I'm fine " she finally responded. " I have to run these test to the lab, go ahead and get dressed and I will return shortly, okay." he said leaving the room.

As she buttoned her flannel her eyes staring incoherently at the wall, not seeing the wall, looking past the wall. The voice inside of her, the voice that lives within the blackest most morbid regions of us all simply said. "JUST KILL HIM " then repeated " JUST KILL HIM"

4

WALKING his route to school, his mind raced with positive energy. He would be trying harder in school, maybe taking Spanish next semester. I will need that for college he said aloud even though he was walking alone.

His goal list increased by the second: Try out for football or track and help out more at home. " I am going to be the best person I can be he said to himself as a smile, a great big smile appeared on his face.

Passing through the pillared gates with the words Madison Junior High School bolted to it he walked with a confident stride making his way to his locker. Saying " Hello " to only a few passing classmates he then took his History and English book and closed his locker door. He paused there and stood for a moment to see if he could see Amber before heading to his first class but did not.

The bell rang while he was finishing his notes on Napoleon. He gathered his things and made his way to the hallway. He knew where to meet Billy, down the stairs by the rear lockers, before getting to 2nd period.

Billy turned and walked towards him. Jessie looking passed him as he approached. He saw Amber further down the hall. Billy was saying something about the game Jessie had missed but Jessie was not listening.

All he could hear was his father's voice as she was right there in front of him with another guy, a guy he did not know or recognize but there she was touching him and introducing him to all of her friends. Jessie had not even met most of her friends even though they just met he felt a great deal of rage starting to build and the voice of his father was drowned out by his own stating " I really thought that she liked me, that fucking bitch"!

Those words getting louder in his head, everyone is so close. His breathe is getting shorter because of everyone around him in the hall.

"I can't breathe. " He says out loud

"What " Billy asked un clear of what Jessie had said.

Jessie turned and started to walk in the other direction. Walking faster and faster until he was running through the hall. Amber turned away from who she was talking to and saw someone running down the hall. She went over to Billy to ask him who or what that was about because he was closer than she was. " Who was that? " she asked him

"That was Jessie " he told her

"What happened " she asked now a little concerned

"I don't know! " Billy responded in a manner that she was suggesting it may have been something he had done.

Jessie was running down the hall passing everyone, knocking books from the hands of those he ran into. Out of the gates he had passed a little over an hour ago with such optimism and not knowing his destination, he just kept running.

He lay awake that night in his bed. The sheets all off of him and the room filled with darkness and silence.

The silence was first broken by the sound of his troubled and angry heart beat pounding from his chest. Minute after minute passed on his clock, impossible to sleep and every time he started to or felt like he was going to fall asleep a barking from outside his window would wake him.

That dog would bark then the others in the neighborhood would bark. Minute after minute bark, bark, bark. "Oh god please make it stop " thought's inside of him

"Why is this happening to me", " All I want to do is sleep".

He arose from his bed placed on foot on the floor and then the other. He stood and walked towards one of his speakers. Jessie pulled the front cover off of one of his speakers and pulled from inside the knife he had gotten from Kevin and since nicknamed " The Key"

He then went through his dresser and took from it all of the black clothes he could find. He used the clothes he had changed out of and stuffed them with other clothes from the dresser in order to make a mannequin style body double.

He stuffed socks with other socks until he formed a foot and attached it to the bottom of the leg that would be exposed from the covers. Standing back he then took a minute to admire his quick and crafty work.

Jessie then turned to the window and began his exit. He slowly lifted the screen once the window was open and left the house leaving behind a model of himself in the bed in the event anyone woke up and checked on him.

He made his way around the darker side of the house so quietly even tip toeing. Jessie removed all of the horrible thoughts of not being able to sleep or seeing Amber with that other guy and exchanged them with fantasies of being on the run from the law or going into war to rescue p.o.w's just like Chuck Norris or Rambo.

He made his way into the Steller's backyard cautiously hugging the wall. He ran in between cars and behind tree's and proceeded up the block to where the maddening sound of bark, bark, bark that prevented him from sleeping was coming from.

He quietly made his way to the fence and pulled from his jacket some of the leftovers from dinner that night. He located the largest boulder from the rock quarry of the house next door and carried it to the fence. He then started to dig slowly and quietly under the fence until there was enough of a space to slide or tunnel those leftovers to the dog.

The hole was dug the food is in place and the boulder was aligned with the hole so Jessie then begins to make meow sounds to attract the attention of the dog to where he is waiting.

"Meow-meow".

The dog starts to bark again but comes closer to where the meow sounds are coming from then picks up the scent of the food. Jessie hears the dog licking the stuffed peppers he had placed for him. He lifts the 30 pound boulder to the top of the fence directly above where the food was placed and let it go.

The boulder crashes down and hammered the dog's skull.

The dogs were barking and causing other dogs to be barking so it made it difficult to hear if anyone was listening to what was presently happening.

The defenseless creature cried into the night " Arghhh-Arghh " The animal only cried twice before Jessie had jumped over the fence, grabbed the dogs snout, to avoid any further crying or barking, turned the dog over and using his key he opened the beautiful creature like a suitcase.

Jessie had trouble waking up the next morning and so did his mom which sent James through the house in anger first thing. Jessie could hear him in the bedroom yelling.

Out of bed now Kelly scrambled around the room locating a top and shoes to wear. James grabbed her hand and pulled her to him in a circular motion then grabbed the back of her head as her body came tumbling into him.

His hand was holding the back of her head with such a tight grip. He starred into her eyes, her body trembling and tears streaming like a river flow down her cheeks. " I'm sorry" crying harder and her voice cracking "I'm sorry" is all she could get out. James still holding her trembling body loosened his grip and simply said " Don't be late for work " as he let her go and walked out of the bedroom door.

5

J ESSIE had left the house without eating and just felt like his day was going to be shit. He was hungry, his dad was being an asshole first thing in the morning and he still had to go and face Amber

On his way to school Jessie fumbled in his head with questions and sayings. " Tomorrow is a new day " was what was running through his head and he just felt like whoever had made that one up did not think it all the way through. If something is wrong than you what deal with it all day because tomorrow is a new, meaning better, day but today you're fucked.

What he kept thinking was that it is more the minutes and hours instead of a day meaning your outlook or attitude can change in minutes and seconds good or bad. Like yesterday how fast he went from optimism to running out of the school and today is a new day but still not better so instead of it being tomorrow that will be better he was hoping for one of those minutes or seconds that could change it back or at least better how he felt.

He entered the school with a low profile making his route to his locker. He deposited what he did not need into the locker and took from it his History book. He closed his locker and saw Amber walking down the hall in the opposite direction with her friends and the stranger he saw yesterday.

The clock read 5 till so he took the long way to his class using the stairs instead of just walking down the same hall they were. He was again trying really hard to concentrate on what explorer went down what river or sailed what ocean to discover whatever. Lunch came and he purchased 2 packages of chocolate doughnuts and 2 chocolate milks and walked towards the courtyard hoping to not see anyone.

He heard someone calling his name from not so far away and behind him. " Jessie " " Hey Jessie wait up " they called again.

Turning around he saw Amber, Elaine, Janet and this stranger. Amber was smiling uncontrollably and trying to fix her hair from the blowing breeze.

"I have been looking all over for you "Amber told him " Where have you been and what happened to you yesterday" ? She asked in front of everyone

"You should have tried out for track as fast as you were running " Janet added and got a laugh from the audience that was present.

"Jessie, this is my cousin from California, Michael" she said " He is going to be staying with us for awhile" " What's up the stranger." Michael said stepping forward and extending his hand.

The relief inside of him was somewhat like every alarm clock in the world going off in unison. Taking his hand he erupted " It is nice to meet you Ambers cousin" She was worried about me he thought to himself and could not be happier.

Never before would he have suddenly had the guts to walk to her, grab her hand and pull her toward him until no space or air fit between them.

Her eyes looked into his and he kissed her taking her breathe and the breath of those around them away. She had always dreamed of being kissed that way and Jessie had always dreamed of having the guts to do it. Jessie did not know where that came from but finding that courage and using it made him feel more in control than he had ever felt.

As the moment started to fade Amber and Jessie could each hear clapping and someone saying

"Did you just see that? " and " Uh huh ".

Pulling away from her with their eyes still staring into one another she asked him " What was that for?"

"I just really missed you " he replied

"Jessie. " she said with her eyes moving down to the ground embarrassed and flattered then back to his " What happened yesterday?"

Still meeting her gaze he said " I will tell you later, it is kinda personal.

Ambers 2 friends standing there started laughing when one of them said " you can see a doctor for that " personal thing ."

"Shut up " he fired back but joining in on the laughing that everyone there was enjoying from his afternoon entertainment.

Walking Amber home that same afternoon Jessie was stumbling through an effort to explain what happened yesterday and the feeling of jealously he had when he saw her with Michael. Amber's first reaction to Jessie's confession was laughter and then she felt flattered again by the sweetness of his affection and his honesty to tell her.

"Jessie " she started while they walked together eyes not on each other more so on the road ahead of them.

"I just met you and I do like you. " I like you a lot and I cannot believe that you kissed me today " She said in a exasperated voice but still not making eye contact.

"That was the best kiss I have ever had!"

"Really? " he erupted asking excitedly.

"Yes, I would not say that if I did not mean it"

Jessie found himself searching inside of him for the guts that consumed him earlier to ask her "the big question" and not sure of her response found himself throwing it out there.

"Do you want to go out with me, you know like boyfriend and girlfriend ?" he exhaled and then began holding his breath waiting for a response.

"Well we do not really know each other that well yet " Jessie's smile began to fade and he returned to breathing.

"But I would like to go out with you again so we can get to know each other more. Maybe you can ask me again later."

"Fair enough" Jessie replied with his smile beginning to return. " I want to take you out on Friday night, maybe dinner and you are going to tell me your life story then I am going to ask you to marry me " he added which made her smile and laugh again

Kelly looked at the dashboard clock on her Volvo and noticed that she had been sitting in her car, in the driveway with the engine running and starring out the windshield at nothing for about a half hour.

She shut of the engine still no thought of what to do with her life, her body and her baby.

Her mind filled with the memories of her first pregnancy. How supportive she wished that James would and should have been. He chose instead to be verbally abusive with name-calling, being insensitive and threats. He backed those up with physical force that she was subjected to time and time again.

She felt so sad thinking of all of those memories, she was still a newlywed and felt that she it should have been the happiest of times for them. Married and my first child on the way was all that she had wanted but the thought of returning to that with another child did not only make her sad but it terrified her too.

Maybe this time would be different she asked herself, if that is possible.

I know he does not mean it. Maybe it was the pressure of work and the first child that was too much for him to mentally endure. He was the only one working and having to take care of everything there was no one for him to take his anger, fears and aggression out on but me.

"Maybe this is what we need" she was telling herself.

"I know" she continued out-loud still in the Volvo in the driveway with the engine now off

"I know he feels bad about the way he treated me and the things that he said but it is difficult for him to talk about it, so we don't"

Leaving off on that thought she left the car and made her way into the house. She walked through the front entrance and turned to shut the front door.

Turning back to face the beautifully decorated home she tried effortlessly to imagine the glow of what a child could bring to The Harrell Home.

While picturing that portrait she is hit with the reality of her problem. She stands frozen in that same spot, lip shuddering and tears streaming down her face.

The real nature of her problem, the truth is her fear, her terror of being able to stand up and walk out of the crippling shadow her husband has placed her in.

She starts to take steps backward almost removing herself from the situation and not even a half step behind her, her back meets the door she closed as she came into the home. Her back flush against the door her legs give out from under her as she begins to slide to the ground.

She curls up her legs so that her knees are in her chest. Her arms wrap around her legs. Her eyes closed tightly but no match for the tears that surpass streaming to flowing she clutches her uncontrollably trembling body. She has never felt this cold in her lifetime and there is nothing and no one there to keep her warm.

6

JESSIE had coordinated a football game after school and invited Amber's cousin Michael in an effort to get to know him better. The boys all lined up to be picked by their delegated captains for teams so Jessie made small talk asking Michael why he had come to Arlington but since Jessie was usually picked 3rd the conversation fell short.

Michael was the last one picked, of course but only because he was the new kid. For a bunch of 8th graders playing football in the park you would think they were professional athletes worried about the draft or a Super Bowl ring.

There was a coin toss, shotgun formation, play calling and routes being run. It was all in fun though. Jessie was one of the receivers and Michael was just asked to rush until the others saw how fast he was and then asked to run some routes to see if he could catch. Jessie and Michael each had good games with plenty of plays worthy of discussion after the game. Michael had gained instant acceptance for his game performance,

Every-one liked him.

Walking home Jessie and Michael continued their conversation they started earlier but it was mostly Michael that was doing all of the talking. " Man it is great to be out here " " In California everyone is so worried about the brand of jeans or shirts they wear or how their hair looks and who they talk to".

"I mean " he continued no room for interjection anywhere yet " The girls in California pretend to be so prim and proper and don't get me wrong they are pretty just like in the movies you know? "

"and they give really good head, do the girls here give good head? " he asked Jessie and the sudden pause was so quick and he was still stuck on the question or knowing what he meant he just responded with " Yeah "

"Good " Michael started right back in " I like getting my dick sucked and all but seriously most of the girl's there are so full of whining and complaining" he finished shaking his head.

Jessie walked beside him in amazement. He had never spoken to anyone like Michael before. The guys in the locker room would brag about the girls they claimed they had been with or wished they had but something, he thought to himself, told him that Michael was not kidding or making it up.

Jessie was also grateful that Michael had revealed what he meant when he said the word " head " therefore avoiding having to ask him or Michael thinking he did not know.

They came to where their paths would end on route to each of their homes and ended with a "later " and " I'll see you tomorrow".

Jessie lay on his bed in his room thinking about what he and Michael had said. Man on the Silver Mountain was playing on his radio and the room was dark with the exception of the remaining sunlight from the fast fading sunset.

The room becoming darker and darker by the minute. He just kept asking himself how Michael knew so much more about girls than he did if they were the same age.

I have had girls shirts off he thought to himself "But I have never had my dick sucked" he said out loud.

He then picked up the phone and with all of the sexual frustration in the world running through every part of his body he dialed the numbers 963 – 7079 and waited for a response. " Hello " the voice answered. " Is Amber there?"

"Yes, who is calling? " the voice answered.

"This is Jessie " he stated

"Hang on a second please " and you could hear that person that answered the phone call to her "Amberrrr". " She is coming " the voice came back onto the line.

"Thank you " he returned.

"Hello " she said into the phone.

"Hi it's Jess"

"What are you doing? " she asked him but sounded pleased to hear from him.

"Wanting to talk to you, what are you doing?"

"I am working on some history homework for Mr. Jansen that is due tomorrow".

"Do you want me to call you later so that you can finish?" he asked.

"No " she said " I can finish it later I am glad that you called.

Jessie asked her what homework or assignment she was working on for Mr. Jansen but she quickly told him " let's talk about something besides homework". " Tell me about your parents " She asked him. He loved the sound of her voice on the phone.

"What would you like to know? " he asked

"What do they do? " she inquired.

"My father inherited money from his father and invested it into some stocks I think but he did well with it and then used that money to start his contracting business which did even better."

"So he like designs buildings? " She asked to clarify

"yes he will do the design and the building of them till they are complete"

"Has he done any building's here that I would know?

"He has done quite a few but the Veterans Hospital is one that you probably see or drive by a lot".

"I know that one " she said like she was competing on a

game-show. " it is nice " she added and finished with " now every-time I drive by it I am going to think of you"

That made him smile " I helped build that you know " he said boastfully. "

"Did you?" she remarked

"Maybe not all of it but I spent a good amount of time in there while it was being built acting like I was helping "

"What about your mom?" she changed

"She works at the mall making all of the people that shop at one of the stores happy.

"Are they unhappy when they shop there ? she asked him making a joke.

"She is the one that you would go and see anytime that you did not find what you wanted or if it was the wrong size, things like that"

"What about your parents " he asked.

"My father is an ocular surgeon" she said and then the phone went silent.

"What does that mean?" he finally asked.

"He does surgery on people that have problems with their eye sight."

"He operates on peoples eyeballs!" he said loudly.

"Oooooh " she responded with that sound " oooooh I have never liked that word and he could picture a sour look on her face like she just ate a lemon.

"Wow that is interesting, what about your mom?"

"My mom takes care of me, my dad and her garden".

"That sounds really nice, you guys are close huh?" he asked her.

"Yeah, I love my parents." " I hope that we are always close." She said wishingly.

"You will " he added reassuringly " you will be"

At the opposite end of the hallway underneath the same roof that one person lie in a euphoric and nirvana state of mind. The other lies in fear.

Kelly Harrell lay in bed waiting for a man in which she fears and loves to come to her.

The sound of the garage door closing and the entrance to the house opens and closes. The bed she is in begins to feel like the cold steel slab of a morgue.

The sound of a man pulling his way up the stairs. The sound of his breathing tunneling through the walls and increasing as he reaches the top.

The bedroom door opens and the smell of a man that has been drinking since he came home has come to empty his manhood into a woman to afraid to say no. he approaches the bed.

Kelly pretending to lay in a innocent slumber can feel him behind her in the darkness just watching her. " What is he doing and what is he thinking just standing there watching me? " she asks herself.

He strips himself of his clothing and comes to the side of the bed still opposite of where she is facing. He then peels back the covers just enough to expose what lie underneath.

She is dressed in pajamas lying on her side facing the wall away from him. He climbs into the bed and begins to slide his hands in between her 2 thighs and moves them upwards. She stirs for a moment and the warmth of her body melts his ice cold hands.

Her mind is screaming, fighting and yelling but no words come out. He is slowly starting to slide down her pajama bottoms down to her knees.

The voices now yelling louder: FIGHT, STOP and VICTIM. VICTIM, VICTIM,VICTIM they repeated. She turns her body over in a fury and thrust herself into the headboard.

She is wrapped up in the covers that she pulled with her and is coiled in a snake like position beneath them. Her hands clasped so tightly to the sheets that the white of her knuckles and her eyes are glowing and cutting through the darkness that filled the room.

"What are you doing? " she asked so angrily yet silent only to avoid waking Jessie. She is staring at him as he still lay in the bed but his head is down buried into the covers so she could not see his face.

"I hate it when you are like this " You don't talk to me all day then you're drinking and you come here and try to take my clothes off while I am sleeping, WHY?" " What in the hell is it that you were going to do?" she asked him still keeping her voice down and still coiled in that position against the head board.

He then raised his head and began to laugh. He started to laugh uncontrollably and to the point than he had tears coming from his eyes.

She clasped the sheets tighter and met his eyes. She said the one thing that she was certain would stop his laughing and wipe the smile right off of his face.

"James,,,,,,,, I am pregnant ."

7

THE next evening was Friday Night and the friends from Madison Jessie, Billy, Sheila, Cathy, Michael and Amber had all agreed to meet at Bennigan's restaurant for dinner. " Table for 6 " Michael announced entering the restaurant. The host instructed us to wait for a table and Michael then told her to check the reservation " it's under the name Top. ZZTop" they all started to laugh and even the host thought that was funny but told them again that they had to wait and she would seat them in about 10 minutes.

The table side manners were all antics of seeing who could make who laugh the hardest mixed with all of the grown up maturity they all felt going to dinner on their own on a Friday night so they all were immolating those around them and the ones seated at the bar.

Jessie, sitting next to Amber, turned to her and looked at her until she turned to him to make eye contact. Jessie liked talking to her, hearing her voice and looking at her.

"What ? " she announced " What are you looking at Mr. Jessie Harrell?" she asked him with a touch of a southern draw which he had not heard her use before but he loved it.

"I like to look at you " he answered and she immediately leaned over from her chair into his and kissed him. This was only the second kiss they had shared.

"Did you get one of those cocktails?" Jessie asked her smiling which again made her laugh and her smile grow wider.

"No "she said " You are very sweet and you are not even trying. That is what makes it so sweet " I think that is the nicest thing anyone had ever said to him he thought to himself " Don't change that " she commanded which now drew the attention of the others sitting at the table with them.

Dinner was finished the bill had come and gone and they began to stare at one another unsure of what to do next. "Well, if no one else has any ideas, I have one" Michael presented to the table.

The table remained silent so he continued " Is there any newly built homes around here that have not been sold?" They each looked at one another as if a mystery were unfolding.

"Yes " Billy chimed in " There is a bunch of them " " New Granada is about 20 minutes from here and they have a lot of those homes still up for sale".

"Perfect " Michael said " So I say we head down there find one of those homes that is vacant and the ones around it that are vacant. We get inside one of them and we have our own place".

Some of the faces around the table smiled and some didn't. Jessie and Amber again looked at one another waiting for a reaction from the other. "No" never did come from her lips he was saying to himself when Michael rose to his feet " We're off "he said addressing the table and then pointing to the door he said " To New Granada " and they were off into the night.

Jessie and the others arrived at the bottom portion of the homes that have been built.

"You guys wait here and don't make any noise " Michael instructed the others " Jessie come with me " he said flatly " You guys stay here, stay out of sight and again don't make any noise we still have to see if there is any security or others around here " he repeated to make sure that everyone did not start howling at the moon or something like that which would make a lot of noise.

Michael jumps up to the brick mason wall that surrounds the area to see if he can see anyone. The street lights were not on or working so the only light there was to see anyone coming was the thumbnail moon in the sky and the stars that surround it.

He pulls himself over and before letting go called to Jessie " Cmon " They approach the house but very slowly. There are no fences that separate all of the homes from one another so someone down 3 or 4 homes may be able to see them and they are listening for any sounds of someone walking through the dirt or whistling.

They make it to the house. " You go around that way and see if you can find a possible entry " Jessie was instructed by Michael and went around the opposite way that he did. Jessie checked the slider on the back door first and then to the windows of the dining area looking for a " possibly entry " he was not even real sure what that meant other than an un locked door or window but as he was checking one of the windows he saw Michael already in the house. He started to smile and Michael pointed back towards the back door in a motion to say meet me there. He opened the door and Jessie asked him " how did you do that " he brought him to the window he came in and showed him 2 screws that anchor in one side of the window " ok " Jessie replied " well you un screw those and that allows the opposite side of the window to move the other way

"Still amazed " Jessie stopped him as they were walking back towards the back door to get the others

"you just happened to have a screw driver ?" " No " Michael said smiling

"The window was open Sherlock " and they both started to laugh " We got us a house, hell we got us a city " Michael said with his eyes wide and fearless.

This guy is amazing Jessie thought, just wow. " Let's go get the others. They jumped up to the wall and got their remaining friends.

Once inside the home Michael again had a plan and they all started to pair up. Michael awarded everyone their suites for the night and Jessie and Amber watched the other 2 pairs walk away into the darkness leaving them in the living room,,,alone.

Amber walked towards the slider and the kitchen windows to look out and see if there was any one coming or out there. Jessie, still in the living room, could see her silhouette from the curtainless windows. The room was dark from no light but what little moonlight came through the curtainless windows bounced off all the white walls and provided some.

She turned to face him with her arms crossed but the silhouette now facing him has no expression as it approaches him moving away from the window. Her walking towards him in the darkness of the room offers him only visions of seeing her naked and touching her.

They embrace in the living room. Amber is still a little frightened about getting caught or getting into trouble but when Jessie kissed her it was different from the other 2 quick ones they had shared. The other 2 were affectionate and this one was far harder and more primal.

This shocks her at first and then her own angst and curiosity gives in as Jessie bends his knees which the shift in weight causes her to fall with him towards the floor.

On the ground the 2 hands and tongues discover one another. The searching and exploring is intoxicating them both when

"What are you 2 kids doing in here" is said in a loud voice but not shouting. The 2 of them leap from the ground in what would be considered Olympic speed and form.

Their hearts racing Amber seeing so many visions of being brought home in handcuffs for trespassing and Jessie still intoxicated from what was happening. The voice steps closer towards them and both can now see that it was Billy. " Oh my god you asshole " Amber screamed.

"I did not mean to scare you " Sheila apologized.

"I have to get going so I am not late getting back to my house ". She said " You guys stay and finish by all means" Billy added as they both headed towards the door they came in.

"No " Amber said " I should get going too " she looked at Jessie to see his reaction then added " I will go and get Michael ".

Amber started down the dark hallway that led to the bedrooms.

The shadows of the living room had stopped and the area was almost black.

She heard moaning from both of them and had to cover her mouth from laughter because she had never heard sounds like that other than on t.v.

"Michael " she called through the door in an effort to scare him the way Billy had scarred them. It failed and it was her that was really scarred.

"Yeah " a voice returned.

"Sheila has to get home so come on"

"You guys go ahead and I will meet you back at the house, if I am late just cover for me"

Amber stood at the door with so many emotions going through her. The sounds returned and she felt cold. She felt cold all around her and inside of her running down her spine. Trespassing in a house far away in the dark no one around and she almost just fucked Jessie.

8

BEEP, Beep, Beep her eyes open. There is noise all around her and there are flashing lights over her that look like a strobe light. They keep passing one, two, three. She raises her hand to cover the unbearable light and feels the restrictions coming from or what looks like out of her hand.

"Where am I " Kelly asked " " Just relax Mrs. Harrell everything is alright".

"How did you know my name?" she asked with anxiety coming from her voice.

"Mrs. Harrell you are in the hospital." the voice returns in a calming but informative voice

"You were in an accident and we are going to take care of you please just relax".

"What kind of accident? " Kelly asked not remembering anything.

"A car accident ". " A car accident, where is Jessie, my son, is he hurt?" she asked alarmed

"Mrs. Harrell please try and relax we are still not certain of all of your injuries". The woman said looking into Kelly's eyes.

"Your son is fine dear, it was only you and your husband".

"We are going to sedate you just relax, this will help you rest"

"Where is my husband?" Kelly asked

"He was released not long after your each arrived". Kelly looked at the nurse puzzled and already started to feel the effects of the morphine. Trying to focus, remember or hold a thought she was again embraced by the darkness of slumber and fell asleep.

Trying to formulate a thought or a sentence the nurse stopped her " He is fine, his injuries were minimal compared to yours but he was wearing his seatbelt

The four of them left the house leaving Michael and Tiffany there.

On the way home Jessie made several attempts to make conversation with Amber but she was distant and un-interested. She insisted that he go on towards his house vs. walking her. Jessie and Billy watched as the 2 girls made their own way in the opposite direction.

Billy asked if he wanted to go do something else since neither had to go home just yet but Jessie was more interested in getting home to call and see if he could find out if she was o.k.

He started off walking and then found himself again running to keep up with the thought's running in and out of his head.

"She was enjoying it".

"Why did Billy have to go and do that?"

"Why does Sheila have such an early curfew?"

"How does Michael do it?"

The street lamps shining on and off of his face as he passed them. Running out of breathe but still running now re enacting each moment he had shared with her tonight.

He reached the top of his block and stopped hunching over to catch his breath. His heart pounding, spit coming from his mouth and his lungs burning but the images and thoughts continued.

You could see the entire street from the top of the block and it was the top. If he had a bike he could coast the rest of the way at a good speed. The car or truck was not in the driveway he noticed as he was now half way there.

He opens the door. The house is pitch black as he headed to the kitchen to turn on the light. He takes one deep breath, exhales and then picks up the phone to call Amber.

"Hello " Amber answered quickly on the 1st ring.

"Amber what is wrong?" Jessie said " I thought" he continued then interrupted by a 3rd voice " Hello, who is this?" The voice commanded!

"This is Jessie" he said apologetically.

"Well Jessie it is almost 11:00 and phone calls at this house end at 9:00" the 3rd voice said hanging up the phone.

"Amber " Jessie started again " Listen I will call you later but I have to go or I am going to be in trouble " she told him.

"O.K I am sorry" he said to the sound of the phone hanging up.

Amber hung up the phone walked to the mirror and takes a long look at herself. She stares deeply then turns away. She goes to her stereo turns on the radio and sits on her bed staring out her window into the darkness. "Still no Michael" she is thinking.

The sound of that dial tone filled in his ear and it filled the empty house. " Is the house empty" he said to himself and went to the garage to see if for any reason one of the cars was parked in there. No car so he went upstairs to see if one of them for any reason was upstairs in their bedroom. He knocked softly but no response. He placed his hand on the knob to turn it but it was locked.

Curiosity getting the better of him and his adrenaline was pumping from everything tonight.

The house they broke into, being with Amber and almost getting caught. He wanted to see if he could do the trick that Michael had taught him earlier with the window. His parent's room was on the second story so getting a ladder was probably not the best idea in case they came home and could be home any minute. The idea of getting into their room was more interesting to him than trying the window trick downstairs so back upstairs he went to get passed that lock.

Jessie loved to pretend ever since he was a kid. He was always pretending to be someone else like the characters he watched in movies.

He would stand in front of the mirror in his room and say all of those lines from his favorite movies and television. The fight scene to rescue a girl, hostage negotiation, gangsters you name it and he had said or re enacted those scenes in his room.

Outside the locked door of his parent's bedroom he tries to think of what Michael would do but cast his imagination to being a cat-burglar. He picks at the lock with a unfolded paper clip and then makes an effort with a butter knife slid in between the frame and the lock. Not a very good cat burglar he thinks to himself he then switches to a detective.

Placing his hand on the door knob and positioning his body to the left so that he can apply pressure from the shoulder into the door itself. He takes one soft shot it not sure of what to expect. Nothing, so he takes another step and places his shoulder into the door a little harder and to his amazement, it opened.

He is inside of the room. Listening for every sound coming inside and outside of the house he looks for clues.

The bed was not made and that was strange, she always made the bed.

"Slam " he heard and it was the sound of a car door shutting and it was close. He looks around the room to make sure nothing is disturbed, his heart pounding " Shit " he says out loud then "if my father catches me in here" to himself.

He runs out of the room passed the door and then turns back around to shut the door and push back on it to make sure it is locked.

That sound outside is definitely here at this house. He runs down the stairs taking 2 and even 3 at a time to get to the bottom.

He lunges to the bottom and hits the tile hard enough it makes his knees buckle. " What the hell? " he says out loud under his breath.

There is no sign of The Volvo but there is a car there that he does not recognize. " Why is it in the driveway?" and then the front door starts to jingle. He turns towards the door not moving as he is still standing in the front of the window that faces out to the street and the driveway.

The door opens and it is his father.

His father did not see him in the living room and walked right by up the stairs towards the bedroom's.

When he walked into Jessie's room and did not see him he called to him " Jessie" " Are you here?"

"I am downstairs he answered" His father came back out of the room and headed back down the stairs to Jessie " Get some things together for me."

"Things? " Jessie asked puzzled.

"Your mom was in an accident and is in the hospital" his father told him.

"is she okay?" he asked immediately

"She is okay but I want you to go and see here so get some things in case we are there late". Jessie started to walk towards the stairs which he was still standing at the foot of and when he got closer he could see dried blood on his father's hands.

On the way to hospital Jessie was asking for the details of what happened.

"I took your mom out for dinner and on the way back we were driving " he started " the guy was weaving in and out of the lane so I sped up to pass him because we would rather be in front of him than behind in case he did crash" Jessie studying him still starring at the blood around his fingernails and the expressionless face as he told the tale.

"When I passed him he slammed into us and it sent us off of the road " "Was he drunk or something?" Jessie asked " I don't know I don't think that they caught the guy but the police will let us know" Were you hurt " wanting to know if that was the source of the blood on his hands " No" his father said " I am fine but I was wearing a seatbelt. Mom always wore her seatbelt and he never did he thought again staring at the blood on his hands.

9

THEY both get on to the elevator at the hospital and his father hits the number 6. Jessie must have the look of being ill on his face because on floor 2 when the door opens and a man walked on he looked right at him and said

"you okay kid?, if you're gonna be sick you're in the right place " He nor his father said anything in fact his father never even looked down at Jessie or at the man.

When the elevator door opened on the 6th it floor it felt like a hole was alas pocked into the bag that was placed over his head. He, finally able to breath, walked with his father towards the room his mother was in.

They walk in to a dark room only light by the many lights coming from many machines in the room and the glow of a television that is on with no volume.

She is not awake and Jessie is unsure of what to do or say. He has never seen her this way. His father makes an effort to talk to her and see if she is awake but there is no response for awhile and then she would open her eyes.

When opened James motioned Jessie to the bed to see her and say hello. She smiled when she saw Jessie's face but her words sounded like they hurt when coming out and she did not stay awake for long. She drifted back off to sleep and James asked Jessie if they should stay the night there or go back home. He did not know how to answer that question so James said they would go home so she could sleep which did not look like she was having any trouble doing.

Jessie went to visit his mother off and on with his father. She was in the hospital for about a week maybe longer and the house was very different without her being there. His dad was not there very much either.

He saw Amber in school that week in passing and they did talk but it was always quick and she seemed to be so busy to talk after school on the way home or phone.

She found out about the accident Jessie's mother had had from some of the others in the school and found him during lunch. " I did not know about your mom " she told him.

"How could you" he responded somewhat sharply " you don't talk to me and I do not even know what I did."

"I know" she said to him and told him how sorry she is for them not talking very much since that night at the house.

"Is your mom okay?" she went right into " what happened?" Jessie went on to tell her what he was told about the accident.

How they we were run off of the road after dinner and they never did find who had done it.

"Jessie, I am so sorry " she kept saying " about everything "which made him feel better.

"Are you doing okay? " she asked him lifting his head up so they could make eye contact

He loved looking at her and could not help but smile " I miss you " he said and no one has been at the house since the accident so there has not really been anyone to talk to about it.

"I am here" she told him " you can talk to me about it"

Jessie had already made plans to play football after school so talking with Amber would wait till later that night. Michael was there telling everyone, that he had not already spoken to, about all the things that he and Tiffany had done that night in the house.

He captivated the audience because most of them had wanted to be with Tiffany and the most any of them had gotten was a kiss. Hearing him describe her body without clothes and how willing she was to offer it to him for the taking that night held everyone's, including Jessie's, attention.

Jessie arrived at home by about 6:00 and his father was home. Going into the house and getting something to drink his father met him in the kitchen. " I am heading to the hospital in about 30 minutes " he announced " you can do your homework there and see your mom.

"I don't have any homework tonight" he told his father and asked if he could stay home because he has not really spoken to Amber that much all week and they kind of just made up. His dad placed each hand on each hip, dropped his head and began shaking slowly back and forth.

"Your mom is in the hospital Jessie" he said then elevated his voice " You do realize that don't you?" "Of course I do" he said back

"I told you before about dropping everything every time she calls, didn't I?" he questioned " So you have only been at the hospital because you 2 have not been getting along and then when she speaks to you again you drop everything including visiting your mother in the hospital?"

Jessie standing there in the kitchen with nothing to say " No way mister" his father said and then continued " you get your books and you get your ass in the car right now."

The visit at the hospital was tense. James and Kelly did not really speak to each other a great deal and Jessie was just mad from the argument earlier. He wanted to see her just not in the manner it came to be and the scene was awkward. His father would ask her questions and she would respond with one word answers again and again.

James finally questioned her on it with " Why are you being so difficult, we came here to see you? "What is wrong?" Jessie stood there in silence when she fired back at him with.

"I don't know James maybe because I was told I had a miscarriage" silence filled the room then "I was told yesterday and I know you were told the day after I got here weren't you?"

Jessie stood there in silence watching his father take a step towards her saying " Kelly" then "No!" she shouted loud enough to draw the attention of the nurses to come in and check on her.

"You stay right there "she continued. He turned to address the nurse that had come in asking" is everything alright Mrs. Harrell?"

"Everything is fine,,,, thank you" he snapped.

The nurse moved around him to again ask her " is everything alright?" Jessie still shocked that she had said she was pregnant, watched his mother looking right at his father with a different look than he had ever seen on her.

"yes " she replied " everything is fine thank you" but her gaze on him never wavered.

He turned to face Jessie and told him to say goodnight as he walked passed him and out the door.

Jessie walked to her in the bed and that new look faded fast as he approached. It changed back to how he always saw her but after seeing the other one he couldn't help but feel sad because even though it was a smile on her face she shared with him. That look, that same look she always wore looked like defeat when compared to the confident, strong and in control look she just wore.

"You were pregnant?" was all he could think of saying because it was the first time he had heard it,, ever.

She pulled him in with a hug that was as strong as could be for her at that moment. " For the best, baby " she told him as she held him moving her hands back and forth on his back. He did not want to leave that embrace.

"I will be out soon honey don't you worry now go on home before it gets too late and next time I see you I want an update on Amber" she finished with him raising his head and a simple " okay mom, I love you ". " I love you too".

————————

The car ride home that night was silent then filled with rhetoric about him being a provider, always making sure that she and I had everything we needed then silent.

He was angry but Jessie could not tell if he was angry about the accident, the fact that she was in the hospital and not at home, the nurse not listening to him, that she just stood up to him or that he just was not in control of anything the way he normally was.

What Jessie did not know was just how in control he was of about everything going on around him.

The night of the accident, while Jessie was on the phone with Amber talking in their very own self absorbed world, Kelly had stood up to James.

He had come upstairs to once again take what he felt was his and she refused to let him do so. He began to laugh and she used what only weapon that she had at the time, her words.

She told him she was pregnant. The news of that pregnancy did in fact stop his laughing and his smiling but it did not stop him.

The news focused and amplified his intent.

He arose from where he was on the bed upon hearing her news. He stood tall over her looking down at the bed. She still coiled in that same position unaware of his thoughts going through his mind. She waited, coiled in her position, for an embrace, an apology or his rage.

He went to her side of the bed calmly. She stirred and shifted still unsure of his actions as he took to one knee on the side of the bed that she was still pressed up against the headboard.

His face was blank like he was still processing what she had said. She saw the color return to his face. His eyes return from an intoxicated state and even a smile appeared.

He reached over to her with his arms open, in a hugging motion and manner. "Come here" he said still with his arms extended.

She studied him and wanted so badly for this to be the redemption she wanted him to express. She wanted this to be the new start and it did not even matter what the past had been if there was a new start that would be and stay.

She went to him. She let go of the sheets and she went into his arms.

Inside of his embrace she could feel his heartbeat and again the man, the vision she fell in love with and has always dreamed of.

He moved his head from her shoulder in an attempt to make eye contact with her but she was still lost in that dream once again. " Hey" he said softly calling her back to him. She moved her head to meet his eyes. His eyes were full of color and he smiled again.

"We're not having another baby Kelly, are you out of your mind"

"How could you let this happen, you know how busy I am " " She started to move back towards her previous position but his arms tightened as did his stare.

"This can be good for us " she started " This can be better " being careful in her words but honest

"Better " he said again his arms tightening " so everything that I have built and done for you and Jessie has been not good therefore it needs to be better" " Is that right?" " No " she replied with her voice still low in an effort to make sure Jessie was not hearing any of this.

"A baby can help you if we try. It can help you be a better man and us a better family"

"A fucking better man? Better family? " " You are not keeping that baby, we have way too much " before he ended that sentence " We need this baby she said with her voice elevating louder. He takes one hand from around her and covers her mouth. " YOU ARE NOT KEEPING THAT BABY " he says again " LOWER YOU VOICE" and she began to scream.

She began to scream through his covered hand. This was not about the baby. This was about the control of a situation and the will over who will be the victor in another situation. She had yielded that control time and time again for years. She was or had reached the point in which a stand was to be made. She continued to scream and louder.

James, shocked at the volume, did not want Jessie to hear or the neighbors calling the police. The police at his home would not be good. The shock gave way to anger which clouded everything else until nothing else was visible but his blind rage.

James moved his head back and with every ounce of velocity his 6"1 208 pound frame had. He slammed his head right into her forehead.

The origin of impact was slightly off center and actually hit the right side area of her head. His holding her back and mouth during the impact prevented her from being thrown into the headboard. Her head fell back in a whiplash state then bounced back into his shoulder where it stayed,,,, not moving.

10

NOW he had a situation. James and Kelly had had their share of battles in which Kelly had to explain a certain mark or discomfort.

This, this was different because most of the other times if not all of them Kelly never fought back. The physical aspect was quick rarely as visible as the contusion erupting from her head not to mention how far it had split upon impact. The swelling was pushing more and more of the blood from the open wound as if she was breathing out of her head.

He quickly grabbed what clothes were on the ground in the closet and applied them to stop the bleeding while he thought.

"What am I going to do, think, THINK" he said to himself.

He does not know how long she will be under.

"Make sure the bleeding is stopped".

"What she will say when she wakes up"." No police, oh god no police it will ruin me" His mind racing.

"The Car " he thinks to himself. " I can take her into the car get on highway 40 and find a place that if an accident were to occur would do enough damage to corroborate his story and her injuries, that's it " he surmises.

His adrenaline moving now he goes downstairs to see where Jessie is . Jessie is in his room on the phone. He checks his watch,8:30. He keeps his hand in his pocket and peeks in the door to let him know he can talk on the phone for another 20 minutes then it's lights out. Jessie was pleased with that because he normally would have said something or wanted him off now for some reason but didn't so Jessie replied " okay, thanks dad".

That will occupy Jessie for that time period.

He opened the garage and pulled the car in to avoid anyone seeing him carry Kelly into the vehicle. He ran back up the stairs to get her. He checked her breathing and proceeded to carry her to the Volvo. He backed the car out and set off in search of an accident scene.

He drove for about 30 minutes west thinking of the story. " Why were we out?" "We had dinner and returning home we were run off the road he said out loud to hear how it sounded if questioned. " Where did we eat?" He found a Grandy's not far from there and ran in to get $20.00 worth of take out so it would be in the car when the police question him.

While waiting for the food he brings in the shirt he was using as the bandage or tourniquet on her head and flushes it down the toilet in the men's room.

Now it is just the place to stage the accident because he does not know how much longer she will be under. He scouts and finds a location and waits till there are not enough cars to get an idea of what is happening other than just a car that already wrecked.

He reaches over unbuckles her seat belt and fastens his. Hits the accelerator on the Volvo until he is at a speed of 45 and plants the car off the road, but still visible from the road, into a tree.

The impact sends them both thrusting forward but as he was secured to prevent him from contact, she was not.

Kelly's unprotected body was sent hurling into the dashboard and windshield before she slumped over to her left side and in the lap of James.

The wound re opened and now bleeding in the vehicle James

removes his seatbelt and runs onto the highway of the now approaching vehicles yelling for help.

The approaching motorist, driving a Ford pick-up, stops and is motioned by James towards the accident scene. " We were pushed off the road, please help me, my wife is bleeding " he yells to the driver.

The 2 men remove her from the Volvo and into the pick up and take her as fast as they can to the nearest hospital.

James, when inside the pick-up, is talking to Kelly " Stay with me honey, you're gonna be alright just stay with me " and then begins to tell the tale to the pick-up driver about the other driver who ran them off of the road and asked him if he saw the driver or the accident. " I did not see you guys go off of the road " the older driver tells him " Damn people don't know how to drive anymore, " I too have been almost run off this road myself" he offers.

They arrive at the hospital and drive right up to the front door area where there is already hospital personal outside smoking.

"My wife" James begins to yell to them " My wife and I were in an accident!"

The staff immediately begins to bring a gurney for her transportation.

They remove her gently and begin her transportation inside while another asked if the pick-up driver was involved or has knowledge of the accident

"I was just coming up on them right after someone ran them off the road" the man said.

"We're going to need you to stay for a moment so we can get your statement and an officer is on the way, should not take too long". The doctor explained

James quickly walked back around to where the pick-up driver is now standing and thanks him for being there in their time of need. Walking away he could not help but smile inside as the man had just told them and would tell the police exactly what he wanted him to say.

While inside the hospital James began to make his presence and the significance of his wife's safety known immediately.

He made sure that everyone knew he was the owner of The Harrell Development Firm in order to establish a level of priority and cooperation.

He also did not know how much Kelly would remember when she woke up so his intent in establishing himself at the hospital as a prominent business man would be to make sure that the doctor and nurses were to be providing her with ample morphine to reduce the pain. He demanded this immediately and each time he spoke with anyone regarding her condition this was a question just to make sure that she was resting and pain free.

James concern for Kelly's rest and pain was genuine but he did have another agenda. He felt confident that the morphine bed she would lay in for a few days would reduce any memory of that evening prior to the accident and in the event she did remember.

It would be more viewed as either nightmares from the accident or trauma following it.

James was looked at that evening but not treated other than some $5.00 aspirin and was released. He was taken home and slipped right in while Jessie slept.

He spent the evening removing the sheets and blanket from the bed to remove the blood. He would wash them in the morning when Jessie went to school.

He called in for work the next day explaining the situation that had transpired which his team offered their full support and wished Kelly a strong and quick recovery.

He contacted the officer that had left him his card last night after taking the pick-up drivers statement to make arrangements to provide his own account and file a formal statement.

"I will see you at 1:00 " he told the officer hanging up the phone.

James finished the statement with the officer and waited for an update on his wife. Dr. Helms whom he had known, as well as Kelly, since Jessie was born came to him in the hall and with the great misfortune of telling James Harrell that his wife had miscarried during the accident.

James,face flush with grief, presented the demeanor of a man who had no knowledge his wife had been pregnant.

"How far along was she? " he asked him.

"She came to see me about 2 weeks ago and I called to follow up with the results about 5 maybe 6 days ago" " She was probably waiting for the right time to tell you James, I am terribly sorry" he offered.

"How is she doing, is she okay?" he switched.

"She will be, could have been far less serious of a head injury had she been wearing her seat belt" The Dr. explained " I know" he said " I know

James leaves the hospital feeling confident, for the moment, that he was able to cover his tracks on all accounts.

11

AMBER had started to come over to Jessie's house more and more during the time his mom was in the hospital because he had kept telling her how there was never anyone there and how empty it felt. She could never stay long because her parents wanted her home after school to complete her homework.

They never knew it was Jessie she was spending her time with after school and would not have approved if they knew it was with a boy.

Amber's parents liked Jessie and had spent some time with him. In- between her time at his house getting to know him more. He was at hers when her parents were there. They had all had dinner a few times that week because they knew his mother was in the hospital.

Jessie liked spending time at Amber's house, it was just like his house when his mom was there.

They ate together, they all asked about her grades, shared laughs and they seemed close. He missed having his mom in the house and the cooking.

Amber's dad was less vocal than his father was. He had noticed he was much more quiet.

The mom was who was the vocal one but she was nice and

encouraging while the father made general conversation and commented on things he felt the need or passionate about. He also enjoyed spending time with Michael, who was getting close to returning to California for school.

Michael's father was divorced and in construction so during break from school his father had the opportunity to make more money doing some piece work on a job site in New Orleans. Michael's father asked his sister which was Amber's mom if they would not mind watching Michael for maybe a month while he was gone. Michael had been and continued to be the most interesting person his age he had ever met.

When dinner was over we helped clean up and Michael asked him to come outside for a moment. They went down the street a few houses where there was an electrical box that sat there by the curb. He asked Jessie how well he knew Cathy Tierney " I don't know not very well I guess, why?"

"No reason but I think I'm in love" he said laughing out-loud. Amber came skipping up to them just as Jessie was pushing his hand away.

She jumped and landed right at the face of the box, turned around in place and fell backwards right into Jessie's open arms on cue to catch her.

"When are you guys gonna finally do it?" he said walking away as she turned her head, still back to him and pulled his head down to kiss her and then turned around in his arms and kissed him more.

Jessie loved Ambers body pushed up against him and what Michael had and was always telling him about all of the girls he had been with in just the month of being here.

"Amberrr" her mother had called to her from the porch not sure of exactly where they were so she never saw them kissing.

"Does Jessie need a ride home?," it is time for you to come inside"

"I can walk" thinking it would do him good "but thank you Mrs. Clevinger."

That night in bed going to sleep all he could again think about was Amber.That night at the house on the floor and how it was just as Michael had put so willing to give itself.

———————

That next morning he is up and see's his father before he leaves for work. " Sleep alright?"

"yes " Jessie replied, "you?"

"I am good how are you and your girlfriend doing, you had dinner there last night right ?" His father asked which is the first time he had asked about Amber but he knew about dinner because he had given him permission.

"We are good " Jessie say's

"Good –I don't want to always bring it up but is an important lesson for you " James begins while holding his coffee and gathering his things for work " you cannot leave or drop what your doing when she want's or calls or ask's, I mean it """ I have said time and again you have to make sure that she is aware that you are you and you do not bend and you do not move." " You are a strong and confident man son period, understand!"

"Yes sir " he offers but not with as much enthusiasm as what his father's speech had been presented with.

"Good. I will see you tonight. Do you have plans?" he asked

"I don't know yet it's Friday so maybe" Jessie responds

"Well I am taking some of the team out to Reunion Tower tonight to celebrate landing a client and will then stop by and see your mother-she is getting released this weekend."

"I will see you when I get home which should be around 10:30."

School was always great on Fridays because you did not do very much but review and you would have testing. If you were prepared then you were fine and if not well then Friday was not as fun.

When school was out Michael was there by the football fields that they would walk through on their way home. Michael kept asking Amber to get one or some of her friends for tonight " Cmon lets go out and do something I am leaving in a week." " Call Melissa or Drew please." She just kept walking holding my hand swinging it back and forth with each step.

"and where are we going to go? " she asked him

"What about those houses that we went to that one time, that was fun" he responds quickly and is now in front of them walking backwards as they walk.

Michael is looking back and forth at each of them " Cmon, Cmon-please-please " he is saying like a dog begging for a treat and staying right in stride with their pace even though he is walking backwards.

"lets see if Billy can get his brother to get us some beer and who else can get something for us to drink there and we can have a nice cocktail party." Michael said pleased with his gameplan. " I can see what I can come up with " Jessie added

"Alright I will call the others and see what they are doing tonight, I don't know about the houses though you guys scared the shit out of me last time we were there" Amber said.

They all went home and spoke to all of their friends to make plans for the night. The consensus was to go to the houses out at New Granada once we had something to drink. Billy's brother was able to get some beers but would only do it if everyone chipped in and bought him a 12 pack as well which was agreed. Jessie went through his parent's bar and poured portions of a Smirnoff Vodka bottle and a Jack Daniels bottle into some jelly jars that his mom had under the counter.

Jessie's mom liked to make jam and always put them in these sealed containers and she had a lot of them so 2 missing would not be a big deal. Jessie did not take the whole bottle of Vodka or Bourbon so no one would see that it was missing and Michael had told him to pour a little water back into each of the bottles in case anyone was looking at the level and would not know any was missing.

They had made sure to leave one or more of the windows unlocked on the same house they were in before just in case they wanted to return.

It was still unlocked and in the house they were. Billy had brought the beer as promised, Jessie had his end, Sheila had brought a radio and batteries, Michael had brought cups and a flashlight so their cocktail party was on. Amber brought Michael and her friend Drew.

The radio played but not so loud because everyone was still a little on edge about being in the house and it was starting to get darker. Round and Round by Ratt was the song playing as the flashlights came on to provide some light and drinks were made. They all talked about the teachers at school, what it is like in California, what bands and songs everyone liked- disliked and what everyone wanted to do when they grew up.

Talking led to truth or dare more drinks and the radio getting louder. Cmon feel the noise by Quiet Riot filled the house and the girls started to dance. Truth or dare would resume when the song finished as did the drinks. The Moosehead beer was getting warm but everyone was drinking it anyway and the vodka was all gone. The truth or dare to Michael came with a dare by Billy, as instructed by Michael before getting there, to take Drew or whoever Amber came with into one of the back rooms for 10 minutes.

Back they go and when the 10 minutes had ended they had not returned. The 4 of them feeling the effects of the drinks that they had and were still consuming sat in the living room laughing at each other.

Billy asked Sheila to accompany him somewhere and she responded with " I have to use the restroom " followed by Amber's " my god me too."

Billy walked them both back to where the restroom was but did not return himself. Jessie stood up and went to the kitchen to see what was left and played with the radio. REO Speedwagon's Keep on loving you came on the radio when the door opened and closed down the hall. He turned and it was only Amber who had returned.

She was smiling as she walked back into the living room " I love this song " she said starting to slow dance with herself then " Come here Jessie Harrell " she said to him with a waiving him in kind of motion.

Jessie walked towards her in the same living room that they began to discover each other the last time they were here. Stepping into her space to become part of her dance she wrapped her arms around him and drew him closer .

"And I'm gonna keep on loving you, cuz it's the only thing I wanna do " she sang so softly right in his ear as they turned in their tight circle.

He moved his head and she looked right at him and they started to kiss just as they had before. The guitar cried out it's solo and he brought her to the floor. No Billy interrupting, no one crying her name to stop them she was giving herself to him.

The song had changed Journey's Don't stop believing now filled the house that seemed to control everything within it.

The song, the house the alcohol it all consumed them.

He had been dreaming of this moment from the moment he met her and she felt so right.

Jessie had never been here before, where he was right at this moment and just did not know what he was doing but his primal instinct's did.

His father's words " You do not bend, you do not move, you are a strong and confident man son, period " and all of the things Michael has told him again and again about the girls he had been with. It all just felt so right.

Jessie moved directly on top of her and again it was alarming, fast like it was setting of the clocks within her body and were ringing all at once rapidly waking her up from her daydream that was in fact a reality.

Jessie was on top of her!

"Jessie wait " she said but he did not hear her, his eyes closed.

"Jessie"., she said louder and tried to slide upwards in an effort to remove him and her from that position.

Nothing.

His hands were positioned directly on each side of her head which made it difficult for her to move and he was not hearing her. She grabbed onto each of his forearms hard and began to scratch at his arms and back but again nothing

He looked down at her at that moment. Her eyes filled with a lack of control, confusion and terror and his with primal fulfillment. She saw his eyes close and could feel every part of his body tense up as he moaned and almost screamed.

His body went limb falling on top of her and then and only then did he feel the weight of her body and it's effort-panic to remove him and free herself.

Amber got up immediately and frantically started to search for her clothes. Jessie sat up completely released from what was occurring and still wide awake in his nirvana and sublime state. She began to dress and it was not until she had enough clothes on and was starting to run towards the door did he awaken

"Amber " he called " Where are you going? " and out the door she had ran with shoes in her hand not even wearing them. He stood up and searched for his clothes or enough of them to go after her and as he made it to the door she was gone.

12

KELLY awakened in her bed from a nightmare she was having. All of her dreams and nightmares felt so real she thought to herself.

She was able to move around and was up looking at herself in the bathroom mirror.

Staring at the bandages that all but masked her face and head. She starts to peel one of them back to expose the zipper of stitches that is on her forehead.

Twister, her nurse, coined by the Arlington Memorial Staff due to her ability to make a mess just about everywhere she was walks into her room.

"Good Morning Mrs. Harrell " " You are going home today." She proclaims cheerfully.

"Maggie", twisters real name "what did the accident report state when I was brought in?" Kelly asked as she was making her way back to her bed.

"Car accident sweetie " " Not a bad one but bad enough because someone wasn't wearing her seat belt " still with the cheer in her voice.

"Do you know what time it was or where " She is having trouble concentrating and a headache is beginning just from the attempt to process the q and a.

"Close to 10, I think and off route 40." "Good thing that driver was right behind you too, he got you both here right quick"

"You feeling alright?" Maggie asked her with some concern.

"I am scared " she tells her " and I don't know why ".

Maggie consoles her with a hand holding gesture " Honey it is a little of the medicine, the concussion and you just had an accident that you don't remember all of the details."

"Perfectly normal but you are okay and you are safe now and that is what is important " Maggie offers her a wink and then off she goes to complete her rounds.

Leaving her in the room Kelly still does not feel so safe or okay and she is not sure why.

She is brought home by James that afternoon and is met by Jessie who stayed home to cook breakfast for them all upon their return. "This is a nice homecoming". She says to them both as they take their place at the table.

They are all seated at the table enjoying a very nice moment. The food Jessie had prepared, Kelly has returned home, James feeling confident his plan had and was working and then the door bell rang.

Jessie gets up " I'll get it" he offers smiling at everyone seated at the table.

Opening the door he is met by 2 uniform officers and a man wearing a suit. " Jessie Harrell ?" The man wearing the suit asked " Yes " Jessie replied as he flashed his badge approaching him inside of the house with one of the officers. " Please turn around and face the wall " the man in the suit says " I am detective John Ramsey."

James Harrell is now at the door way with his son who is facing the wall as one of the uniform officers pats him down " What is the meaning of this " he demands.

The officer begins to read Jessie his rights as he completes the pat down search for any weapons on his person then removes hand cuffs from his back belt and places them on him as the detective tells The Harrell Family that Jessie is under arrest for rape.

"What!" Kelly shouts

"I want an explanation right now!" James tells the detective and can see a crowd of neighbors beginning to form on some of the lawn's outside.

"We are arresting Jessie for rape". The detective informs them.

"He is being transported and will be detained at county now so you may want to call your lawyer." They lead Jessie from the home on Saturday morning in broad daylight to one of the 2 marked cars on the curb in front of close to every singly neighbor on their street. James slams the door furiously walking passed Kelly who is still looking at the door, now shut, where her son was just standing with handcuffs on.

James immediately contacts his attorney. " Roman, this is James Harrell." Roman McKinnley, Romey to his friends because he was one of the most eligible bachelors in The Dallas area and roamed relationship to relationship, was the top defense lawyer in the area.

"James, it's Saturday morning " " I understand but there is a matter that requires your immediate attention, I need you at the county detention center right now my son Jessie was just arrested for rape."

"County it is then, do you have any of the details?" " No, just get there. " he said hanging up the phone.

James went to Kelly " Honey stay here and rest, you need to rest. I have Roman on it."

"I don't understand " she said " It will be fine, I am going down there right now and will not come back without him." giving her a hug in which she did not return he left the house. He could not help but feel mortified making eye contact with the majority of his neighbors as he got into his truck and made his way to Jessie.

Jessie is fingerprinted, stripped, given new clothes to wear which was an orange jumpsuit and then left in a room with a desk and 4 walls.

"Hello Jessie my name is Roman McKinnley and I will be representing you." Roman sits down at the table placing his briefcase on top, opens it and takes a large yellow legal pad and a pen from it. "Let's begin, shall we?" " Who is Amber Clevinger?" he asked

"I didn't do it " he said not answering the question and then repeated it " I didn't do it!"

"One thing at a time okay son, who is Amber Clevinger?"

"She is my girlfriend."

"How long have you been dating?"

"about 6 weeks"

"Did you have intercourse with her prior to last night?" he started then added before allowing him to answer " you did have intercourse with her last night didn't you".

"Yes " and then " No"

"Yes to the last night " he asked clarifying as he wrote.

"yes to last night and I did not rape her!"

"Can anyone help you prove that, anyone else there?"

"yes but they were all in other rooms"

"Well I am going to need their names, where you were, what you were doing there everything okay so get comfortable and leave nothing out better for me to know now than find out later you understand?"

"yes" he replied and settled into a grueling series of questions that would last almost 2 hours before beginning the same process with the detectives which would last close to another 2 hours.

Roman was good, possibly the best and he held the detectives at bay but the bottom line that would come to fruition is that they had Jessie's semen found inside of the "alleged" victim and they had his skin under her fingernails not to mention a statement from her that this was rape and not a consensual act.

Jessie was going to be held there overnight until they were able to get him in front of a judge to make bail while they decide how to proceed. That night was the longest of his entire life and it was shared by each his mother and his father.

The next morning when he was to meet and stand before a judge in his orange jumpsuit he was informed that he will stay in the custody of the state with no bail until the trial. The gavel fell and echoed forever.

Mr. and Mrs. Clevinger were present in the courtroom that morning alongside Jessie's mother and father when that decision was made and the only other sound that Jessie heard following that gavel falling was the voice of Mrs. Clevinger shouting " YOU ARE GOING TO PAY FOR THIS !"

The trial would go on for only 2 weeks as the prosecution had compelling evidence against Jessie. They had the semen, the skin, the statement from Amber and no witnesses to say different.

The day had come for the sentencing and Roman was hopeful for a probationary sentence due to no priors and his father being prominent in the community.

That did not happen.

The judge was Evelyn Rosemont and the only thing she despised more than murderers were rapist. She sentenced Jessie Harrell to the maximum allowable sentence by the state. 5 years in The Dallas Correctional Facility.

Jessie was allowed to have a final embrace from his parents before being led to his new life. His mother cried and his father held him terribly hard for that brief moment.

He was then taken and led to a door and upon his exit the only other faces that he saw were the Clevinger family including Amber who had been there that day to testify.

They all seemed so happy, celebrating what he felt like was the end of his life. He did not make eye contact with Amber or her father only Mrs.Clevinger who smiled at him with great confidence as they removed him from the courtroom.

13

JAMES and Kelly Harrell were met outside of the courtroom by reporters from all of the Dallas / Fort Worth and Arlington area news teams.

"No comment " " I said no comment " Roman demanded as he bullied his way through the reporters to escort The Harrell Family to a waiting car.

At the opposite end of the steps was The Clevinger Family whom also had a large audience of lights, cameras and microphones all pointed in their direction.

They used them and addressed everyone " Justice has been served! This affirms that the system works here in our great state of Texas and we want to thank everyone that supported us and our family during this very difficult and trying time in our lives."

Amber was not present at the press conference and it was again Mrs.Clevinger that did the talking with Mr.Clevinger and their attorney at her side.

"What the hell Roman, what the hell did I pay you all of that money for when my son is still in there and will now be in there for another 5 years?" James yelling in the town-car as they made their way to a safe destination. Kelly, still wearing her bandages to conceal the stitches and bruising, felt ill and asked to roll down the window for some air.

"James, Roman pleaded, I believe you are aware of my winning track record and have been known to get just about anything in a courtroom done in my time but you have to understand the case they had against him. The evidence, the testimony of that little girl with her wonderful family being torn apart and nothing, I mean nothing on our part to say it did not happen other than his word for it"

"5 years Romey?" James stated but it came out like a question which made Kelly feel like he was suggesting that if Jessie had done what they said. The idea of giving him 5 years for doing such a terrible thing to that little girl was wrong and that thought made her feel more ill.

"Please pull over " she said to the driver as Roman and James continued the conversation not even hearing her.

"I will get him out in a couple of years, I will get him early parole" Roman stated " All he has so do is his time without getting into any trouble while he is in there and I will have him home back to you both in half the time, I promise." The car came to a stop and Kelly made her way from the black town-car. She desperately tried to breathe holding her chest and her head feeling dizzy.

James came from the car to console her but before getting to her she had lost consciousness and was on the ground. She fell right into the grass onto her side

PART
TWO

14

JESSIE walked down the long brick corridor. Hand-cuff's around his waste, hands and feet.

Shackles was the term that he was now familiar with. He was led out of the courthouse building to a bus along with some of the others that were there being held or were there to see the judge.

The bus ride was and would be the last trip he would see of the country side for some time. He would view that country side through a window that had a cage mesh over it. Passing stop by stop that was familiar to him on his way to his new home.

The trip was over an hour and he wished it would have been longer but they did eventually arrive to The Dallas Correction facility or "The D.C. Each of the passengers would exit the bus and be placed in a line.

Jessie looked at the facility that was engulfed in high walls, chained fences and guns. There were guns in every direction everywhere you looked.

A guard approached and stood at the front and center of the small line of passengers. " Boys, my name is Duncan and I am the one person here you don't want to fuck with!" " I make a living squishing shit like you into the ground as if you were a cigarette I just finished smoking."

Moving to the left he went to each person in that line to make closer eye contact as he continued his greeting.

"You will be assigned to a cell, you will be assigned 1 hour of yard time each day, you will dine in our facility 3 times a day and you walk in a single file line that has been displayed for your viewing pleasure to and from that facility with no talking each day" " deviation from that line or any policy is when you and I become more acquainted with one another." He finished now looking Jessie right in the eye

"Welcome to D.C now let's get you boy's checked in" he said motioning to the guard holding a large riffle and wearing dark aviator glasses.

"You see the green line in front of you, you", he said to the one boy closest to him" get over here, then you, then you" forming a line " start walking!" he began to lead them into the facility.

The walk in was right by a fenced in area that all of the guys inside were in, like recess he thought except the kids looked a lot different than they did at Madison Junior High. Jessie looked away not wanting to make eye contact with any of them that were up against the fence staring and making comments to the new arrivals.

His eyes focused on the green line approaching the front gate. His ear's were focused on the sounds.

He could hear the sound of weights clinking and slamming up and down. He heard the sound of a ball bouncing back and forth off of a wall, a basketball game was happening, guards, whistles, a bell, racial, sexual slurs and profanity all filled the air as the gate closed behind him. He was now inside.

This place is cold. He thought to himself making an effort not to shiver. He was issued a number and the clothing he and the others would be wearing then led to his cell. The facility was a 2 story with rows and rows of cells just like you see in the movies.

Jessie was assigned to cell # 237 and once there it was the one place he was glad to see and the only place he actually felt safe.

There was 2 bunks in the cell but he was the only one assigned to that cell so for the time being he was alone. You could not lay down on the floor and fully stretch out your body in width without hitting the other wall. There was no seat on the toilet and there was again the sound of threats, violence and racial slurs that filled the air around him.

The longest night of his life in county was nothing compared to this. He had only been here for 2 hours and would be doing this for another 5 years he thought to himself as he sat himself on the bottom bed with his head in his hands.

The Clevinger Family had placed their home up for sale and decided that the media and attention at school would not be the best environment for them and Amber to move forward with their lives.

Amber said goodbye to a select core of friends and vowed to keep in touch not really knowing if she would or not. These were the only friends she had ever had but she could not stand the way everyone looked at her when they saw her.

The father could work anywhere and the mom would place all of her focus on her daughter healing and moving on. The trial even though brief took a lot out of them. The day Amber testified had been the worst day of her life.

She came home that night of the incident and it was still early so her parents were up and in the living room when she got home. Her mother, never to let things go, could sense something was wrong when she got home and did not stop until Amber let her in her room and told her the truth.

Her mother, enraged, had called the police immediately and they were there that evening to interview Amber for all accounts of the evening.

She told them everything about the evening including breaking into the house and the alcohol. She told them the others had gone into other rooms and that her and Jessie were dancing together, then kissing and it led to their clothes mostly being off but not all the way and that she was willing up until he moved on top of her.

It scared her the way it happened so fast and she tried to stop him and asked him to "wait" or "stop" she could not remember her exact words but she did not want to and it was like he could not or chose not hear her. It was over and she ran from the house was the story she had told her mother and later the police.

The house did not take long to sell but they did not wait in Arlington during the sale nor did they tell anyone where they were moving. Her father resigned at the hospital he worked, Amber was removed from the school, a truck showed up one day to move the belongings and they were gone. Just like that.

James Harrell was having his own issues to deal with. He went to work to face all of his team and even though they seemed loyal and supportive he knew there was doubt. It was written on several faces not to mention some of the clients he had just landed had backed out fearful of media attention being drawn to them and their business.

His clients that he had done business with stayed with and beside him though and continued to use his expertise and team on future projects.

He also had to face his neighbors which did not either know what to say to him at all or simply did not want to speak to him and would turn their backs and go into the house upon his arrival home.

He then had Kelly that he had to face and even though she had no knowledge of the incident that took place that night he could not help but feel terrible every time he saw those stitches and her pain that she wore. The pain, not from the accident which still had a lingering effect but the pain of not seeing her son every day.

Every day made James wonder why it took this much time and all of this to be such a wake- up call. Kelly was right that night about him being able to be a better man. He could admit that now but for some reason did not know how to say or express that to his grieving wife.

Kelly had resigned her position as well. The bandages and scar that was setting in was one thing but the looks on everyone's face was not something she wished to endure each day or till it passed. She never really liked the job anyway and all of her focus right now was going to see Jessie every chance that she had so she could be there to help him through this. He needed her more than ever right now and that is what she was going to do.

15

A LITTLE time had passed and Jessie just trying to stay like a ghost in this place. He wished he was invisible and made every effort to stay that way and just let the time pass. Each day in the yard that was not so easy because he did stick out in this place. The facility had about 700 youths in it and it was not the kind of place that they sent kids that did not go to school or shoplifted. These were the worst kids in Texas. These kids had robbed, assaulted and killed.

There were clicks in here, just like in school but these clicks were mobilized, dangerous and conglomerated in the yard. There was 30% African American 30% Spanish, 5% Native American, 5% Asian and then 30% American but the majority of American or white youths had their head shaved or tattoos every-where . Jessie did not look like anyone here and he knew that. The kids in here had muscles ripping out of their uniform. Tattoos everywhere and the way they spoke made his language ability even though he rarely said anything seem superior. Everyone in here spoke with slang and profanity as if it was a language all its own.

The way he looked and the way he never spoke earned him a nickname pretty early. " Spook " they called him because he was always trying to pretend he didn't exist. Jessie had never even been in a fight and knew that anyone in here could and would kill him probably just for the bragging rights so he continued to do what he could to not exist.

It was visiting day and again his mother was there to greet him and do what she could to make sure he was surviving. His father was not here on this day so he would ask how his business is going and how the 2 of them were doing. He was glad to hear that she left her job since he knew she did not like it that much and made a small joke that she could dedicate more time to making jam which made her smile. He about started to cry telling her how much he missed having meals with them and did actually cry when he told her how sorry he was for everything he'd done.

He had not yet done that since this had happened. He had not yet apologized to anyone. His mother tried to fight back her tears and did so for the most part until she made it back to her car where she would come apart.

Kelly had, each day, blamed James more so than Jessie for what happened and where Jessie was. She had felt that enough years of James demonstrating his will over hers had done some psychological damage that had finally found its way into Jessie and his actions.

This was the thing that stopped her crying and gave her strength.

Jessie had a great deal of time on his hands day in and day out to think about every detail of his life and how it led him to this point. He felt, truly felt, he did not belong here. His father had money, we lived in a good area and had nice things, I have a trust fund and would one day follow in his fathers foot- steps with his business.

"How in the fuck did I get here? " He would question often. He would think about Amber and that night or even the nights that led up it but that night in particular.

He reflected on all the conversations his father had with him. He played them countless times now as well as the arguments and things he saw his father do with and to his mother. These thoughts were the only emotion he showed in this place but he only did so when he was in his cell where he could be alone and express his anger.

Kelly went to bed early that evening after seeing Jessie and was already in bed when James arrived at home.

She was not asleep but did not want to really speak to him so she turned off the television that was on in the room and rolled to her side away from the door and his side of the bed. He came up the stairs and opened the door but waited to enter for a moment. She is stewing in anger still for that moment had a feeling.

She was not sure what it meant but it was something. He came in the room and began to change his clothes into something more comfortable.

When he was finished he came to the other side of the bed where she faced and went to one knee in an effort to get more to her eye level.

James nudged her a little and whispered her name. James continued to search for the things that he could do now to help salvage his family and make right. Jessie was away with no way to help him so he focused on what was in front of him. He continued to work hard and poured himself into his business which was again making financial gain and helping them with the attorney fees and he focused on trying to reach his distant wife.

"Kelly" he whispered again this time her eyes opening. She rubs them to pretend as if she was sleeping and then sits up in her position on the bed keeping the covers over her and in her hand.

"I wanted to talk to you, I missed you." he said and he extended his arms open and moved towards her to hug her. He wrapped his arms around her still under the sheets and squeezed tightly. He then moved back, his arms still around her and met her eyes and smiled at her longingly.

Her mind reeled and filled with a vivid memory of the night of the accident. Where he knelt, how he held her, how he smiled and what he said.

"Kelly" alarmed " Kelly what is it?"

"You did this " she said prophetically his arms around her immediately lost their grip and let go.

"What?"

"I know you did this! " her eyes wide and her face clear with that same confidence and control she had when in the hospital.

"Kelly, wait a second. You're upset and we have been through a lot" he said now standing and walking away from her

"I have done this and stood by you for years" her fearless confidence in full stride " I am grateful for what you have done for our family but this is over!"

"What do you mean?" " Kelly " almost pleading

"Our son is in prison for rape James. How do you think he got there, is that a coincidence, is that an accident?" she says now standing up in the bed dropping her shield of blankets to her feet and begins to step from the bed and walk towards him.

"You did this, ALL OF IT!" " but it is and will be the last time you ever touch me again do you understand me?" She turned and left him in that frozen position as she walked to closet to retrieve a suit case to pack some things.

"Kelly please" he pleaded and could feel the earth move beneath him. " I know you were right, about everything please not now, please you can't leave."

"I can't stay here with you, I can't even look at you! Don't worry I am not going to the police about however you covered it up but I am not staying here." She finished packing as he sat on the edge of the bed with his head in his hands and she left the house.

16

THE next visit that Kelly had come to. Jessie noticed that the look she possessed at the hospital when she stood up to his father had returned.

"You look great " he told her as they made their way through the usual and same conversation. Kelly found the strength to tell her son how sorry she was for everything he may or may not have seen over the years between her and his father.

"Is everything okay?" he asked " Yes " she replied or so it will be "Jessie, I am leaving your father."

"What" he said " you guys are getting a divorce?"

"I have allowed your father to control me for several years Jessie and now my greatest fear is that you seeing all of that has not only found its way inside of you but may have something to do with why or how you ended up in here." " I feel terrible and responsible for that and will not allow it to continue."

Jessie not sure of what to say or believe. He has always trusted his mother, always but this seemed so much, divorce. " it has not been that bad. Everything was fine, normal" he told her

"No Jessie not fine, not normal. That is what I mean you need to know that what we have done or what I have allowed to be done is not normal

"He just" Jessie started to say in defense or an attempt to make this go away before she railed " A man does not hit his wife again and again Jessie. He does not stage and accident to get rid of a baby because he is not in control of the decision to have it!" " MEN DON'T DO THAT AND IT IS NOT NORMAL!"

"What do you mean?" "What are you saying?" He asked sitting back in his chair flattened by the news and seeing his mother upset.

"Your father who has done a great deal for us since we have been married and since you have been born." She said calmly " but he has physically abused me for years placing me in a weaker position to stand up to him or for myself "

"This I allowed to get so bad that when I am became pregnant I thought that it would be the one thing that could save us like maybe he would be able to make up for the terrible things he did when I was pregnant with you." "I told him that I wanted to have the baby to make him a better man and us a better family." " He became irate and I am not sure what exactly he did because I blacked out but the next thing I know I am in a hospital with and had a miscarriage."

Jessie was speechless. This is the most candid his mom had ever been. This was the most honest she had ever been but when he really thought about it was the most candid and honest his father ever let her be. She was telling the truth.

"He told me you weren't wearing your seat belt and he was. I thought that was strange since you always did and never did." He offered to show her that he believed her.

"Jessie I truly am grateful for everything he has done for me and I don't want you to hate him and I did not tell you this for that reason our marriage is our problem. I need you to understand that what happened or what you did that night was not your fault." " Not entirely, she added

"I am going to be here, in here with you till you get out of this place and then we can start over where no one knows who we are.

Everything is going to be alright." Her face still held that confident and in control look. It looked great on her and she wore it well.

The next day Jessie was assigned a bunk mate for the first time since he had been at D.C. Randall " Mack 10 " Humphries came into the cell and had to walk sideways to get through the front. He was in the cell when he arrived and said nothing to him when he came in.

Once the guards had departed he looked at Jessie and asked " This your bunk down here?"

Jessie looked at him not sure of what to say and said " I have been using it"

"You using the top one now!" and threw the book that was on the bed up there making the piece of paper book mark fall out losing its place. Jessie climbed up to the top bunk still saying nothing.

They called him Mack 10 because of his frame built like a semi but when he hit you it also felt like a truck or a mack 10 machine gun.

He was in here for " all of the above on the sheet ". He has robbed assaulted and even killed in The Dallas area and was a known participant of a white gang called the Arian Brotherhood. Jessie watched him blend right in when in the yard with the others that were just like him. Not long after his arrival in the cell he was in his top bunk reading from a novel. It was mid afternoon and there was plenty of action going on in the general population of the 1st level so it was noisy.

A hand came over the bunk and landed on his chest hard like a pounding paw from a polar bear. The hand clinched its fist and with it the shirt that Jessie was wearing and began to drag his body over the bed railing. He resisted but to no avail. The strength was relentless and it sent his body hurling into the concrete wall that lay in front of the beds. " Come here you little bitch " the voice said in a growl as one hand grabbed the back of his hair so tight he could not move his neck and the other his pant bottoms as it threw him face first into the floor.

"You like to rape girls you little bitch " the voice said still in that growl and he never actually saw the face of who this was that was on top of him.

"I hate rapist! " he said " I hate people that would do such an act to another member of your own race but I do believe in King James an eye for an eye so I will show you what that girl that you raped went through, let's see how quiet you are now spook" The hand ripped the pants down from the waste and used his foot to keep them around his ankles.

"Wait " Jessie screamed " Wait please – whatever you want" he pleaded.

"I already have what I want right here" now using his legs to spread Jessie's legs despite the pants at his ankles.

"Money " he said " I can get you money" The hand pulled the hair back lifting his head from where Mack 10 had is shoved into the concrete.

"You don't have any money in here stupid."

"Not in here he said desperately trying to keep his attention".

"Well what am I going to do with money in here if you really do have it anyway?"

"You are going to get out eventually just as I am".

"I have a trust fund and can get you money, plenty. " he had his attention " More money than you have seen " he continued " please" he pleaded. There was a second and then the incredible weight and grip was off of him.

"Get up " he commanded and Jessie as quickly as he could was on his knees then his feet pulling up his pants.

"I am listening " he told him " This better be good spook."

My father has set up a trust fund for me that I get when I am 18 which is only 4 years away and I am in here for 4 so it's perfect. " If you would make sure that nothing happens to me when I am in here then I will make sure you get $50,000 when you get out.

"Not good enough " he said. I have already been in here a while I just got transferred to this facility due to overcrowding here so I will get my release before your little birthday party". " You will have to get me that money sooner my man or I and everyone in this place is going to have their way with you daily once I tell them what a treat you are, you feel me?" " How much sooner?" he asked.

"How soon can you get it, hell it may motivate me to break out of this place if I knew I had a couple of quarters waiting for me on the outside."

"You don't understand he tried to say without upsetting him, it is a trust fund I don't get it till I am 18 but it is guaranteed."

"Unless something happens to whoever set it up right?" he said looking at Jessie

"The way I see it is that you get rid of whoever set that up and you are having an early birthday party". Jessie was pretty certain that he still had to be 18 but there was no point in arguing if he had his attention now at the moment and it prevented him from doing what he was going to do.

"How do I do that, if I am in here?" he asked him still not trying to piss him off.

"That will cost you more but I have some people that can help you with that". " I get $50,000 and I will set up a hit on whoever it is in the way for an additional $10,000. I am in here for another year no matter what so I am willing to entertain your business proposal as long as you are able to provide some more details."

He had no choice. I will spend the next few years getting raped every day by various inmates or I work out a deal that puts a hit out on my father he thought to himself.

"I am waiting" said Randall Mack 10 Humphries. " Okay " Jessie said thinking to himself okay, what choice do I have.

The details that he wanted were to satisfy his curiosity. He wanted to know what his father's name was, where he worked, what he did, how much he made, what he looked like the bank the trust was set up with but he was not writing it down.

Jessie did not know if they were just talking at this point or that he did not need to write it down as it may incriminate him in the crime when and if it was done.

The discussion bought him a night.

There was no attack for the remainder of the evening but he did not sleep at all that night either thinking that the potential for someone to murder his father was out there or in here.

The thought of being responsible for killing his father. Killing him for money just made him feel like he was on trial all over again. I am in here for 5 years, my parents are getting a divorce, I was almost raped and now there is a discussion on ending my father's life to literally save my ass in here is all that kept going through his head.

Then, a revelation.

He was not able to jump up in his bed and he was not able to pace around in his cell to think it through because one thing he has and continues to learn in here is to conceal and not show your hand.

He lay's in his same position, in his upper bunk and formulates a plan with reasoning to justify the action and he does so without making a sound or a move.

17

JAMES had convinced Kelly to stay at the house and he would find a place in order to keep it quiet so it did not affect the business. James had done an amazing and diligent job in keeping the good name of the Harrell Development Firm in tact during and after the trial despite all of the media attention and just felt more news attention surrounding the name and the family would do more damage than good.

He was hope-full that this would be just a separation and could not argue the point regardless. He had been a poor husband and he knew that and he felt terrible it took this long to figure that out. The idea of giving her space to find herself and discover what it is that she wants was well worth the wait and she deserved that.

The business was going well so again his plan was to pour himself into it to ensure that it continued to thrive. He had new clients he was still working with that when complete he knew would lead to more business from them and again others. He opted to not share the news of the separation and asked that Kelley did the same and in return he would give her as much space as she needed. He would not call or come by the house without calling or her knowledge just so she felt he was committed to giving her what she wanted.

He did not speak with Roman McKinnley, their attorney, regarding the matter either so the only people that had knowledge of the separation was: Kelly, James and Jessie.

Jessie's plan was like most of the other things he had learned throughout his short lifetime, taught by his father.

He had listened to his advise his entire life and even if he felt like he was not listening. He was, he thinks to himself in silence.

He had heard one of the many conversation's with his father that same day as the night he was with Amber, right before in fact.

He did have something to do with my being in here. He thought to himself beginning to seethe in his bed still not moving and still not speaking.

The conversation he had with his mother on their last visit, his hands on his stomach with his fingers dancing in a domino effect starting with the pinky then to the forefinger. Up and down right in motion again and again was the extent of his movement.

His father had tried to cover up beating her with a car accident.

So his plan was that simple and poetic he thought.

He would ask Randall to stage a car accident that would end his life therefore putting in motion a trust fund that would await him upon his release and offer an insurance pay out for his mother that would start immediately.

He would be able to give her that new start she spoke of, that starting over that she deserved.

He would be able to have it all so to speak but he would have only one small request for Randall and his crew, only one.

James was leaving work later than everyone else once again. He had really been putting in the hours but it helped pass the time while doing something productive and it was the only thing in the world he felt good about.

Rubbing his eyes he rolled down the window to get some fresh air and then turned on the radio to have something to keep him awake for the ride home. It was 10:30 and no traffic which was one good thing about working late as he made his way to a hotel he was checked into.

He stopped at a light that just turned red as a pick-up pulled next to him. The passenger had come from the vehicle before it had come to a stop on his left side, right in front of him. The passenger opened the door which James did not lock and ripped him from his seat which was easy because he was not wearing a seatbelt.

The passenger then throws James into the back of the pick-up and a middle passenger comes from the cab that had pulled up beside James and into the driver's seat of James truck putting the truck in drive and moving forward when the light turned green.

The man that threw James into the back was now back there with him keeping James in a bear hug and headlock to prevent him from moving or being seen by any passing cars.

They drove for about 45 minutes to a location they felt comfortable to carry out their deed.

They pulled James from the bed of the pick-up and the 3 men stood before him. " What do you want?" he asked them

"I will give you anything, just tell me what you want?"

"You don't have to give us what we want, we came to take it" one of the men said while the other 2 stood there. " I do have a message for you." The man said

"I don't understand" James said. " I said, I have a message for you " the man repeated as James tensed up fearing that the situation seemed more than random. " please " he said " please don't hurt me

"James " the man continued " be a man, that is all I am saying"

"What?" James asked "What did you say?"

"I said" the man continued " Be a man, don't bend, don't move, you are a strong and confident man James and don't ever let anyone stand in the way of your dreams"

James, on the ground in the middle of nowhere just stared at the man speaking with a bewildered look and then it clicked.

"Jessie? " James said as his eyes went to the ground.

The 2 other men approached James and started to grab him when he jumped up and started to run " What are you doing?" he screamed.

One of the men jumped on top of him quickly and the other grabbed his legs.

"Help!" James screamed as loud as he could.

"What are you going to do, why are you doing this?"

"We are going to take a ride " the man said then finished with ***"Don't forget to buckle up!"***

The 2 men hit him enough times that he was not only unconscious but barely breathing.

They placed him in his pick-up lodged a paint stick into the accelerator and popped the emergency brake sending the pick-up truck hurling off of a ravine.

The distance to the bottom was a couple hundred feet and the explosion was seen for a good couple of miles in the midnight air, if anyone was looking.

The coroner's report would state that the body was charred from the flames and severed in 2 parts (literally in half) upon impact.

The impact mixed with the rate of speed upon collision with the ground would be the reason for the severed parts but not to forget that although he would still be dead from the impact he would certainly have not been ripped in half had he NOT been wearing his seatbelt at the time.

18

JESSIE your father is dead!" his mother told him immediately when they met for their next visit.

"What?" he said surprised which was good because he actually was surprised. He was a lot of things at that moment and had a number of feeling's going through his mind and body. They did it, he thought they actually did it.

His mother before him crying but he felt responsible, he felt sad he felt in control and he felt rich.

"Did you guys have an insurance policy on each other?" he asked coldly and with poor timing.

"Jessie Harrell" she said almost embarrassed " Your father just died.

"I'm sorry I am just thinking of you" he explained " What happened " he figured should be the next question.

"He was leaving work late, he was always working so late now that we had separated".

"Did anyone know you guys were separated?" he interrupted.

"No " she said.

"Your father was hopeful that we would get back together and he did not want the negative attention on us after everything else.

"You didn't tell anyone?" he pushed.

"You"

Jessie did not think of that before. A separation and how it may look on her in the event of a death and insurance pay out but if no one knew then no reason to be concerned and he wanted to get back on track because these questions seemed to be aggravating his mom.

"Are you okay?" he asked her

"I don't know how much more of this I can take I mean you are in here, we separate and now he is dead" her hands visibly shaking.

"Mom" he says " Listen to me please, I am in here and I will get out. You guys separated for the right reasons and it may not be a bad idea to not share that with anyone, the separation I mean."

"Why?"

"I don't know if there was an insurance policy and they do investigate then you don't want them to deny it because you guys were getting divorced because of physical violence you know think about it."

"What is happening to you in here?" she says looking around the place, do you realize how you sound?"

"Forget how it sounds and just think about it. You deserve that money. You deserve a new start and in a place that no one knows your name, remember? If they investigate a battered wife who is leaving her husband and then a death occurs it may prevent them from paying it out."

She did not know what to say. How his focus and attention was on this matter and not the death and the most horrible part about what he was saying what that it was true.

"I don't want to talk about this anymore, do you understand me? " No more."

"Okay" he said " I'm sorry mom I am just thinking of you. Let's talk about something else"

The conversation shifted to the idle chat of how things were going, the food and reading but her mind, as well as his were each still occupied on the insurance policy. Now what?

The phone was ringing off the hook for a week straight. The team from the development firm, friends his family, newspapers, Roman and then John Slessinger.

John Slessinger was their agent for all insurance needs and Kelly had always been the one to pay the bills or call him to change, transfer, add or just general questions. They had always had a good rapport.

She had answered the phone that day as his call was much later in the week when she had grown tired of it ringing all day and not answering it.

"Hello." Kelly answered.

"Kelly, it's John" he stated " John Slessinger, how are you doing?"

She did not know how to answer that question because she simply did not know how she was doing at all.

"Kelly, I am terribly sorry to bother you but one I want to first express my deepest condolences for you and Jessie."

"Thank you John, I do appreciate that "

"and second " he continued " we have to discuss his life insurance policy."

"John, he was just buried 2 days ago and I do not think I can have this conversation right now." she explained.

"I completely understand Kelly again I am sorry for the intrusion and your loss. I would like you to contact me next week so we can schedule some time to discuss it please it is important for you and your family." He stated then hanging up the phone.

James was buried in a plot next to his mother father and grandfather in The Forever at Peace Cemetery in Arlington. His ashes and bones as they were from the accident were laid to rest in a plot, as his will instructed and as Kelly knew he had wanted.

The funeral was large enough that he would have been pleased and a eulogy given by The Senior Manager at The Harrell Development Firm. The things that everyone knew of him in public and the outside is how we will be remembered to everyone else, she thought

Kelly had secluded herself in her home following that service. Thinking of the words in the eulogy and how they were everything she had dreamed and wanted in her entire life to be true.

She missed him still despite those words not being totally accurate.

She did not know if she missed him because she did not have Jessie, because she had no one at all or because she really still loved him despite all of his faults.

A bottle of wine later and she had concluded that she had loved him.

There was a time that she had loved him with all of her heart and that he was the answer to all of her prayers.

He became another man over time and one that was no longer who she had loved.

Not by choice or by design but just because she thought but still here in this house that he helped build and all of the things they purchased to furnish it she could not help it, she missed him.

Opening the 2nd bottle of wine now her conclusion had changed and her missing him was in part because he was never coming back. She was now talking to herself in full conversation and out-loud.

"He was a terrible man that did not deserve those wonderful things said about him. At least the ones about his family anyway", she said.

She walked around the house with the glass of wine in hand and looked at every corner of the house that a incident took place in which her will was reduced to fear and it made her angry.

Jessie was right she said out loud a new start, a new beginning where no one knows who I am. She did not realize those were her original words to him but it did not matter her confident and in control look was returning and Jessie was not the only one that thought she wore it well.

"You have a debt to pay Spook " he said to Jessie walking up to him in the yard.

"I know " he replied " I heard, I can't believe it is already done"

"You can't believe what is done?" he said looking at him as if nothing had happened.

"Your debt." he repeated.

"Okay but this just happened, exactly how fast do you think something like that takes before it is paid out" he was reasoning

"There is paperwork and signatures, lots of them that have to be documented and like you said you are still in here no matter what. It is only a matter of time which is the one thing you and I have" He said smiling which was not returned.

"Did you give him the message?" he asked as Randall walked away"

"loud and clear" he said not turning around.

Jessie had some time but Randall would bring up the debt as often as they were in contact which was a lot considering he was his cell mate.

In the shower a few days later they were wrapping up and all of the boys were heading in. Randall Mack 10 Humphries took long showers and in came an assailant with a shiv or shank which is a prison made sharp weapon and plunged it into the coraded artery in the neck.

Pulling the weapon from the neck quickly caused the artery to explode onto the bathroom wall and Randall to grab his neck with his right hand as he came eye to eye with his assailant. It was Jessie.

Randall grabbed Jessie by his neck and started to squeeze with his one hand. Jessie while in close enough started to plunge the shank into his heart again and again and again until his grip loosened and eventually let go. Randall fell to his knees and then to the ground as blood erupted from each his chest and neck.

Jessie washed his body quickly. He only had a few minutes before the guards came to clear the shower area for the next session of inmates.

The area was clear and only with a towel and robe he made his way to a laundry shoot where he cleaned the knife with the towel and dropped it into the laundry transporter.

Randall was found and a siren was alarmed for a lock down of all inmates so that an investigation could take place.

Investigations inside were not taken very seriously because for the most part they did not care if all of these guys in here killed one another.

It only made more room, less to feed and one less criminal inside or out.

They would determine it to be a homicide and due to where the weapon was found the Arian Brotherhood blamed the African crew's because they had most of the laundry detail inside so they assumed it was a hit and an effort to get the shank into the laundry where one of their crew could dispose of it later.

The case was unsolved and Jessie was never looked at because of his spook status. He was unassuming and smaller in size meaning that no way could he have taken Randall Mack 10 in a knife fight but what they did not know was the research and events that let up to that day.

Randall had befriended Jessie in a sense because he viewed him as a meal ticket while inside and was counting his cash when he got out already. He did not share the business deal he made him with anyone because he did not want anyone getting in on his action Spook was his, he thought.

Spook was white and so was Randall so no reason they would have a beef and again even if they had, god Randall would kill him easily everyone thought.

Jessie read a great deal though while he was inside in fact it was all he did.

He had been reading from the encyclopedia Britainica version of h. Human body is what he was looking at to understand if he did have a weapon then what would be the major arteries or kill points on a human being that would inflict death in the quickest manner.

He studied and studied and he knew or had observed enough while being in here the weapon of choice for people when they wanted to do a hit. He located some re-barb outside and was able to get it into his cell and spent as much time as he could un-detected sharpening the end to a point on the concrete and the wall.

This also allowed him to remove his everyday debt to Randall and the $50,000 less he would owe upon his departure from D.C. Jessie too was counting his cash when he got out.

The one last thing Jessie had to do before taking his one and one shot only at Randall was to find out more about his connections outside.

If he was unsuccessful then he would not only be spending more time in here but Randall would make it torturous before killing him but if he was successful then he had a whole other plan he was putting together based on the successful business transaction between He, Randall and his father.

Jessie was able to keep Randall up at night from time to time by asking questions about his connections. He did this by appealing to the egotistical side which was something else he had read about.

He wanted Randall to feel superior and to allow him to feel like his status as a gangster was immortal. Randall speaking was like he was tutoring him and one night he was able to get Randall to talk about a guy in El Paso that he knew that did fake i.d.'s. "This guy does passports, driver's licenses and birth certificates you name" it he said.

He was planning on using him for some work when he got out of here and it would help him get into Mexico so they could not ever find him because they would be looking for another name and another face.

"How another face? " Jessie asked him that night " Because they also do plastic surgery ' he said almost whispering it and then laughed.

He had planned on doing 3 big bank job robberies on route to the border then a stop in El Paso for his guy and a quick face lift, new i.d and a new life.

The guy operated a bar in El Paso that was a front. His name was Nelson Pritchard "and the bar?" Jessie asked.

"Heaven's Gate " He said laughing again, "get it? It is your ticket" laughing louder.

Jessie got it and again did not sleep all that night until he had thought this all the way through.

19

KELLY awoke that next morning with a pretty good hangover and was asleep on the couch in the same clothes she had on the previous night.

She stood up to fast and the dizzying effect brought her back to the couch and then a near vomit experience right there. She clutched her mouth and composed herself.

She went to the kitchen to get some water and make some toast to at least put something into her stomach and absorb the alcohol she had consumed.

The slammed down another glass of water as the toast was buttered and devoured. Feeling better she went to the restroom to take a long hot shower.

Felling even better from her shower she wiped the mirror freeing it from steam. She sees her face in the mirror and tries to recognize or identify who it is staring back at her.

She placed her fingers on the scar that is still very visible to her and makes the decision to call John Shlessinger.

They arrange to meet at his office because she felt that the drive out with fresh air would do her some good. He is pleased to see her and again expresses his deepest sympathies for all of the matters that he was aware she was dealing with.

John made every effort to make this pleasant and efficient.

"I have some things for you to sign, regarding the pay out." He explains and produces the file marked with where her initials and signature would be required.

"What is it that I am signing " she asked him trustily.

"These are the papers to the life insurance policy you and James had taken out on one another right when Jessie was born, remember?"

"Yes. " she replied

"Well in order to finalize payment and create a check I need your signature and I should have the check to you within about 3 day's"

Still feeling the effects of the wine she asked him " How much is it?"

"Its 3 million dollars Kelly!" " Again, I am terribly sorry, for everything you have gone through."

She just started crying not sure of how to react or what to feel. She could not believe it.

He grabbed her a tissue

"I am so sorry." She apologized " I just don't have any control over anything or any emotion right now."

"If there is anything I can do, please don't hesitate" he ended.

The first call she had made was to Roman McKinnley to thank him for the kind words regarding James and to discuss where the appeal or parole process was on Jessie's case.

Roman reiterated his condolences for her and Jessie's loss.

"Now" he said moving on " Jessie has only served a year of his sentence so we are making progress. We can appeal but it is really the parole hearing I like best considering he is conducting himself proper up there in D.C which from what I have been told, he has."

"What does that mean then exactly?"

"We continue to make sure he is model in his behavior up there and when the hearing comes up in about 8 months we should have a fine case to present that time served warrants the punishment and that it is time for this young man to move on with his life" he explained with great confidence.

"8 months then" she said " How are you doing Kelly?" Roman asked her.

"I don't know, I really don't know?"

"I understand" he comforted but some pressing matters that will require you and I to discuss.

"What matters?"

"The business for one, you will have decide the direction that it will take remaining in your name under new management or a sale out right".

"What about Jessie's trust?" she asked him

"That is fine, still there, not going anywhere. Can we schedule a meeting here this week to look at everything because that business of his is still doing well and there will be competitors interested in buying not to mention the team he has there that will want to know their fate or future, you understand?"

"Of course, you are absolutely right. Thursday?" she asked

"Thursday then. 12:30 and I will take you to lunch you could probably use a good meal. Come by my office and we can go from there." He offered.

Let's meet because I will be visiting Jessie that day and want to be near a car" she told him partially true because she really did not want to be alone with a man nick named Roamey for longer than she had to.

"Kennedy's it is then. 12:30 I will make the reservation."

"That's fine Roman, thank you. See you Thursday " she said hanging up the phone.

She had found herself again behind the wheel of her Volvo, that had since been repaired from the accident, sitting in the driveway of her home staring at the dash board.

She did not know what she was going to then and she did not know what she was going to do know even though the circumstances were entirely different.

She went inside and really had some things to figure out so she got some paper and pen and for the first time she made a list starting with the house. Did she want to live there anymore with all of those memories? Did she want to stay in this neighborhood with these neighbors? Was it fair to sell the house that Jessie had grown up in? She would ask him those things at their next visit.

What about the business, his legacy? She thought. That was the one thing that he had done and done right. He cared about this place and was to be we had hoped where Jessie would be to carry it on if he wanted to.

She did not know anything about development, architecture or running a business and in being honest with herself she did want to go there and be a part of the place that portrayed him in the manner she had always wished he had been. That was not fair to them or to her so selling was the thing she felt in her heart but would ask Jessie's opinion before going over with Roman.

She wanted to pack now. The longer time went on waiting for Thursday to visit Jessie and Roman she just wanted to start packing what she wanted and leave the rest or donate it but something to begin a move forward.

Right now she was still stuck in the now which was still the what was and not the what will be.

Selling the house and selling the business and just waiting for the parole to come then the 2 of them somewhere else living another life is all that she really wanted to do.

———————

Thursday was a big day. The morning had started with a call from John to say that the cashier's check was ready to be picked up at his office, she was seeing Jessie today and she had Roman to discuss the future of the business.

She had told John Shlessinger that she would be there following the visit to see Jessie if that was alright and he had told her that he would be there all afternoon.

The meeting with Jessie was different from the others they had and shared. This one had hope.

She shared with him the burial and the service. She shared the words that were spoken and who came. She shared with him the meeting today with Roman to discuss the selling of the business, the house, the parole board in 8 months and then the check that awaited her at the insurance office.

Hope.

They each had it and they each exuded looking at each other. Jessie agreed with selling the house and it did not bother him that he would not be going back there when he did get out.

He also agreed with selling the business just because he would always feel like he was living in the shadow of his father, who built it, in the event he did decide to go into architecture.

Jessie was also optimistic about the parole hearing in 7 months because his spook status had kept him out of trouble or getting killed. " Does Roman have any suggestions for me to help with the parole board while I am still in here?" he asked

"Great idea, I will ask him today"

"Are you excited about the check?" he asked her

"I don't know, I don't know how I feel about that. I have seen money like that before but I am happy right now for the first time in a while so I want to focus on that."

"You deserve it he told her, you really do and I will use that check as motivation to get through the next 7 months."

"You do that she told him, you probably need all of the motivation that you can possibly get"

Hope.

She met Roman as planned at Kennedy's at 12:30. He was there when she arrived.

"Kelly" he said standing to greet her and then reached out to pull her chair for her before the server had.

"Thank you Roman" she said thinking how good he is at this and flattering as it may be the idea of being with him even for lunch just gave her the creeps.

The server had taken their drink and lunch order and was off
"Have you thought about what I said? About the business?"

"yes" she told him sipping from her water and then taking some bread from the center, she was hungry she thought to herself.

"I spoke to Jessie today about the house and the business and the memories of each" she stopped " I just think it would be best to sell. I don't know anything about the business he built and would not want to do anything to damage the name he worked so hard to establish."
" You said that there was potential buyers?"

"Yes, I am sure that there are and you never know maybe someone on his team may buy it out but its best if make that public so we can begin the process and you can then start to look at potential offers."

"I will need your help in that field again not knowing a thing about the business I would have no idea of what its value is or is not."

"You thinking of selling the house too?' he asked

"I want to focus on the parole hearing and Jessie getting out of that terrible place. We can start again new somewhere else is what feels like the best medicine" she explained. " he asked me to ask you if there is anything he can do to better his chances from now till then with the board?'

"Stay out of trouble." He told her "that is my advice."

"Do you have a realtor to help with the house, moving company things of that nature?" he asked as the meal was being delivered.

"No but I am on my way to the insurance company for a check that will help pay for those things until the house sales."

"Good, great news I am glad you both took care of each other" he said biting into New York strip steak.

Next stop was the office of John Shlessinger to pick up the cashier check that was now ready.

The exchange was brief as before and she was offered a seat in his office. She waited for his return and upon his return he had a check.

The check was made out to her in the denomination of 3 million dollars.

She did not know what to say and she did not know how to act or if she should even take it as he held out for her.

She accepted the check stood and just hugged John Shlessinger, to his surprise. "Thank you John, for everything " she said to him and then walked out of the Fidelity Mutual Insurance Company offices.

She went to the bank and deposited the check to make sure it was real and to also make sure it was not on her even though it was a check it made her incredibly nervous having that piece of paper.

For the first time in her life, she had money of her own.

Month after month went by while Kelly was selling the house and packing up the boxes Jessie was serving the time remaining on his sentence.

They met every week and Kelly also moved forward with the sale of the company. The timing on each was impeccable because shortly after the sale of each. The market took a turn for the worse sending homes into foreclosure and businesses into bankruptcy.

Roman marveled at her timing because she truly was one of very few people in The Texas market that had survived a perfect storm.

She not only survived she did very well for herself but still her focus was on the parole hearing that was not far away.

The day had come for Jessie's parole hearing and he was ready. He had served one year and 7 months of his 5 year term but had established himself as a ghost inside that was trouble to no one.

He was ready to address the board with his reason for his ability to be released and move on leading a productive life having learned from his crime.

To his surprise upon entering the room he was met with the board member in which he was prepared to face but he was also met another one he had not anticipated.

Mrs.Clevinger.

"Jessie Harrell" the board stated addressing him. " Yes " he replied.

"Do you wish to address the board regarding your rehabilitation and why you feel you are fit for release?"

"I would " he said and presented line by line what he had rehearsed earlier regarding the ability to lead a productive life learning from his crime but they then gave the floor to Mrs.Clevinger.

She had some words for the board and some for Jessie Harrell as well.

She gave a heart wrenching tale that captivated every member to the point of tears and anger.

She told them of the therapy in which Amber is still involved in, the nightmares, the self consciousness and fear that she lives with every single day of her life.

She detested that Jessie was having an opportunity to be set free today when her daughter had not in fact been set free of the cage she is in and was placed in by him. She said pointing to him.

His parole was denied that afternoon and he was returned to his cell # 257.

20

JESSIE'S time of standing still and saying nothing had left him today.

His return to that cell was like a cage now even more so than it was when he had arrived.

He paced back and forth furiously and screamed as loud as he could again and again with only laughter coming back and howling along with him from the other youth inmates.

He was on his way out he said out loud. They had money and he was closer to his trust fund which would have meant more money and "no more cage!" he screamed! "FUCK!" another scream

Ohhhhhh that fucking lady. He thought to himself. Still pacing hands on his hips breathe in and breathe out he attempted to compose himself.

"Oh that fucking lady, with her smiling in that court room. Like Amber had nothing to do with this, NOTHING, please. She is in a cage I AM IN A FUCKING CAGE!" He screamed again.

"Shut up" and " Howlllll" or " Spook is getting spooked " you could hear all through the walls.

Therapy, she wants therapy. I will give her therapy thinking to himself not pacing as much after that last scream.

Fears and Nightmares huh, I will give this fucking family some fears and some nightmares when I get out of here now holding his fist balled up against the wall moving his head in-between them like he was doing push up's with his head barely touching the wall.

So began the next chapter of what would consume him for the remainder of his time in D.C. Getting even with the other family or person that put him in here. Hitting both fist's on the wall just hard enough to bounce him back to his feet where he was standing up straight. He went to the bars that led to the remainder of the facility and looked around. "fears and nightmares" he said under his breath. " fears and nightmares."

Kelley came to see him as scheduled and she was visibly upset. She had planned and prayed and wanted so badly for him to be coming home with her that day.

Jessie was reserved, he was cold and he was distant like he was not in there at all.

"Honey, I am so sorry" is all that she could say.

"Is there anything that you need or that you would like?" she asked to help soothe the situation.

Jessie did not have a great deal to say but he did ask for some romance novels and maybe some detective books too.

"You want some romance novels?" his mother asked and he cracked a smile to say that he has been reading the whole time probably learned more in here than in school which made her smile a little.

"Romance?"

"Maybe it will brighten it up in here and the detective ones will add some excitement. Not that that is lacking in here but in the cell it may be lacking, will you bring them?" he asked.

"Of course, anything else that you need or want?'

"I think you should start now." He said

"Start on what sweetie?"

"The new beginning. I think you should leave and start now so you don't have to come here each week. You could start now and I will be there when I am out and it's okay."

"I am not leaving you, are you out of your mind. You are the only thing that makes me smile."

"That is because you are not looking at anything else. It does not mean I don't want you to write or visit still or send the books and things like that but you coming every week staying in some hotel around here for another 3 or 4 years is a sentence on you too and you did not do anything."

Every time she spoke to him she was amazed at how mature and almost beyond his years he was or was becoming. He did not belong in here she thought.

"How did you get to be so grown up?' she asked him

"A cell 4 x 8 allows someone a lot of time to think " he said making a laugh but he was serious.

"I am not leaving you " she said again wiping a fallen tear.

"I am not asking you to leave me, I am asking you to start and there is a difference. This is no different than when I was born and you already had a head start on life. Well, its like that you go and get a head start and I will catch up because one of us in here is enough." He said again being dead serious and looking her right in the eye.

"I want letters, lots of em because I will need them to get through this" he was saying

"You're serious" she interrupted but he never heard her.

"I want to see pictures of where you are so I can see it and visualize it as if I am there with you but I need the books please before you go."

Kelly left that visitation and felt like she had almost for 2 years just on a roller coaster of emotion's.

There was a time when things had a place and an order and she was asking herself if she would trade this time now for those.

She did not know. She did know that Jessie would get out and the money that they have now was beyond the 3 million in life insurance, there was another 10 between the business, stocks and the house.

She was stuck here still in what was just like he said and it killed her to think of starting now or over without him. "Why in the hell was he right all the time" she said out-loud. We are both being sentenced she thought and one of them could end today.

Kelly's next visit to see Jessie would be her last for awhile. She had thought a great deal about what he had said and she felt that he was right.

She had brought him several romance and detective novels just as he had asked. He was so happy to see her and her gifts.

Jessie played it very strong for her sake. He was encouraging her to start a new life but inside he was really going to miss her more than anything.

She was the only one he had left and the only one that visited him here. He looked forward to those visits. Seeing her face or hearing her voice, it gave him hope.

He listened to her idea of going to Italy and staying for a while. He listened to her tell him how she had never been but to a few states outside of Texas and never out of the country and he could see her enthusiasm on her face, in her eyes and her voice.

"Maybe you take a turn at making wine there instead of the jam you made here." He told her which again encouraged her on her new journey and next chapter.

She watched him again get brought back to a door that would lead him somewhere she could not go and it pained her beyond measure.

She left the room then the parking lot and went right to the airport where she boarded a plane that would take far away from this place and its memories.

Jessie back in his cell began to read the jackets on the book to see which one would interest him.

He decided on a romance novel based on a woman who fell for the wrong man and just started reading. He read and he read day in and day out to pass the time and to educate himself on other topics and areas.

He had created a new identity upon entering this place so he was in search of his next identity because a "spook" was not going to get into The Clevinger family so he had create one that could and would

He read of characters with powerful names like Jack Cauldren or Nick Anoir unlike his name which sounded childish. He read about the stunning features that the lead characters had which made them stand out in a crowd unlike his spook personality that was designed to blend and not exist.

He read about the charisma of the characters and the verbiage they would use to lure woman to him. He read about the wit and the confidence. He read and he read all the while practicing just as he had done in the mirror at home. No mirror here so observe the facial expressions and features but the words and mannerisms he would learn and he would master.

He started to work out each day in his cell doing push-ups and sit-ups. He was going to change those features as well because Jessie and Spook had small frames that would be considered un attractive to woman but his new character would have the wit, charm, charisma, education and physical appearance that all of the characters he was reading had.

Jessie,for an entire year, built another person inside of himself and the physical appearance that had changed on the outside that allowed that new personality to become the dominant personality.

He now spoke, walked, acted and looked different than the 13 year old boy that had arrived here.

The pictures and letters his mother had sent him from Italy also played a role in his new persona. The travels and experiences she was on were translating to him as if he were there with her. He was becoming well versed and traveled right alongside her.

The inmates inside were seeing a different side of the person they nicknamed spook. His chest and his arms were much bigger in his shirts than before and he spoke much more now. Since they never heard him speak a great deal before no one had noticed the accents he played with turning them on and off.

They really did not know how to take him. He spent almost 2 years in the far corners of the yard when they were outside and he never challenged anyone to play hand-ball or basketball and now here he was.

He spoke the slang of the inmates when challenging and beating them on the courts. He did the weights and he did not back down if there was an altercation.

Jessie had never been in a fight in his entire life until being in here and he made it 2 years without one. His character on the other hand was not afraid and he showed it. He began to get into several fights over that next year. Some won and some lost but his persona was a force, a force to be reckoned with.

21

THE day had come for Jessie to be released from The Dallas Corrections facility.

The day had come where he would follow that line or hear that whistle for the last time.

He was issued the belongings that he had on him when this all started 5 years ago. The clothes no longer fit so he was issued a standard pair of khakis size 29 and black shoes size 10 compliments of the state.

He came into this facility as Jessie Harrell. He survived inside of it as Spook but he was coming out of it someone different and pretty soon that new person would have a new face and name.

He was met outside by his mother who just hugged him with every ounce of strength she had within her. She pulled herself back to look at him and his physical transformation.

"You are huge Jessie my god how many times a day were you working out?" she said breathless and in disbelief.

"I cant's believe its you, you are here, you are out " she said almost twirling around on the spot"

He could not help but look at her as well and all of her new features that were probably there all along and he just never noticed.

She continued to dawn her confidence which alone was what made her more beautiful but she had more than just the confidence.

She was living now and living for herself. She had color in her face, her eyes were alive and she had cut her hair from the long way she wore it before to a fashionable shoulder cut with long bangs. She was radiant he thought and told her so which the compliment from her son made her blush but it made her smile. She was so glad he was home now.

"Do you want to get something to eat?" she offered thinking that would be the first thing and she was right.

"I am starving" he replied and they found the nearest place to go sit down and eat.

Jessie devoured his hamburger and fries while his mom watched eating nothing.

"You are going to be 18 in a few months" she said watching him wash it all down with the remainder of the coke he had ordered.

"I did not forget" he said

"What do you want for your birthday?"

"I already have what I wanted, I am out!"

"So where do we live now" he asked curiously

"Wherever we want to. Where do you want to go?" She said with enthusiasm.

"How was Italy? Did you like it and are you still there?"

She went into detail and painted him the same picture he had seen from the letters and the photographs she had sent him.

"Would you like to go there? We still have a villa there if you want."

He did not know where he wanted to go other than El Paso but through that would not be the best travel plans yet. They settled on Italy so he could see if it was as beautiful as he imagined in his mind all of those times and it would allow them to get as far away from here as possible.

She took him shopping first to get clothes so he could get out of the state issued ones and then to a hotel so he could shower.

Jessie could not wait for them either. He was never very much into clothes when he was going to school. He wore what he had and if looked good then great and if not well it did not matter but after reading all of those books he felt compelled to dress more to draw attention to himself and impress.

He picked out 4 different outfit's that he could interchange to keep it interesting and while trying them on his mother again could see and tell a difference in him.

The mannerism's, the way he spoke, his vocabulary and his physique. He seemed sophisticated was the only word that she could think of to describe him.

He asked if they could stop so he could get a haircut as well. He had let his hair grow while he was inside.

He had longer hair to begin with 5 years ago, close to the shoulder but after 5 years it had grown to the middle of his back.

The stylist asked him for sure if he wanted it cut after all that time of growing and she told him how good it looked him but this too was part of his past.

This was another part of Jessie and Spook which he wanted to rid himself of.

He, the stylist and his mother all looked in the mirror at the transformation. His hair was now very short and parted on the side but now brought the confidence and sophistication he was exuding even more to life.

Jessie looked in the mirror in his new clothes and his new appearance. He was excorsising his past, shedding the skin and removing weight after weight from his body but he never once stopped thinking about The Clevinger family.

He never stopped thinking about why he was transforming and changing and soon enough his transformation would be complete.

The doorbell rang to the room they were staying, which was a very nice room entitled the presidential suite. Kelly approached the door asking who it was

"Fresh Towel's mam?" The voice returned.

She not even thinking about it and figured it was Jessie who had requested them and opened the door.

In came 3 large men with the first carrying the towels and threw them onto the bed. Kelly stunned stepped back and kept walking backwards till she reached the glass door leading to the balcony. One man looked at her and the other looked around the room. One of the men went to the restroom and walked right in bringing Jessie back out with him.

"Spook" the one man said who carried in the towels. " I do believe you have a debt to pay for a certain service that we provided!"

"Of course he said" then his mother interrupted " What debt?"

"Mom, don't" he fired back and gave her eyes that were an attempt to say let me handle this.

"You are spook, correct?,I mean you look a little different than Mack described you?

"No that's me I just had no way to get into touch with to settle. You know he set it up and I did not know when it was being done and did not know it was that would so I had no way."

"And then", the man interrupted him " Mack had a little accident up in the showers, right? Convenient too" his head nodding up and down.

"That had nothing to do with me, I have your money let me settle and we can be on our way". Jessie reasoned.

"You know we did not know if it was you but you were the only Jessie Harrell being released today and that was his name correct?" The man paused.

"Who's name?" his mother asked not sure of what his meaning was

"It was" Jessie said " $10,000 right, that is what I owe you?"

"There is going to be a slight interest penalty on the loan as it is past due a year plus" he said grinning.

"How much?" he asked

"We want 50k and we want it today, is that going to be a problem? You see we figure there has been no investigation so the deed was clean and there is no more Mack so we get his share too for doing all of the, you know, dirty work."

"Mom" he said looking at her and then going to her " I need 50,000 to be taken from the account."

"Are you crazy she said under her breath, who are these guys and why do you owe them $50,000" her eyes bulging and scared.

"They protected me when I was inside and I paid them for it otherwise I would have been dead in there. We have to go and get them the money."

"So" the large man said " Are we ready to go take a ride to the bank?"

Jessie got dressed quickly and wanted this to be over right away. He was not out even 4 hours and the past had already found him.

They drove to the bank and had to go inside with the large man with her the entire way. The other 2 remained in the car with Jessie as they waited.

While they waited for the teller to complete their transaction she removed herself from the desk to obtain a managers signature" Please excuse me for a moment " She said to Kelly and the large man seated at her desk.

"Why did you ask if that was his name when you spoke to Jessie ?"Kelly asked the large man.

"Spook, because the deed we did involved a Harrell and if spook's last name was not Harrell than we would have had the wrong guy."

"What exactly is it that you did?" she asked him and he responded with a " you don't wanna know, I got the right guy here and we are getting what is owed and you don't need or want to know anymore than that lady." He said as the teller returned with her request.

They left the bank with the $50,000 as promised. Once in the car Kelly remained silent while the men celebrated their score on route back to the hotel.

"Spook, you didn't have anything to do with Mack's knifing did you?" The large man asked ceasing all of the celebration that was taking place.

"He was a friend of ours you know it wasn't just business and if you had something to do with it we may have another problem and another debt" He said turning his body around to the seat looking at Jessie seated in the back in between the 2 other men he brought with him.

"Do I look like I could have taken Mack in a knife fight" he said jokingly " seriously!" he added

"You don't but your eyes do " he said staring right into them from the front seat.

"You have your money, it is what I owed you and him and then some. I did not have anything to do with his death. They told me."

"I know I know " the man interrupted " I know what they said" he said still looking nowhere but into Jessie's eyes.

They pull back into the hotel they were staying and the men pile out of the vehicle as Jessie and Kelly follow suit.

"This concludes our business then, have a nice life spook" the large man said as they turned to walk in the opposite direction as the front door to the hotel.

Jessie and Kelly do the same except into the front door to the hotel and before the door shuts " One more thing spook" The large man shouted so they could hear him. "We buckled him in real tight just like you asked and the message was loud and clear!"

Jessie went to the elevator and hit the top button with his mom right behind him. She waited till they were in the elevator and the doors had shut before all of her nerves came apart

"Who was that?, why were they here?, what did they do?, how are you mixed up in it? and buckled who in real tight?, what message? She rambled with a high pitch shout done while whispering.

Jessie said nothing on the elevator ride he just listened until they got into the room and he had no choice but to explain a few things to his mom.

'They protected me inside, you don't know what it's like in there and what they did and do I made a deal with them to protect me." He explained

"Who is Mack and why are they asking if you killed him?"

"He was my cell mate for a while when he got there and it was actually him that I offered to pay to protect me, so to speak on the inside, and then he was killed so maybe they thought I may have something to do with it which I don't. It was a gang thing"

"Buckled who in tight" she asked going right down the line of questions that she had.

"That one I don't know, these guys do drugs and they do a lot of things for a lot of people but it was protection money which I would not be standing here right now talking to you had I not made that deal 3 years ago."

"We cant stay here" she said panicky they found you, they found us right here so quickly. We have to go" she told him

"Get your things. Anything that you are taking and if not we will get them when we get where we are going" and they left the hotel as fast as they could into a cab to the airport.

They were headed to the airport now and he was leaving all of this behind just as his mother did 2 years ago. The plane ride to Pisa gave more of that solitude time to think but with a much better view.

He sat in his comfortable 1st class seat and thought about the monotony he had just spent the past 4 years in. He thought about his father and his last thought's or words, and he thought about the look on Randall Mack 10 Humphries face as the shank when in and out of his heart.

He thought about how good he felt right now and he thought about the Clevinger family. What were they doing right now and where did they go?

22

THE Clevinger Family had packed and left their Arlington home, work and friends for a new life.

They had decided on San Diego to start over mostly because of the medical facilities there and they were interested in gaining the work of Norman Clevinger, Ambers father.

Norman was and still is a great surgeon. He was attending Princeton University when he met Nancy Clevinger, his wife now of 20 years.

They had been married for 2 years when Nancy greeted Norman with the news of their first child. The 2 of them could not have been happier and they named her Amber after Nancy's mother. Norman graduated from Princeton. He married Nancy, he took on a job at Boston's Mass General and then he was having a child. It was truly a wonderful time for them both.

The news of the baby and their car being broken into followed by a home robbery made them look at where they lived. They were not home when the home was robbed but the sheer idea of coming home to your things ransacked and damaged left them feeling violated and unsafe particularly Nancy who was 6 months along.

They researched where they could go and found that the smaller town life of an area like Arlington Texas was a good place for them to go. The market was doing well and they felt it was a place that was on the move.

Norman accepted a job with Arlington's surgical team and Nancy gave birth to Amber in that very same hospital.

They brought her home and they never looked back.

The San Diego move proved to be the right idea for each of them.

Norman was right back to work as was Nancy taking care of her daughter and her husband. The only real issue here is that Amber was now fast becoming 18 and she loved her mother with all of her heart but also began to resent the control she had over her.

She had to know everything. She was invading and unbearable at times. Amber had gone through a great deal with a rape, a trial in which she testified and then being moved away from all of her friends she grew up with there. It was a lot so she agreed to go to therapy to work on discussing and dealing with all of the emotions.

Dr. Elliot Feingold was her therapist whom she saw twice a week for the past year.

When they moved to San Diego they felt as they had hoped it would. It felt like a new start and a breath of fresh air.

The trees, the greenery and the ocean. Miles and miles of the ocean for you to enjoy and it staring right back at you. They found a home that spoke to them in Carlsbad and it was close enough to everything they needed to be close to.

The house was a corner lot with grass everywhere out front. The flooring was wood with bright yellow and coffee browns painted on the interior with white trim. Single story house that was less than 2 blocks to the ocean.

Amber and her mother found beach cruiser bikes in the garage when they moved in and went for a long stroll around the area to discover their new home.

The air was so fresh and had a fragrance all its own. Everyone here seemed so happy. There were people running, roller skating and bicycling everywhere every day even the dogs out here were riding skateboards and on the front of bikes.

The day to day majestic sunshine, waves and sand were just not enough for Amber to move on so they found Dr. Feingold and she began seeing him twice a week on Tuesdays and Thursday for an hour each visit.

"How are you sleeping?" " Is it better?" he asked her

"it depends" she replied " I have times when there is no issue sleeping and with no nightmares and then there is times when I will not sleep all day." I am taking what you prescribed but it does not help"

"Okay we will find something that will help you relax more during bed time, tell me about the nightmares."

"Do we have to talk about them?" she asked him

"Are they the same ones you were having or are they different?'

Amber had a re-occurring dream since that night in the house. The dream varies from time to time but the message was the same and she was always being chased. It seemed it was the only dream she had. If she slept at all then she dreamt of being chased in some form or fashion.

She dreamt about the test the medical people ran on her after she left the house. She dreamt of the way they opened and poked every part of her body and the questions she had to answer that night by total strangers.

She dreamt about going to the trial to say those things to an audience and how if she did not say anything that night how she might have been pregnant because he did not use a condom.

Nightmares and dreams consumed her in the evening and she had taken every pill that was on the market or being developed to remove them.

She liked Dr. Fiengold and he was helping her. He at least was a person besides her mother to talk to and this was the basis of which many of the session's they would have would be about.

"She is always there." she said getting away from the nightmares.

"Have you been making any friends in school, ones you would consider to be friends?' he asked her to see how her socialism was coming.

"Not really but that is mostly because I don't know if we are going to move again and even if we don't move my mom would never let me go out with them or come over unless we are where she can see us" she replied angrily.

"What about school, your grades are still top honors?"

"Yes. " she replied and added that she would graduate soon.

"What about college then, have you considered that college and dorm living would free you of your concerns with your mother?"

"You will be 18 and you will free to decide the things that you wish to do as long as they are sound decisions there will be no reason for your mother to interfere" he said now elbows on his knees vs. sitting with his back to the chair and his legs crossed."

"Your mother wants the best for you and for you to feel safe which is why you are now."

"How is your relationship with your father going?" he continued

"We have always been closer in certain ways. They are both great parents and I am grateful but my dad does not demand or impose his will the way my mother does. We talk and he will listen instead of her talking and my listening."

"What would you like to do? If you went to college what profession would you like to pursue?" he asked getting back to her

"I don't know" she said and asked him " is that terrible, I should know shouldn't I ?"

"Perfectly normal to not know what you want to do with your life at 18 Amber I was just curious if you had some thoughts. You see if you are able to see that profession and yourself in that profession then you will begin to occupy your mental state with the tools to achieve that goal and therefore leave behind the objects that consume your mental state presently and in this case. The Past."

That did make sense to her and was another reason she liked coming here. She was able to speak her mind about her mother and get the advice she wanted without a discussion of why it is right or wrong.

The plane ride was long but the landing was smooth. They landed at The Galilei Airport in Pisa Italy and would take a train into Florence where the villa Kelly had been staying was still available.

They had some time before the Frecciargento train left so she showed him some of the sites.

She showed him the water and explained how beautiful it is at night when you walk over the Ponte Vecchio bridge and see the lights from the city and building reflect off of the water.

She showed him the Accademia Gallery which is where Michelangelo's famous statue of David was kept. "There a so many museums here Jessie, you will love it".

They boarded the train to Florence and she asked Jessie to sit at the window so he can drink in the sights before the sun had gone down.

The ride there gave him all of the images she wrote about while he was gone and inside of that place. She spoke of the area as healing and full of energy.

He saw rolling hills that extended forever and were the greenest shade of color he had ever seen.

There were fields of what looked like Sunflowers with horses and running streams but pretty soon the darkness had come and the only thing he saw in the window was his reflection staring back him and he closed the shade.

They took a taxi and found their way to the villa she had spent so much of her time in starting over. " This is your special place now Jessie " she told him as they left what items they had brought with them at the doorway and closed the door.

He did not sleep well that night and was not sure if it had to do with the not being in the place he had slept for over 4 years or the visit from Randall's friends.

The thought that those guys were able to find him today was unsettling and who is to say that they would not attempt to shake him down later for money because he saw that it was obvious to them that his mother had no idea what had transpired.

That is worth money to them. They come right after us for more money or go to the insurance company if we failed to comply.

He did not like it at all.

Yes they were gone now and yes they were far away from Arlington or Texas for that matter but who knew what length these guys would travel especially if they saw today that she was able to accommodate their request for $50,000 with little hesitation.

They could be doing more research on her now to understand who they were dealing with and once they knew about the business being sold on top of the insurance there is a good chance that they come back for deeper pocket money.

All he kept thinking about was El Paso.

He woke the next morning and wanted to do some research on El Paso. He was looking for Heaven's Gate which was the bar that Randall spoke about and the guy who ran it named Nelson Pritchard.

This was how they would not be able to find Jessie Harrell or Spook ever again. This is also how his next plan unfolds.

There it was, he thought to himself, this is a moment I have waited 5 years for. The smell of breakfast being cooked filled the air.

This was a symbol that better days had arrived. He ran into the kitchen to meet his mother as she worked inside of the kitchen just as he had remembered her but this kitchen was far smaller than the one they had in Arlington.

"Would you care for some help" he said to her

"No go outside look at the view" she told him.

He walked towards the French doors which were open and walked onto the balcony.

The sky had no clouds and was blue as far as he could see. The sun was shining and it felt like home on his face as he closed his eyes. He could hear the sounds of nature all around him. The birds singing and the water running. He could feel his mother in this place even if she were not here right now. This belonged to her and it will soon be time to find a place that would become his.

He returned and sat on the bar that was directly in front of the kitchen.

"Have you made friends since you have been staying here? He asked.

"I have and I look forward to introducing them to my son" she returned with pride. "

"I want you to stay and relax by the pool today and we can decide what to do later but for now it is food and then more food, no arguing."

No argument here he thought and he reveled in watching her in the kitchen.

He remembered many of her meals and her being in the kitchen at home but again the face she once wore made what she was doing look like work. Here in this place not only was her face different but so were her actions.

She danced in the kitchen as she listened to the flamenco guitar coming from the speakers. She danced and she lived. She was doing because she wanted to and not because she had to. It was inspiring and he could not help but smile.

"Do you want to eat by the pool?" she asked him and without him answering she grabbed his plate and led him out the French doors. Jessie followed her and the plate out the door and to the right where a smaller wooden gate that was rounded at the top opened.

There was the pool, private pool outside disturbed by no one and surrounded by lemon trees, flowers and a section of grape vineyards. The pool overlooked the same breathtaking view he saw from the balcony.

There was a table and 4 chairs set up on the deck and Kelly sat his plate there for him to sit and eat. " I will leave you to yourself for a little bit so you can enjoy you breakfast and the view." She told him as he sat down.

"This place has been good for me Jessie and I hope it is as good for you, enjoy your breakfast sweetie." And she was off.

He dug right into the breakfast omelet she had prepared which was full of garden tomatoes, mushrooms, spinach and topped with cheeses.

This was the best omelet he had ever had in his life.

The view may have had something to do with it and he again closed his eyes to let the sun kiss his face as he chewed.

23

AS the plane was boarding and then departed from Dulles Airport in Dallas bound for Pisa the large man that had escorted Jessie and his mother to the bank to retrieve his debt owed to him was watching.

He watched them board the plane and he made sure there were no layovers along the way. They were going to Pisa and although he was not sure where they would go from there he was confident he and his team could locate them upon their arrival.

The debt was paid but knowing that the mother had no idea of what plans were made for her husband and allowed her the fortune she now was spending made him feel that there was more than $50,000 they could afford.

Something in his eyes also as he looked at him in the car something told him Spook knew more than he was admitting about their fallen friend Randall. The money was the true purpose of the tail to the airport though and Randall would understand that, it's just business and his business sense told him there was more money to be earned.

The large man made a call " Pack some things, get Randy and meet me at the Dulles Airport by The American Airlines check in.

We are going to Italy for a few days" he told the man on the other end and hung up.

Graduation day had come for Amber and although it was another day that should mean more to her and be amazing she was saddened that she was not with her friends that she had grown up with.

Her mother had a difficult time understanding Ambers discontent because she herself was loving San Diego.

Mrs. Clevinger dove into the society aspect of the area and was heavily involved in the school, volunteer work, community service and felt a little celebrity in the area due to her ability to be so unafraid and vocal. She was a hit in San Diego.

She pressured Amber to do the same things she had been doing and it would produce the same results should tell her but Amber was and had become far more introverted and each time she saw her mother in public almost performing like an entertainer on stage in made her further retreat inside of herself.

This would be again communicated in her next session with Dr. Feingold.

"She is driving me crazy" she told him

"It is getting worse, it has never been like or am I just loosing that much control over who I am?"

"Give me an example" he would tell her to have an understanding of what she is feeling.

"She asked me to go with her door to door and do volunteer work for Senator Patrick Gray and I said I did not want to so she tells me how not going out and doing things if this nature are what is wrong with me, like it is my fault. I don't want to go to do stupid door to door or cold calling people. Just because it does not interest me so how is that my fault?"

"Okay" he starts " this gets back to us finding something that moves you like we talked about before. You interest need to be fed. Did you think about some of the things we talked about last time and are there interest that you have to pursue?"

"I thought about painting." She told him half expecting some criticism or a why painting comment.

"Excellent" he said and repeated " Excellent."

He was almost excited. " What style of painting do you want to pursue?"

"I don't know yet, the painting decision alone was all I could come up with."

"Doesn't matter, this is a great step. This is what you do know Amber you research what style moves you and I can help with too."

"I have a good friend that I went to college with many years ago and she was an art student and now is a fairly accomplished painter here in town. I will get her number and call her to let her know that you and I know each other and see if she will spend some time with you and your new interest."

He excused himself for the moment and went to his desktop rolodex and writes the name and number for her to take with her.

Lillian Caufield was her name and her office / studio was located right there in Del Mar.

"You call her by tomorrow, she will be expecting your call?"

"Are you going to tell her I am a patient?" she asked concerned.

"Heavens no. You are a graduate student whom I met and was interested in the pursuit of art to explore and that is what I will tell her, the rest is up to you Amber."

———————————

Amber went to the library after her meeting with Dr. Faingold and checked out various books on painting. She researched water and oil, abstract and expressionism's she had no idea there were so many forms.

Looking at the full color and thumbnail portraits page after page made her feel better. These people expressed themselves through the canvas she thought they expressed themselves using color and a brush to tell a story." I could do that" she said.

"Hello Caufield Stuidio, May I help you?" the voice answered and was so pleasant.

"Yes, Lillian Caufield please."

"Speaking" the woman said with again the warmest voice Amber thought. Her mother had a commanding voice. One that demanded attention but this voice was tranquil and calm like one who would read bed time stories or books on tape.

"My name is Amber Clevinger and I met Dr.Feingold who said that I should call you to see if you had some time to sit down with me so I could ask some questions to learn more about art"

"Elliot, yes of course. I have been expecting your call dear. When would you like to stop by?" She offered the address and location of her studio and then accepted Ambers day and time for tomorrow at 3:00.

"Would you like me to bring anything? Amber asked

"An open mind and heart" the woman with the wonderful voice said" You just bring an open mind and heart and let's see where that takes us."

Amber for a moment thought that Dr.Feingold had told Lillian about herself hence the open heart and mind comment but even if he had she felt intrigued none the less.

It felt good to be feeling something besides her staple anxiety, anger or fear feelings and if going there gave that to her it was worth her travels.

24

I T was a beautiful shop she owned. It was in a shopping area beachside in the town of Cardiff located near Del Mar.

The building was a 2 story narrow Victorian with windows filling the front entrance.

Walking into the shop felt like a peaceful light and if you stopped right there at the door it felt like a conveyer belt brought you the rest of the way if your feet wanted to or not. It called you like a playmate wanting to play.

She was greeted by a woman at the door "May I help you dear?" the woman asked.

Amber responded if she could speak to Lillian Caufield.

"Is she expecting you?" " she is Amber replied and as the woman was walking to get Lillian from the back somewhere the woman turned back and complimented Amber on her top saying " that color looks very good on you" with a smile.

Something about being in here made her feel welcome and at home. She walked towards some of the painting hung on the wall and she dove into them, all of them. The colors, the message, the vision, the detail and the stories they told.

"Amber" there was that voice, she turned as Lillian introduced herself.

"Hello Mrs. Caufield, thank you for taking the time to meet with me."

"Lillian dear, you call me Lillian and this is my assistant Jayne."

"Hello Jayne, how do you do my name is Amber Clevinger.

"Well Amber Clevinger, Welcome to The Caufield Studio." Jayne said with the grandiosity of a Ringling Brothers Circus as she took a bow.

Lillian walked Amber to her office which was located up the stairs and into the back. This room was darker than the walls lined with white wall to wall in the studio downstairs.

The white truly accentuated the color in all of the paintings and up here it was wood but rich in colors as if a rainbow had crashed right inside of this very office. She was organized and her manner was warm.

She had shorter hair that was naturally silver but looked very comfortable on her. She wore jeans that had tiny specs of paint as if they had been through a few canvasses together and a top that was billowy and moved as she did like an octopus in the ocean. The top was purple which highlighted her silver hair and blue eyes.

She was beautiful Amber thought to herself and not in the way that many people in San Diego were beautiful. This woman was beautiful inside and out and she was glad she had come here today.

"Elliot tells me you may have an interest in art, is that true?"

"It is but I am not sure. I just graduated and I guess like many others I am not sure what it is that I want to do and he suggested that seeing some of your work or talking with you may give me some insight if this is what I could pursue." She said honestly.

"Have you ever painted before or wanted to?"

"I have never painted before but to be able to do some of the things that are on your wall downstairs is moving and interesting."

"Why is it that you feel you want to paint?" Lillian asked her.

"Do you have a story to tell or a vision you wish to share with the world or more for yourself to keep?"

"I don't know" she said starting to feel the anxiety again and not the peace that greeted her upon her arrival here. " I think I want to get some of the things inside of me out and I think putting them on a canvas to see what they look like face to face would be good for me and if the work I produced was good then maybe it would be good for others too."

"Does that make any sense? She asked Lillian.

"In-deed it does dear, in-deed it does" Lillian repeated looking at her and studying her.

She did have some demons within her, she could feel them as well as see them on her demeanor but she liked her poetic honesty. She liked that this girl was not trying to be anything other than what she was and who she was even though she probably had good reason to.

"Okay" she declared "let's talk about your schedule then. When do you think you could come in here and dedicate at least 2 hours each week?" Lilian asked her

"I just graduated and I do not work so my schedule is free except Monday and Thursday at 10:00"

"Then you will come here tomorrow, which I know is a Saturday but if we are going to do this then we should start right away and see if there is something there."

"I can be here tomorrow" she said excited. I did not have plans anyway she was thinking but kept that to herself.

"Tomorrow it is then. Let's say 11:00, dress down a little so you do not ruin anything and don't forget the heart and the mind as those 2 tools are the most important for what we will be doing"

Ambers anxiety had gone away again. Defeated in battle it seemed in this place like it was no match for what was inside of this studio or the company of Lillian Caufield.

"Thank you Lillian, I will see you tomorrow" she said leaving the studio.

Amber drove down the strip of highway that looked out to the ocean on her way home and with the windows down and her hair blowing around her face she for the first time in a very long time felt a place or a person besides the Dr. and prescription's that made her feel good.

This was a place for her and she was truly grateful.

25

JESSIE was celebrating his 18 Birthday in the villa with a number of people he had never met before. The friends or new friends his mother had made during her time spent here.

There was no mention of where Jessie had been or what happened only that he had made the decision to join her and them there which was great cause for celebration.

There was food and drink in every portion of the villa including the patio outside. Food he had seen or heard the names of before but tried all that was present for the sake of " When in Rome". He thought to himself.

Hand shake after hand shake and hug after hug he was dizzy which could have been the wine as well. He had not drank anything for some-time now and even though he was eating the enthusiasm, the festivities, the people, the laughter and then the wine must have been a little too much for him.

He excused himself and went for a walk down the rolling green hillside he looked at from the balcony each morning. It was different at night but even the moonlight and darkness could not suppress the colors that radiated.

He took it in for about 20 minutes just lost in a daze and catching his breath and decided to return. Up the stairs that lead to the pool deck right outside of the house he saw a girl his age but older maybe 20 or 21. The old Jessie would not have been able to go and speak to her but this one that had been reading and reading for a moment just like this saw it as an opportunity to perfect his new craft.

"Hello" he said warmly approaching her as she sat on one of the deck chaise chairs with the sling back to the almost a lying down position so she could stare at the star's.

"Hello." she returned.

"I am Jessie Harrell" extending his hand to greet her.

"The birthday boy" she said smiling.

"I am and it is. I wish to thank you for attending this milestone." She laughed

"You know my name and you are here to celebrate with me yet I do not know your name" he said taking a seat at the end of the lounge chair where her legs were and shoes off.

She sat up more situating herself on the chair and introduced herself and Franchessca. " Franchessca" he repeated.

"it is a great pleasure to meet you this evening. How are the stars treating you thins evening? I assume you are here outside by the pool for them, no? He said with a touch of an Italian accent.

Franchessca's eyes squinted a little in an effort to look at him more closely.

"I will leave you to them, do enjoy" he said getting up from the chair and now looking down at her. " I do hope we see each other again and you continue to see those star's" he said to her walking away to the gate which led inside of the house.

She was stunned, what a cutie she thought and found herself getting up from the chair and walking to the same gate that led into the house.

She stayed at the gate though and did not go inside. She instead watched him from outside making his way from guest to guest. He was smiling and he was entertaining and it was effortless she thought.

She wanted to get to know him more and as he made his way to the kitchen to pour another glass of wine he saw her. His eyes met hers and it startled her that she was watching him and was caught. He did not startle or say anything. He simply raised the glass of wine he had poured and toasted it to her then drank from the glass. She felt a tingle in her toes as he walked away from her for the second time.

The 3 men departed the plane in Pisa and made their way to a pub where they would begin to work on locating their business partner's. They had no photos and they did not speak Italian but they did have a persuasive way of obtaining information.

They described each the woman and the boy to everyone they came into contact with and even mentioned their name in the hopes they were using their real name. No luck at the pub so they checked into a hotel and obtained 3 rooms while still continuing their search.

They called all of the hotels near the airport in search of a Mr. or Mrs. Harrell and again no luck.

They had some time and were committed to spending at least 5 days on their crusade and in the event they did not find them then it would be considered a vacation of sort's.

The 3rd day had come and they decided to travel to some of the other towns in case they did not stay in Pisa. They were in Pisa eating at a small bistro by the museums when they decided to look at the wine selection to go along with their sandwiches. The large man went from selection to selection and found one that very much wet his appetite. A Siena from The Harrell Winery.

He put the menu down and smiled. The waiter approached and he began to ask the broken English speaking waiter about the wine and where it was made.

He stumbled through what he knew about it a cross between a merlot and a cabernet grape then " No" the large man said interrupting him " where is it made?" The waiter took the bottle and read the back to find it was produced in a family winery in Florence.

The men then asked that their sandwiches be wrapped to go and they departed out the door taking the bottle of wine with them.

Next stop as they boarded the train,,,,, Florence.

Amber arrived at the studio and said hello to Jayne who was perkily at the counter answering the phone and greeting every guest that walked in.

She watched Lillian come down the stairs to greet her and she led her to the back room where the studio to paint was. It was a small room with 2 windows which were open. There was a breeze and the sounds of the ocean and passing gulls danced in and out of the room.

A blank canvass and drop cloth was set up and before her. Lillian offered her a coverall to wear and dressed her.

"Are you ready, dear?" she asked her as if they were setting off on a journey or if as if she were about to face an opponent."

"I am" she said affirmingly looking right into Lillian's eyes

Lillian turned her around to face the blank canvass again with her hands on her shoulder and standing directly behind her so she could not back up and escape.

"I would like to start with oil and an abstract painting today."

"What do I do?" Amber asked her not sure

"Did you read or research anything before starting?" this was a test in itself to see if she were committed to doing this.

"I did and abstract is shapes and images, correct?"

"Correct, dear. Now paint using your brush. Paint any image or shape that comes to mind and use any color you wish. Open your mind and your heart. Put the brush to the canvass and let it guide you. If you trust yourself then you will find what you seek and from that search will come an amazing portrait." She said to her leaving the room.

Amber stared at the canvass and again here came the anxiety and here came the fear.

She closed her eyes and listened to the sounds of the ocean. She breathed in and she breathed out. She dipped the brush and then placed the brush to the canvass and let it guide her.

Lillian did not disturb her or check in on her nor did Amber leave the room in search of anything. She painted and she did not stop until an image was complete.

She stepped back to look at her sequence of colors and the image's it formed all on its own with very little direction from her. She felt fulfilled as she looked at this. Lillian entered the room and stayed in the door where curtains were parted to enter.

"What do you think" Amber asked her.

"I think you have a talent." "That is what I think." She said and went closer to observe the still wet strokes on the canvass.

"How do you feel about it?" she asked turning her head back.

"I feel whole she said" without even thinking about what she said and then tried to back track that statement " that sounds corny".

"No-No-No Lillian said waiving off the gesture literally through the air with her hands and stood before her closely looking into her eyes. "if it makes you feel whole then you embrace that gift child, that is not corny. Art is an expression and an extension of your being. Let it make you whole Amber it is okay."

"Then I love it" she said her head up and producing a smile

"So do I" she told her smiling. " I think that our next visit will be impressionism, are you okay with next Saturday same time?"

"I can't wait"

"Do you want to take the painting home?"

"Not yet" Amber told her " I want to get good enough where some of my work is hanging on your walls. " Can I keep it here for now?"

"Of course you can, I will see you next Saturday."

The morning after Jessie's 18 Birthday was a good one. He had met several people that evening and demonstrated his ability to work a room. To hold an audience, to make people laugh and to enjoy his conversation.

He had also held the attention of a very beautiful Franchessca whom he would set out in search of today. He rode into town to look around the shops in search of her and it was not long until he had found her waiting tables in a small Café.

He took a seat outside under the umbrella and waited for her arrival. She approached and was surprised to see him and he too acted surprised even though he had spent the past 3 hours looking.

"I am so happy to see you, I was not sure I would have the opportunity although I truly wanted to and here you are." He said lifting both hands towards her as if she were a gift and a surprise.

"Frencehessca, yes?"

"yes Jessie she said looking at him like a cat that ate a canary.

"Can I take you somewhere, out maybe on a date, you know " he said again playing with an Italian accent.

"I get off at 5:00 she told him"

"Then I will be here at 5:00 he said walking away.

"Aren't you going to eat she asked?"

"No, thank you I already ate." He told her with an expression that he was not there by accident. She again felt that tingling in her toes.

Jessie arrived at the Café at 5:00 and was greeted by Franchessca who was looking forward to seeing him again.

They walked along the water front next to the shops looking at the buildings and talking. He told her of his mother's triumphs coming to Italy to start over and how he would join her as well to start over.

"Are you running from something, is that what you mean when you starting over?" she asked him and explained that what he meant was more of a searching than a starting. They stopped walking over a bridge and he told her he was searching for the places and the experiences that will fulfill him and enrich his life.

"We look for things constantly, we are searching always for maybe the perfect recipe, the best glass of wine or the most beautiful girl." He said leaning in to kiss her.

"My search is over" he said and kissed her again but bringing her into him.

"Would you like to see where I live?" she asked as it was starting to get dark and before they left the bridge he looked down at the water. "What is it?" she asked him

"My mom always told me how beautiful the lights were when it became dark and they reflected off of the water, she was right."

He told her again looking into her eyes. She grabbed his hand and directed him at a quick pace towards where she lived.

Her apartment was small and not furnished with a great deal of things but it was hers alone and comfortable. She explained that she had to take a shower and to make himself at home.

She departed to the back bedroom and he could hear the water running. He went to the kitchen where she had several bottles of red wine and he opened one.

Carrying the wine and 2 glasses he walked into the bedroom. He poured 2 glasses of wine and began to light the candles that were in her room.

She emerged from the shower and placed a robe while she dried hurrily but when she came from the bathroom into the candle light room she closed each end of the robe tightly and nervously.

"Jessie what are you doing?"

"I brought you some wine" he said bringing the glass towards her and he could sense her being uncomfortable.

"From the moment I saw by the pool under the stars all I could think about was seeing you by candle light. I was in search of the most beautiful woman and I have found her."

He raised his glass to toast her." To seeking what you desire and finding it" he said to her and she raised her glass to his clink, they sounded.

He moved in to kiss her as she put her glass down. His hand gripped the back of her head pulling her hair slightly so her head went back and he kissed her neck.

He let go of her hair and her head came back again he kissed her lips. She unfolded the knot in front of her robe and he removed it dropping it to the ground.

She began to take his shirt off and un-buttom his pants dropping those to the floor as well. She backed him up to the bed until he hit and feel into the center bringing her with him. She guided him inside of her and looked down at him while she found the spot that pleased her the most.

Searching, he thought to himself and almost laughed but her enjoyment was far from funny.

She moved back and forth, up and down and her long dark hair with her. He loved how it felt when her hair came down over him as she bent down to kiss him moving her body faster and faster.

She moved back up with both of her hands digging into his chest and her head back far enough as if she was again looking for the stars.

She and he moaned until they had each reached a climax which sent her body crashing down to him and then rolled to her back beside him in search of catching her breath.

He turned to her and told her "that was the most amazing experience he had ever felt." this pleased her because she too was enjoying his company. They laid there for some time before either spoke after that exchange just satisfied.

The candles danced and flickered when she rolled over to look at him and asked " What are you doing tomorrow?" he smiled and said that he was probably spending time with his mother since they were away for so long and that he should get going because he was supposed to have dinner together."

She did not like him leaving so soon but found it endearing that he was interested in spending time with his mother. He dressed and went to the side of the bed where she still laid in the bed.

"I am not kidding, that was the most amazing experience." She blushed and said" we will have to do that again, you know where to find me." And he was off out the door and into the night.

He felt incredible and he felt like all of those characters he read about. He rode on through the town and it was only 7:00 so he stopped quickly at a café to get a coffee. He was parking his bike when through the window he saw the same 3 men that were in the hotel a few days ago.

They were asking questions and did not notice him outside the store. He slowly got back on the bike and as he started to ride away one of the men looked through the window and asked the other 2 " is that him?"

They walked out of the store and could not tell because they last saw him with longer hair and his hair was short now. He rode as fast as he could to the Villa where his mom was waiting for him. "I knew it" he said aloud while he was riding " I knew they were going to come after us, how do they keep finding me?" That is it he thought to himself we have to get to El Paso.

26

M OM" Jessie shouts upon entering the villa. " Jessie, I am out by the pool she says."

"We need to go" he tells her running to her.

"What, what do you mean we need to go, where are we going?"

"Those men from Arlington, the ones I paid to protect me."

"Yes"

"They are back, they are here and they are looking for us."

"Why would they be looking for us, you paid them."

"Mom we need to go, I need you to trust me and listen to me and lets get out of here right now."

He tells her grabbing her hand and leading her up from the chair she was seated in. She stops him mid way to the gate " What are you not telling me Jessie Harrell, I want the truth this minute!"

She demands as he is still trying guide and direct her inside.

He stops trying to guide her and looks at her " I will tell you everything I promise but we have to go right now or they will find us here before too long okay, please."

She listens to him and goes inside to pack a few things and calls a cab to pick them up. They wait for 20 minutes till a cab arrives to take them " Where are we going she asked Jessie sitting next to her in the back seat of the cab?" " Take us to the airport " he tells the cab driver. " Where are we going Jessie?" He explains that it is not safe to say right at the moment fear-full that the 3 men will locate the cab driver and get it out of him so right now all the cab driver knew was the airport and there is a world of possibilities from there which were far better odds in their favor to not be found.

Ambers next visit to Dr. Feingold was different from the previous ones and he could tell right away. " I see that you met Liilian" I trust that it went well. What did you think?"

"I think she is amazing and I love her studio. I love how she carries herself. Thank you so much for setting that up I really think this is good for me."

"Excellent". He says "Excellent!" and how does your mother and father like the idea of your painting?"

"I have not told either of them yet because I did not know If I would like it plus the time just has not come up but I will tell them soon"

Their session went on to discuss what she had worked on that day and how the sounds in the room and Lillian's encouragement seem to rid her collected thoughts of anxiety, fear or depression.

This was what she was looking for and it was not on a couch in Dr. Feingold's office and it was not in the circles of friends she would or would not have and was not in pharmaceutical form. This was simple and raw she told him. She was on her way to healing.

She had told her parents about the new experience at dinner that evening. Her mother was the first to comment " When did you decide that you want to become a painter?" the tone was comical and almost condescendingly.

"I did not say I wanted to become a painter, I just said it was thing I discovered and was honestly the best thing she has felt in a long time."

Her father jumped into the conversation and told her how pleased he was that something she found was bringing her that type of fulfillment,

"When do we get to see some of the work?" her father asked and before Amber answered her mother jumped right in

"Where did you get the idea to paint and where is the studio is this a class is there a professor?" she clamored

"Dr. Feingold" she said " It is not a class, this was a friend of his. Lillian Caufield is her name and she owns a studio in Cardiff up by Del Mar.

"I have never heard of her" her mother said acting as if she were a connoisseur of fine art.

"I just went up on Saturday and did some abstract work to see if I liked it and she said she would work with me on other pieces if I chose to move forward with it. I am not kidding it was the best I have felt and she is amazing."

Nancy Clevinger was not crazy about the Dr. putting ideas into her head without her knowledge and she would make a point to discuss that with him in the near future. She also had made a point to drive up to Cardiff in search of the studio and Lillian Caufield.

Dr. Feingold had checked his messages and one left for him was from Nancy Clevinger asking him to return a call as soon as possible.

He dialed the number left for him and he reached her at home " Hello" she answered.

"Mrs. Clevinger, yes this is Dr. Feingold returning your call."

"Thank you Dr. I wanted to schedule some time to meet with you at your office if possible, the sooner the better.

"Is this a therapy meeting or a social one? He asked to clarify

The idea angered her that he implies she need to see him for therapy" No Dr. this is about Amber. I want to get your thoughts on how she is doing. When can we meet?'

He was not interested in meeting with her to discuss this matter but agreed to in the later afternoon tomorrow if that were convenient with her and she agreed.

Her next stop was to Cardiff to visit The Caufield studio.

At the airport Jessie searches for a airline that will take them to El Paso. They purchase the tickets and waited to board.

"You had better tell me what the hell is going on right now, Why are we going to El Paso and what are those men after you?"

"They are not just after me at this point you do need to understand that they want you as bad as me."

"WHY?" she said with her voice escalating

"Okay' he says and takes a deep breath " When I was inside one night one of those guys tried to rape me and he was going to kill after he let all of his white supremacist friends take a turn." "I told him I had money and if he didn't, then I could pay him"

She was holding her mouth not breathing as he told the tale.

He agreed and it was protection but he wanted the money right away and I tried to explain that my trust fund would not happen till I was 18. That was not good enough and he thought well if the person in control of the fund was out of the way then it would happen sooner and his money he would have."

"Oh my god Jessie" she said

"I told them where he worked and they went to see him. I did not know it was going to happen that soon I really thought they were just talking you know I mean I still had 3 plus years and so did he so I figured it was just talk for now but it kept him from doing what he said he would. I had to protect myself."

Her eyes closed and she covered them with both hands that were over her mouth.

"The next thing I knew you told me he had died." I did it for us you have to believe me. I wanted you to start over and live a different life and here you are doing just that. Look how happy you are. I did it for us."

"Yes look at my life right now being chased by 3 men that I don't know and look how happy I am just finding out that you had something to do with this."

"What did he mean when he said he was buckled in nice and tight?"

Jessie turned around his back now to her as he looked out the airport windows.

"ANSWER ME!"

"The story you had told me about the accident, the night he covered up beating you with the car accident. Mom you have to understand I was sitting in there and they were going to kill me and I started thinking about the things he would always tell me and how he treated you. I felt like he was somewhat responsible for my being there so if I was able to make that right and give you a new start or a better life then that is what I did."

"I told them to make sure he was buckled in tight so when the truck crashed he would know and understand why it was happening to him, he deserved it."

She slapped his face and she did it hard. " That was not your choice to make. You are not god!"

"I would not be here right now nor would you if I didn't make that choice and I don't regret it either.

"So who are the 3 men?" " They were the ones I guess that carried out the order.

"Why are they chasing us?'

"Because they figure there is more money in it for them. They probably figure they could blackmail me by threatening to tell you or they could blackmail you by going to the insurance company or authorities."

"Do you have a plan then or are we just going to go airport to airport looking over our shoulders."

"I do have a plan as a matter of fact."

"Did you kill their friend? The one that you said you shared a cell with?"

He said nothing staring into her eyes just as he did when the large man asked him in the car after the bank. She saw the same thing he did. The possibility inside of him.

"What have I done." She said Oh my Godddd, what have I done?"

"stop it, please calm down" he said grabbing her so she could not run away. He held her while she cried and the announcement came for them to begin boarding a flight for El Paso.

"Everything is alright" he told her " Lets get on the plane so we are away from here and there is someone in El Paso that can help us where this stuff will not find us again."

He held her hand and led her onto the plane where she consumed a few drinks to calm her nerves not really sure of who she was seated next to her.

"Who is in El Paso and how does he help us?' she asked him after 4 screwdrivers.

"When I was inside I learned about a guy there that owns and runs a bar called "Heavens Gate".

"His name is Nelson Pritchard and the bar is a front. What he really does is fake passports, birth certificates and things of that nature."

"We get to El Paso we find him and we are able to get new identities so we can go anywhere and never be found again."

"We still look like this though, if they go to the insurance company or the authorities they could release a photo of us and that will eventually find us wherever we land" she said

"That is where the other service he provides comes in. he is also a plastic surgeon. He will change and alter our appearance so when we leave El Paso we not only say we are different people but we look like different people too."

She had to admit he once again seemed to have the answers. She was feeling the effects of the vodka and everything he just told her was making her ill. She went to the restroom and vomited several times before rinsing her face off with water from the tiny sink.

She was on a plane with her son. She was being chased by 3 men who killed her husband and could turn her and her son in to authorities which would create another level of a manhunt and she is pretty sure her son killed a man while serving time for rape.

This was a great deal to take in and she did not know if she was able to go along with this. They were going to El Paso to get new identities on paper and flesh, ohhhh she felt nauseous again and then right back up in the toilet.

She did not have a choice. " I don't have a choice!" she mumbled at herself in the mirror of the tiny bathroom. She left the room and returned to her seat. She shut off the light and turned up the air located directly above her. She did not say anything to Jessie. She just closed her eyes and tried to sleep.

27

THE 3 men arrived at the Villa that evening. The large man knew that they were not far behind because the tea pot that was on the stove was still warm. They waited there in the event the 2 of them had stepped out and would be returning shortly. They waited all evening and there was no sign of them.

While they waited they did go through the items inside as well as help themselves to the items in the kitchen. Nothing except a sketch -pad with some scribbles.

"Look at this" one of them said to the other 2.

"What is it?"

"Looks like a drawing of a face ."

"Kinda looks like the kid, don't you think?"

The large man takes the drawing and begins to walk around the abandoned living room. "If I had money and I had someone possibly chasing me what would I do?" he says out-loud to the other 2 then turns around to face them tapping the sketch pad on his left hand like cop holding a nightstick.

He then held the sketch up to his face so it was side by side and say's " I would change my appearance!"

The other 2 look at each other with satisfaction.

"Who do we know that does such a thing?" He asked.

"Heavens Gate" one of them said but the other interjected " they could go anywhere though. They have the money and it is not unlikely that a woman would get some work done right?"

"No" he said plainly. These 2 will not be just getting some lift's and tuck's. If he has a drawing on this that means he was looking to alter his appearance which means he is not looking to stay the same person now does it? That tells me they will need some identification to go along with their new features and the only person I can think of right off the top of my head is in El Paso."

"What other leads do we have? Either of you have any objection to a trip to El Paso?"

"Not at all they each agreed."

Back to the airport they went by cab and were booking the first flight to El Paso they could which was only about 8 hours behind the one Jessie and his mom were presently on.

The only difference here was that The 3 men knew where they were going and who they were going to see and the others did not nor did they know that 3 men were right behind them.

Mrs Clevinger located the shop Amber had described and walked in.

"Hello" a cheerful voice bellowed " Welcome to The Caufield Studio, please enjoy and let me know anything that you need."

Nancy looked at her with a slight smile and Jayne then answered the ringing phone in the same tone with the exception of adding this is Jayne and how may I assist you.

She looked at the work and not sure what she was looking for or at but just looking. She went piece to piece and had to admit that there was a calming sense about the place and she did enjoy the location, so close to the sea.

Jayne finished up her call and went to Nancy to ask if she was enjoying the view. Normally she would not have enjoyed being bantered by this woman called Jayne but she was looking for some information and came here for a reason." I am curious about the artist, do you know her?'

"Well of course, would you care to meet her?" Jayne offered.

"No. Perhaps another time. What can you tell me about her" Nancy asked.

"Lillian. Words would not do her justice best for you to meet her and base you own opinion and as far as her work we can let that speak for itself but I can tell you when the piece was done and where if you would care to know?"

"Simple question, and it was not about when what was painted." Nancy said quite bluntly.

"I don't understand." Jayne said looking at her.

"What exactly is it that you would like to know Mrs.?" And she turned to go to her desk where her phone was located. She picked up the receiver and called Lillian's office to inform her someone was her to see her.

"Excuse me!" Nancy said to Jayne for turning her back to call for Lillian.

"That will be enough" she turned and said to the woman in the gallery.

"I have called Mrs. Caufield for you so if there are further questions that you wish to ask in regards to her than I suggest you ask her, thank you!"

Jayne turned and returned to her desk. Nancy Clevinger was not used to being spoken to in that manner at all. She was also not one to let the other person get the last word so as she was heading towards the desk of Jayne to continue that discussion she heard a woman's voice.

"May I help you dear?" Nancy turned to see who was speaking.

The woman was atop the stairs leading to the 2nd floor." I am Lillian Caufield and what is it that I can do for you Mrs.?"

"Mrs. Clevinger "she said making eye contact with the woman. Lillian began her decent down the stairs and was placing the name and towards the middle of the stairs she said " Amber Clevinger's mother?"

"Correct, may we go somewhere private and talk?"

"Of course wont you come upstairs and we can talk in my office."

Nancy took a seat in the bohemian styled office as Lillian sat across from her." May if offer you something to drink?"

"That will not be necessary, thank you" Nancy replied.

"My daughter came to see you this week?" Nancy asked.

"She did. lovely girl and with a good talent in her hands there." Lillian complimented

"Why did she come to see you?" Nancy again asked bluntly

Lillian unsure of what the meaning behind the question was but abliged her with an answer " A colleague of mine referred her to me in an effort to see if painting interested her and I agreed to meet her."

"Dr Feingold?"

"That is correct" Lillian stated not wavering from the eye contact that Nancy Clevinger was so good at.

"Mrs. Caufield."

"Please call me Lillian."

"Lillian." She said. "My daughter had been through a great deal over the past 5 years and Dr.Feingold is her therapist. Did you know that?"

"I did not." "you do know that Elliot Feingold is a therapist?"

"I did but the reason of the referral was of no concern to me. I respect his opinion and if he said he had a young woman that may be searching for something in which I may be able to assist then I was more than willing to meet her and base my own opinion."

"Do you have an opinion?"

"I do, I like your daughter although I known her for less than a day but I like the talent in her hands and agree with Elliot. She is searching. I think if she finds what she is looking for then she will make a fine artist."

Lillian continued to honor the eye contact that Nancy Clevinger enjoyed so much and for the sport of it she added " is this the reason you have come all the way here? Does Amber know that you're here?"

"That is none of your concern and a rude assumption I might add"

"So she doesn't, is there a reason you're here then without her knowledge"

"How dare you" Nancy says coming to her feet as a guest in your establishment.

"You are not a guest Mrs. Clevinger." She interrupted her and until you purchase something you are not a client either. I do not care to speak on matters with other people I do not know without the knowledge and consent of whom we are speaking about." I do hope you understand" she said smiling to the rapidly departing Nancy Clevinger.

Her rapid departure down the stairs and out the door would not have been complete without the cheery Jayne offering her to "have delightful day."

"The audacity of that woman and her assistant" she said to herself getting into her car."

Amber returned to the studio that Saturday and was looking forward to it. She was wearing some old jeans and a Bon Jovi T-shirt with her hair tied back when she arrived to be greeted by Jayne.

"You're looking quite youth-full today and it looks great on you if I may add". Jayne told her

"You may" Amber replied " Jayne do you know how nice is to be greeted by you each time I walk in here." Then Jayne stops everything and leans over on her desk with her head in her hands almost like a puppy dog and says. "Tell me how nice it is and leave nothing out.

"This place would not be the same without you" Amber tells her and is then joined by Lillian who tells her from the top of the stairs " It most certainly would not be the same without Jayne,I agree." "Are you ready to begin Amber?"

"I am." Lillian leads her to the studio in the back where again another blank canvas is and she is again greeted by those delightful sounds that for some reason she would hear every day but they would not have the same effect that they do in here.

"Impressionism, is our task today now do you have your tools she asked her?" This was her implying that her mind and heart was open.

Amber closed her eyes for a very brief second to take in the sounds once again then opens and replied "I do."

"Okay then I have set up a fruit basket here on the table let's see your impression of that basket here" she said pointing to the canvass and departed with " I will leave you to it."

Lillian left Amber in the studio and never once mentioned that she had met her mother here the previous day. Her focus was Amber and not her mother.

Nancy Clevinger was seated in the reception area of Dr.Feingold office reading a copy of Travel Magazine as she awaited the Dr. She had been there for almost 17 minutes and was growing in patient when he came to the area to greet her.

He escorted her back to where they had first met a year ago. She had been in this office only once before which was when he felt it would be good to meet the parents.

"Nancy, what is it that I can do for you?"

"How is Amber doing in her therapy?" she asked him which was a question he was uncomfortable with.

"Have you asked her how she feels about the sessions or how the direction they are taking her?" he returned

"I did not ask her I am asking you, how is she doing."

"My opinion is only mine. It is her opinion that matters the most Nancy. It is her that has to feel that they are helping her not my opinion."

"So you don't know or you don't have an opinion?" I just gave you my opinion but if you must know I do feel that we have made some progress. She at her last session was more vibrant than any other visit to date and I feel that it was a result of an exercise that we discussed."

"Lillian Caufield?" She asked him " This was your exercise?"

"Amber spoke to you about it then, good." He said to her.

"What was the purpose of the exercise exactly?" He did not like her tone and it was becoming uncomfortable once again.

"Mrs, Clevinger your daughter continues to focus on things that are the past which conjure her anxiety, fears and nightmares.

"My suggestion was to pursue something new that will fill those mental spaces with present and future aspiration so she no longer is focused on what was and this frankly is all I am going to comment on the matter."

"Lillian Caufield?" Nancy asked. "I did not care for her so how is she supposed to be helping Amber?"

"Again" he said " You will need to speak with Amber with how this is or is not helping her. She is 18 now and is free to make those decisions on her own but please understand that my interest is entirely focused on her and her healing. I felt that Lillian would be good for her."

"Talk to your daughter Nancy, she will tell you." He ended " Now if there is nothing more that I can help you with"

This concluded her visit yet she was still unsatisfied with the end result.

28

THE plane landed and was headed to the terminal. Jessie woke his mother who now seemed to be suffering a little from a hangover, jet lag and cabin pressure.

Collecting herself they made their way into the airport and then to the curb to retrieve a cab.

"Heaven's Gate" he tells the cab driver hoping the driver knew that location. The cab driver turned in his seat to look at them both and then put the cab in drive. He studied them in the mirror on the way there. It looked as if he was studying them to know if he was going in the right direction or not.

"1st time in El Paso?" "yes" Jessie replied while Kelly held her head in an attempt to keep it from falling apart.

"How did you hear of Heaven's Gate?" " Friends in Arlington and The Dallas area had mentioned it to me a few times and it was a must see, is it far?"

"No, not at all" the driver said still studying them.

They arrived at the parking lot which was dirt of the bar. He paid the cabbie $60.00 for a tab that was $47.00 and told him to keep the change and the cabbie could not help but see the wad of cash Jessie had on him.

He and Kelly enter the bar and blind a few patrons on the inside by the sunlight when the door opened. They each walk saying nothing but a few nod's to people they pass as they approach the bar. The sight of the alcohol behind the bar and the smell of the place was making Kelly nauseous again and she was trying to prevent herself from throwing up there or even dry heaving.

"What can I get for you?" the bartender said " We are here to see Nelson" Jessie says.

"I don't know a Nelson, Can I get you anything else?"

"He is the owner Nelson Pritchard, he is expecting us."

"You may have the wrong place then a guy by the name of Sonny own this bar not Nelson and Sonny is not here either." "Sorry" the bartender said walking away.

Jessie looked at his mom and she was not doing well and to be honest he kind of felt ill as well. This was their ticket just like Randall said.

Unsure of what to do he was thinking maybe they should go back and get a hotel then try and figure out another plan. They go back outside to get some fresh air and the cabbie is still there.

"Can you take us to a hotel?"

"Sure, did you have one in mind?" he asked them as they got back into cab.

They drove for awhile but the cab was not going back into the direction they had originally came, it seemed to going further south and away from everything.

"Where are we going?"

He asked the cabbie and his right hand had come back into the back seat and slammed Jessie into the face with a gun sending his head smashing into the backseat and he continued to do it until the cab came to a stop.

"Get out" the cabbie said to each of them and when they were out of the cab they realized they were in the middle of the desert and not too much around.

"Give me your money" the cabbie said to Jessie who was holding his head where the gun had struck him.

The cabbie pointed the gun at his mother and said "Ill shoot her, give me the money that is in your pocket,now!" Jessie emptied his pocket with the wad of bills he had and walked to the man to give it to him.

"Just throw it. "He said. " If I throw it the wind will blow it and then neither one of us will have it." he said to him still approaching.

He handed him the money and with the same vengeance he had when putting Randall Mack 10 Humphries down he went after the cabbie.

He struggled to get the gun but this was Jessie's one and only shot just like that day in the shower because they were in the middle of nowhere with people after them and they had to find this guy Nelson.

The gun shot off a few rounds in the air until Jessie put a few knees into his stomach which lowered the gun then he put an elbow into the face of the cabbie sending him back.

Jessie took one hand off of the gun and hit the man in the face, in the nose again and again and again until the cabbie had fallen back enough times to lose his balance. He fell on his back. Jessie jumped on top of him and again continued to hit him in the face.

His mom went after the gun that was in his hand but was let go when he was trying to protect his face and nose from the blows. She screamed to Jessie" Stop", "Stop it!" and he removed himself from atop the cabbie.

Jessie entirely out of breath walked in tight circles to get it back all while looking down at the cabbie that was still on the ground.

"Who is Nelson Pritchard" He said still out of breath. Jessie walked over to his mother and took the gun from her hand. ' Jessie No" she said and was again on top of him but this time with the very gun he used to strike and rob him.

"I have done some time, I have people chasing me and I have killed someone before so whether you live or die right now is of no concern to me. The only thing standing in the way of that is the answer to this next question." He loaded the barrel by clicking the hammer back and placed right in the face of the cabbie.

"Where is Nelson Pritchard"

"I will take you to him" the cabbie said with his mouth full of blood.

"I am not fucking with you!"" You take me to him and there may even be some in it for you so don't be stupid just take me to him-NOW!"

Jessie helped him up and put him behind the wheel this time with Jessie in the front with the gun and his mom in the back seat. They went back to the bar and back in the door not exactly sure of what to expect. The man had been cleaned up a little but you could tell he was worked over and they could also tell that the young man in earlier was now carrying a gun.

The cabbie went to the bar and told the bartender to get "*Jefe, hombre es mucho denero.*"

The bartender looked at Jessie again for a few seconds and then picked up a phone to call someone and then hung up.

"Can I get you something to drink while you wait?"

"Get the cabbie what he wants and we will have 2 waters please." He told the bartender and they took a seat at the bar so Jessie could keep the gun on each the cabbie and the bartender all while seeing behind him in the mirror.

His heart rate was pounding out of his chest as they waited in this place where once again anyone in here could and would kill him just for the bragging rights.

The door opened and in came a man with 3 behind him. He was in his late 40's to early 50's well dressed with a silk shirt tucked into his black slacks. He had dark hair with threads of silver throughout and was well tanned.

"We don't allow gun's in this establishment. He announced.

"Are you Nelson Pritchard?" he asked the man

"That depends on who is asking, you are?""

My name is Jessie and this is my mother Kelly." He said pointing to her next to him.

"Your mother?" the man said and some of the patrons in the bar started to laugh while the expression on the man yet to identify himself had not changed.

"I am here to purchase something, something of great value which is a benefit to us and you." He said to the man interrupting the laughter. He had his attention.

"Won't you come with me somewhere more private for us to talk."

Jessie looked at the cabbie and told him if they make it out of here then an envelope will be left for him here at the bar and walked towards the man with Kelly at his side.

"What is it that you wish to purchase?" The man said seating himself behind a large poker style table and gesturing for the 2 of them to join him. The 3 men stood at the entrance which they came so no point of exit unless told to them by the man seated at the table.

"Are you Nelson?" "That depends on what you wish to purchase."

"We need new identification and we need surgery to match the identity" he said staring at the man.

"Then I am Nelson Pritchard". He said to them "but how do you know who I am?"

I was in Dallas Corrections with a guy named Randall Humphries, they call him Mack 10 and he told me about you and your service."
" We are in need of your service and we have money to pay for it, will you help us?"

"My service will be available to you for the sum of $150,000 each. You pay half of it up front and then other when complete. Do we have a deal?"

"We do" Jessie said shaking the man's hand.

"Arturo" he said calling one of the men to him" Please escort these 2 to our offices and do make sure they are able to obtain their funds so that we can begin right away."

"I assume that you wish to begin right away?" He said confirming

"Please." they each said and walking with the man called Arturo out of the bar know as Heaven's Gate.

They made their stop to obtain the required $150,000 and were then on route to a destination neither of them had any knowledge of. They did not know if at any point they would be killed because they were out-numbered and they were out gunned but in order to obtain what they came for they had no choice but to continue on.

They arrived at dusk to a place that again was in the middle of nowhere. The door opened for them to get out of the car and they were walked inside of the building. It was a large warehouse looking building with sections that looked like an office but they had no partitions to separate any of them.

The far corner had a table that was similar to what you would see in a dentist office. There were X-ray machines and computers, printers and faxes. Nelson walked into the room greeting them" I see that you arrived safely, did you not think you would?" he asked smiling.

"Actually we did" Jessie returned "because I know this is of interest to you as well as the balance we owe once this is complete." He said to him showing the $150,000 he had requested.

"Then let us begin, who wants to go first" he said and motioned to Kelly as if to say ladies first but she stepped back and told Jessie to go ahead. Jessie stepped forward " I will ."

"Right this way, please join us through" he said to the woman in an effort to make her more comfortable.

"I want you to see what we do, you may like it." He said to her.

Jessie was sat a desk like you would find if you were being interviewed for a job. Nelson on one side and him on the other.

"First things first, do we have a name?" He asked Jessie and oddly Jessie had not thought about the name of his new identity. He searched back to the novels he had read for a name, a strong and powerful name.

"Jack Rodan" He said. " Well Mr. Rodan how old will you be?" and Jessie decided to go ahead and be 21 now instead of waiting another 2-3 years.

Nelson went down the list of questions that would define his new existence which included a driver's license, birth certificate, passport and school transcripts in the event he wished to attend college.

Jessie had all of the information that said he was Jack Rodan but it was now time in which to change the one thing that would complete the birth of him and death of Jessie Harrell and Spook.

He was sat in the chair as it reclined back. He looked up at Nelson who was wearing scrubs and a mask so all he could make out was eyes of a man that appeared to be upside down.

He administered a local and then waited for him drift off and then proceeded to prod his face with needles in order to numb all of those areas in which he would be cutting and slicing.

The surgery lasted about 5 hours and he would awaken. The room was dim in light so not to agitate the eyes and he was heavily bandaged because his vision was not only blurry but obscured from them.

"This is where you will stay and rest until you are ready for them to come off. It will take a couple of days but your transformation is complete. How do you feel? He asked him

"Dizzy." He replied even though he was not moving he still felt dizzy.

"Where is my mother?" He asked.

"I am right here" she answered.

"Is everything okay?" he asked to make sure they and she was safe.

"Every-thing is fine Mr. Rodan" he said to him answering his mother's question.

"Again you will rest and you will heal while I take your mother and we begin the same process for her."

She was terribly nervous after seeing what they did to him but he did not seem in pain but it was just too much she thought.

"I am scarred " she said to the man she did not even know.

"Of course you are but you came here for a good reason and you risked a few things I might add to get this far. I will only proceed if it is your wish."

She stood there frozen as she had time and time again with her past. She had been enjoying this amazing time in Italy and already felt as though she had transformed just not to this level. Those men did find them and would continue to just as Jessie had said they would.

This is the defining moment for you, she said to herself. This is where what was becomes no longer and all we have is what is and what will be.

"Okay" she said to Nelson taking one deep breath " I'm ready"

Nelson had let her know that it is in her best interest to wait till the morning so she could retrieve the money in her account and he would assist with the set up of a new account under her new name via his banker in The Cayman Islands otherwise after her transformation she would be able to gain access to her account.

She did not even think of that. All of her money would be untouchable because she would look like someone else and have that name.

"Thank you" she said to him " I did not think of that all-Thank you."

"You are welcome. I will have a car take you there in the morning and this will give you time to think of who you want to be and look like."

"I do not know that time to think about it is the best thing I would rather just do it but the bank thing I am so glad you said something."

"You must be hungry?" he said to her " I am, very much how does that work?" she asked him.

"I will have them prepare something. There is a kitchen and we have a very good chef."

"Here" she said " you cook it here?"

"Yes this is also where you and he will be staying until our business is complete, should only be 3-4 days. What would you like for dinner?"

"I don't know" "do you like meat, do you like vegetables, do you like Italian?"

"Anything she said would be fine thank you."

He ordered (2) petit Filet's with a peppercorn sauce accompanied by sautéed vegetables and a light salad. The salad came with a selection of dressings to accommodate her taste. Nelson asked if he could join her during dinner and she did not object not that she would have had any idea how to considering where they were and who he was and not to mention the men in the corners of this warehouse with guns.

They finished their meal which was amazing and he showed her to place in which she would able to sleep for the evening safely. She did not sleep that night at all for many obvious reasons but he was true to his word about her safety.

She awoke the next morning and again he had a small breakfast prepared including fruit, toast, coffee and juice.

"Good morning" he said to her " I have prepared a few things for you to start you day and while I follow up on your son I will have Arturo take you to the bank as we discussed." He motioned her towards where a seat was at the table that housed all of the items that were prepared.

"Did you think of a name so we can start that portion of the process as well for the banking?"

"I did" she said biting into a piece of buttered toast and drinking from a coffee cup.

"Camile Harrison" she said to him. "Enjoy your breakfast Mrs. Harrison" he returned as he walked away.

She finished her breakfast and was taken to the bank which was close to a 50 minute drive one way. She entered and signed in then sat while she awaited for a branch member to assist her. She was approached and escorted to the desk where she explained her need to close the account under her name.

The individual and even the manager spoke to her a few times in an effort to prevent her from cashing out the account that was over ten million in it's denomination.

The money was placed into 2 separate cases and she was escorted by each of the guards of the bank, the manager and Arturo to her car.

The 2 of them made their way back to the warehouse and she felt incredibly uneasy being in this car with this man and all of the money that she had in the world. " What am I doing?' she thought to herself as the car drove out into the middle of nowhere.

29

THE 3 men landed in El Paso and immediately went to the curb side to hail a cab. They flagged down the first one they saw and piled in with one of them sitting in the front seat.

"Heaven's gate" the large man said and they were off. They arrived in the dirt lot and paid the driver.

They walked into the bar at night time and saw that it had a pretty good occupancy. They looked around the room first to see if for any reason the 2 they were searching for were there and they were not so they went to the bar.

He ordered 3 shots of bourbon and 3 beers then asked the man if he had seen a boy and a woman in there that would not look like they belonged.

"Who does belong in here?" the man asked setting up the shot glasses and began to pour."

"I mean they would have stuck out a bit more than others?" he replied

"You stick out in here as much yourself." He said moving the shots forward and then beginning to pour the beers.

"Do you know who I am?' the large man asked the bartender

"No" he replied " You're someone who owes me $24.00 for the drinks, have we met?"

"No, is Nelson around?" he asked placing 2 twenty's on the bar.

"Nelson who?" the bartender said. The large man looked at him hard and was demonstrating that his patience was thin. He leaned on the bar closer to where the bartender was standing and said.

"Nelson is a guy who does things, things for guys like me, guys with money so tell Nelson he has someone here to see him." He stayed in that position on the bar staring at the bartender who did not move from his leaned stance against the back bar with his arms crossed.

"He is busy", the bartender finally offers.

"So you do know him" the large man say throwing back one of the bourbon shots on the bar.

"He has a couple of clients he is working with and is not available."

"Those clients happen to look like the 2 I described?" he said smiling at the bartender.

"I don't know man, I was not here all I know is that he is unavailable."

Reaching into his pocket he pulls out 5 $100 bills and unfolds them onto the bar. He slides the bills over towards where the bartender is and asked.

"See if you can reach him." then takes the beer's and remaining shots to the other men seated a table. When he got to the table with the drinks he saw the bartender had removed the bills and was now on the phone.

"Now what?" one of them said "we wait." The large man answered.

Amber had finished her impression of the fruit bowl and again stood back looking at the detail she had placed into it. She picked up the dimples on the orange and the lines on the banana and she felt good. She liked it. She liked the feeling of getting lost into the images and colors and finding a souvenir of her journey when it was complete.

She went to get Lillian to show her and saw her in the gallery area talking with what was either a customer or a fan. She watched her and how she spoke. She was calm, she was open she was educated in her craft and spoke of it with passion. Lillian saw her and excused herself from the conversation she was engaged in.

"I did mean to disturb you" Amber apologized.

"Not at all dear let's see what you came up with" and she walked back to the studio with Amber directly in tow.

"Well, well, well" she said approaching the work " our confidence is growing Amber, can you see it?"

"What do you mean, how can you tell?"

"Because you did not settle for the outline or the color you went deeper and you gave the fruit character and depth, you see." She said pointing to certain details and areas. " This is confidence, this is exploratory and this is another fine piece of work from a young amateur.

"Do you really think so, you're not just saying that?" she asked her.

Lillian approached her and stated "It would never be my intention to harm your feeling's but I must have the ability to critique your work when necessary and I shall also have the ability to compliment what I find to be worthy of such a comment." Honesty" she continued " Honesty is what will tell us if we are moving forward or backwards Amber and I see steps forward."

"What do you see?" she said pointing back to the painting and then looking at her as her finger still faced the canvass.

"What do you see?"

"I see progress." She told her

"And feel? What do you feel?" Lillian asked not moving from where she stood looking at the painting and then her.

"I feel the progress. I feel the steps forward" Amber stated and feeling like a bathtub full of water that the clog had just been released sending all of the water spiraling down the drain she stepped toward Lillian and she hugged her.

This ultimately surprised Lillian but she welcomed it. " You're going to be alright dear. "She said to her hugging her back. "You're going to be just fine."

Lillian returned to the front with the canvas to show Jayne who began to praise Amber for the work she was doing after only visits.

"We should enter her in that amateur competition, don't you think Lilly?"

"What amateur competition?" Amber asked after thanking Jayne for her kind words about her work.

"There is an annual competition for all ages of amateur painters that is this month. You can paint whatever you wish it just has to be done the day of in front of the judges, what do you think?" She said looking at Amber who looked at Jayne's nodding head.

"Okay, couldn't hurt right." Amber said standing between each Jayne and Lilly.

"Progress " Lillian said looking at her and then " looks like you may get your wish of getting some of your work on these walls you keep this up little miss."

She left the studio once again feeling release. The shop gave her strength. Lillian and even Jayne gave her strength and she once again drove home with that ocean breeze blowing through each open window of her car.

A man approached the table of where the 3 large men were seated.

"You guys waiting for someone?" The large man looked and him and said "yes" keeping eye contact with him while the others looked around the room to survey it in the event this went sideways.

"Who are you waiting to see? The man asked him

"Unless you are him I don't see how it is a concern of yours."

"Are you him and no offense but I don't think that you are.

"I am an associate of his and he wants to know what business you have with him?'

"We have business with the people I believe he is working with presently, is it possible to speak to them?"

"What business do you have with them?"

"Again and this is of no offense to you but I prefer to speak with them regarding that matter but it is money related."

"They owe you money?" he asked

"They do."

"Go to a hotel, there is a motel 6 that is 20 miles from here. Stay there tonight in room 6 and I will call you tomorrow to discuss if there is business to resolve then I will contact you." He said getting up from the chair he was seated in.

"If I don't hear from you?"

"Then there was no business to resolve." And he walked away.

The 3 men had another drink while they waited for a cab to taken to the destination he suggested.

Kelly and Arturo returned to the warehouse.

"Ah a safe return " he announced in an attempt to make her feel better.

"Your son is doing well, he is healing. Let's set up the accounts for you and we then can begin your procedure."

Nelson dialed the phone and contacted his accountant in The Cayman's. It was his direct line. "Arthur, this is Nelson. I have some crucial financial business that needs your immediate attention. I have a client here which wishes to deposit some money into your bank so we need to establish an account and I will have her there in 3 days to sign the papers."

Nelson completed the call and hung up." This is additional to the service that has been started. The $300,000 would be for what we have discussed but in order for me to continue to assist with the banking matters that will cost an additional $300,000 and for that I will fly you to the Cayman's and introduce you to a man that specializes in off shore accounts.

The account will be set up in your new identity and we then part ways. Is that satisfactory?"

"Of course, your help is greatly appreciated. Shall I pay you now?"

"That will not be necessary. You will pay as the service is complete, are you ready to begin?

"Yes"

He began typing and preparing all of the documents that he had done for Jessie earlier and was ready to have her lay down.

"What about the money?"

"The money?'

"The money" she said again when you place me unconscious then you can take the money and leave us here. We do not even know where we are and that is all that we have in the world besides each other." She said looking into his eyes.

"I could, this is true, you could already be dead and so could your son but you are not. I am a business man and you have come for a service and you have paid and paid well so I will fulfill my obligation to you and your son." "You money will be here when you wake up."

She closed her eyes and slowly drifted off to sleep.

Jessie woke the next day with Nelson looking at him. " Who are the 3 men chasing you? He asked

"They are here? Jessie asked trying to get up a little in the bed

"No but they are here in El Paso. In the same place I found you.

"Why?" he asked

"They want money and they think they can blackmail both of us by going to the authorities but they were paid for what they did."

"What did they do?" he asked

"My father used to beat my mother and did it pretty often but one of those nights he hit her really good and covered it up by a car accident." Nelson listened as Jessie continued

"I had to get some protection when I was in D.C and the guy in there, the one who told me about you, came up with the idea to kill my father for the money so I could pay him to protect me while I was inside."

"Did you, pay him I mean?"

He put out the order and the 3 men were who killed him and the reason I did was for my mother so she could start over and get a new life. That is why we are here."

You did not answer my question, did you pay them?"

"Yes we paid them in Dallas hours after I was released. We paid them $50,000 and now they want more."

"I see." Well lets take a look at the work tell me what you think."

Nelson started to peel the bandages from his face slowly until none were present and then produced a mirror for him to see.

He had changed the nose, the jaw, the hair color and his eyes from the brown they were to a deep blue. He really looked different. He looked strong and masculine like he had imagined in the stories he read. He had rid himself of the boyish Jessie and ghostlike Spook. He was now Jack Rodan.

"What do you think?" he asked Jessie staring at himself in the mirror exploring all of the new details in his face.

"Its incredible" I don't look anything like I used to, I cant believe it."

"Where is my mother?" She is resting from her procedure.

"Did she get all of her papers?"

"She did " he answered " she is now Camille Harrison and once the 2 of you have healed entirely we will fly to The Caymans to set up the account your mother emptied and place it into her new name. We agreed on an additional $300,000 to do so which is fair considering it is my accountant, contact and plane we will be taking. Don't you think?" he asked

"You have been more than generous and we both appreciate what you have done, this was our new life like I said."

"What about the 3 men " He asked Nelson

"Don't worry about them, if you paid them then your debt is clear and you have given me no reason to think otherwise."

"You won't tell them where we are will you?"

"I cant" Nelson said laughing " you don't exist."

He could not stop looking in the mirror and could not believe the difference. The changes.

"Can I see her, see how she is doing?"

Nelson led him to the area where his mother Camille was resting. He looked at her bandaged face just as he had years ago when this all started but he was not afraid or scared this time.

These bandages, unlike the ones in-flicked upon her out of anger, would be removed leaving the past for her behind forever.

PART
THREE

30

THE annual Cardiff amateur competition was under way and being held at the beach. There were 15 contestants present that day including Amber. They each were instructed to paint what they wished and would be judged on all aspects of the originality and detail.

Amber thought and thought for a week leading to this competition trying to decide in advance what she would paint and just kept coming up blank and now here the day was, here she was still blank.

Here came the anxiety and the fear and this time when she closed her eyes it was different from the studio room she painted him. She listened to those same sounds she heard in the room but the strength of the studio Jayne or Lillian were not with her.

Then she closed her eyes again and listened to the last conversation she had with Lillian Caufield and she began to breath.

She then dipped the brush opened her eyes and did what she did the pervious times before. She opened her mind and her heart and she let the brush guide her.

When she was finished and the judges came to view the work it was met with a unanimous reception of accolades.

She had painted the wet sand on a beach with 2 feet. One foot in front of the other and a simple signature that said *progress*.

Amber won the completion that afternoon.

She was met by local media that wanted to interview her for the positive message that she had envisioned and painted vs. the traditional ocean or city landscapes being done that day which were good as well.

They took her picture along -side her painting and Amber did get her wish. Not only was she making progress but the work would be hung on the wall in The Caufield Studio.

While Jessie was eating and waiting for his mom to heal from her procedure he did what he had become very fond of doing. He read and while Arturo or the others were out he had asked if they return with some local and world newspapers or magazines for him.

He ran through the staple crime stories that plague each city as well as some sports items but then he came across a uplifting article that was done on a girl just outside of San Diego who won a amateur painting competition with a piece entitled *"progress"*.

The article had a picture of the girl standing next to the piece she had painted which is what drew his attention to begin with. The face on the picture was Amber and the name in the article was Amber Clevinger.

Carlsbad girl takes 1ˢᵗ place in a amateur competition with a message that reaches all . Was the heading as he read the story.

Amber was in a town called Carlsbad near San Diego.

He stood up and began to pace inside of the warehouse just as he did the day they denied his parole thanks to Mrs. Clevinger. That name created a faster rate of pacing which drew the attention of the other men inside of the warehouse.

"Hey" one of them said " Are you okay?"

"Yes" he replied.

"Then stop you're making me nervous and you don't want to do that." The man holding a gun near the entrance said.

He sat back down and controlled his breathing just like he did when he was inside D.C

His hands on his head then moving over his eyes his mind raced with the opportunity to pay her and her family a visit when they concluded things here and The Cayman's.

They won't even see me coming he thought and that made him smile which was still making the guy with the gun nervous.

The 3 men in the hotel did not hear from anyone at all. " What do you think " one of them asked the other 2.

"We could stake out the private airports around here to see if we spot them leaving or will they fly commercial? The other asked.

"Where would he be able to do what it is that he does, what type of building would we be looking for?

Cmon man are you kidding that could be a million different places, let's take the $50k we got and chalk the rest up to a vacation like you said.

"He would have called by now."

"Man we are right here, they are right here we are so close to huge pay out. I bet we can get 5 times that if we can find them."

Amber returned to The Caufield Studio following the competition along with Jayne and Lillian. They all 3 stood back and viewed the new addition to the gallery hanging right on the wall entitled " Progress."

"This is a good day " Lillian said to both of them and then " you have managed to reach yet another plateau there dear" to Amber.

Jayne jumped right in there with " We are both so proud of you, it's really good work."

"I can't thank each of you enough for allowing me to come here each week and be a part of what you 2 have created here. It means so much to me." Amber said to both of them.

Amber returned home to share the news of her day when she was met by her mother. " I won. " she announced smiling

"You what?'

"I won." She said again and continued " I won the amateur competition today for my painting."

"You did?' her mother said smiling. Pleased as well as surprised. " When do I get to see what you have been painting?" Then " That is wonderful news."

"The papers interviewed me and Lillian even hung the piece in her studio ahh it was amazing, I can't believe I won." Her energy was unlike what her mother had seen in years. She really looked at her and how this was something that seemed to be helping her.

"I am proud of you honey, I can't wait to see it." She said and instead of leaving on the positive note that existed right then and there she went and asked.

"Does this mean you will become a painter?"

"What do you mean?"

"I mean, does this mean this what you will pursue this painting thing or are you going to look at schools to move forward with your education and a career."

"I don't know what it means, why do you have to do that?" Amber looked at her hurt.

"I didn't do anything I just asked a question a legitimate question at that." Amber took from that and turned to walk towards the front door." Where do you think you're going?"

"Get back here" her mother said.

Amber stopped halfway down the steps that lead to the street turned around and returned to the front door where her mother was.

"I am not a child anymore and you telling me when or where I can go is over. I am happy with what I am doing right now and this is the first time in a very long time that that has happened and I will not let you take that away from me." She said storming back around and down the steps.

Her mother stunned stood there watching her daughter walk away down the street. She sat at the table waiting for her husband to come home which was not long from when Amber left. She was crying when he arrived and he came to her aid asking " What is it, what happened?"

"I had a fight with Amber" she told him and went into detail about her winning the competition, her comment about school and even fessed up to seeing Dr. Feingold and Lillian Caufield.

"Nancy", he said to her holding her hand while she cried.

"This has to stop. You love her and you have always been there for her but if you don't allow her some space to grow you are going to lose her and I can't let that happen."

"I love her so much " she said crying harder.

"I know you do but if she is telling you that she is happy then you have to trust her and her decisions because it was her decisions that led her to the point of happiness to begin with, right?"

"I know she said I know." He continued to hold her while she got it out.

"She won huh" he said to her to switch it up.

"Did you see it or have you seen any of what she's done?"

"No" she said "Then that is our first step" he told her.

Nelson woke Kelly and it was time to remove her bandages as well so that he could see how she was healing.

One by one he un-wrapped while Jessie looked on. He was equally impressed with her work as he was with his.

These still have to heal but we are right on schedule he said to her and she looked to find Jessie.

"I'm right here" he said figuring she did not recognize him

"You are going to love it." He said smiling and she smiled back when she saw it was and was not him at the same time. She became excited to see the end result's.

He presented her with a mirror to see for herself and just as Jessie had done she could not recognize herself in the mirror.

"What do you think?" Nelson asked her.

"I don't know what to say, It does not look like me."

"But do you like it?'

"I don't know, it is hard to say I just look so different."

"You look beautiful." Her son said to her "this is our new life."

It was not long till they were boarding a plane that nelson had in a hanger located next to the warehouse they were in. They stood outside as they watched him pull the jet from the hanger using a cart. The cart dragged the jet to the tar-mac where a door would then open for them to enter.

Nelson invited his guest aboard and followed them in as they found their seats. They sat low to the ground but were in leather seats located directly behind the cockpit where he himself sat.

"Will you by flying us there?" she asked him

"I will, sit back and enjoy the flight he said as he started the engines.

The jet reached its speed for take-off and then lifted high till it reached its altitude to continue on to The Caymans.

The 2 of them held hands seated next to one another while she looked down to the ground from which they just came and did feel better that the past was quickly behind them.

"How are you doing back there Mrs. Harrison and Mr. Rodan?" he said from the cockpit " I trust you are enjoying the flight."

"Yes we are she said to him looking down at the ocean below" yes we are."

They marveled at each other on the way there as they pinched and stared into each other's new features.

"How surreal it is to hear your voice yet be looking at someone so different from whom I known my entire life" She said looking at Jessie.

―――――――――

They touched down and departed the jet. There was a car on the tarmac waiting. They both quickly looked around and could feel the heat of the sun beating down but there was an ocean breeze as well that took some of the temperature away.

They drove and drove while looking at the tree's that would be in front of the ocean view then gone again.

They arrived at The Hotel Montecito where valet opened their door and offered to take their bags. They followed Nelson into the lobby where they checked into their rooms. He turned and handed them their keys and said they would meet here at the concierge in an hour where they would be introduced to Arthur and conclude their business.

They had 2 separate room located next to one another. The door opened and you had a spacious living room complete with couch, chair and balcony. To the left was the bedroom complete with a queen size bed and restroom. The balcony doors opened and allowed the ocean breeze to fill the room while you stood watching the sun fade into the water.

They each needed clothes. Jessie went next door and knocked on her door to see if she wanted to go to the gift shop downstairs and get a set of clothes to change into and she agreed. They purchased enough items to feel new again after a shower.

They dressed and returned to the concierge desk where Nelson was already seated with another man.

Mrs. Harrison and Mr. Rodan this is Arthur Branson. Arthur stood to introduce himself and asked how he may be of assistance to them. Nelson stated that an account was to be opened.

He walked them to the valet where a car picked them up and took them to the Bank of Cayman and Arthur's office.

There was an account set up in each of their names with checks, pin numbers and debit cards so that they would each have access.

They withdrew from the satchels they were carrying prior to the deposit the remaining $150,000 then followed by the additional $300,000 owed to Nelson Pritchard for his services.

The car took them back to The Montecito Hotel. Nelson Mrs Harrison and Mr. Rodan exited the car and entered the hotel.

"I feel as though we should celebrate" she said to the 2 men and nelson agreed to at least a toast to each of their new start's.

They proceeded to the bar and ordered 3 Red Stripe's. The beers arrived and there Nelson proposed a toast " To new beginning's!" he announced and the clink of the 3 beers was just that " a new beginning.

They spoke as they continued to finish the beer and ordered another round. Nelson asked them each what their plans would be moving forward with their new life. He knew this was none of his business but the majority of his clients were much more high profile criminal types that never spoke so he was intrigued by their plans.

He was intrigued by their dynamic. A mother who was beat and a son that removed the person who did the damage in order to manifest a new life for his mother. They were likable, they were personable and they were grateful for the gift that Nelson had given them.

They paid for the service just as the others before them but he found it endearing and could not help himself but be drawn into their enthusiasm and even inspired by it.

He also enjoyed the company of the woman that now called herself Camille.

"What do the 2 of you have planned now that your past is behind you?" he asked ordering another round.

"I had hoped to return to Italy but as quickly as those 3 men have been able to locate us both in Texas and there then here again I just don't feel safe there." She explained smiling at Nelson.

"How confident are you that anyone one of the men that were in the warehouse with us while our new identities were being created will not talk?" Jessie asked Nelson straight faced and before he answered.

"They are the only ones besides who is at this table now that could ever communicate that to anyone if they were being asked or paid.

"You mean by the 3 men?" Nelson asked him

"I mean by anyone and I do not mean any dis-respect."

"I understand your concern and all of my previous clients have and continue to be anonymous, you are safe Mr. Rodan as are you Mrs Harrison. Again I ask what are your plans?"

"I agree about Italy and I am sorry that the place you were able to find yourself and some peace is now a threat to us but we can find another I promise." He said to her as the second round of beers had arrived.

Nelsons next toast was " To unchartered territories." And again the clink that made them each smile.

Jessie had an idea of where they would be for their new start but did not feel the need to share it with Nelson. It was not that he did not trust them but the less people that had any knowledge of where they would be than the better. They looked different, they had different identification and the funds to finance their travels but it did still make him nervous that if the 3 men got a hold of one of those guards in the warehouse and offered them some money that it would not be hard for them to get the names they had created right there in that warehouse.

He would save the discussion of San Diego for later with her when nelson was not present but the way he was looking at her and the way they were laughing he did not give him the impression he was in a hurry to say goodbye either.

She was enjoying the attention Nelson was paying her. She was given attention in Italy by men and had 2 lovers while there but those were more or less part of her discovering who she was as Kelly.

This was different and he was different. She was now discovering who she was as Camille. He was a very attractive man, especially after 3 or 4 Red Stripes, who had many secrets. He created new lives for people and he flew a jet so his attention was her pleasure she thought to herself.

"What about the trust fund?" Jessie asked Nelson

"I am sure that if you spoke to the attorney he could perhaps just wire you the money here to the account you have set up."

"Wont he ask why I am putting money into an account of another name?"

"Possible and I am not sure about you having to sign anything. It seems that the trust being set up has been established and the record of your birth date is known so you are legally over 18 so the funds inside of the trust would now be yours to do with as you wish." Nelson concluded

"I will call him tomorrow to discuss it." She said still staring at Nelson.

Jessie was interested in discussing San Diego but he could tell that his mother was not ready to leave so he either stays with her and him or finds the concierge who can help him with locating some information on San Diego.

"It think I am going to go do some research on something, are you guys okay here or are you ready to go?" Jessie asked them each who both replied " I could have another round and continued their conversation." Jessie kissed her and shook Nelsons hand and was off to find the concierge.

31

C AN you help me?"

"Of course Mr. Rodan."" the concierge had said and was the first time anyone outside of Nelson or his mother had used his new identity and it felt good. "What is it that I can assist you with this evening?" The concierge continued.

"I am wanting to do some research on San Diego,California."

"We have a library that can answer many of your questions but it is closed at this hour."

"Is it on property?" " No, Mr. Rodan but I can have a car ready for you by 9:00 a.m. to take you there if you wish."

"That would be excellent thank you Remy" he said returning the name recognition the concierge had graced him with."

"It is my pleasure Mr Rodan good evening to you."

He returned to his room and went right to the restroom where he could again study his new features under the bright vanity lights.

How appropriate he thought to himself to be looking at himself so closely under what are called vanity lights.

He truly was another man, he was Jack Rodan. He began a monologue of who he was, where he was from and what his goals and ambitions were.

He played into the night with his new identity, getting to know, understand and memorize it for it will be soon when he would be reciting passages from it as if it were a great American novel or film.

While one of them played with their identity. The other played with the man who created them and brought them to life. She had woken up the following morning with Nelson in his suite.

She was awakened by a multitude of breakfast options, coffee and juices. He greeted her with a simple" I was not sure of what you liked so I had them prepare everything."

Her eyes were groggy as well as her head but she was sure the man sitting at the edge of the bed in front of her in his robe was in fact Nelson Pritchard.

"Oh my god, Oh my god" she said " I can't believe that I did that, I don't know what to say."

"Kelly did not know what to say." he explained to her and smiled as he went in very close to her to gain eye contact and kiss her forehead "But Camille,,,,, she say's good morning and rises to embrace her day." And he reached out for her hand to assist her from the bed while having a robe in his other hand for her to slip into.

The view was breathtaking, the meal was magnificent and he was charming. " This Camille has quite the life, she thought to herself looking across the table at him sipping his coffee.

Remy true to his word had a car ready for Mr.Rodan to take him to the west Cayman Library and precisely at 9:00a.m.

He went in and spoke to the woman at the counter who referred him to the reference clerk. He was shown the areas in which he could spend hours if he wished doing all the research he desired on San Diego California.

He took out books on art as well to begin to learn the differences between oil, acrylic and water colors and then the different types of painting.

He began to work on an in with her once he arrived and was getting there quickly. He had to first find out where Carlsbad was as well as the mentioned Caufield Studio where the art would be on display.

He found an atlas to scout some areas but would purchase one of his own from the concierge. His plan was simple. He had to fly to San Diego and either rent or purchase a car. He would drive to Cardiff where the Caufield Studio address is and wait.

He would wait for her to arrive there and then begin to study her habits. From there he should be able to understand a way to make contact and test his identity. This would tell him if he was able to pursue his long awaited interest and plan.

The 3 men would spend at least one more day in El Paso and call it a vacation if nothing turned up.

They ended up back at Heaven's Gate considering this is the place they came for a new identity so someone in here knows something and if they didn't then they knew someone that did.

They each ordered round after round while making small talk with anyone that would until it came to the young man and older woman who were here a few days ago and have not been seen since.

That question seemed to scare off the majority of everyone in the bar until a man approached the larger of the 3 men at the bar

"What's it to you? The woman and the kid?" The man asked

"Well if you know something about how I can find them then it's not what's it to me it is more of what's it to you because there is a benefit to each party in this scenario." The large man offered removing the sunglasses he was wearing inside of the bar.

"Okay then what's it to me?"

"Do you know something?"

"I do and considering the warm reception you are getting in here I see that it elevates my worth substantially but this is not the place for us to be having this discussion nor is it the place for you to be asking the questions you and the others are asking."

"Worth has many meanings so if there is another location you wish to continue this conversation then I suggest we do just that."

He looked at him and the others assessing them and the potential that this could be for him vs. the headache it could cause if he is discovered trading information with people other than his primary employer Nathan Pritchard.

"What hotel are you 3 staying in?"

"Motel 6 not far from here."

"I know it." He told him.

"There is a restaurant right up the highway from there and off the side, it is called Grand Torrito. You and your friends need to depart now with no more questions and I will meet you there in 2 hours." He stood from the bar stool he was occupying seated next to the large man and walked to the restroom.

Upon his return the man he was speaking to at the bar and the 2 others had departed. He sat back down and looked at himself in the mirror across from the bar. He took a long look as he finished his longneck beer. He waited a good amount of time, even finishing one more, before he left the bar and again taking one last look at himself as he paid the tab and walked out the door.

32

AMBER walked down her street until she reached the end of the block and kept walking. She went down 2 more streets and curved around the one way till she reached the beach access and started down the stairs to the sand.

She could hear the water crashing down as she took her shoes off to walk towards the wet sand. The breeze was blowing right off the coast and the starts filled the sky and yet with all of this wonder around her that was endless.

The sky, the sea and the sand all endless with possibility it was her that felt so trapped and isolated.

She called Lillian and she felt terrible when doing because she had never spoken to her for anything personal or anything home related.

Their relationship had been nothing but teacher and student up until this point but her faith in Lillian and the strength that she felt when around her she needed right now desperately.

"Hello." Lillian answered the home phone that she had given Amber.

"Hello." She said again as there was still no response.

"Hello Lillian, It is Amber and I am so terribly sorry to bother you at this hour." She clamored nervously

"Don't be silly Amber it is only 9:00 how old do you think I am dear, is everything alright?" she asked her to sense the hesitation in her voice.

"I don't know who else to turn to and I have been so helped by you since you have come into my life and just" she paused from tears beginning to fill her eyes and her throat " I just feel that I need some of that now."

"What is it Amber? What is the matter dear?"

"I don't know if I can talk about it over the phone, I am sorry I should not have bothered you Lillian, I feel terrible, I am so sorry."

"Nonsense Amber. If you cannot talk about on the phone would you feel more comfortable meeting somewhere?"

"It is late and I do not want to trouble you at this hour."

"Amber, if you have nowhere else that you feel you can go to discuss that which is troubling you then I will get into my car and drive wherever it is that you feel you can go to discuss it."

There was silence on the phone

"Amber, where are you now?"

"Carlsbad beach 22nd street beach access by the lifeguard station."

"Well then Carlsbad beach it is. If this is where you feel comfortable then I don't suppose a walk on beach in the moonlight with a friend would harm either one of us right now. Can you give me at least 30 minutes?"

"Lillian."

"Not another word unless you answer my question. Will you be there in 30 minutes if I drive there to you?"

"Yes."

"Then I am on my way honey, you just stay warm and safe and I will see you soon."

They each hung up the phone and as Lillian dressed a little warmer and heated some water in a thermos for hot chocolate Amber felt awful that she was bringing her into her troubles but so much better for the moment that she was coming to listen to them.

Lillian arrived at the 22nd street beach access that Amber said she would be

And found her in the precise area she said she would be. She came with a blanket for her in the event she was cold.

"Now, it has been my experience at least that in times of trouble a little blanket and warmth does not hurt." She said as she arrived. Lillian held out the blanket and thermos of hot chocolate for her and sat next to her in the sand.

"Tell me what is troubling you dear."

Amber went into not great lengths of detail but enough back story on her time in Texas, the trial, what the trial was for, the move here, Dr. Feingold and the stranglehold her mother had had on her ever since the incident happened.

Lillian just listened and let her get it all out and it helped her understand what the purpose of the painting was and why she was there in the first place.

"You did not know any of this, Dr. Feingold never told you anything?' Amber asked her.

"Heavens no. Elliot and I are friends but he is helping you and would never betray you Amber.

I did not know anything other than what I saw you paint I felt had purpose and wanted to explore it more with you, to help you explore it more."

Lillian did confess to Amber the meeting she had with her mother and went on that she can understand and sympathize with Amber and the validity of the feelings she has but also made note of the fact that she herself would now have compassion for the mother who was protecting her daughter due to the awful and traumatic experience that she had.

"You each have your side and the right to feel what you are feeling right now but your mother has probably never forgiven herself for not being there to protect you that night and is compensating for it now."

"What she was doing before made sense to me and the move i did not like at the time and still miss everyone but understand why they did it." She explained

"Now it just feels the extent of her protection is unhealthy for both of us."

Lillian had to marvel at the depth of her perception and felt that if she did not have some clarity to support what she felt it then it would blur and she should never really know what is real, right, wrong or unhealthy.

"How do you feel right now about where you are in your life?" Lillian asked her and turned to face her then continued

"I am not talking about the fight tonight either I mean the girl that I met a month ago. The one who has come and painted each week and the one that won an award earlier today and even fulfilled a goal she had set to have one of her paintings hanging in my gallery."

This made her smile and again here came her strength.

"I have been happier and stronger than I have in I don't know how long. I have found something that is helping me heal and is helping me channel as well as fulfilling me. I have found strength in your gallery and with you."

"Then you continue on that path but the new plateau of that path is the independence you gain as you walk it." She told her

"What do you mean?"

"I mean that you found something that was yours and not your mothers or your fathers. That is part of the fulfillment and the healing because you are regaining your identity through your own self discovery so the more that you find that is yours then the more you that you become." This does not mean that you are leaving your family or that you don't love them but you loving yourself right now is what is important because there is no loss of the love coming from either your mother or father and nothing would make them happier than to see you strong, confident and fulfilled."

"I don't see that making my mother happy." Amber said laughing

"Don't confuse fear with happy. It will delight her to see you strong, confident and fulfilled. It is only fear that you see right now because she feels it is her responsibility to provide those things for you when in reality they are your items to claim as part of your path to discover who you are."

"So what do I do?" she asked

"You keep doing what you are doing because everything you have said tonight tells you that it is working.

You continue to come in and you continue to paint. You continue to channel, express, explore and heal. You do that and you will find that next plateau in your life that you are in search of. I promise!"

They finished the hot chocolate and stared out to the sea but the air was not as complicated and her emotions not so thick now. She felt as if she were a screen that had been dirty and the ocean air was now cleaning and blowing right through each of those tiny spaces.

Lillian started her car and began on her way, just as Amber had, home.

Amber met with each of her parents when she walked in the door but this time it was her father that did most of the talking.

He promised to make sure that each of them support her with this new experience and they each could not wait to go to the gallery and see the painting for themselves.

Whatever happened that night felt very much as if it were meant to be as she was in her bed getting ready to drift off to sleep.

She was so grateful to have each of her parents in her life and Lillian helped her see that tonight as well as the other things she had not considered.

She would continue to go to the gallery. She would continue to paint, explore and heal just as Lillian explained.

Amber felt the optimism and confidence now that the next level of her life would appear through doing these things just as they discussed.

They had finished eating and still sat on the patio looking out to the ocean. They were each still wearing their robes and he the smile he could not contain each time he looked at her or her him. They said nothing for the longest time until.

"Nelson." She finally started " I don't know what to say.

Last night, this morning and you they were all amazing but everything to me is so complicated. More so than anything or moment I have had in my lifetime. She sank her head away from the ocean view to the floor.

"You speak with a tone filled with a lifetime of troubles that existed and were owned by a woman who no longer exist. You do understand that?"

"I don't see how a week of change on the outside removes a lifetime of who I am inside. Can you understand that?"

"Of course I can and it was thoughtless of me to have said that. Please forgive me." He said now looking at the floor himself then quickly lifted his head and scooted his chair closer to her.

"I am used to nefarious and criminal characters. I make a living blurring the lines, if you will so that was attempt to make you feel better. A poor one at that." He apologized.

"What I meant to say is that I see a woman who dreamed of a family and fell in love to achieve that. She worked hard to create what she had seen in her mind time and time again as she grew up and the man she married did not reciprocate."

"He may even have cracked that beautiful image that you saw in your mind yet you forged on to fulfill that image for your husband, you son and yourself."

He reached for her hand and continued "What happened to him was not your fault. You did not even have knowledge of it but if the things that your son told me about the man you spent half of your life time with then the woman who sits before me deserves this view.

She deserves the comfort that we feel right now."

He then stood up and then knelt before her which startled her because it reminded her of James but continued on.

"She deserves this opportunity, she deserved her pleasure last night and she. You deserve to rid yourself of the weights that deprive you from being happy right now and tomorrow!"

She sat there crying with tears running down her cheeks and dripping onto the cotton robe. He embraced her which again started her. He felt this in her body and he just felt terrible how all of these emotions lived and consumed this woman's body to where she was frightful of being held so she could weep.

"Its Okay" he began to rock her in an effort to allow her to let what was inside of her out and no longer fear what was preventing her from doing just that.

"Please It's Okay. I am not going to hurt you I promise." He told her holding her just a little bit tighter to see if she was ready to let go and then he told her

"You deserve to mourn Kelly, you deserve to mourn his passing and all of those things that you have kept inside and concealing for all of those years afraid of him or anyone else ever seeing. I am so sorry."

She let go. She crumbled and he felt her body first let go as if she had lost consciousness then in the wake of that came the trembling cries which made him grip her tighter in an effort to hold her. She cried harder which was still part fear and letting go but it was the first time she had ever done that in the presence of another person besides James in her lifetime.

He said nothing more.

He just held her for as long as she needed and the funny thing was that he was a guy who could have just about anything or anyone he wanted. He was drawn to the fragile state of this woman.

He was drawn to the value she had in family based on the extent she would endure to preserve it. He wanted to help her because it was one of the first things he had felt good about in a very long time.

He had helped several people but they were all evading and running from something because of something they did and deserved to probably be caught but their evasion was his financial gain.

33

NELSON was a very good plastic surgeon who was all about the work for most of his life. He dated when he could but his hours and dedication to his craft was what moved him and not the emotional baggage of a relationship.

He was moving into a field that had little interest at the time but was on the cusp of becoming one of the most sought after and lucrative professions that there has ever been.

There was once a client that had come in for a pretty routine consultation. He was the owner of a bar in Los Angeles and had been in a fight which led to stitches.

He had 37 of them on his right side and he came to Nelson to see if he could better his profile from its current state because he was a lady's man and the stitches gave him a complex.

Nelson completed the procedure and it was not long till the scaring was non-existing. That was that and he had a very pleased client once again.

Then a year later this same man came to see him again and was in some trouble. The trouble had to do with narcotic distribution and tax evasion in which he would be sent to prison. He was released on bail, pending trial and he had a proposal.

Nelson listened to the man propose if he could change his features enough to alter his appearance he could become another man and flee the country with a new identity. He was willing to pay him 3 times whatever the number Nelson had in mind and it would be in cash as well as tax free.

Nelson did not know what to say. " Your face is your face but the identification you have will not pass as what you will look like later." He told him

"I got that covered and is not a concern but I need someone to make the changes so I look different otherwise no matter what the identification says they release all of those wanted posters and they get me sometime, you know?"

"This is time sensitive so I need an answer."

"I need 24 hours."

"I need an answer now doc." He snapped

"Your hearing can't be tomorrow, wait it is not tomorrow is it?" he asked panicked.

"No I have a week but there are details to work out."

"I need 24 hours to think about this, it's a lot."

"You right doc it is a lot. It is a lot of money that I am offering you that is what it is a lot of so I will tell you what. I will give you 3 hours.

"You make your decision by 7:00p.m. today. I will call you at this office at 7:00 for an answer." He said getting up. He then turned to the doctor before opening the door.

"If you go to the police during that time doc I promise you that even if I am inside the joint or out I will have several men visit first your mother and then you. I already checked on her and know she is a resident of Palm Villas in Palm Springs so don't do anything stupid. There is benefit to everyone involved if you think about it. Talk to you at 7."

Nelson was a wreck.

He had never been threatened and he had never had his mother's life threatened. His career was at stake everything he went to school and worked so hard for. Everything he cared about. He canceled the remainder of his appointments and went for a walk outside for some fresh air.

Think Nelson think, he said to himself as he made his way to a grassy spot at the park. He thought about where he was in life at that moment. What he was doing, where he was working, who he was working for and this city.

He had always been more natured than Los Angeles had to offer. How much money would he pay? What he could do with that money?

He could move, he could start his own practice, he could always be able to take care of his mother but what if he was caught.

He could never go to prison, he would never survive. His mind raced but the air outside, although riddled with smog, helped.

He made his way back to the office after an hour and a half and felt he was ready to speak. He walked past everyone that was still at the office and went directly to his. He paced back and forth until the call came.

Nelson agreed to meet him and to perform the surgery for $200,000 in cash and wanted to know how the identification was going to follow.

"What do you need to know that for that has nothing to do with you."

"If you had another surgeon you would have called them before calling me."

"What makes you think I haven't?" he asked him

"Because you know my work. You know how good it is and that I will succeed." Don't you?" he said confidently. Nelson did always have a great deal of confidence in his work.

The phone was silent.

"I want the information in case this sort of thing comes up again." He said into the phone which was still silent.

"I want to think I am helping you and if the opportunity arises for me to help another then I could offer the service of your friend as well, that's all."

"175,000 and I introduce you to the other person involved but we do this tonight and we do it fast. Do we have a deal?"

"We do."

Nelson said into the phone and his life was never the same. He would take the money and start over in Austin Texas still performing his role as a surgeon.

Over time enough referrals would come to see him that he would leave the license of practicing in a facility behind. He feared that if people started to investigate his own practice then it would be to easy to connect the dots.

If he were a bar owner with a facility to perform his craft to a select clientele then it would reduce his potential for being suspect.

He had made enough money and in addition to the bar he started to evolve his business through amenities such as providing the identification himself vs. outsourcing which shrunk his cost. He also had his money in off shore accounts so if clients did not already have such a plan in place that too was available.

The problem was that the art of performing his craft was still mostly all that moved him. He had not planted anything that grew and would impact the world positively he felt.

He was surrounded by drug runners, gun traders, pirates, drunks and thieves.

He found this woman though. He found a woman that he felt he had some things in common with. They each had opportunity thrust on them when neither had sought it out.

They each felt guilt about the role in which they currently exist.

It was more than just the circumstances in which they had in common though. He did find her attractive and her pain made his heart ache which is not something he had felt since his father passed away.

He wanted to help her even if they did not stay together but he enjoyed last night and wanted to see her again.

She was still in his arms when she finally had felt better. The fear returned and she was afraid to pull away and face him. He did and it again made her tremble and her eyes actually close.

"Kelly" he said and then " Camille, you are alright now. I am not going to hurt you." He let go and stood back to give her some room now in hopes it would alleviate her fear.

"I am so embarrassed"

"no-no-no-no-no there is nothing to be embarrassed about and that gets back to what I was telling you. You are alright okay, you are safe and you have every right to feel the way you do. I just want to be here for you if you need me."

"Why are you doing this?"she said plainly

"Because you deserve it" he said again and offered to tell her a story that may make her feel better.

She agreed and he went on to tell her everything that got him into this business. He told her how it makes him feel and how meeting her was the first real connection he had had with another person in such a long time.

"You and I are a lot alike and although I do not know all of the things that you have been through to get here. I choose and wish to be here with you right now." He said to her

"I will help you if you let me and to be honest with you I feel that you are helping me as well." He stood there waiting for a response of some sort.

"I choose to be here with you too." She said smiling " and I am glad that I am able to be doing something for somebody." She added exhaling a long breath

"We will go slow. We enjoy. We learn and we grow but no more of this I am going to schedule you a massage right now." He stood and went right to the phone

"What? A massage?" she said never having one before.

"That is right" he was now on the phone ordering a bottle of champagne and a therapist to join them in the room within the hour for a deep tissue massage.

When he completed the call he announced that she was to have champagne with fresh fruit and the finest deep tissue massage to remove every ounce of negative thought being held in her body.

He held out his hand which she grabbed and he pulled her to him and he began to slow dance.

See he said to her" slow."

34

H E had finished what research he could do at the library and was on his way to his mother's room to discuss the idea of going to San Diego.

There was no answer at her room so he decided to go to Nelson's suit to see if he had knowledge of where she was.

2 knocks at the door and he waited until Nelson answered the door wearing a large cotton robe.

"Mr.Rodan" he said with cheer and a smile " What brings you here Jack?"

"Good afternoon Nelson. Have you seen my mother?"

"I have Jack she is here." He said moving to his side with a gesture for him to enter the room. " She is having a massage, wont you come in."

He walked in and was not sure what to think. The room smelled of lavender and there were several breakfast plates and carts throughout the room. He was trying to figure out why she was having a message in his room.

He approached her as she lay on a table face down near the balcony. There was a robe like the one he was wearing on a chair located next to the table she was laying on.

"Mom" he said and she lifted her head slightly but she did not appear to be moving very much. She turned her neck to where she could see him. " How are you?" she said still fighting the urge to call him Jessie.

"I'm good and you?"

"This is my first massage" she returned " I cannot believe how good this feels." and then her head was back face down.

"I want to talk to you, how much longer do you have?"

The therapist answered the question with "another 20 minutes"

"Do you want to go for a walk after?" he asked her then Nelson interjected " May not be a good idea to walk right after, can it wait till maybe 5:30 so there is time to relax after?"

"Is that Okay honey?" she asked him

"That's fine just come by my room and we can go down to the beach."

"It will be an amazing sunset." Nelson offered

"I will be there, 5:30." She said still not moving from where she was on the table.

Nelson walked him to the door still full of cheer and gave him a more serious look." Is everything alright?" he asked him in the hall so she could not hear.

"Everything is fine, just feel like taking a walk and talking."

"That is a great idea and I think she could use it too." Nelson said to him with one hand on his shoulder. He ended the conversation there and went to his room.

He was grateful to Nelson for everything he had done but he did not like the way he put his hand on his shoulder just then at all. It reminded him of his father way too much. He did not know how to take the dinner last night either. Was there something going on between them he wondered? If there was, is that wrong?

He waited in his room till the knock came. It was after 5:30 but seeing her when he opened the door continued to take some getting use to for both of them. She did look relaxed, lighter and more comfortable.

"do you want to go for a walk?" He asked her

"I would very much" she said back and they made their way down to the sand. The sun was almost sinking away bringing nightfall to the island.

"How was it?" he asked her

For a moment she felt terrible because she did not know what "it" exactly was he was asking. Was he asking about last night with Nelson or

"How was the massage?" he said again, "you look great."

"Thank you honey, It was amazing. You should get one tomorrow."

"I have an idea." He began as she laced her arm through is while they walked.

"What is that?" she asked him admiring the fading light.

"I think we should go to San Diego. Get a place and start over there."

"I have never been to San Diego" she said very calmly looking up towards the sky still walking in pace. " I don't believe you have either, why San Diego?" she continued

"I don't know, I did some research on it this morning at the library and it sounds perfect." She clutched his arm and shuttered briefly like she had a chill run through her.

"It is by the ocean and on the border to Mexico. It has a great school, sports art and museums. It has everything that we need and a place that no one would think to look for us in event anyone was looking for us.." What do you think?" he asked her

"I don't see any reason why we could not go there and see if we like it, when did you want to go?"

"Tomorrow, maybe the next day."

"What" she said now settling out of her post massage relaxation. "Why tomorrow?"

"I don't know. I am just excited I guess. Why what is wrong with tomorrow or the next day? We got what we came here for, right?"

"I don't know. "She answered him " I like where we are right now or at least the moment."

"I am getting to know Nelson and I don't want to rush that or walk away from it either. Does that bother you? The getting to know nelson part I mean?"

It did and he did not know why but he said " no, I just want to start again you know. I have been away and since I got out we have been running." He explained.

"I want to find somewhere that feels safe, like what you had in Italy before all of this happened. You felt safe right?"

"Oh Italy was amazing baby but it was different at the same time. I too was still running and the fact that I did not have you or knowing if you were safe never left my mind."

"This is different" he said "We are together and safe. I like it here too but it does not feel like home. It feels more like we are on vacation. I just want to find a place that feels like home again."

She understood that especially after where he has been.

"We do still have some things to talk about" The massage relaxation was now definitely gone.

"Did you do that to your father for the money?" she asked stopping him in the sand and pulling him to look her in the eye.

"yes and no." he answered her " I did do it for the money because I did not feel like I had any other option. I thought about it a lot when I was there and all of the things that I saw him do to both of us seemed." She looked down to the sand avoiding eye contact.

"I did it for us." I did it for both of us and here we are."

"Did you tell Nelson about your father?"She asked him

"Yes but it was because those 3 guys from the hotel had found us in El Paso and were in Heaven's Gate looking for us. They figured out that we were going there so they knew we were looking to get our identity changed." She looked back at him again not knowing that last part.

"They followed us?"

"I think so and I think they want more money but I had to tell Nelson because he was asking why they were in his bar asking questions."

"Do you trust him?" he asked her squarely

"Yes" she responded

"He said they would no longer be a concern once I told him everything. I told him what they did to him and why. I told him for how much but the debt was paid so they were looking to extort more from us after the fact." He could see that she was thinking and taking this all in.

"I hope we can trust him" he said

"What do you mean."

"He is the only one that knows what our new identity is and he is the only one that could get that information to those guys."

"He would never do that. He does not need the money for one and he seems to want to help us."

"I hope you are right because it does not matter where we go if those guys find out who we are now then we will see them again regardless."

"San Diego huh." She said feeling quite worried that this still was not over. " I have a better idea Mr. Jack Rodan." She continued now smiling.

"Why don't you go to San Diego and see if this is a place that we would each enjoy. I will stay with Nelson so we can continue to get to know each other and it will give me a chance to make sure that what you are concerned about does not ever happen."

"How are you going to do that?" he asked her looking for re assurance.

"I don't know but we do have to make sure that no one finds out who we are and if he is the only one than he needs to have an eye kept on him, agreed?"

35

H E drove to the diner where the 3 men awaited him. He did not want to go inside. Fear-full that someone he knew would see him speaking to these men that had been asking so many questions that should not be asked.

He had to find a way to see them but in a place that was not so public or private because he did not know these guys or what they were capable of. He just wanted a payday plain and simple. Get a nice chunk of change and flee but it would have to be enough to disappear too in the event that his boss Nathan figured him for the leak.

How much do I need to disappear?

He was trying to figure that out in addition to how to meet with them. He decided on a note to be left on the door of the room they were staying with a more remote location near dark so no one would see them together. This would give him time to get some more artillery in the event that he needed it against these 3.

The 3 men finished ordering and then the meal. The waited till they no longer had patience. They paid the bill and departed back to their hotel where they were surprised to find a map on the door.

The map instructed them to walk a distance behind the hotel and into the brush where they would be found from there.

"Found how?" is what the large man asked the others."What do you think" the other asked?"

"I don't know." He said " The way I see it is no one would speak to us but him so it is possible there is a few guys out there waiting for us to end any further questions from being asked or it is just him looking to get paid for the information we need."

"do you think he knows anything?"

"There is only one way to find out." " Are you guys with me?"

They went into the room and collected what weapons they had including ones they could find in the room in the event it became hand to hand.

They went on their way as the map instructed to this secluded spot behind the hotel and in the brush. The large man instructed each of them to spread out a little so they were not all together. He would go in to where they were asked and the other 2 look for anyone else out here.

"I can't see a shit out here, how in the hell am I supposed to find someone else?"

"You will know it when you see it I guess, figure it out." He told each of them and continued towards the destination.

It was dark alright and the only things he was seeing in front of him were the brush when it was already hitting his face. He was waiting for his eyes to adjust to the darkness when he heard a voice

"Where are your 2 friends?"

"They are here, don't worry. You have to understand that not knowing where I am or who you are that this would be considered insurance."

"Fair enough." He said " stop there that is far enough

He was trying to identify where the voice was coming from. He could tell the direction but not the distance or closeness.

"my insurance policy is the m-16 that I have pointed at you" he paused " just in case I miss on the first shot I will have another couple hundred chances.

"Why are we here?" he asked the man who's voice he could not find.

"Safer for me to not meet you in public. Why do you want the boy and his mother?"

"Money, why else." 204

"Do they owe you money?"

"you could say that"

"Why do they owe you money."

"What difference does it make you either have information for me or not. I am prepared to pay for it. I know they came here to get out of the country and I know if they came here they did it to get a new identity so all I need is the name and location of our 2 friends."

"How much are you willing to pay for the information?"

"Listen how much do you need to give me what I want?"

"$200,000 " he said

"wow cmon man wait a second. They do not owe me that much money"

He said in an effort to stall hoping one of the 2 would find him in the darkness and get a hold of him so they could get this information and a much better rate. Like killing him after he told them what they wanted to know.

"I was thinking more along the lines of $50,000." He said looking for a response.

"You thought wrong then. You should leave and not return to ask more questions because what will happen is I and many others will get sent after you till there is silence. If you have nothing more to offer than this conversation is over."

"Wait-wait a second" he said still stalling. If they don't find him then how much is this stuff worth. They got the 50 and felt there was the potential to get 500,000 so was it worth 100 to this guy then split the rest with the other 2? Why can't they find this guy he was thinking to him-self.

"$100,000" he said and then heard crackling but other than the brush moving which could have been his 2 or that one with the machine gun, there was silence.

"All I want is the name they are using and where they went and

I will pay $100,000." Still silence with the exception of the crackling which sounded like it was coming closer.

"Are you there?" he called out and was turning to face the sound of the crackling but had now pulled out the revolver he had in his waist.

With the gun at his side he cocked it and did not move to prevent any glare or shine that may come from what portion of the moon was present. If this guy saw that he had a gun he may take him out right then right behind him was a much louder crackle and then a hand on his shoulder and he squeezed the trigger firing a round off into the ground. He turned in a fury with his hand waving as a turned to prevent the barrel of a gun from being in his direction and started to fire.

The person that was behind him was one of his men and now had 3 holes in him from the gun fire.

The first round in the ground made him back up but when his friend turned to face him all he saw was the white powder coming from the barrel and in his direction until he hit the ground.

"Fuck" he yelled " What the fuck man–Where are you" The large man screamed and there was only one voice that returned a comment. It was the 3rd man yelling " Where are you?"and "What happened?"

"I am over here. Just follow my voice" he said to the 3rd but he still could not find him. He stood over to the man he had just shot in the dark and was now trying to figure out what to do with him because they were not far from the hotel. It was possible someone heard those shots and called the police or where around looking for what may have happened.

"Go back to the hotel but don't let anyone see you" he whispered trying to avoid if anyone was listening. " I will meet you there."

The cracking of the darkness was completely rattling his cage now because he could not tell if it was his guy going,the machine gun guy who may or may not still be there or if it was people to investigate what they heard.

He sat there in the darkness as silent as could be just trying to get his bearings and thoughts. How do I even get back to the hotel and what the fuck do I do with this body? He thought to himself.

The crackling faded and did not continue after that so it appeared that he was alone with his dead friend. If he left and went back to the hotel for help it was possible he would not be able to find this spot again in the darkness which means it could get discovered in daylight so he had no choice but to start moving dirt and brush with his bare hands in an effort to cover and conceal as much of the body as possible.

He worked on it for over an hour until he felt that it was good enough in the event of someone walking in this area, hoping that no one actually did that.

Now that he was covered he then had to figure out how in the hell to get back to the hotel. He was turned around a few times searching for the voice and the crackling and then the adrenaline from the gun shots so he really had no idea from what point he came in. He stumbled on through the night and the whole time he was trying to figure what had happened and where the guy from the bar went.

He made his way out to a rode but was not sure if it was a side street, driveway or a highway. He picked a direction and started in the hopes of a car or familiar something. He would not reach the room until the next day when a car did finally see him and got him going in the right direction which was a good 12 miles in the wrong.

He told a tale of taking a walk then the sun went down and he just got lost. The driver was kind enough to get him to the hotel with some friendly advice advising not doing that again.

The other man was there asleep but awoke as soon as he banged on the door. "What happened?" 206

Nelson, Camille and Jack enjoyed a lovely meal and it would be there last for the time being. They spoke over dinner about the trip he would be making to San Diego and all of the things he hoped to find there leaving out the actual reason that was drawing him there.

He saw a chemistry that was there between them. There was a comfort and familiarity that was growing.

He still did not like it but she was right. If he was of any threat to them at all than it was better that Nelson enjoy their company and want to help them. Her staying would allow her time to work on whatever it was between them that was happening and maybe even speak to him about the concerns they had of anyone ever finding out who they now were.

Nelson volunteered to fly him there in the morning but he felt it was better to fly an airline and explained that he did not want to burden him if he and his mother were enjoying their stay. Nelson agreed that he was in-deed but it was not trouble or bother at all.

"I insist" Jack said " You have been of tremendous assistance and as I said before we each are very grateful for the gift you have provided. I am forever in your debt already and will not have you pulled from this moment to fly me to San Diego."

He raised his glass and awaiting for the other 2 guest at the table to do the same .

"To Nelson. " he said and clinked the other 2 glasses.

The toast made him blush but it also stopped the conversation of Nelson flying Jack there and it also re kindled the spark between her and Nelson. She had not seem him blush before and found it endearing on both he and her son's part for making the perfect toast.

Nelson asked the waiter over and instructed him to contact the hotel concierge where he wished to have a car ready for Mr. Rodan in the morning.

He parted company in the morning with Nelson and his mother. He purchased a flight bound for San Diego flying first class and boarded the plane.

He sat in his chair and was greeted by the lovliest sound " Good morning Mr. Rodan, may I get you anything before we take off?"

"I am fine thank you." He said to the flight attendant.

He was Jack Rodan and he was on his way to San Diego he thought to himself smiling and putting on his sunglasses .

The plane touched down and he proceeded towards the car rental section of the airport. He asked for a convertible because he had never driven one or driven in one. He did not even actually have a license and was not sure if he was a good driver but if he was going to find out it was going to be in a convertible.

He placed his bag in the trunk removed the atlas he had and shut it.

He could not believe the amount of roads or highways that there were her. He had never seen anything like this in Texas or even in Italy or The Cayman's. This felt like a test to him when he was back in school and had to pull over several times to make sure he was going in the right direction.

He was on the 5 headed North, looking for his exit and getting frustrated that everyone was driving so fast around him. He was frustrated that every wrong turn he made he had to go several blocks out of his way with no way to make u-turns without it being illegal.

He was not in any hurry to test that portion of his identity so the frustration went on and on until he found the city of Del Mar. He knew he was going in the right direction according to the atlas and the directions so he felt better. He kept his eyes on the road taking an occasional glance at the homes, people and the ocean which was right there on his last.

He passed a sign stating Welcome to Cardiff so he knew he was closer. To the left was all beach and ocean and up ahead was a shopping center. He passed the 2 story restaurant and pulled right in the first entrance. It was busy, everything seemed so busy.

He drove around looking for a parking space and could not find one which again was starting to frustrate him but then he realized he was not even sure if this was the shopping center so he kept driving shop to shop.

Looking at each sign on the door or above until he found it. The Caufield Studio.

He stopped immediately and then a car behind started to sound their horn. They then were getting ready to pull around him when he started to accelerate again and just drove and drove until he was able to find a parking space.

He could not see the shop from where he had parked so he got out and went closer towards it so he could see it but be far enough away. He stood there for a while and could not stand it he had to see if for some reason she was there now. He went closer and closer until he could see inside the windows and because it was dark out he felt certain they could not see out.

There were people in the shop looking at the art on the wall but no one inside he recognized so he wanted to go back further away.

The passing aroma of food in the air made him aware that he had not eaten in a while and he also needed to get some idea of where to sleep so he found one of the at least 5 places to eat in that area. He walked to the door of one that looked not to nice to where he could not get in or feel uncomfortable. He looked at the menu that was posted outside to make sure that there was some food he would enjoy and went inside.

He asked if he could eat at the bar instead of taking up a table and they showed him to where he could eat in that area.

"Perfect" he said and waited for the server. He was greeted by the quintessential California girl named Dakota and "What can I get for you?"

He ordered a California Burger complete with avocado and Swiss cheese and then asked if she knew of a hotel in the area that he could get a room.

She told him of a place that was not far up the road from where they were now but looked at him funny like he was trying to pick her up and it made him feel uncomfortable so he stuck to little conversation until he finished his meal and paid the check leaving a nice enough tip to make up for any misunderstanding.

He went up the road in the direction she gave him for about 10 minutes and pulled into the first place he found. He asked for a room if there were any available "You are in luck my man, we have one left." The smiling clerk wearing a bright orange t shirt which made his very blonde hair stand out even more said.

He took the necessary information and payment and checked in Jack Rodan.

He showered and then relaxed on the bed. He held in his hand the article he had found and kept on the painting she had done. The picture of her smiling for a camera holding a piece entitled *"progress"* made him glad he had made the trip.

He was glad he was here. She is smiling for cameras enjoying her progress huh he said to himself in a low voice. He then placed the article on his chest face down and closed his eyes remembering that night. He remembers her coming from the back room, she was dancing and she called to him. She sang to him and she never stopped him or said no.

"*Progress*" he thought to himself.

How much progress do you think I have made being sent to that place for all of that time? For something that you and I did, not just me. The voice in his head getting louder but not leaving his lips. Not just me Amber, you and I., you and I.

He was now working on his breathing to get control of his demeanor just as he had done countless times when he was inside. He had this entire conversation in his head and never moved from his spot on the bed.

He got control of it, got under the covers, shut off the light and went to sleep.

The next morning he was dressed and grabbing some Danish and coffee from the complimentary breakfast amenity the hotel offered. He was back up the road and in the parking lot of the shopping mall and this time he had no issue getting one this early. He found that would allow him to stay in the car and see everyone coming and going.

He saw a middle aged woman with a key opening the store followed by a older woman with shorter silver hair half hour later. The middle aged woman was who opened the door earlier and was now at a desk located in the front. It would be 2 ½ hours before anyone else would come and it was a couple holding hands each wearing shorts and flip flops.

He waited there all afternoon and there was no sign of who he was waiting for. It was 7:30 and the older woman was leaving so he decided to leave as well. He wanted to eat before going back to the hotel but did not want the girl from the last restaurant to see him and think something so he ventured in the opposite direction a ways to see what was the other way.

Not that far down he came across another shopping center that was much busier than the one he just left. He tried to pull in to park but was met by the same challenges he was having anywhere he went so he turned on the next street which was residential and combed up and down until he found a place to squeeze his convertible in. he decided to walk because pizza sounded good and he could take some back to the hotel for later if he wanted,

There was as many people outside on the curb as inside. The menu was in chalk above where you order and the place was loud. He looked at what to order and decided on a build your own. When he finished paying he noticed to the right there was a bar with several taps and again the various selection's written in chalk up above. The artist had a good hand with the letters he thought but had never heard of a single one of these beers.

"What can I get you" the jovial large bellied man behind the bar said .

"I don't know" he said nervously

"Got it, your first time here what type of beer do you normally drink?" he asked him

"Budweiser" he answered and watched the grimacing face of the man behind the bar

"These here are microbrews, they are crafted beers by people right here in Cardiff for you." He picked up a glass and poured from the tap a few ounces of something and slid it to him " try that one."he said slapping a towel over his right shoulder and crossing his arms awaiting a victorious agreement.

"That's good" he said " it taste a little like honey" he added " that is our Cardiff Honey Lager and it is good isn't it. $6.00" he said sliding over a pint to him. He paid with a $10 and told him to keep the change

He waited for the pizza and studied the people in the place. There were families in there with their kids in the back by the arcade games.

There were bikers with the Harleys parked on the curb. There were people in their on what looked like a 1ˢᵗ date, study groups, fitness people on break from bicycling because their bikes were on the curb too. The place had everyone and every kind in here. It smelled great and the beer was pretty damn good.

He was reading though some of the several free publications and magazines that were at the door when they called his name for his pizza. He took the pizza and the magazines back to the convertible to head back to the hotel.

While he ate the stuff in the magazines was full of information. It talked about all of the things going in all of the areas around and including San Diego. It talked about upcoming concerts, politics, festivals and art shows including one that featured graffiti artist.

He decided on calling his mother because he had not talked to her since he had arrived and did not want her to worry. He also wanted to know how it was going with Nelson. The phone rang and rang with no answer. He did not know if it was too late there or if she was just not in her room. He was the one that was now worried.

He awoke the next morning and walked to the front desk to ask if there had been any messages. He had one and it was the one he was awaiting. It said for him to call her whenever he could today, she would be in her room waiting and it did not matter the time.

He went back to his room and made the long distance call to The Montecito Hotel. It would ring 3 and a half times then she answered " Hello."

"Mom" he replied

"Honey" she said. She had not exactly gotten used to calling him Jack and he wanted her to get away from calling him Jessie so she opted for Honey. " I am glad you called, how was your flight? What have you been up to? How is San Diego? Are you enjoying yourself?"

He could not answer any of the questions before she asked another but he had one of his own before getting to answer the barrage she asked.

"How are things there with you and Nelson?"

"Fine honey, we are great. We have been talking and getting to know each other a little more."

You like him don't you" he asked her curiously. They talked about this before on the beach before he left and he saw them together knowing there was something but it was not until now that it clicked. He was not that comfortable with the fact that she may have an interest in him and it has bothered him a little but at the same time it made him happy that she was happy.

He did not want her to get into a situation with a guy that could be dangerous considering all of the time she spent with someone who appeared to be so normal on the outside but was dangerous on the inside. This guy was just plain dangerous inside and out he thought.

"I don't know how I feel about him. He is interesting on many levels and seems to have not just my best interest but yours as well." What do you think about him?" she asked him

"I love that you are happy but I don't want you to get involved with someone that is dangerous after everything you have been through."

"Do you think he is dangerous?" she asked him

"I don't know but considering what he does and who he deals with I would think he is or is capable of being dangerous. The guy had armed guards all around the warehouse we were in.

"He was protecting himself and us." She added

"I know, I know it is just the business he is in I mean dad was in a very well liked business and everyone respected him so here this guys is in a whole other business where I would image people fear him." "We went to him for his service which he provided and we paid him for I just do not know what good may come now from you and him spending time together."

"He said that he is getting something from the time spent with me. It makes him feel good or better than the other people he does business with like he was really able to help someone instead of contributing to them fleeing or running." She explained

"He is the only person who knows everything that has happened besides you and he is still here and he feels genuine when he is talking to me and letting me talk, letting me work through these feeling that I have never shared or shown anyone. Honey that does make me feel good and it is something that I need and have needed for some time." The phone was silent because he did not have a response to that.

"Okay" he finally said and she then went into " Tell me about your trip."

"Are you enjoying yourself?"

He went on to tell her about the flight, the first time ride in a convertible which made her smile because he was now doing things and experiencing things for the first time just as she had and knew the positive effect it had on her. She listened in delight to every detail he shared with small questions for him to elaborate on.

He did not mention anything about the art gallery other than he wanted to stay longer with an unsure amount of time until he would be ready to leave.

"What about you?" he asked " Are you guys going to stay there?"

"Actually he asked me to return to El Paso with him for a while if I wanted to." She told him

"What did you tell him?"

"I had never been to El Paso other than when I was a child and it was for a weekend with little memory other than a bridge, some cobblestone and The Alamo." He continued to listen

"I don't know but he said he felt that it would be good for me to return to Texas with some strength and sense of healing in my soul."

He still listened definitely not sure what that meant but he could not help but hear the tone in her voice that made him feel like she was better there with Nelson than here. How else could he do what it was that he was doing if she was here so at least she was there with someone and she felt safe.

"When would you leave?"

"He has to return within a day, I don't think he likes what he does for a living and I think he has not for a while then we came along and really made him see it." "With as much effort as he has put forward to listen and help me I feel like I should be there for him as well. I think he too is going through some changes that he just can't talk about with anyone else."

"Will you leave a message like before with where you will be and a number for me to reach you and I will call you as soon as I get it." He told her the hotel and location he was staying so in the event if she ever had to leave she would know the city and address of the hotel to find him.

They each exchanged I Love you's and hung up the phone.

He opened the front door to his room and stood in the doorway leaning up against the frame. The breeze and fresh air was one of the many things he missed when he was away but this breeze had a fragrance with it unlike anywhere he had been.

There were flowers, grass and salt in the air that when mixed together like that with the breeze it truly felt and smelt like freedom. He stood there for several minutes thinking of so many scenes in his life as if they were passing before him. His eyes closed taking them in, all of them the good and the bad and what collectively has brought him here today to this moment.

His eyes opened and looked at the colors that surrounded him from the paint on the hotel, the shrubs, bushes, trees, grass and the different colors of the vehicles in the parking lot.

"Time to go to work" he said and shut the door.

36

H E was on his way to the gallery and again found a spot where he could park but with it now being a weekend the lot was already fuller than before and it was only 10:30. The gallery was already open and he decided to take steps in to see if she was there and if not at least see what was inside that led her there to begin with.

He was immediately greeted by the same woman he saw opening the store 2 days prior

"Welcome to The Caufield Studio" she said with more enthusiasm than anyone he came in contact with in The Cayman's. The store had 2 other patrons inside none of which were her so he went piece to piece on the wall and looked at them. The place was bright and had something about it that he could tell or feel.

The colors coming from the walls, the natural light, the happy person at the front whatever it was he could see why she liked spending some time in here.

He located what brought him here as he made his way around the room. He stopped there and looked at the piece longer than any other. Jayne approached him at that time to offer a comment on it " Doesn't that just say it all?" she said standing next to him as they each shared space looking at the piece.

"It does" he said agreeing but she did not pick up on the sarcasm in his voice.

"Lovely girl that did too, she won an award for this exact piece about a month ago."

"I understand why, it kind of speaks to you" he said still looking only at the painting.

"Everyone" she announced " it speaks to everyone that sees it " she giggled and nudged him " funny you would say that. Is there anything I can help you with?"

"No not at the moment, I saw the place and was drawn to it, very glad I came in too. Specially to see this." He offered now facing her with a contagious smile and holding out his hand to introduce himself and make an impression.

"Jack Rodan" he said

"Miss Jayne Woodall " she returned " Well Miss Jayne Woodall you have been an absolute delight, the work in here is inspiring and the place itself just as comfortable as a blanket." He said to her still holding her hand and continuing to smile.

She now letting go of his hand but again giggled at his charm.

He started towards the door and before leaving the gallery bid her a wonderful afternoon and she him and he was off. He returned back to the car feeling confident that he made the right impression on her and this place that he was hoping she would return to soon.

Shortly after noon there she was. He could not believe it. He had not seen her in 5 years, aside from the picture but even that was smaller in size and black and white.

Here she was walking to the gallery wearing white shorts, a light baby blue short sleeve button that was tied in the front so it did not hang so low on her. Her hair was still long and brown. She looked great he thought.

She had grown up and her features matured but she looked really good. He waited in the car for 5 hours until she departed again and she was never visible from the window upon her arrival except for what looked like a warmer greeting from The Miss Jayne Woodall that just any customer coming in so again he felt good that he had made the impression he did on her.

She was gone from that moment till now so he wondered what she did there. None the less he would save that matter for another time. He wrote down the time and day she arrived at the gallery into a notebook he had purchased to record some notes about his plan. He started his convertible and placed the top back up and followed her out of the parking lot.

She was driving a rose or almost wine colored V.W. Kermagee and was heading in the direction of the pizza place he had discovered the night before. He followed behind her for close to 20 minutes turning here and there and he was beginning to hope he did not get lost on his way back but he kept behind her. He pulled into a shopping center some-where, he was not sure where he was.

She parked her car and walked into a book and music store. He decided to get out as well and stretch since he had been in the car the entire day and go inside but not be seen. He took a San Diego Charger baseball hat he bought to wear and conceal himself a little.

He went in and just went aisle to aisle until he located her. She was in a section that was art based. He went towards the music selection so he could see her and pretend to look at some things.

She picked out 4 books from where she was and took them to an area that looked like someone's living room. He really kind of looked around to see where he was.

He had never been in a place like this come to think of it. The only place he had looked at music tapes was at small store in Texas and this place has rows of C.D.'s, aisles and aisles of books with labels like in a library but there was music playing throughout the store.

You could smell coffee in the air and there were places to sit but not the traditional wood tables like in a library. These were large leather chairs and couches with coffee and end tables. This place was incredible he thought and apparently so did she.

She sat in those chairs for another 2 hours just reading and looking at the books she had selected and when she was done with those she went to get others.

She returned all of what she had taken stretched out by placing her hands together, raising them to the sky and arching her back. She then headed out the door without purchasing anything. Back to her car and on the road.

It was a little after 6:00 and the sun was going down but the car she was driving made it easy to not lose sight of.

Turning here and there it appeared that she was heading home because less and less business areas and more homes were around. The streets were wide and everywhere he looked there were people walking, jogging, bike riding or kids playing in the streets. This scene along with the sunset was so domestic and was what everyone around the world that did not have it dreamt of.

Her car slowed near a stop sign and pulled into a very small driveway so he slowed down to avoid the car being seen as she got out. He sat on the curb there for a moment while she collected her things and went inside using the front door.

He then pulled up to the stop sign which was at a 4 way but the house was located on a corner lot. He moved forward and continued to the end of the next street turned and came back towards the corner so he could see the car and the front door from where he parked.

The house had green all around the front, side and even in between the tire spaces on the driveway. It was single story with a balcony on the front that was like a porch and had a table setting complete with an umbrella.

The street as well as their home was lined with Palm trees and again he could smell the domesticity in the air from the various barbeque grills that were being used to prepare the evening meal.

He sat in his car again now hungry and growing agitated from where she had lived. The entire time he was in a cell fear-full of rape, being beaten or even killed all the while eating shit food and drinking water that you could see the rust in the bottom of the cup she was here in this sunshine parade.

He wrote in the notebook the car, color, license and address which he could see from the 4 way stop.

The problem was he did not know where he was. He was not

worried about how to get back to where his hotel was as much as being able to find this place again. He did not want to chance having to wait however long for her to return to the gallery so decided to stay.

He knew there was a 7 eleven about 2 block away because they passed it before turning onto this street so he locked the doors to his car and decided to take a walk and take in the block she lived. This would not jeopardize losing his parking space too considering how hard those were to come by he was learning.

He left 7 eleven with a buffet of items to eat and get him through at least the day or even the evening if he had to and returned to the car. There were no books at the convenience store so he settled on local and national newspapers as well as another one of the free publications he found at the pizza place just to have something to read and kill time.

He waited there all night with no sign of her. He had drifted off to sleep after midnight feeling pretty sure that she would not be going anywhere at that hour but was awaken by the many cars starting and the bright sunlight of the 7:00 hour.

He was tempted to go back to the store and get a coffee but he then saw a woman leaving the home but it was not Amber. It was Mrs. Clevinger.

This was the other woman he spent a great deal of time looking forward to paying a visit to or getting even with in the near future.

She had come to the front lawn to clip some of the flowers that were growing on the side of the house and bring them inside. He waited another 2 hours and would finally see Amber.

She was again wearing shorts but these were cut off's and she was wearing a solid white t-shirt. She was pulling the hose around from the house towards the driveway and started to spray down her car.

It was Sunday he thought to himself as she started to wash and rinse her car. He studied her and her new physique which had grown in the 5 years he had not seen her.

He had not really looked at her yet because he was more concerned with being seen or recognized and now for some reason he felt confident she would not see or recognize him.

She was becoming a woman. She still looked fragile and youthful because of the way she was dressed but her clothes revealed a very sexy side to her. He did not know if it was watching her bend, stretch or if it was because she was getting wet.

He did not know if it was because he had not slept but there was still the same attraction to her that he had before. Her legs looked amazing in the shorts and even though she was wearing a t shirt he could see that her breast had become larger. He again was glad he made this trip.

She completed the task of washing her car and returned inside but it was not long till she returned to her car and placed a few items inside that he could not make out. Her father and mother then outside as well as she was getting into the car and starting it.

They each leaned into the vehicle to kiss her goodbye as she backed the clean vehicle out of the driveway. The car heading down the block with each parent still on the front lawn watching it disappear he then started the car and made his passing them as they turned their backs to head back inside.

She did not drive far, maybe a few blocks and pulled to the curb a beautiful house that sat on the edge of the earth looking out toward the ocean. The house was either being built or remodeled because it had construction things everywhere.

It was a canvass and supplies she pulled from her car and went towards the house. She did not go inside or even the front yard. She set up the materials there on the sidewalk but you could still see the sand and ocean before you and started to paint.

He again had to drive a ways to find a place to park and then walk but she was till where she was when he made his way back. She painted what she was for what seemed like forever but probably because he had not eaten was still agitated.

She worked so contently and patiently studying what she saw and then applying it to the canvas. He could see what it was that she was painting but anyone that passed by here made reference to it positively which seemed to further inspire her.

He wanted to be one of the people to see it and stop by with some words. This could be the moment to make his introduction but given the way he looked and smelled there was no way he could make the right impression.

She finished or stopped what she was working on and then returned the materials and piece to her car but she did not get in and drive home. She locked the door and then ventured down the beach access way so he followed.

She found a comfortable spot that was her own and occupied by no others. She sat there looking out to the ocean and the sun. He was curious what she was thinking but whatever it was she was again content with what she was doing because she was able to sit there for another hour just watching.

She returned home after watching the sun tuck itself into the ocean for the day and he again right behind her. He returned to the 7 eleven to fill up on some evening fuel but his spot was now occupied and he settled for a further spot until his next sighting the following morning.

37

THE large man shut the door behind him and went right to the sink to get water and wash his hands then splash some on his face. "Well." The other man said again " What Happened?"

"I shot Mickey." He said calmly and plainly " he is dead and I spent the night first attempting to bury him then getting lost until someone finally saw me and helped me get here.

"Why did you shoot him"

"I didn't do it purpose idiot! It was dark I heard the crackling or something then he grabbed me from behind and this was after the guy we went to meet told me he had a m-16 pointed at me so I turned and put a few in him thinking it was our bar friend."

"I can't believe he is dead. What now?"

"I think this vacation is over. I think we get the fuck out of here and back to Dallas. The last thing we need is them finding him and tying us to him so get your things. I will take a quick shower and then to airport."

The man from the bar who went there to meet them was not far from the hotel and awaited their next step. He saw them depart the hotel into a cab with what appeared to be luggage or a couple of small bags.

He followed the taxi they had taken to the airport and just as they had located where Jessie and his mother had gone when they left Dallas for El Paso. He watched them board a plane bound for Dallas. He left it that for the time being but he had to return to where he arranged to meet them near the hotel.

There was a decent mound of dirt obvious enough to draw attention to anyone walking through here if they were to be passing through but not as obvious as the hand being dragged from the dirt by animals in the night.

He had brought a shovel with him and began to dig a hole large enough to swallow the body into the earth and prevent the animals from continuing to eat off more of the exposed hand that they feed off of last night.

He returned the shovel to his pick up and in he went as well back to Heaven's Gate where his boss Nathan Pritchard was returning today.

The following morning he was awakened again by the light but there was also the sound of engine after engine starting like it was a Nascar race. Car after car was pulling from their perspective driveways and everyone dressed in their Monday morning clothes were off to fight the good fight.

This included her father but no one else from The Clevinger family emerged until 9:15. Amber was now wearing blue jeans and a form fitting long sleeve shirt that had something on the front he could not make out. Into her clean car and she too was off.

He followed behind and this time they made their way to a free way which he just did not like driving on at all. He followed her to the exit and another couple of miles and into what looked like very nice business buildings.

A sea of cars in the parking lot that led to a wall of tall glass towering buildings. The buildings were at least 15 stories high. He had to follow her to see where or which one of these places she was going. He grabbed his notebook and hat so he could continue to write in an effort to look busy if anyone was watching.

They enter through the front doors and it is large, circular with

2 series of elevators leading up and then walkways lined with offices on each side of the elevators. She walked to the right of the elevator and proceeded down the hall passing 3 office buildings each having a marquee or plaque out front acknowledging what one was.

He stopped at the door that she did walk into and read the name on the door.

Elliot Messner. Clinical psychologist.

He continued to walk down the hall which had no exit other than an emergency so he returned towards the lobby and front door their entered.

This would be the only exit and it would allow him to see her when she leaves. He recorded the name in his notebook and again the address then walked towards a large fountain and some tables that were in the front.

He recounted what he knew about her at this moment. She left Arlington after the trial more than likely to escape the publicity from the news and probably school. Who knows why they chose San Diego but they end up here.

Her parents send her to see this guy to work on some things probably related to that night at the house or the trial because he knew first hand what it did to him. She paints now and is interested in art and goes to this gallery.

He knows where she lives and that she looks great it cut off shorts and a t shirt. He needed a little more time but he needed to get back to where his hotel was so he can check to see if his mom called and get changed and showered.

He decided that was the best idea because no matter what he would find her again at the gallery and from there this time he would write as he drove the steps and roads to her home.

Off he went to the nearest gas station to fill up and ask directions to Cardiff or Del Mar because he could figure it out from there. He headed off towards his hotel and eventually reached it. The shower felt incredible as did the change of clothes then he headed to the front desk for any messages.

He had no messages at the moment so he took that to be that

things continued to be well and she was now back in El Paso so he
had no choice at the moment but to wait to hear from her and obtain
a number to reach her.

He then went to a clothing store he saw when coming back to
the hotel that was maybe 10 minutes away. He needed to get some
shorts and maybe some different clothes to fit where he was. The
things he bought when he left DC were dressy and the items in The
Caymans were a little touristy so he wanted some comfort like he has
seen Amber wearing.

He returned to the gallery each day but no sign of her until the
next Saturday. He had packed clothes with him in the event of seeing
her each day so today he was ready for wherever she would take him.

Her trip to the gallery that Saturday was longer than the previous
and she would not leave until after 6:00 going on 7:00 but she had a
canvas with her as she went to her car. The older woman he saw last
week walked with her to the car and hugged her before she drove
away. One of his next steps was to return to the gallery and make a
similar impression on her as he had done and needed to follow up on
with Miss Jayne Woodall.

He had notes in hand and wrote furiously while desperately
trying to keep up with her and not get into an accident. He was not a
great driver or experienced is the better word but writing on a piece
of paper against the steering while turning the wheel and holding a
pen was just asking for trouble.

She went straight home which made his task of mapping the trip
from the gallery to her home a perfect a,b,c. reference. He waited
though for about 3 hours just in case she was leaving for the evening
to go out on Saturday night or if someone was coming to pick her
up but she never left and no one came. He added that to his at least
mental list of items to know about her. She was a homebody and not
dating anyone.

11:00 arrived and decided to return to his hotel by back tracking
his notes and testing their accuracy. The great news was that he was
getting his bearings because he was back at the hotel in no time.

He rested and was up showered early in the morning dressed in some of the clothes he purchased which included a pair of surf shorts and a popular surf company t shirt. He was comfortable and felt good. He was headed back to her home and arrived just after 9:00 and as he drove down the street he saw her car coming right at him. He passed the car and attempted to make some contact but she never looked away from her straight ahead stare.

He made mental notes of the direction the car before coming to quick complete stop and turning around. The car had a little distance but not incredibly far. It went through 2 straight ahead stop signs and then veered to the left onto a one way street that looked to the ocean and was lined by houses. She had found a place to park and was now his turn. She had returned to the home she was at last week. The house that had all of the construction material scattered throughout the property.

She again set up and began to work on what she was painting last weekend. He went to the same spot to watch her and observed several people walk by with their dogs and even a older man on roller skates wearing no shirt and suspenders.

This was it he thought, this is when I approach her to see if she recognizes me. A couple of deep breathes and a visualization of the words in the books he read and the impressions he had made on the girl in Italy and even the girl at the gallery. It is time he said to himself and began to walk towards her on the sidewalk she was using as a studio.

He walked closer and closer and the visual of what she was painting became clearer. She was painting the house in its state and the view of the ocean beyond it. When he got close enough to make out each vivid detail and speak he said.

"What does it mean?" She never looked up from what she was doing so his guard went down a little.

"What does what mean?" She asked back still brushing with

her face close to the oils carefully seeing how they interacted and interpreted what she was trying to duplicate.

"The painting. What is the interpretation?" he asked with more detail to his question.

"It means under construction." She returned still not making eye contact "There is a beautiful home here with a breathtaking view that most people would find to be perfect just the way it was but even the most perfect of things sometimes need construction to make them whole.

"She finished smiling at her definition of the work she was doing then made a quick small stroke and faced the inquisitive voice that did not continue on like the other passer by's of the morning.

He continued to stare at the work getting what her interpretation was considering his own family was perfect by the perspective of many people on the outside yet required construction which was also ironic considering his father was in that field and they killed him as form of that construction.

The irony did not end there because in order to make it whole they themselves were physically reconstructed in order to lead new lives so he truly felt like he got this concept.

He then shifted his smiling gaze of understanding and admiration to the artist. She senses his appreciation and it gave her confidence that the interpretation was present so she said " I call it *under construction.*"

he actually placed his hands together and applauded. Her confidence and smile grew from that reception.

"My name is Jack Rodan" he said to extending his hand " Amber" she said back not offering her last name then made a squishy face realizing that the hand she was shaking with still had wet paint and began to apologize and offered him a towel that was covered in dried paint. " I am so sorry."

"Not at all, I could use some color." He said and the squish returned to smile.

"Have you been painting long?" he asked with comfort because not once had she really looked at him with alarm or question.

"Not really almost 2 months but I have been taking lessons from a woman. I don't know,I like it."

"I see why" he said " I love that you can duplicate something like that but give it such a different meaning, one that speaks to you even though it is just a house like a hundred others." He said flattering her and then went for the kill shot.

"You know what. I saw this piece the other day that was like this or had the same effect. " He said to her and began to use his hands and fingers to point to the strokes and the ocean while she listened intently. I was in a gallery that was filled with other pieces that were all good in their own way but then I came across something that was simple but the words. The words just stopped me and I could not stop looking at it."

"What did it say?" she asked just as drawn to the conclusion as he was to offer it.

"*Progress.*" He said to her "It was remarkable" he added."Oh My God!" she said just like she used to say when he knew her before and something excited her. " You saw that? You liked it?"

"The best one in the gallery" he returned folding his hands across his chest and nodding his head up and down.

"That is mine too." She said "The gallery belongs to a woman named Lillian, she is who works with me. I did that painting about 3 weeks ago. I can't believe you were there and saw that, how funny."

"Funny, what is funny is that I see that there then you here that is funny."

"I can't believe it." She said

"What are you doing now? Are you finished do you want me to leave you alone so you can finish? Do you want to go for a walk on the beach?"

"I am finished actually" she said "and I always like sitting on the beach when I get done working so a walk sounds good."

"Cool" he said back " Can I help you with this stuff? Where does it go?" he offered and he assisted with taking back to her car. She locked the door and down to the sand they went.

38

THEY returned to El Paso and Camille was uncertain of what would be the next chapters to come. Nelson had invited her back with him but offered little detail to what would occur when they arrived.

She watched him instruct several people that appeared to work for him to re-fuel, clean and store the plane into the hanger and he escorted her to a waiting car where he held the door for her to enter.

"Where are we going?" she asked him

"I have something that I want to you see." He returned while grabbing her hand and placing it in his from the back seat. She was nervous and she was not sure why. It could have been that this was her first return back to Texas since getting Jessie and then having these 3 guys plow into their hotel room and then follow them all the way to Italy and then even here to this very same place.

She held his hand apprehensively as they drove to their destination. The man in the front seat next to the driver spoke with Nelson during the drive regarding matters of business that transpired in his absence which made her feel better because it was a buffer of sorts so she did have to hold a conversation at the moment. It gave her time to think but once she started doing that she then wanted to talk to now take her mind off of everything.

They pulled into a gated and guarded entrance. The gate was tall iron and filled in between brick pillars that ran all around the front of the house that was set behind the walls. She could see the guards were armed as one of them approached the car to greet Nelson.

"Good afternoon Mr.Pritchard we trust you had a comfortable return sir?" Then finished with "Welcome Home Sir." The man removed himself from the window taking with him the large revolver that was strapped to him inside of his jacket.

The gates parted as well as the remaining guards in front of the gate allowing the car to enter. Welcome home she thought so far a very different impression than the typical welcome mat you would find at the front door.

"This is your home?" she asked him

"It is Camille, please won't you come inside" he said to her as the man in the front that was seated next to driver opened her door and offered her his hand to assist her in departing the car.

"Thank you." She said to the man who was yet to speak to her directly

"Arturo."

Nelson said " Please see to it that the bags are delivered to the guest room for Miss.Ritchards as well as my things returned to my room. Ask Santy to prepare some lunch for us and you and I will meet today at 3:00 in the study to continue our conversation."

The man, called Arturo, said nothing but returned the request made by Nelson with a nod which must have been enough to appease Nelson because he had taken her hand once again as he walked her towards the door but with no other from the car ride or the guards surrounding the home behind them. He opened the door to a sparkling white marble floor and foyer that was large and oval in shape. She immediately noticed that the acoustics in her voice and his traveled so far or echoed. She almost laughed out loud but settled for a smile when she was noticing the booming sound in his voice that she had not heard before. Each room was cool to the touch and very open or roomy.

She studies things briefly taking in each item or detail here and there going from room to room on the tour he was offering her.

"What do you think" he said with his arms open and extended out like a wing span as he turned slightly side to side.

"It is not you, or it does not feel like you." She said quickly without even thinking.

"Nelson, that was rude, I am sorry It is beautiful and possibly the nicest home I have ever seen in my life." She attempted to make up

"Not me how? Camille." he asked with curiosity now folding his left forearm underneath his right elbow which elevated his thumb and forefinger to his lips.

"This home is the home of a man that is comfortable but the man I have been speaking with and getting to know doesn't feel like he lives here."

"I don't understand?" he said wanted more clarification or detail.

"Comfort in the home, through his business and all that it has afforded him but not comfortable with himself. In his own skin and maybe for the same reason that the comfort exist to begin with!"

"WOW!" Nelson said looking at the ground in the same pose.

"I know no one else that would either have the insight to make that observation nor the courage to say it if they had." He said now looking directly into her eyes now and again not moving from his pose.

"Brave, smart and beautiful." He said to her taking step by step slowly towards her.

'That is not brave Nelson. Brave is when you fear someone like how I feared the man I was married to for all of those years. Standing up to what you fear would be brave now I will give you the smart and beautiful part because you're right there but I don't fear you because you won't hurt me and that is because I won't let you." She said with that confident and in control face she has become more and more accustomed to wearing.

He reaches her meeting that confident expression on her face with her arms crossed. "There are many more words to describe you Miss Ritchards and I am going to enjoy all the time that it takes to tell you each and every one of them." He slows and quiets the boom in his voice quieter and quieter as he gets closer to finish those words and moves in to kiss her and she greets his embrace by opening her arms to pull him in.

"I love that you can see that." He says to her following their kiss but not leaving the embrace.

"You are better than this place, you are more than this in so many ways. Where are you in any of these rooms?" she breaks away challenging him to offer her some warmth amidst all of the cold features and décor.

He thinks for a moment and the moment grows to an uncomfortable silence that continues to make her feel victorious in their playful discussion and yet hurt because he too is living inside of a person that is not truly who he is,,,,, just like she is.

"I've got it" he proclaims.

"This way" he takes her hand leading her down a hall. He opens the door to a wall to wall wooden room that has one window with the curtains open.

"This is my study" he announces with pride and stand's beside the door with it open and a gesture for her to enter.

She walks into the room that has a dark hunter green thick carpet and a very large L shaped wooden desk. The desk is wide in depth and has a great deal of workspace on each portion of the desk and is very well organized. The room is different from any other part of the house so far because it is darker. The dark carpet and the wood created a darker feel but the natural light coming from the window with a view of 2 large trees in the yard make the room feel much more organic than any other room she has seen.

He stood at the door leaning against it as she makes her way from corner to corner discovering the plaques, certificates, degrees and accolades hanging on the wall from his surgical and flight achievements.

This room was him. This was a room that he was comfortable

in his own skin in and where he was surrounded by the things that moved him.

She looked at him standing in the doorway enjoying her enjoying this discovery.

"How many woman have been in here?" she asked him straight out.

He smiled at her still enjoying himself " None " he responded. " This has been a place of privacy and sometimes business but it has never been a place of pleasure."

She paused for only a moment and began to walk towards him where he was still leaning on the door. She kissed him to get his attention and then smiled very big at him and said " Till now" She kissed him again and her kiss was full of passion for him wrapping her arms tightly around his shoulders. She pulled him all the way into the room shutting the door behind him and made love to the man she was slowly falling in love with right there on the carpet floor of the most personal room of his home.

He was speechless when they had finished and was still even partially dressed. He up until that point had been the one in this, whatever this was, he thought had been the one with the answers or the guiding hand but now here she was in his home, in his study and was just making his head spin.

"How can you see me so clearly?" he asked looking at the ceiling

"I don't know Nelson, I think I see so much of myself in you that it makes it easier for me to see the things that I do.

"Are you mad?" she asked him unsure if he was or was not

"No, of course not it is just when you say some of those things I guess I don't know who I am anymore. You really got me thinking about things like that and I don't know the answer.

"You are and have always been Nelson Pritchard. That person is still in there even if he is lost that person still exist and can be found if you want him to. It again is just like I told you before a week of changes on the outside does not change a lifetime of who I am on the inside."

"But this is the life I have built, this is who I am now."

"If this life makes you happy and the person you have become you are proud of then your search is over. I think it is hilarious that I am changing who I was to become someone new and you are trying to find who you were. Cmon Nelson, that is funny what a pair we make."

They shared a good laugh while locating discarded items of clothing but he could not help it what a pair they were indeed he thought, what a pair indeed.

"Enjoy your stay in Dallas Mr.Santor." The rental car agent said to him handing him the keys to a car to be determined when he arrived outside at the curb. He shoved his more than 6 foot body into a Ford Tempo and adjusted the seat to a tolerable comfort level. He turned the ignition and made his way towards Main Street. After his visit to the airport a few weeks ago to watch the 2 remaining of the 3 men board a plane to Dallas Airport. He had done some research on the 2 remaining of the 3 men he had encountered in Heaven's Gate and the woods later that evening.

He learned from liaisons that Nelson had in the Dallas area that these 2 were part of a fairly organized gang in the area known as the Arian Brotherhood which specialized in anything that made them money and fed their propaganda agendas. The larger of the 3 and the one he had the conversation with in the woods was called Knight " as in White Knight" his source tells him.

He gave him a location of the area and buildings that these guys would be seen so Nathanial Santor found himself in search of the men that had expressed interest in bidding on the information he had. He thought to himself that as far as an insurance policy goes maybe it was not enough to disappear but again if they were willing to pay $50,000 for just the kid then he could do that to make some extra money and make sure the leak was never tied to him.

Nathanial figured since the woman had returned with Nelson to his house that it was not in his best interest to give her up but if he stayed close to them both he would learn from the woman where the boy ended up going since he did not return with her. He already had his name from being there the night they did the paperwork so he just had to patient on the location. He first did however have to locate the men he met with and get something to them to let them know of his continued interest to make an arrangement.

After a few days of calling back to El Paso offering an update regarding the ailing family member he had offered up as the excuse to leave town for a few days Arturo did want a return date prior to hanging up the phone.

"I should be able to be back by Friday evening if that is good with you guys?" he asked Arturo with today being Wednesday afternoon.

"That is fine, do you need me to send someone to get you from the airport?" Arturo asked

"Please, that would help I will confirm Friday with the flight details and again Thank You." He said to him hanging up the phone.

There was still no physical sign of wither of the men he remembered from the bar but he was in between a few places a day so he decided to pick one and stay there.

He chose the building that appeared to be 4 stories of apartments in the hopes that they would eventually come there to sleep or meet whoever it was that did live there. Thursday evening he was sitting in the parking lot in the back of the building looking at every car that came and went until a large bronco 4x4 with black tinted windows pulled into the parking lot and fast. There was music coming from the vehicle that was loud and has fast paced as the driving.

The music continued for a second after the Bronco came to a stop then went silent as the driver killed the engine and out came the passenger side the man he knew now as Knight. He did not want to follow them in because they did know who he was and would recognize a figure as tall or large as he was so the attention was not what he had in mind. A message was what he had in mind so after waiting a good period of time after the men had disappeared into the building he approached The Bronco passenger side and slid a note under the wipers and returned to his car to wait.

He thought about being in the parking lot in the event that they came back found the note and went immediately through there knowing he was or had been there. The idea of a large confrontation when again he was outnumbered did not agree with him so he left the note to speak for itself and returned to his hotel and made arrangements for a flight. He then called Arturo once again as stated to offer the flight details for a pick up on Friday.

The large man Knight would find the note the following afternoon. He opened it and as the others with him clamored on with "What is it." And " What did it say?" because he read it, smiled for a moment till the smile faded and then crumbled the note in his right hand.

It said $35,000 for the name and $35,000 for the location. I'll be in touch!

39

E was pretty pleased with how that went he though driving back towards his hotel with the top down and the cooler evening ocean air blowing all around him. "She had no idea it was me." He said out-loud in his car. " No idea!" He returned to the hotel and his routine of going to the lobby for any messeges and his mother had left one. It was only a phone number but the area code meant she was back in Texas so he would wait till tomorrow to call her due to the time it was here and there.

He figured his next step was to go back to the gallery to meet the older woman Lillian that she spoke about tonight. He needed to make an impression with her and follow up on the one he made with the other woman. No pacing around the room he just laid in the bed going over his plan for tomorrow. Even though he was no longer incarcerated and had the ability to move around or make notes he still was used to laying in one place playing out the details in his head all through thought.

He fell asleep not long after thinking back on the walk he had taken on the beach with her hours earlier. The sound of the water and the darkness all around them. Just the 2 of them and their conversation. Free.

He awoke and was immediately ready to begin his day. He first was in need of calling his mom for an update on her and Nelson so following a cup of coffee he dialed the numbers left for him at the front desk.

"The Pritchard residence." A woman answered.

"Yes, I am calling for Camille. She left a message for me to contact her at this number." He asked

"One moment please." The voice returned followed by a silent pause

"Hello." She said knowing it was Jessie but still slightly uncomfortable with any other name so she again continued to use the endearing honey.

"Hey mom I am glad you called. How are you?"

"Really good but I want to hear about you. How are you enjoying San Diego?"

"I like it here and I am thinking of staying for a while, see what happens."

"Where are you staying and what have you been eating?"She quizzed

I am in a hotel near San Diego in a town called Cardiff and mostly Pizza to be honest with you but so far I really am enjoying myself. What about you?'

"I am at his house."

"I got that from whoever answered the phone but what does that mean?"He asked her

"I don't know right now but like you I too am enjoying myself."

"Are you going to move there or stay with him the whole time?"

"I really don't know honey about anything other than right here and right now. Right now I am enjoying myself so for the time being I am going to stay here until it is no longer time to be here. Are you making any friends where you are?"

"I am" he said " I am getting a little culture too? He added

"I like that, what kind of culture have you been getting?"

"A little art and a little psychology."

"That sounds wonderful, how have you been introduced to those things?"

"I met someone who paints and I was thinking of seeing a psychiatrist."

"I can see you with a painter, how did you meet, what is her name, where was your first date, what did you wear? She hit him from all sides and he was not ready for that. He could not tell her anything right now so he settled on " let's see if there is a 2nd date before I go into all of that."

"okay then tell me about the idea to see someone." She asked

"I heard about a guy here and thought maybe I would go a few times and talk to see where it leads. What do you think?"

"Oh honey I want you to be and do what makes you happy. If you want to talk to someone about everything that you have been through then I want you to do that."

"Thanks Mom" he said finishing up the conversation and looking at his clock. It was time for him to get ready. He knew there was no way to tell her the truth about what brought him here or why he is still here. He was not sure himself on a couple of levels. He did not have to be here doing what he was doing. The psychiatrist was partially true in wanting to talk but the real motive was he was more interested in seeing what information he could find out about Amber from his perspective by using seeing him as an excuse to gain access somehow to his files or notes.

Drying off out of the shower and dressing he made a note to himself to arrange a meeting at her house sometime in the near future.

He wanted to see her mother face to face and soon. She was the only person aside from Amber that he felt would be able to recognize him, she sure spent enough time staring at him in court with her penetrating stare.

He looked into the mirror at himself and admitted truthfully that he wanted to be here and he wanted to play this game with them all. He was good at this game and he felt he could control it just far enough to square up a few things with The Clevinger Family. Off went the lights then locking the door behind him as he made his way to his car. He was ready to meet Lillian.

It was almost 9:30 and he knew that the first woman would be arriving soon to open the gallery and it was usually not long after that the other woman would arrive. He wanted to get there to make sure that the older woman would be there before going into the gallery. He found a space as always and waited. While he waited he went over the reasons he would be able to schedule an appointment with Elliot Messner and what he would talk about. He would have to change a few things but definitely enough he had to get into the office and see if he could somehow find where he kept his notes. He knew many things that Amber might talk to him about but he wanted to see what she liked and disliked now in her life.

There was the first woman he met and looking at his notes said her name out loud to affirm it. Jane Woodall so now he waited for the 2nd woman. There was not one visitor until after noon and Lillian arrived shortly before that. He studied her quickly before she made her way into the place she called The Caufield Studio. She wore Khaki Capri pants, comfortable white shoes and a shawl wrapped around here that was multiple light colors. She looked strong he thought and wondered how old she was. He waited a while longer, almost an hour so she had time to settle in which is what most people did when they first arrived. He went and got another coffee and waited till he finished it and freshened with a mint before going in.

That sound he remembered from his last visit was the very enthusiastic and contagious greeting that Jane offered him and remembered him from his previous visit.

"Welcome back to you kind sir."

"How are you Miss. Woodall" he offered with equal enthusiasm and shocking her at the same time that he remembered her name.

"That is quite a dangerous memory you have on you, do you know that?"

"I had to come and see you again. I have the most amazing news." Sounding as if he was bringing home a report card of straight A's to show his mother.

"What is it, this amazing news then?"

He went to the painting again and she watched him from where she stood at the door. He looked at it and then called to her. " Come here please." Still full of enthusiasm.

She came from around the podium and approached him standing in front of the painting.

"Do you remember when I was here last time and this is what I liked the most." He said pointing to the painting.

"I do" she replied smiling at him and waiting for his news.

"You will not believe this." Now facing her and he could see out of the corner of his eye that other woman was now at the top of the stairs on the 2nd floor looking down to see who she was talking to.

"Believe what?"

"I met her."

"You met Amber?"

"Yes, it was amazing. I still cannot believe it. I was here last week and stopped cold after seeing this and then I am walking and see a beautiful girl painting on a sidewalk. Did I mention she was beautiful." He asked and this made Jane cover her heart with both hands.

"She was painting something and as I got closer the picture became clearer and clearer so I stopped and asked her what it meant. When she explained what it meant it reminded me so much of this piece right here so I told her about it and she then told me it was hers and all about you and Lillian. Can you believe that?"

"I don't believe it, that is such a sign. You 2 are going to get married, have children and then have stories written about your first encounter." She said still poised with her hands over her heart. He could hear the foot -steps coming down the wood stairs due to a slight squeek.

"That is an amazing story." The voice from behind him said as he turned to face her.

"I am afraid I have not had the pleasure." She said now at the bottom floor walking towards him taking him in and extends her hand. " Lillain Caufield."

"Jack Rodan." He says gripping her hand firmly but not too tight. "Mrs Caufield." "Please call me Lillian."

"Lillian, I was in here last week and had a delightful 1st impression of first Jane here and then the discovery of this piece right here."

"*Progress*" she said smiling at him

"It just spoke to me and then to meet her just on the sidewalk. Have you seen what she is working on now?"

"No " She replied" I have often liked to see a finished product after all of that person has been applied to the work but she does seem excited to show us when it is done."

"She is amazing, I don't think I have ever met anyone like her before. She told me so much about you both and I had to come by and meet you in person."

"Well Jack Rodan it is very nice to meet you, do you live here?" She asked still taking him in but enjoying the young man's enthusiasm.

"No, I was looking to move here. I have been here for about a month and have never been here before. I was a traveling military son you might say and this was just one of the places we did not happen to come."

"What brought you here, if you don't mind my asking?" and Jane interrupted his answer with a "Get used to it now because I have a ton of questions when she is done."

He laughed and presented a blush before answering. " I lost both of my parents to a car accident last year and I have just been traveling and searching for a place or something that spoke to me or felt like home. "This." He said turning back and pointing to the painting. " This and then meeting her just seems so right, like a sign. You know?"

"Well I have taken up enough of your time, I just had to come and tell you the story."

"Do you have to go?" Jane asked him

"I do, Will you tell her I stopped by though?"

"I will " Lillian stated before Jane did

"It was very nice to meet you Jack." She ended as he approached her extending his hand once again first to Lillian then to Jane before his departing salutation.

The door shutting behind him with the bell jingling until it silenced was broken immediately by Jane and the various compliments of Jack and not being able to contain herself till Saturday when Amber was to arrive and hear them for herself.

Lillian was always entertained by the very contagious and optimistic Jane. She took in all of the words, smiles and laughs before turning back to the stairs and making her way back to her office on the 2nd floor. Half way up the stairs the phone rang which then occupied Jane to answer and entertain the caller.

Lillian stopped and turned towards the piece hanging on the wall that was Amber's "*progress.*" She always enjoyed looking at it and found it to be such a compliment to her gallery. The work had won her several praises from people that shopped in the store and she herself absolutely understand the message and why it did speak to many people. It made her happy that another individual had found the message and spoke of it in such light so why was she cautioned?

She continued up the stairs and into her office to sit in her chair behind her very, at the moment, cluttered desk. She was not sure what it was, she had no idea but it was something she thought. Something cautious.

40

AMBER was on her way to the studio on Saturday afternoon as she had done for a few months now. She had intended on finishing the piece she had been working on and showing it to the others today. She had seen the house enough times over the past few weeks that she had it memorized clearly in her mind to finish in the studio.

Her arrival into the gallery was met with an immediate barrage of words, adjectives, motions and sounds all coning from Jane to describe the visit from Jack earlier in the week. Jane sounded like one of the friends she would have had in Junior High with as high pitched as her voice was, it was an octave that she had not yet heard on her.

Amber could not really make out what she was saying at the beginning and did not know right away what the context of her excitement was." Who is Jack?" she asked to slow her down and get some clarification so she could share in her good cheer.

"Okay." Jane says catching her breath and slowing down for just a moment but was clearly just ramping up another set like a dog that has been brought to a park and was getting ready to be let of the leash.

"Jack, the guy that you met. The one that was here last week and saw your piece then met you while you working on something else a few days ago?" She pauses

"Oh my god Jack, how did you know that?" she asked her but is smiling now understanding more of why she is excited.

"He was here!" "He came in the other day to tell us about meeting you. Lillian met him and he was so cute and the story of how you both met ARE YOU KIDDING ME, they cannot write stuff that is that good.

Amber is beside herself and smiling a smile that Jane has never seen before. This is different from even when she either won the competition or had the painting placed on the wall by Lillian. Jane is looking at her and again has each of her hands clasped together and over her heart but cannot contain even for a second the smile that is on her face while looking at Amber.

"What did you think of him?" Amber asked her

"Oh my god,I want to date him." I thought he was so handsome the first time he came in, he was so courteous and the way he carries himself. He loved that painting and you should of heard him tell us the story about meeting you. OHhh the look on his face, wow sweetie he is a keeper."

She could not help but agree with just about everything that Jane had said. She did like the way he carried himself and could not believe how they met considering he was just in here a few days before looking at her painting.

"Are you going to ask him out?" Jane asked her and now beginning to sort of bounce then it slowly turned into a slight jumping up and down.

"I can't ask him out!" she said

"Why not Amber? You cannot ignore those signs and he is adorable you have to admit."

"I don't know how to get in touch with him for one and I have never asked anyone out in my life."

"Do you like him?" Jane asked her

"I don't know, I don't know him really. We took a walk on the beach. Then Jane interjected with that octave again " You took a walk on the beach?"

"The night that we met just after he asked about what I was painting. When I was finished we went for a walk on the beach but I still don't know him that well."

"That is why people go onto dates or more walks on the beach so they can get to know each other better. You are asking him out!"

"I can't Jane I don't know how to even find him."

"You did not get his number?"

"No we had just met."

"Then you go back to where you were on that day that you met okay and continue to paint. If he shows up again that day then you know. You just know right there more signs." Waiting for Amber to agree it was the only moment that Jane was silent long enough for her to think since she arrived that afternoon. Amber looked at Jane who was no longer the dog being let of the leash but her smile and posture gave way to what now looked like a jack in the box that was being wound up and ready to spring from where she was and create more excitement.

"Okay she agreed." And there it went she sprang from her position and actually left the ground then ran to hug her. It was tight and full of energy.

"You will see Amber, these signs don't lie. I just know it.

Lillian had not arrived yet so Amber finished hugging Jane and began to set up in the studio so she could finish the work she had been doing in time to unveil it later today before leaving. She was again in the place that gave her comfort. She closed her eyes, as she always did, to capture the sounds and scents of what brought her to the place of comfort and strength. She then did what she was taught by Lillian and just put the brush to the canvass and let it guide her.

She worked and worked on the detail of her memory while

adding what elements she felt were necessary to translate the meaning but the entire time she was painting he was on her mind. She could not deny all of the things that Jane was so excited about and she too felt them. She agreed with her that she would go back to the place they had met and let fate produce what was to be and if he was there that day she would ask him out.

She worked for 4 hours and finished what she called "*under construction .*" She had not seen Lillian yet so she went to search for her and found her upstairs in her office.

"I have something that I want to show you, if you are not busy?" Amber said to her.

"Is it ready?" Lillian asked with some excitement. She did get excited seeing something for the first time but this had even more anticipation to it because there was a part of Amber that very much wanted to please her and Lillian knew that. She knew that Amber was driven to create something that justified its compliment which pushed her particularly to complete what her vision was and to be honest Amber had not let her down yet.

"It is." She said with confidence and a dare in her eye to come and see it.

"Then off we go." She said standing up from her chair behind her desk and as she approached the doorway Amber actually bowed her head and gestured for her to exit first as a doorman would. Lillian let out a play-full laugh and grabbed her arm to walk together down the stairs.

Taking each step towards the studio Amber asked her " Did you meet Jack too?"

"I did." She responded " That is an amazing story the 2 of you have at the moment with the meeting and all. What do you think of him dear?"

"I was going to ask you the same thing." Amber replied

"Why do you want me to date him?" Lillian said play-fully

"No" she said back giving her a nudge " Did you like him?"

"He made a very nice impression to say the least."

"I love him!" Jane shouted, hearing their conversation from the lower level as they continued to make their way down the stairs.

"Would you care to join us" Lillian offered to Jane

"Where are we going, are we closing early to celebrate Ambers new love?" She asked which produced a smile and blush on the face of Amber.

"No Amber wishes to show us her latest effort, would you care to join us?"

"I would in deed."

Amber was not as nervous as she had been in the beginning with showing these 2 anything she was working on. She had discovered some confidence in her ability and a challenge for her-self to do things that were appreciated. She was ready and held back the curtain to allow the 2 of them to enter before her. She wanted to see if they could find the meaning in the title without explain its meaning as she had done with Jack that afternoon. He truly seemed to understand it after the fact so the next achievement would be people being able to understand it without the explanation.

They both took it in for a moment and then went closer and closer to study it all the while the room being silent. She waited at the entrance and then became a little nervous because this was the longest for either of them to comment to date. She waited and waited until Lillian turned to her and removed the glasses she was wearing to make eye contact.

"It seems the plateau you seek is becoming closer!"

"Do you like it?"

"I love it."

"Do you understand it?"

"Well it may have different meanings to the many people that view it but the true meaning behind what you are seeing here is moving. The detail is authentic and probably the most difficult work you have done to date. I also think it is your best."

"Me too, that is good Amber." Jane finally added.

Amber had loved these moments she was able to have. The feeling of starting and finishing some- thing that these 2 well trained mind and eyes deemed moving or good really gave her the finest sense of accomplishments she has ever felt in her lifetime.

"Is it good enough to be wall worthy?"

"At this rate we may have to expand the gallery to accommodate your own section." She answered her and meant it.

41

A MBER was at that place they first met the next day. She had her supplies and her imagination. She sought opportunities to be inspired to paint but she simply was not there to paint and she knew that.

She was waiting for Jack to return period. So in the interim of waiting for what may be a sign she made her first attempt at an ocean landscape. It was not long into the skyline setting on the canvas that a voice was heard.

"I was hoping that you would be here." He said to her from the curb

She turned to see what she too was hoping for and the sight of it made her smile. He started to take steps from the curb towards her now smiling as well and added " I really was and last Sunday by the way was a very long time to keep me waiting if you would be here."

"I was kind of hoping you would be here too."

"So you are glad to see me?" he asked wanting to hear her to say it just one more time.

"Let's just say that I had never before had an interest to paint the ocean before last Sunday."

"Is that what you are working on now and does that mean you're

finished with the one I saw last weekend? Before he let her answer
he started back in with " You know I went back to that shop to see
your other painting and also. She stopped him in the middle of what
he was saying and just let the words fall out of her mouth. " Do you
want to do something with me maybe?

"Do you want to go for another walk?"

"I do yes but I mean like at night like maybe this week if you are
not busy or this weekend?

"Are you asking me on a date?"

"I guess I am so what do you think?"

"I think I would love to" and he continued to tell her about
meeting Lillian and Jane at the store and having to go to them and tell
them the story of the amazing meeting and what he felt was a sign too.

This walk on the beach went further than the last one, was longer
than the last one and gave them a chance to get to know each other
a little more than what felt of like courteous conversation of 2 people
that were already walking in the same direction on the beach that
day and just made conversation. This time they asked questions and
sought answers. They listened and laughed. It was a wonderful sunset
that evening that they shared.

Upon arriving at the car he opened the door to her " So where
are you taking me and when?"

"Where is guess will be a surprise and does tomorrow night sound
okay?"

"I have to tell you I hate surprises but " Dinner." He interrupted
quickly.

"Dinner?" she asked making sure she heard him right

"Dinner then no surprises, do you like pizza?"

"I lovvvve pizza." She said making longing sound almost wanting
to go right then.

"Pizza it is then, I can meet you here if you want or at the pizza
place. It is not far from here and then we can just go from there. No
surprises."

"Where is your car?"He pointed down the street further than she
could see but described it. " Pull up here and you can follow me to my

house. Just remember where it is from here and then pick me up there tomorrow night." He ran down the street towards his car and then drove it back to where she had parked and proceeded to follow her to her house. She pulled into the driveway and he the curb parking directly in front of the house. He looked across the street opposite the stop sign at the spot he spent almost 2 nights in watching and seeing where he was right now.

"This is beautiful and you are so close to the ocean."

"Can you remember how to get here?" she asked him

"I got it." He said confidently

"Take down my number just in case you do get lost or have to cancel."

"I have not been clearer than I am right now so lost is not an option." He said smiling and complimenting her. That was good she thought to herself, he is smooth. She gave him the number anyway and asked "Is 6:00 good for you? Right here tomorrow."

"I will be here tomorrow at 6:00, save your appetite." And back into his car he climbed. She started to walk towards the door and as he went through the stop sign and made a u turn to come back down her street he saw her on the steps before going into the house waiting for him to pass for that one last look. He waved again and made a loud enough comment to her standing on her step before it faded into the night air.

"I waited all week to see you again,,,,,,,,,,, I can wait one more night."

She looked down at the ground with her hand on the door handle. Big smile on her face as she turned it and went inside.

———————

Monday early morning and she was inside of her regular scheduled visit with Dr. Elliot Messner. He found her to be in good spirits as she discussed all of the good things that were occurring around her.

"You still working with Lillian Amber?" She went to tell him all about her latest *"under construction"* piece. The meaning really pleased him.

"This is good Amber. Very good and very healthy. I am so glad that you continue to *"progress"* yourself through " *construction"* he said using her painting's to reference their own work together. They shared a laugh over his wit and she then went on to tell him the amazing story of meeting Jack and how he had seen the painting in gallery,etc,etc.

He was impressed. It was an impressive story and all in all she really was doing well and he could see it in her demeanor and eyes. " I am very happy for your good fortune Amber, how is everything with your mother?"

"Everything has been fine. We had a good blow out almost a month ago but she has been better. I am seeing Jack tonight and it will be our first date." She told him.

"Does your mother or father know about Jack or the date?" he asked returning to his serious Dr mode.

"No I have not told them yet."

"Do you think that you should?"

"I don't know why I mean I am over 18 so when do I get to make such a decision on my own without involving them or their approving my having Pizza with someone?"

"I understand clearly and you do have that right to make your own decision. I am just asking because we both are aware of the relationship dynamic between you and your mother."

"I will go out with him tonight and will tell them if they ask!"

"Okay fair enough. You have great, positive things happening. You have done really well Amber so let's stay right on this path."

"Agreed."

The session ended as well as the discussion.

She returned home that afternoon and decided to lay out in the backyard before going out later. Her dad had come outside to the back yard and took a seat at the end of the lounge chair. She was not aware that anyone was home and he explained he was just in between some things and came home to get something to eat and clear his head. He asked her about the session today with her doctor and if she felt good about still seeing him.

She told him also everything that she had told Elliot earlier including the pizza tonight with Jack. It was easier to talk to her dad for whatever reason but bottom line she felt comfortable, safe and not judged. This was another re assurance of that as he just listened to her amazing story of the latest painting, the meaning, the meeting of Jack, how he had seen her other painting.

"It's all incredible sweet-heart." He said smiling and happy for his daughter "Will you bring him in to meet us when he arrives tonight?"

"Will you be here at 6:00?" she asked him

"I will now." He said still smiling and left her to continue tanning.

She showered and got ready for Jack to arrive. Her father had not arrived but her mother was home and came to her door. She knocked and asked if she could come in.

"Your father told me about your session today, it sounded so nice." She had already had the conversation with her father earlier and with the Dr. before that so she really did not feel like having it again right now. She knew that did not seem fair to her mother who probably just wanted to be a part of the great new things that were happening but she also did not want to fight about anything that her mother may not approve of.

There was silence for a moment while she looked in the mirror at the angles of her-self with what she was wearing.

"He also said that you were going out tonight." Her mother added breaking the silence while she sat there uncomfortably on her bed watching her daughter study herself in the mirror.

"I am."

"He said that you and this guy had this amazing meeting, where are you going tonight?"

"Pizza, I told him no surprises so we are just going to have pizza and talk."

"Where?"

"Mom, I am not getting into this right now."

"I don't want to fight with you I am just asking where this boy we have never met is taking you."

"I don't have to tell you everything that goes on in my life!"

"Why are you acting like this?" Her mother asked.

"You don't have to know everything."

Norman Clevinger walked into her room to try to see what the noise or argument was about "What is going on?" he said walking into the room but in the calm voice that he always spoke with.

"I can't keep doing this. She has to know everything about everything." Amber tells him but with her voice elevated.

"Calm down sweetheart." He says to her but looking at his wife who has her arms crossed tightly and passing back and forth in very tight steps maybe only 2 steps in each direction.

"I'm sorry and I don't want to fight with you I just wanted to know where you were going."

The doorbell rang and the 3 of them looked at each other as the ding-dong faded to silence. Amber was who moved first towards to the door of her room and then to the front door. Her parents left in her room for only a moment to gather their facial expressions and speak to each only in a whisper.

"You found it." She said opening the door to greet him.

"I can be very resourceful when I want to, may I come in?" he replied and walked into her home where he was met by each member of the Clevinger Family. Here it is he thought to himself but just as he had done all of those days and nights in DC. He was composed and he was calm. He was ready for this moment so in the home he went and greeted first the mother.

"Mrs Clevinger." He said extending his hand " My name is Jack Rodan." Taking her hand and smiling. She looked at him hard and there was a squint that appeared in her eye like she was looking very hard at something so he removed his hand from hers and then to her father.

"Mr Clevinger." He said shaking his hand firmly.

"Jack" he said while shaking his hand " Call me Norman, please."

"Norman." He returned and then faced Amber to compliment her then returned to each of the parents to thank them for inviting him into their home as well as a quick compliment on the home.

"Thank you Jack. " Norman said then "Well,do enjoy your evening." Winking at his daughter as they made their way towards the door.

He opened the door for her to exit and then turned to face them one last time before leaving the home with their daughter. " I look forward to seeing you both again."

"Goodnight" he said waving to them both and watched his front door close. Mrs Clevinger did not speak another word during the brief transaction but did move towards the window to watch him again open the door to his car for her to enter. She stayed there while he joined her to watch the tail and headlights light up as the engine started and then off the car went.

"I do not know as many places as you do so work with me tonight but I do know a place that I like for Pizza so I was thinking we could go there and as promised no surprises."

"Pizza sounds great."

"It is not that far from here so just enjoy the flight and I will tell when we are close to approaching our final descent." He said to her jokingly and it worked as he could see her smile and even laugh as he looked over towards her."

The place was crowded even on Monday just as it had been any other night or afternoon he had been here but at least tonight he saw table opportunities for them to sit right as they walked in. They went to front counter and he indulged her in the opportunity to order whatever it is that she wanted. They joked and laughed back and forth over what they did and did not like on pizza and settled on a pepperoni and onion. They made their way towards a table to sit near a t.v. that was showing the Monday Night Football game that was on but the sound was off.

"We have been here a few times." She told him

"I love this place myself and I have high expectations." He replied with a confident tone.

"Do you?"

"Of course I do, I am here with you aren't I?"

Another smile followed by a long stare at him all the while the smile remained. They sat there and talked about anything and everything that came up. He asked every question he could but kept them to positive topics and never delved too much into her past to remove any uncomfortable feelings from happening. He left the door open for her to ask him any question she wanted. He had gone over the details in his mind a thousand times leading up to this moment so all he had to do was be it. He was charming. He was charismatic and vulnerable all at the same time. The conversation went on for hours and well after the pizza had come and was eaten.

Looking across the table at her he could tell she was close. He did not have her yet but she was close.

42

NATHANIAL Santor was back in El Paso and performing his role in security for Nelson Pritchard in any capacity that was delegated by Arturo who was essentially his boss. He had not seen Nelson yet but there was talk from the others about Nelson not being around very much at all lately since he returned with the Texan Camille. He needed to obtain the 2nd part of the information that the others in Austin would pay for. He had one part which was the name so all he needed was the 2nd part which was the location.

He had to be patient and not raise attention so in the event that the boy is found there is no question on behalf of them as to how it happened. He found out that the woman was staying with Nelson at his home so he made an effort to get any of his assignments from Arturo towards the home in the hopes that she was there.

The September morning was warm to him and he hated wearing the sport-coat but it did conceal the 44 that had shoulder holstered . He had been wearing a weapon of some sort for so many years of his life that he simply felt like he was not wearing pants when he did not have one on him but the coat in this climate just felt cruel. He was assigned to the perimeter detail which simply meant walking the property line all afternoon to ensure that no one was attempting to access the land from any other means than the guarded front gate.

He was given a break around 1:30 and went to the air conditioned 1,400 square foot house on the property that served as essentially what you find at a Fire-station. There were places to sleep and included a kitchen, restrooms and living area all used by the security team. He did not see Arturo in there so he decided to take a walk to the main house and see if Arturo was there but he was seeking the woman or someone that knew where she was. Inside the main house he went room to room reaching 3 of them before he saw a single other person. He considered the temperature of the day and made his way to the pool to see if she was there but again no sign of her.

He then went to the kitchen to Santy who was their Chef who again was not there but did find Mary, one of the housekeepers.

"Como estas Mary." He said to her

"Bien e Too" she replied to him

"Bien-Bien. How is the new house guest treating you?"

"She is very nice. Does not need much of anything and even helps. Have you met her?"

"Once but I have not seen her since they came back from The Cayman's. Are they here or did they go onto another trip?"

"No, no they are still here. They have been together the whole time. It is good to see him so happy." She said smiling and he returned in agreement.

"Is she going to stay here, like move in?"

"I don't know but like I said she is very nice and he is much happier. More than I have ever seen him."

"Does she call anyone or is there anyone else that will be coming with her to live I mean?"

"I don't know. She has a son I hear but he has not been here and they only talk on the phone."

"Do you know where he lives?"

"Nathanial, Can I help you?" a voice asked with a stern tone to it. He turned to face the voice that was coming from behind him which also made him jump when it happened. The voice belonged to Arturo and was curious as to why Nathanial was in the main house.

"I was told you were up here so I wanted to come by on my break and tell you again how grateful I was for the time off to take care of that family emergency." He said thinking quickly

"You are welcome now let's go. I will walk you back. Mary" he said nodding to the house-keeper as he waited for Nathanial to join him.

"Buenos Noches a asta menyana Mary." Nathanial said to her and began to walk with Arturo out of the kitchen. He had to find another way to get the location of her son and it seemed the best place was probably from her. He knew that Arturo was always with Nathan and if he wasn't then he knew where he was. Mary had told him that the woman and he were always together so he needed to get on the detail that was with Nathan and where he goes. He made small conversation, which was about the only kind of conversation you could get, with Arturo on the way back towards the main gate.

"Do you need any help with anything outside of here? I want to say thank you again so what- ever you need."

"I will let you know." Then saying nothing more he continued to walk to the gate where a car was awaiting him. The front passenger door was open and in he climbed shutting the door behind him. The car sat there running for a few minutes where an apparent conversation between the driver and Arturo was taking place. Nathanial continued towards his perimeter post but could still see the Crown Victoria sitting there and then sped off with Arturo still inside the car.

---

5 days would pass before he would even have seen Camille for himself and she was again with Nathan. They did seem happy he thought and she did not look really anything like she had before because he had remembered the 2 of them that afternoon when they arrived and were brought to his place of business so to speak. He had to hand it to Nathan and how good he was at what he did with a surgical knife.

They both were healing and then gone before he got a chance to see the final result on each of them so he was not sure if he would have recognized the boy even if he was here. All he remembered was that day when he was pacing and he told him stop because it was making him nervous.

They were going to a political dinner and Nathanial was asked to accompany the detail to and from. Nathan Pritchard was a frequent campaign contributor to certain parties and kept relations close with them when-ever the chance arrived. Tonight would be one of those nights where he was taking Camille to a $10,000 a plate black and white dinner function for The Governor. She had never been to such a thing and as nervous as she was he was enjoying the opportunity to partake in something that was again a first time thing for her. Nathanial Santor was searching for any opportunity that he could to inquire the woman Camille Harrison directly regarding her son in the hopes that some detail would deliver his whereabouts.

The dinner table was a cruise style seating that placed 5 parties of 2 all together at one table . Camille,seated next to Nathan and a slew of business professionals, moguls and athletes, found that trip to the restroom would be appropriate just to get a moment alone before the dinner had taken place. She had already endured a single file line in which people were awaiting the Governor to come in and shake hands with every person as well as more photographs than she can remember.

"Wont you excuse me?" She said while every male seated at the table joined her rising from her seat. " I will only be a moment."

"Of course dear." Nathan said and continued to seat himself and carry on listening to a tale from one of the other guest seated at the table.

Nathanial saw her heading to the restroom and figured it be the best opportunity to date and went towards the area. He looked at the front door where Arturo was observing each guest as they arrived and were searched discreetly by secret service. He did not notice that Camille had left the table but that is okay that is one of the reasons he was there anyway so him escorting to the restroom would be in the line of his duty.

"Miss Harrison, I am with Mr. Pritchard allow me to escort you please." He said to her smiling and she immediately retuned his smile with a "Thank you ah I am sorry I do not know your name."

"I am Nathanial Santor Miss Harrison and I want to tell you that we are all very happy that you have returned to El Paso with Mr Pritchard."

"Thank you Nathanial that is a very sweet thing to say."

"I will wait here to escort you back to the table." He said smiling to her and waited for her return. A few minutes later she emerged from the ladies room and made eye contact with him.

"You are part of the security?"

"I am, yes mam. Will your son be joining us this evening?" He threw in there just to see the reaction or response and did hope that it was not to forward or odd of a question.

"My son, no not this evening" she responded not thinking anything of it but again she was enamored with the tables of well dressed people, music in the air, conversations being had as they made their way back to their table. She could see Nelson and he was smiling at her return so she did not think anything of the question he had asked or the reply she had given. Not even the "The culture in San Diego or Cardiff I think he said seems to be really agreeing with him right now but I will get him back here soon enough."

"Well we look forward to that as well Miss Harrison, enjoy the rest of your evening." He said to her as she walked the last few steps to the table alone. The men again stood up and the table captain pulled the chair for her to sit. She looked back towards Nathanial and made a small wave gesture to again thank him for the escort.

He agreed with the others that she was very nice and it did seem that his boss Nathan Pritchard was happier than he had ever remembered before. This is not a fun thing he is doing but it was business he said to himself. They said it was only money they were after so no harming the boy other than a tax on his earnings which was not much of a concern to him. He had what he needed and just had to make sure that no connection could be made to him regarding how the boys identify and location was to be known by these Dallas men.

Not a concern of his at this moment because the night was looking up on all accounts. $70,000 he was already counting which would inflate his personal and private account to its highest point EVER!

Thank you Camille Harrison,,,,,,Thank you very, very much.

43

THE night' and days following their first date were filled with many more. There were lunches, dinners, movies, picnics, museums, bike riding and anything that allowed them to spend time together. Amber was hardly ever home yet they never spent time at his hotel either. He sensed that it might have made her uncomfortable so it was just not somewhere that they went but she did know he was staying in one because he was not sure if he was staying in San Diego or not, until he met her.

He told her that several times and she never got sick of hearing it either.

"There is no other place I would like to be."

The only time that they were away from one another was when she was painting. Her next piece she was working was inspired Lillian and Jack titled "*Plateaus*." He was anxious to see it but with Amber there was patience. They did nothing until she was ready and could give that freely and comfortably.

They waited some time before they even kissed for the first time but he knew that was one of the keys to her trust. So he was patient and understanding the whole time then it would be her that would kiss him. It had been one of the nights that he walked her to the door after an evening or afternoon together. He sensed that it was at her house that she had the most rebellion or frustration like she was trying to break free from something but it was on the first step of that house that she pulled him towards her for a very brief yet passionate kiss.

She painted, she was inspired, she was happy and she was falling in love. The only place that she was not happy was at home and that lack of total control or independence that she longed for. This was not hers for the taking as long as she was under the same roof with her mother. The relationship was better and she always knew that she meant well but she began to feel more and more desire to free. To be independent and in total control of her life for better or worse.

Nathanial found himself back in Dallas and back at the hotel he had located the people that were going to pay him $70,000 in cash for his information. He waited and waited for the return of that Bronco and run over in his mind several times how he was going to execute his plan. He was alone again and could not take the chances of allowing them to gather troops and meet him later and he was not comfortable being in the area that was more or less theirs. He needed to get the one they call Knight alone and take him. He needed to find the opportunity where he could get him alone and considering that he was giving something of value to him he felt confident he would not resist. The money for the information and then never to see each other again.

The Bronco made its entrance loud and fast once again. There was his target but again with another person that he had not seen him with before. Does he take his chance with the 2 of them or wait? He asked as he sits in his cramped car, sweat pouring from his body and time feeling as though it is running out.

Contemplating his chances allowed enough time for the 2 men to walk from their parking space and onto the elevator. Nathanial watched the door close on his shot. He pulls the gun from its holster and stares at himself in the rearview mirror. $70,000 he thinks to himself and then repeats it with his eyes closed still sitting in the upright position to see his face when his eyes re open. His eyes reopen because the doors to the elevator did as well. Out comes his target with now a 3rd man as they approach the Bronco. Nate places his gun in his lap and waits to start the vehicle. The Bronco engine and loud music fill the lower level parking garage and off it goes. He starts the vehicle and as he places his rental car in gear he says one more time with an exhale accompanying the words out loud "$70,000

He follows the Bronco and the 3 passengers for 30 minutes and Nate can again feel his time draining like the last sip of water available in a cup and he is thirsty. They pull into a gas station and Nate pulls to the opposing side of the station where 4 other pumps are located and the air/vacuum tanks. 2 of them get out and while one stays to pump the large one they call Knight is who is going in to pay.

Nate leaves the car running and the doors unlocked. He is out of the car and to the entrance to make sure the other 2 are still at the pump. The one inside is getting beer and approaching the counter. He asked for Marlboro reds and 20.00 on #2. Nate waits for the pump to start so the other would remain occupied and goes in to stand right by him. The man turns to see the equal sized man and with each hand full carrying beer in one and a pack of reds in the other his eyes squint to recall and widen because they just remember who it is right in front of him.

Nate has his jacket open to reveal his gun and his forefinger is over his lips to symbolize his request for his to be silent. " I have what you want" he says quietly and now the clerk is paying attention because the man did not leave yet. " Not a word, you and you alone come with me now or there is no deal, understood"? Nate waits only a second for a response and then ushers him out the door. "Turn left and not a word". He has the man drive and gets in beside him with his gun now drawn. "Drive out this exit, make a right and drive till I give another instruction".

As the vehicle is exiting from the station and heading east Knights partner was going in to see what was taking so long. He searches the store and approaches the restroom. He opens the door to find it empty and turns immediately towards the clerk. " Where is the man that was just in here"? "Big Guy/Bald". He offers "He just left" the clerk explains confused. "He Left"? The other asked. "He just left" the clerk repeated. "He bought beer, cigarettes and left with the other man in here. "WHAT OTHER MAN?" he asked with his voice elevating.

"Another guy, big guy." "What else did he look like"? The man asked. Another customer walks into the store to pay for gas while the clerk offers a limited description but it was enough to paint the portrait of a Large Spanish guy wearing a sport coat. The man runs out of the store and looks around the parking lot and even circles it on foot while being approached by the 3rd man that was in The Bronco. "What the fuck it taking so long he asked?" "El Paso is back" he says still looking around the parking lot.

"What?"

"The guys from El Paso who got Mickey killed and has information on that kid and his mom is back!"

"Where is Knight?" the 3rd man asked

"I don't know" he says and then repeats "I don't know!"

44

SO what is your plan EL Paso?" You don't mind that I call you that do you since I do not know your name?" Knight offers because the man pointing the gun on him looks a little rattled. "The deal is simple I want $35,000 for the new identity of the boy and then another $35,000 for the location."

"Okay" Knight says still driving and unsure of where he is going

"I want it today and now. I get my money and you get what you want. We both walk away and this conversation never happened, understood?"

"Sure but how the fuck do you think I am going to get $70,000 right now? Do you think I walk around with $70,000 on me Paso-Huh" he states sounding agitated.

"I don't care how you get it but your window is closing and I am fine with going back to where I came from and leaving no loose ends here if you get what I am saying."

"Okay-Okay just calm down I do have it but I don't have it on me you know. Its hot out and you have a gun on me can you just relax and I will take you to where I do have at least 40". He says to him not ever looking directly at him.

"40 gets you one and if that is all you have then that is all you get." How far?'

Knight agrees to the one piece of information with his left arm on the door and his hand extended upright with his fingers messaging his temple.

He tells him about a safe at one of the bars that they own in Dallas and that he was not worried about being able to find them once they knew the location. The conversation seems to lighten the tension in the air even with the gun and the heat. Nate is working through the fact that he will not have the 70 he hoped for but $40,000 was still better than nothing and worth the very little time he had put into this venture.

What Nate did not know was that Knight and his crew had always had a protocol that if in the event anything ever happened to any of them in his crew that they were to meet at Racks Bar. This way they could work through the details and strategy of retaliation all while in the company of Strippers, Liquor and pool tables. Racks is where Knight was taking Nathanial for his payment and also where Knights crew would be waiting.

Jack arrives at the door and is again greeted by Ambers father Norman. "Please come in Jack how are you"? He asked. Norman was very much in support of anything he felt was helping his daughter be happy and Jack arrived earlier than expected so he would have time to visit with her family.

"Amber is still getting ready, would you care to sit down?" Norman offered enjoying the moment to get to know Jack more. He does not want to ask a great deal of intrusive questions but does realize he does not know very much about him so he starts with " How long have you lived in San Diego?" Jack stays away from any time spent in Texas and stays with the military son that is well traveled with his most recent time spent in Pisa Italy and then finished with "Have you ever been?" To Normans reply of no it now allowed him to provide

Norman with a wonderful mental tour of the area as he remembered it himself. The journey brought Norman to edge of his seat and was accompanied by a delighted smile.

Jacks finished touch involved him telling Norman that of the time he has spent in other places, although beautiful and even educational, it was here and with Amber that he has found a true sense of belonging. He goes on to explain her talent in painting, how her work spoke to him and that it is one of the happiest periods of his life. The 2 of them share that moment together while Norman is filled with pride of his daughter bringing not only her life back but life to another.

"Jack you are early" Amber states entering the room first greeted by her father who extends her a kiss followed by a large smile she has not seen in a while. She smiles back curiously and then moves towards Jack to hug him. "What have you 2 been talking about?" she asked looking back and forth at each of them. Her father stated that while she was getting ready it afforded them an opportunity to get to know one another a little bit and even further offered how much he enjoyed their conversation. As the 3 of them share that moment the front door then opens where they are all greeted by her mother Nancy Clevinger

Nancy was not aware that there would be company upon arriving or that Amber had plans so when met in her living room by the 3 of them she made every effort to be cordial. "Hello" she offered .

"Mrs. Clevinger" Jack returns

"Well to what do we owe this pleasure?" She stated a little less icy than her greeting.

"Jack is taking me out this evening and came early to get to know everyone." This Saguenay to Nancy offering for them both to sit down which Amber was not taking part in. The thought of being seated in the living room on display for her mother to judge any part of whet ever this was between her and Jack was non negotiable.

PART
FOUR

45

WE do need to get going" Amber added while Jack made a assuring offer that he would return again so that the 2 of them would have time together just as he and Norman had shared.

"I would very much like that" Nancy continued and then made the invitation for dinner this weekend.

He approached to shake hands starting with Nancy " It would be a absolute pleasure and look forward to the opportunity." He then to her father where his handshake was firm followed by a smile and his stating his name "Norman".

As they exited the home Nancy asked " Where are the 2 of you going this evening?"

Amber turned to them waving and stated " I am taking him to meet Michael."

Jack drove to the directions provided by Amber while listening to an under tone of discontent being offered by Amber of living at home with her mother and having her involved in every detail of her life. Nothing that was ruining the date but enough to understand one of the ways in which he would repay Mrs Clevinger. They arrive at Underwood's which is a restaurant and bar owned by Michaels dad.

"Where are we" he asked quizingly

"Michael is my cousin, His Dad owns this place and since he was working tonight I wanted you 2 to meet."

Jack was not sure of what to say or even do. His heart started pounding faster. No one has recognized him at all so far. The family had not spent that much time with him and all the time in the courtroom was them behind him looking at the back of his head. The eye to eye contact made by them in the courtroom was from a distance and anything in the paper was distorted by pixels.

Michael he had spent time with and he started to remember the things Michael had said in the courtroom. He started to even remember the letters that Michael had sent to him stating the horrible person I was and what he would do if he ever saw me again. Walking towards the front doors there is 3 black and white police cars in the parking lot.

"Did the place get robbed?" He asked filling the silence in the air while his mind danced over the possibilities of seeing him again.

"Cops are always in here". She replied " His Dad, my Uncle Tommy, was in construction and when he got hurt on the job he sued the company and won.

He took that money since he could not work or at least work like that anymore and he bought this place about 3 years ago. The food is great but because it is also a bar and is open late his Dad loved having Cops here all the time hanging out for lunch dinner and drinks after work so robbed no, not yet. " she answered assuringly and in they went.

"Amber". The hostess yells when they enter the restaurant portion of the venue. The Hostess talks with her on the way to the table and offers to get Michael before departing. "You will love it here" she says picking up the menu. " I should weigh about 200 lbs with as much as I have eaten in here the past year." The air is filled with the scent of garlic and the room looks like a fishing village. There are booths and tables while there is scenery that is painted on the high walls that give it the appearance that there is a 2nd story with windows /balconies and lights. There is lanterns hanging on each pillar, boat's hoisted up above you and netting that stretches out filled with crabs.

He sees the officers of the parked patrol cars dining in the restaurant and looks down at the table where Amber is showing him where maps of the world are placed under the acrylic top. " How many of those places have you been?" She asked him staring into his eyes and her chin resting onto her right hand.

Before he answers they are greeted by 2 people at the table. The server,who again, greets her enthusiastically by name and then the other who he recognizes right away as Michael. Amber stands from the table to hug each of them and then proceeds with her introduction of Jack who is looking everywhere but at the piercing stare of Michael.

They complete their order and Michael then takes a seat at the table as opposed to departing with the server. Instrumental Muzak is playing in the dark sea village they are seated in. Jack is back in DC controlling his breathing and the beating of his heart that he is certain can be heard over anything in the restaurant.

"Jack is it?" Michael asked still staring and almost studying him from across the table." Have we met?"

46

RACKS parking lot was empty and the venue was closed at this hour. They park the car in the front and not the back so the crew that would be arriving would have a heads up not recognizing the vehicle. They enter from the front door using a key that is secured on the premise. " Your lucky day Paso" He says killing some time and setting his at ease as they approach the office.

"I just had that key placed out there for emergencies like kidnapping, get you a beer?"

"You want what I have so kidnapping is a stretch. Get the money and it will be both of our lucky day's? He returns matter of fact and gun still drawn and pointed right at him.

As the 2 inside the bar approach the office the parking lot outside is beginning to fill with cars from Knights crew and as planned they question a Ford Tempo in the front of the bar. Knowing that he left with the individual described as being the man in El Paso something is not right and drive to the back and begin to load their weapons. To them this guy not only has something that is money to them but one of their friends is dead and how he was killed had to do with the person potentially inside the bar right now.

"It is on" one of them says as the clip is clicked into the place and the hammer pulled back placing one in the chamber.

"Where are they at?" Knight asked the man again killing time

"Open the safe" He answered and even cocked his weapon before adding " Now!"

36-6-28 was entered and you could hear each one of the tumblers dialing as the knob moved left to right and then the click. Nathanial moves closer into the office to observe the safe so that no weapons were inside. He instructs him to remove everything from the safe and place it onto the desk and while Nathanial had his entire attention on what was transpiring inside of that office watching Knights every move he was unaware that the bar was slowly and very quietly filling with a small army of people that were only interested in retaliation and money with no concern of how they would achieve getting each one.

Onto the desk was stacks of money and a 38 caliper gun which Knight was not concerned with an attempt to use if his soldiers were doing what they always been instructed to do. Nate instructed him to count out the bills to understand the denomination that was present. His crew could hear him counting as they motioned for each other to areas of the bar in the event when they take him he begins to shoot. Knight counts out a little over $37,000 in cash and then moves it towards Nate on the opposite side of the desk still with his gun cocked and pointed at a very close range to Knights head. "The location?" he says calmly staring into the barrel of the gun.

"Turn around and face the wall" he instructs so he could approach and retrieve the gun and bills stacked on the desk

"Hey man-I gave you what you wanted."Knight states still facing the wall. And then repeats " What is their location?"

Money in pocket and a gun in each hand he slowly begins to back up from the office telling him to remain facing the wall until he is close enough to exit and will then tell him their location as agreed. He exits the door frame of the office walking backwards with still every focus on the large man called Knights facing the wall when he hears something and as he turns half his body with one gun in the office and the other going where his eyes lead all he sees is several men rushing him. Both guns fire but they get that one shot which both miss any targets other than the walls of the club and office. He is hit in every part of his body in a barrage of fist, legs and bottles.

His adrenaline kicks in fueled by the pain of the attack and charges out of the office striking back and you could hear Knight tell his soldiers " I want him alive!" Nate runs over one and then pushes another of his adversaries over a pool table. He turns, making an attempt to locate the entrance, right into the fist of one of them and then another. The 1st blow stalls him and the 2nd one knocks him back flush to the pool table. Both of his firearms go off shooting one of the 2 men that just hit him and as he is about to fire his 3rd shot both of his arms are grabbed by 2 separate men pushing them into the air where they now empty every round into the air as a bottle, pool stick and fist tattoo Nathanial face until all his consciousness has left.

When he wakes up he feels a distinct neck pain lifting his head to discover he is tapped to a chair. The rest of the pain in his body was not far behind as his eyes focus on where he is and what is happening. They have been waiting.

He cannot make out the complete math of how many people are in the room but is certain his idea of making some extra money has come to an end. Knight sits down at a chair that has been placed directly in front of Nathanial.

"What are their names?" and "where are they"? he asked even adding that it is not late for you to still make some money as long as you tell what I want to know. Before Nate can speak one of the others in room belts out " Fuck that Knight this guy killed Mickey, I want to take his ass apart"! Knight turns slowly in his chair towards the man making the comment and silences him without saying a word. The room become silent and Knight returns his focus to Nate. " You do want to still make some money, don't you"? he asked him.

"You're going to kill me either way!" he says defeated.

"No" he says with a long drawl.

"I am going to kill you if you don't tell me what I want to know but I will still honor some of the payment with of course a small tax for the death of another friend and of course pain of suffering caused

by your kidnap attempt. You understand, right?" the room now fills
with some laughter before returning to silence.

What are their names?" and "where are they"? He repeats.

"Jack Rodan and Camille Harrison". Nate says staring right into
Knights gaze.

"Good" he says encouragingly "and their location?"

"You can't get to her. She is with my boss Nelson, the one who
owns the bar and you do not want to fuck with him but the boy is
in San Diego."

Knight is sitting directly across from Nate in the chair turned
backwards and his arms resting on the back with his head knodding
up and down slowly. "Cut him loose" he says.

"What " one of them asked.

"Cut him loose!! " He returns louder and add's " Get him a
drink!" He turns back to Nate and asked him " What will you have ?"

"Whiskey, Neat." Knight jumps out of his chair stating "Whiskey
and make it neat for the man that just offered us one of the biggest
paydays we will have to date."

Nate begins to feel the blood flow back into his arms as the tape is
being cut from him and the chair he was tapped to. He also feels the
pain in his body from the several blows he received but the whiskey
now in front of him and being brought to his lips does offer some
sense of relief. He drinks it all in one shot and grimaces from the sting
it made against the cuts on his lips and mouth. Knight returns and has
a stack of money in his hand.

"This is $5,000 for your travels and our business is not done yet.
You are going to help me get to the woman that is with your boss."
He says returning to his seat smiling and offering another whiskey.

"You are going to get me alone with her so we can discuss a
business arrangement for our silence or hers, either way." I can't do
that" Nate says " My boss is Nelson Pritchard, do you know what he
will do to me?'

"No" Knight says smiling "but I do know what everyone in this
room will if you don't give me what I want. "Okay" Nate says again
with defeat. " Okay!"

47

DARKER lighting, soft music and garlic filled air held no weight to the immediate silence and discomfort of the table that was present once Michael appeared. Michael had a good sense of things and always did. He had a knack with people and trusted his instincts as they had always served well growing up in Southern California.

He was fit and learned a lot from his experiences in school, construction sites with his father and his father's crew. He learned even more in the restaurant industry dealing with and reading people. He learned from working with so many other ages, races and beliefs.

He talked with and learned from everyone he spoke to. He was young but was able to hold conversations with Trash men, Law Enforcement Officers, Teachers, Lawyers, Students, Surfers and all other walks of life that frequented Underwood's.

Michael was also protective of his younger cousin Amber. They were close growing up and were always in each other's life but following her move to California regarding a tragic experience in her life he was always there checking on her to help.

Michael did feel some responsibility for the events of that evening or at least being someone who may have brought everyone to a place for a circumstance like that to happen. He forgave himself but also made a promise to help her move beyond what happened and be there for her with anything she ever needed again. That incident in a way he felt changed his life and somewhat saved it as well.

When he had gone to Texas that summer it was only he and his father. His father worked a lot doing construction and that left him to his own devises whatever those may be. Not many were positive and he felt that if he was going nowhere then he was going to have as much fun as he could along the way.

Her tragedy awakened him to more possibilities than he was aware of before. That in conjunction with the accident that his father would have a few years later would also bring them closer together than they had been in years. He appreciated working with and being with his Dad more now than they had been growing up. Michael was there for his cousin Amber and he was committed to ensure that she would not be in harm's way again.

Michael was not exactly sure why at the moment but all his instinct's felt that "harm's way" was sitting directly across the table from him.

"I do not think we've met" Jack replied to Michaels question.

"I've never had the opportunity to eat here before and have not been in San Diego that long." He offered while Michael still said nothing and continued to study him.

At first Amber did not notice the exchange but became aware now that the silence was awkward. She started to say something and Michael began to lean in more in attempt to shift in his chair but also to take a closer and more in the light look at his guest. The server returned with the drinks but also offered that Michael was needed at the host stand and then in the kitchen to help with expo getting the food out of the window.

Michael smiled, still said nothing then left his chair and excused himself. Amber went for a quick change of topic asking about of the map and places he has been which one was his favorite and why?

The dinner and their time together was to date the most trying Jack felt and could see the constant piercing stare of a watching

Michael from various places he was standing in the restaurant. Jack was very conscious of almost every moment and movement he was making while in the restaurant not wanting to give or offer any tells that could be even possibly be recognized by Michael and simply wanted out of the space.

Michael joined them again as they were partially through with their meal and forbade any pleasantries and bluntly asked " Where are you from"? The question increased the silence of the table and Amber was not sure where that came from but remained silent to allow Jack to answer. Jack returned with the scripted monologue he had built and rehearsed time and time again. Michael just studies his eyes and could not place what it was but it was simply that he did not like him, not sure why but he was going to find out.

Michael remained at the table until his guest were decided to depart which for Jack was not soon enough. The one last thing Michael had of interest was the residency of Jack and where he could find him which was offered when asked and as Jack drove Amber home she offered apologies for the way Michael had acted offering for the first time that there were circumstances in her past that made the people in her life over protective like her mother and Michael. Jack made it clear siding with each of them that had something of " circumstance" happened to my loved one that he too would be overprotective.

"you don't have to live with my mother"! she retorted

"Then maybe it is time for you to move out and start your chapters that are yours alone" he said calmly and supportively.

Amber had never even considered that as an option before oddly enough. Her world had become just that her world and each day there was that foundation that just was but the last 5 years of consistent battling with her mother over trivial things had worn on her and for the first time she did feel she could as jack said " Start chapters that are hers and hers alone"

That evening Jack paced back and forth in his hotel room taking inventory of his thoughts and plans. He was successful in getting out of DC alive, he learned things in there that allowed for him to facilitate a plan of new identity and features which to this date not one person has recognized him even as uncomfortable as the exchange was with Michael he felt confident he would never be able to place that he was Jessie. He was successful even if by accident with making things right between his mother and the way his father had treated her, they had money in the bank and to his knowledge at that moment no one looking for him. His thoughts lightened and his spirits elevated with pride in the manner in which events had played out. His focus would now be on catching up with his mother and settling a debt with The Clevinger Family.

Camille and Nelson have immersed themselves into one another during their time in El Paso. Their conversations were deep and thought provoking as well as filled with laughter and each seemed to be bringing the other a filled void which made them grateful to each other as well. Nathan ponders his business and his successful run not being ever caught and how much longer that would endure if he did not perhaps change his direction. It is hard for them to talk so freely when so many guards are present so their most intimate of conversations take place in the most intimate place of the home, the bed.

"What will I do if this is all I have ever done"? he asked her truly looking for some insight.

"You could always do what you have done just return to doing it legally freeing yourself of the cell and cage you have before you." " You don't need all of these people here, all this security looking over your shoulder and can return to helping people for the right reasons"!

He loved her insight and even though he had not known her long he trusted her far more than anyone in a very long time.

"Have you talked with your son? How is he doing"? He asked changing the topic.

"No" she returned " But I need to, I miss him and want to hear about if he is staying there which means that is a topic of discussion for me to move there with him."

The comment left the room silent in thought when Nelson added

" Another topic of discussion is if you were to stay here with me for us"?

Nathanial returned to El Paso once again only now with far more luggage meaning he had to first explain the love taps on his face but also how would be get Camille to meet with Knight and not get killed in the process. Part of him was angry at himself for ever starting down this path but he thought of the money and was just trying to get some put away into savings for his future so that ambition and partial greed has led to how do I make this all work?

"What the hell happened to you"? one of the guards asked as he reported to work and as he offered a tale of the not so friendly aspects and areas of El Paso he can see Arturo approaching.

"What the hell happened to you"? Arturo asked immediately and before he began his tale of what transpired Arturo cut him off stating " The woman is going shopping and Mr Prichard wants a car and escort detail for the afternoon, you both come with me"!

Camille still had only the few belongings from The Caymans she purchased with Jessie so she felt like it would be ideal to obtain some things while she awaited a call from her son. The weather was hot but still beautiful and as much she did enjoy the shopping part to depart further from her past and deliver her closer and closer to her present she did not care for the armed escort which was there constantly and made her uneasy.

Nathanial waited patiently for any moment that he could to get close to her and since they had an exchange at the Governors Dinner they had some familiarity so when he finally did get close she offered " Sorry to keep you guys out here, I honestly had no issue with going on my own Nathanial". Remembering his name and spoken with a smile he quickly and quietly said

"They know where Jessie is and if you say anything to anyone they will kill him, just keep walking, breathe and be calm but you and I need to talk"!

"Talk then"! She returned turning her head to look at him

"Do not say anything to Mr Pritchard or anyone for that matter or they will kill him, we cannot talk here. Finish your shopping and lets return to the estate where I will find you with a way to talk and until then if you speak to anyone they will kill him"!

Camille said nothing on the return to the estate and knowing that Nelson would not be there she had no choice but to wait to hear from the guard. Should she tell Nelson and what would that lead to how far would this all go she pondered and once again felt anxiety, fear, anger and uncertainty. What if Nelson and his guards could protect Jessie, she hated thinking that the potential for her son to have killed someone while he was away made her ill but she also did not know what took place in places like that and what he had to do to survive. How did the guard know this about the men coming for him?

Knowing men were coming for her son to kill him scared her and she needed a way to warn him.

48

AMBERS latest piece she had been working on also has inspirations to support its message but the timing had been the perfect storm for her piece that was entitled *Plateaus*.

Her evolved work and accolades regarding her talent as a painter was becoming something that fueled and fed her to elevate. Her discussions with Lillian and Jayne supported her evolution as a person and artist which then combined with the meeting of Jack and he too offering poignant messages for her to stand on her own and be free of the shadows of her mother they all captivated her and guided her work when the brush met the canvas.

She felt empowered now for the first time and it was freeing to discuss with Dr Messner whom once again also supported the growth of Amber Clevinger but did caution her to not fly to high during these soaring moments. Their session ended and she departed once again for her car and that drive to The Caufield Studio to unveil her latest work to her dearest friends.

Jack checked the messages at the desk and found several that were from the El Paso area so he returned to his room immediately to call.

"Hello Pritchard residence". The voice answered

"Camille Harrison please, she is a guest there". He replied quickly " One moment please".

He waited patiently but the wait was not long.

"Hello". She said

"Mom, its me, are you ok"?

"Honey it is so good to hear your voice and there is so much I want to talk about but I am not sure how much I can say on the phone but the problem we had when we got back to the hotel when you got out is back and near San Diego"!

"How do you know that"? he asked quizzingly

"I found out today and just wanted to let you know, I think I should come there". She added

"No, as much as I want to see you if for any reason there is a problem not a reason at all for you to be part of it". He reassured

"Then you come here that would solve a lot and I could see you, how about that"?

"I will, I want to, you know I want to see you but I have some things I have to address here and much quicker now if there is the potential of any issues. Lets talk about you and I will tell you about San Diego". He finalized to change the topic because she seemed concerned about saying to much on the phone so they caught up on all the details of each of their time away from one another but he left out all of the things about his true motivation for being in San Diego.

Knight sat a table back at his bar Racks with many of his crew in close proximity milling about the bar and tables. " Whats the plan"? one asked while staring at a cocktail server that just started working there.

"The plan is we wait for our El Paso comrade to produce a window to meet with the mother and rattle her cage because I get the feeling there is interest to her to pay us for not going to insurance company!"

"If she is in El Paso and staying with that surgeon guy isn't that heat we don't want"? he asked cautiously.

"Heat we don't want yes" he stated and then paused while the crew looked and awaited his next response " If we get the son first and have him that is bargaining control and if we get to him before we get

DONNY R. CRAWLEY

to her and convince her that her son will be killed if she tells anyone
that buys us time to relocate and with a lot of seed money to do so"!

"What do you mean, how much money"? One of them asked still
trying to make sense of it all

"I did research on the name Harrell following the death of who we
hit and although it did or would not share anything about insurance
money I feel pretty good that if he had a trust fund set up for the kid
that the wife would have been taken care of but what I did find out
was that she sold his company and that was publicized. She netted 7
million for the husband's business so add it all together and we got a
trust fund, insurance and a business sold for 7 million. We get the kid
and we have bargaining power for a large payday"!

"So where are we going"? another said half laughing and ready
to get paid.

"Cardiff California now lets go get that money fellas"!

Michael now aware that his inventory had a flaw and a big one at that
meant he had a choice to make which was to return to El Paso and
him and his mom discuss a alternate plan of destination or he stays to
execute his plan for revenge which meant moving much quicker as he
did not know how long it would take the Brotherhood to find him. He
could go and know they would not find him or take that chance now.

He takes a long look in the mirror at himself having this
conversation aloud. "We could just walk away and get away" he says
to himself in the mirror " but they have been able to find me from
the minute I got out". He answers.

"I am this close"! is said louder than he had wanted so another
inventory. They don't know where I am staying and if they did I could
check out and relocate which buys time. " I need to get her away from
her mother that will destroy one half of the equation so by getting her
to move in with me, getting her to fall in love and then destroy her
heart, her existence and then I could be on my way knowing each one
of them will again forever be changed, never trust and never forget

what their actions perpetuated. He sets out to unite with Amber and just as he had found the window for the introduction, just as he had found the window for the walk, the dates and courting he can find one for the asking of her to move out and in with him.

He calls her home with no answer and then calls the Caufield Studio and is greeted by Jayne.

"Caufield Studio this Jayne how may I help you"?

"Jayne, this is Jack Ambers boyfriend, is she there"?

"Hello Jack, she is, she is and just brought us her latest work. Have you seen it"?

"No, but can I speak with her if she is not busy?

"One moment and I will get her, she is a real gift Jack and you are a lucky man"! she celebrated.

We are going to find out how lucky I am he thought to himself.

"Hello, Jack"? Amber spoke into the phone with much enthusiasm and anticipation.

"Your painting is done, Jayne told me. I have to see it and you can I come by the studio"? he asked awaiting the response.

"I have to see you too, how fast can you get here"? she says flirtatiously.

"I will be right there"! and he hangs up the phone.

Jack picks up flowers from one of the markets on the way there he knows exactly what he has to say and has to do now all he has to do is get there.

He enters the studio bearing 2 bouquets of flowers and presents one to Jayne offering " For you for always being a source of light every time that I see you". Jayne is stunned and speechless possibly for the first time ever and accepts them wearing the deepest shade of red from blushing she has adorned in a very long time.

"Where is she"? he finally asked and coming out of her haze she walks him to the area Amber always worked where her a Lillian were having a conversation. Jack approaches but Jayne has already made their presence known by loudly stating " Aren't they beautiful"? Both Amber and Lillian break from their conversation to see Jayne holding flowers and then the approaching Jack with more flowers.

"Good afternoon Mrs Caufield"! he states and then all his eye contact was on Amber as she was just taking in what was happening and not sure of what to make of it. Jack extends the flowers to Amber proclaiming "Amidst all of the enchanting exhibits within these walls I see the most beautiful one before me"!

She accepts the flowers with tears filling her eyes, the room is silent and Amber steps into his arms to hug him and then Jack instinctively kisses her softly but it was a kiss that took her breathe away and even made the room spin. The only thing that returned it to reality was the sounds and octave levels Jayne was demonstrating.

"Well Jack Rodan, you certainly know how to impact a room". Lillian finally said restoring the suspended reality. They all laugh for a moment drinking in the intoxication of the room until Jack asks " Can I see your painting"?

Amber points to it and says nothing allowing Jack to interpret for himself. He like all the other ones simply studies in silence then turns to her to say " Like your others they speak to me and they say things I need to hear and want to hear.

He turns to face all 3 of them, smiling and using his hands in an animated manner he begins to share " The progress is what we all seek, one foot in front of the other no matter how small is still just that progress and being under construction is where we spend most of our lives building and growing, learning and evolving and here we have plateaus which is how we measure our growth" his eye contact bounces from one audience member to the next speaking with subtle and quiet tones but passion and conviction that has the attention and perhaps even captivated his audience.

"We have to celebrate Amber, where would you like to go right now"? He insist's.

The last place he wanted to be to celebrate was back at the restaurant Michael worked yet here they were being walked to a table and Michael walking towards them to see them.

Jack takes in the long and loving embrace which reminds him of the first time he saw them together and resulting in his running down the hall and out for the school but not today. Today he smiles and awaits the eye contact that Michael will engage once completed with his greeting of Amber.

"Hello Michael". Jack says extending his hand.

"Jack" his one word response to him and finally shaking his hand before returning his gaze to Amber. " What brings you here"? he ask's leaving out what brings you both here.

"Jack wanted to celebrate so I could not think of anywhere else I wanted to go to do so than here with you"! she says happily.

"Celebrate, what are we celebrating Jack"? now eyes fixed back on Jack.

"How long Amber and I have been seeing each other and just how captivated I am by here talent as well as her beauty"! not wavering from Michaels gaze.

There is an arrogance in the air Michael senses from Jack that is not celebratory it feels cloaked and although not insincere but more rehearsed but why. Jack knows that his own clock is ticking so he has to move fast and be strategic he stays on course with Michael stating the many moments he and Amber have shared, the recent painting and the impact she has made him to make him a better person. Rehearsed, Michael thinks to himself again and just what the fuck is this guy up to. Amber is not super wealthy and she lives at home so what is it he keeps asking himself.

"So you are staying, are you still at the hotel"? he asked Jack

"Staying yes but I have a plan with the hotel but that is where I am staying at the moment". " I am thinking of school but undecided".

"You don't work"? Michael asked mockingly.

"No, not at the moment I inherited money from my parents death in a car crash and am just trying to find myself which at the moment is the closest I have been since being with Amber". He volleys back breaking his eye contact with Michael to look into Ambers eyes making that last statement then asked still making eye contact with her. " Are you ready there is somewhere else I want to take you"?

They end with Jack offering to Michael " well see you soon". Yes you will". Says Michael.

49

WHERE are you taking me" She asked curiously as they
drove through the night.

"Somewhere that is very special to me". He responds
not offering anything more.

As they get closer and he begins to park she recognizes the place
but still says nothing allowing the element of surprise to play out.

"What are we doing here"? She asked softly as he came around
the car to take her hand.

"I wanted to take you somewhere that means a great deal to me".
He says holding her hand and looking into her eyes.

"This is where we met, this is where I found you and I found us"
He stated as they began to walk towards the house she had painted
months earlier that was under construction and continued to lead
her down to the beach access where they would take their first walk.

They were now on the beach walking along the shoreline with
the moonlight above shimmering off the tide and water coming and
out. They walked in silence for a moment that was not awkward at
all just taking in the sounds and energy of the moment.

"Those things I said to Michael I meant". He said softly but
pronounced with statement.

Before she responded he proceeded to elaborate all the depth of his earlier statement to Michael regarding how she has made him think, made him see, made him feel and want to be here like a home. "You feel like home Amber"!

"I have been lost for some time with no one and for the first time in a long time I feel like I am home and with someone that I want to find new plateaus with"! he stated knowing she too had been lost to a degree and searching for something that would make sense again.

"I want us to move in together and start something that is ours, ours together and all the progress that entails with us constructing a life". " I want to have dinner with you in the evening and wake up with you in the morning"!

She was speechless and did not know what to say but the last several months have been amazing and all felt so right to her on all levels.

"I feel like I have known you for so long" she said looking into his eyes beneath the stars

"You have, you were just waiting to meet me". " Say yes Amber".

"I can work or go to school but I do have that savings from my parents". He says with growing enthusiasm " We can get the best place and furnish it and it will be ours to come home to every day, It will be ours Amber and you will be free of your mother"!

"Say yes Amber". Now speaking a little bit softer but both hands on each side of her shoulders staring into her eyes.

"Ok Jack" ......" Yes I will move in with you"! she offers as a smile appears from her face and Jack grabs her bringing her close to him and him howling into the night air as he twirls her in circles.

"I cant wait to tell your mother"! were his last words as he continued to twirl her on the sand of the beach beneath the stars and moon of where they had their first walk together as Jack and Amber.

Michael sat in the family owned bar/ restaurant that he managed and reflected on Amber and her friend Jack. Michael was always close with

Amber growing up even though they lived in different states but that fateful trip and months he spent in Texas with her had brought them closer than anyone else he had been involved with.

He always felt responsible for that event being the person who came up with the idea and brought them to the empty house and felt he provided the forum for such an event to take place. He left her in there with Jessie while he disappeared to serve his own needs and had since the incident felt responsible.

He was not at the entire trial but had to testify to the events or his account of them for the prosecution and did play a role in the justice the Clevinger Family had felt was served.

He had returned to California and it would not be long thereafter the trial had concluded that she and her family would join him and his in California and they would all work to resolve the tragedy that had taken place.

Michael felt he needed to watch over and assist in any capacity to ensure that she was better, she was healing and that she was safe. They grew far closer in the years spent in California and by all accounts had about been inseparable and he also knew that he had helped serve as a buffer or an outlet for her to discuss her frustrations with her mother's increasing and growing grip she was having on Amber and it was also known by Michael that her mother, in addition to his own guilt, felt he was somewhat responsible for the events of that evening and had they not been there they would not have occurred.

Michaels relentless involvement and constant presence in time did allow that to pass and he even had made the confession to her he had felt responsible and would never let her be hurt again which strengthened their bond because they did share the common denominator of Ambers safety and happiness.

So as he sat there pondering the visit and reminiscing on the past he looked at the bar patrons seated and watching the television or conversing with one another and there sat a detective named Tommy Reynolds.

Tommy had gone to school with his father and they had known each other most of their lives. Tommy had been a regular at the family owned bar since his father had bought it so Michael sees the seat empty next to him and a window for an idea he has just conjured up to satisfy the nagging suspicion he has felt since the moment he met Jack Rodan.

"Hey Tommy" Michael says as he approaches the bar.

"Mikey" the jovial detective says in a booming voice as he turns to shake his hands.

"You having dinner, we have done a 3 cheese tortellini with Alfredo sauce broccoli, mushroom and I personally like to add bacon for a special tonight".

"No, No I just stopped in to have a drink before heading home. Anna is making dinner and she would kill me if I had the bacon". He returns " How are you kid"?

"I have a question due to a concern, do you have a moment"? he asked

"Of course Mikey, is this something your dad knows about"? He asked while gesturing for Michael to take the seat next to him which Michael did to make this more comfortable because he has never asked anything like this before but who better than a Detective he has known his whole life.

"You know my cousin Amber, the one that moved here from Texas 5 years ago"?

"Sure, I have heard your dad and you talk about her and met her in here once. Why"?

"What you don't know is that she had a bad issue with something in Texas that brought her here and it hurt her and it hurt me because I was there and felt responsible". He starts while Tommy just listens and nods affirming his retaining of is being said.

"She introduced me to, well I don't know what he is but he is with her a lot and has been for some time now meaning this is not just a date. They are becoming closer and I don't know why but it, he bothers me" He explains.

"Ok"? Tommy says pausing.

"If I give you his name can run a check on him for me and just tell me what you find, Can you do that please I don't want to see Amber get hurt again".

"I can do that Mikey sure. I look at it first thing tomorrow when I get in. What's his name"?

"Jack Rodan". Michael says looking Tommy in the eye before Tommy takes out his flip notebook he keeps in his blazer pocket for moments like this when he needs to write something down.

"Jack Rodan". He says more to himself as he records the name in his notebook.

"I will let you know what I find out okay".

"Thank you". He says to Tommy finishing with " Dinner is on me next time okay"?

Camille is losing her mind running through the events of her life that has led her to this moment. She had a family, even if that family was not the best family it was hers that she had built with a man she fell in love with and stayed with far beyond when she should have.

Her son was taken from her at a time when she had a miscarriage from a pregnancy she was not even sure she had wanted. She had to attend a trial where he son was convicted of rape and would go away for 5 years while her husband would part, now knowing that it was murder and the people responsible for that murder are looking for or now know where Jessie is.

She has fled a country twice, she inherited money now has a new identity including not looking like she has always looked her whole life every time she looks into the mirror and had started to fall for the man that did that to her face and he has armed security guards all around him at all times and performs illegal surgeries to help people like her and her son flee.

"What is happening" she asked herself aloud but in a quiet tone as she stares into the mirror of the master bathroom when a knock is heard of the master bedroom door.

"Yes" she says " Who is it"?

"It is Nathanial Mam, May I come in"?

She opens the door and is met by Nathanial who is alone but she sees the gun peeking out from his blazer.

"What is happening"? she asked in a menacing tone and followed the first question with another " Where is Nelson"?

"Have you spoken to anyone and I know that your son called is he still in Cardiff"?

"I am not saying anything until you tell me what is happening"!

"Mrs Ritchards the men from Dallas feel they have a bargaining point to negotiate with you regarding your inheritance is what I know and that they know where your son is and will him if you do not have that discussion with them because they not only feel having your son would motivate you but also the police in regards to insurance fraud and perhaps even that you had him killed"!

"Where are you in all of this"? Her voice elevating and not feeling that afraid at the moment " You work for Nelson how do you even know anything about these men and we paid them $50,000 which is what Jessie promised them"!

"I do work for Nelson and have for some time. My face". He says pointing to it with his right index finger. " Those men were responsible for this and said to me that if I did not get you to speak with them they would end me and come after my family that is why I am here and how I know them".

"Nelson" She says to him " Nelson will stop them and protect us all". She offers to reason with the request.

"If you tell Nelson, they will kill your son and then go after my family, understand"! he fires back knowing his time is running out being up here.

"Our only option is to get you to them and listen to what they want, I do not know anything about what you paid them or what was promised but they do have leverage here because if they go to the police and the insurance company about murder your change of identity will be evidence of guilt because if they go looking for Kelly who will they find"? He asked then pausing before adding.

"They do have your sons fingerprints on record so it will prove that he had his identity changed and that he fled and he fled with money financed by a murder so if you are both not killed he will go back to jail and this time you will go with him"!

She begins to pace rubbing her temples and then sweeping her hair back with both hands.

"Where do I meet them"? She asked defeated with options that at the moment she sees no other.

"I don't know but I do have a way to reach them and at least this keeps everyone alive and out of jail, it is like a business proposition. I will let you know how we proceed from here but again you have to act like nothing is wrong and everything is fine Mrs Ritchards".

"Can you do that"? He asked to finalize their discussion.

"I did it for years with my husband so yes I can do that but when will I know"?

"I will work on it right away, I want this over as quickly as you do and everything will be fine but tell me he is still in California just so this does not get any more complicated"?

"I don't know where he is and far as I am concerned that makes us in a better position them not knowing because if they don't have him then there is nothing to discuss right"? she counters

"Not cooperating is complicating this and with men like this that usually ends poorly as you know with the circumstances of your late husband, is he still there"?

"Yes"!

Nathanial calls the number he was given when in Dallas which turns out to be the bar he almost lost his life. He was told to ask for Knight and leave the name El Paso and that would get him touch.

There is a long pause until a voice comes onto the line that is first silent but you can hear the bar activity in the background.

"That you Paso"? He says into the phone

"Yes". One word response

"Do you have something for me"? He ask's already knowing the answer but awaits the sweet response.

"He is still in Cardiff and the mother will talk to you just need to know how and when"?

Laughing is coming from the other end of the phone line right into his ear " Well alright Paso I knew we were going to be good friends". " Your almost there Paso, almost there to where you can make some money, you do want that right"?

"Yes"

"Good so lets get mom on a flight with you to California for a family reunion, give me a number to reach you at so I can contact you once my team is there and finds him".

Jack and Amber have been looking at places all week and waiting for the perfect one that will be their own. Amber has never done this before so she is nervous but loving the days that are filled with apartment/home hunting even though it is exhausting the idea of their own place has grown on her tremendously.

They have viewed close to 20 and stop for lunch to talk about what they have seen. They chose In and Out for some Double Doubles and sit outside even though the air is much cooler now with it being Fall time but felt the fresh air would help them think and process

"What do you think"? He asked as they waited for their number to be called

"So many choices, they all almost look alike now but what are we going to do about furniture"?

"That part is easy". He smiles looking at her " We will furnish it with what we need once we find what we want and you will love that part, I know that I will". He adds still smiling.

"Have we found what we are looking for"? He asked her

"I don't know". She moans playfully

"Maybe we need to look further like in Solana Beach or Del Mar, have you been down there:? He offers

"How far is that from here"? She asked

"Not far at all, lets eat and take the drive so you can see the distance and the area and see what we think plus it may give you your inspiration for your next piece".

She liked that idea and loved the lunch it was just what they needed to continue with their search. The drive was beautiful but not long and they remained on the coast. Driving the area to get familiar " So this is Solana Beach" She says looking out the window.

"What about those".? He says pointing to an Apartment community entitled Solana Horizons.

"I like the name and this area is beautiful".

"Do you want to stop and look at one"? He asked

"Yes". She responds enthusiastically

They pull into the front and park. They walk into a small but nicely furnished living area with offices in the back. There is a view of a pool through the back French doors leading to the back and before going towards the offices the head towards those French doors to take in the back area and it's lush landscape. He says nothing but looks at her taking it in and sees her smiling so he takes her hand and they proceed to the offices to ask for a tour.

The woman seated behind the desk was on the phone and offered a finger to gesture she would only be a moment and to take a seat at the 2 chairs before them at the front of the desk.

The woman hangs up the phone and exhales " Ahhh, How may I help you"?

"Do you have any vacancies that we can view"?

"You 2 are in luck because yes I do and what a beautiful couple you 2 are". She adds grabbing a key and making Amber and Jack smile. " Ok you 2 let's take a tour of your new home"!

They exit out the back French doors so they could start with the pool and hot tub area and as they walk past she mentions that with the cooler weather coming for Winter that the hot tub would be a treasure to come home to and enjoy once again making them each smile.

––––––––––––––––––

Grass, foliage, shrubs and flowers line the sidewalks and frame the buildings. They are 3 stories in height and the one they are being shown resides on the 2nd floor. Her key unlocks, opens the door and walks them inside where they are met with a good sized living room with lots of natural light from the patio door that leads to a balcony to the right of them and a breakfast bar and kitchen to the left.

They stay together but Amber is moving much faster excited to see each room. She opens cabinets in the kitchen and envisions putting groceries away and cooking in here. The dining area is right off of the kitchen space and met by the living area which then leads to a hallway where 2 bedrooms are located. They walk into the master first to take that in for some time followed by the second bedroom where Jack, still holding her hand says " This can be where you paint"!

She squeezes his hand at that sentiment then walks back to the living space and out to the balcony which has a view of the many colors nature has provided for them and they both can feel remnants of the ocean breeze that is just blocks away.

"I can paint here too"! She adds now making him smile.

"Have we found what we are looking for"? He asked again feeling much more sound about the question than he had asking it an hour ago. Then before allowing her to respond he adds " It is not far from your parents or the studio, it has a second bedroom for you to paint and we can start furnishing it as soon as we get the key:.

"It also has more beach for more walks together too". She offers looking down at their hands clasped together then back up and into his eyes.

"Did we find what we are looking for"? He asked one last time.

"Yes"! Then moving into his arms as they wrap around her into a hug.

"What do you need us to do"? He says to the woman standing with them in the living room and she invites them back to her office to do the paperwork for their new home at Solana Horizons.

As they drove home excited about the chapters to come and what it all meant she says that she wants to speak to her mom about having him over for dinner so they can tell her family which he is in total agreement about and is at least one part of his plan to settle a debt with The Clevinger Family.

Stay focused he says to himself in the car on the way back to Cardiff. We are getting closer and closer every day to redemption so just stay focused!

Amber has the discussion with her mother regarding Jack coming and staying for dinner but did not ask if it was alright more of a declaration which her mother agreed.

Jack offers to set the table while Mrs Clevinger continued to finish cooking and her husband has not yet arrived. It is almost 7pm when the Dr. comes through the front door immediately taking the scent coming from the kitchen before announcing that he is home.

Amber and Jack were in the loving room and she gets up from the couch to greet him with a hug and " Hello Daddy". He makes eye contact with Jack who is now standing and Jack offers " Hello Dr. Clevinger".

"Hello Jack, are you staying for dinner"? He asked and Amber would respond for him with a " Yes".

Dr. Clevinger walks into the kitchen to greet his wife and asked what she was making as he approaches her for a hug and a kiss.

"I have prepared a Roast with all of the vegetables you love and a salad" She says kissing him.

"Do you want to change or do you want a drink"? She offers.

"No, I'm good thank you do you need any help"

"No, Jack and Amber set the table and everything will be ready in just a moment, How about some wine I opened some Cabernet for the Roast"?

"On second thought a glass does sound good". He proceeded to where the glasses are in the cabinet followed by the bottle on the counter. Nancy Clevinger pulled the roast, separated and plated then called for everyone to the dinner table.

Jack enters the room to enjoy not only the meal that looked and smelled amazing but the show that was about to begin at the Clevinger dinner table.

"How was your day Daddy"? Amber asked to start the conversation which he had replied with what seemed like the mundane task's that any job would take on given the amount of time you have done them. He then asked, to change the subject

"What did you guys do today"?

The room filled with silence only broken by the clatter of silver against china until Amber spoke.

"Jack wanted to go look at apartments". She stated then silence again for a moment and only Jack was the one aware that a anticipation was simmering because their expression was blank or unconcerned meaning it has not hit or registered yet.

"Does this mean you are staying in the area Jack"? Nancy asked him again silence following for just a moment yet the clatter of silver and china continued.

"Yes, Yes it does".

"Well at least that means you will be getting out of that hotel, I could not imagine that feeling very comfortable". Nancy said

"I have made do and although your right Mrs Clevinger it has not been like home I have a plan that will change that". Jack responded.

"Did you find anything that you liked Jack"? Dr Clevinger asked

"I found what I was looking for". Jack says smiling still waiting for that moment of awareness, acknowledgment, the click if you will.

"I have something I want to share". Amber declares setting down her silverware and taking a drink from her glass as to pause and breathe before sharing her statement.

"Jack and I are moving in together"!

There it is Jack thought to himself now lets see how Nancy likes losing her daughter as he makes eye contact with the mother the entire time taking in the click, enjoying the click while trying not to smile but he said it was ok because they are supposed to be happy and therefore no one would think anything about him smiling other than the 2 of them were happy so allowed himself to smile and celebrate the click.

"What"! Nancy says with an elevated tone while the Dr. is trying to make eye contact with his wife.

Jack grabs the hand of Amber that is rested on the table top so it is in view of Nancy while making eye contact and smiling. This makes Nancy seethe.

"We have not discussed this, when did you decide this and why was it not discussed with us"? Nancy voice dominant and controlling while still elevated and clearly agitated.

"Jack and I discussed it and we both really want to do this". Amber said adding " Mom calm down".

"We Amber, this family discussing it not you and Jack"! Nancy's voice much louder.

"I wont have this Amber, I wont"!

"Mom calm down, Daddy tell her to calm down. I am 18 and do not have to discuss everything I do with you to get your permission".

"Amber". Her father says in an effort to deescalate the environment. " We both want you happy when he is interrupted by Nancy " You are not moving out"!

"Nancy" The Dr. elevates his voice agitated he was cut off.

"I am done with you telling me what to do, I can't live like that anymore and I wont" She says rising to her feet taking Jack with her. She stands there at the table for only a moment until Nancy is also at her feet trying to get in the way of the departing Amber.

"Get out of my way"! Amber says her voice now elevated

"This is a mistake Amber we just need to discuss it and you will see". Nancy says reasoning.

"Then it will be my mistake but from a decision I made and not another one you made for me, let's go were leaving". She demands then leading Jack by the hand passed her mother and towards the front door but not until Jack slows her pace to a stop to turn and face the mother and father.

His smile is gone and his eye contact takes one parent at a time before finalizing his gaze on the mother and says " Thank you for dinner"!

50

AMBER would not return home that evening and stayed with Jack rising that next morning with anxiety which Jack comforted with support for her doing the right thing to establish herself as an independent and setting off on her own to be who she is which she found that she liked the idea of that concept

"Do you want to go furniture shopping today so we can get what we need for the apartment"? Jack asked.

"I think I need to go see Michael and Lillian so I can tell them, can we meet after"?

"Of course". He returned then added. " I will find some places that we can go and together we can pick out everything that we want to move in and make a home of our own". He said kissing her. " I will be here waiting just call me here at the hotel when you are on your way."

She smiled at him and proceeded to the shower to get ready for her errands so she could return and wanted to go furniture shopping to as he put it " Make a home of her own".

She drove to the restaurant to see Michael first hoping he would be there this early which he was and she found him doing inventory of the bar before the place opened.

"What are you doing here so early"? He asked surprised to see her.

"I was going to ask you the same thing but it looks like you are actually working"! she said jokingly

"Funny, I do have a role here and take it very seriously when I must, What's up"?

"I told my parents I am moving out last night"! she said flatly looking right at him where he stopped everything he was counting to return her eye contact.

"Wow, How did that go"? He said curious about the answer.

"How do you think it went, you know my mother". She returned sitting in a chair with each of her hands under her thighs while one leg bounced up and down in a fast repetition.

"Are you Okay"? He said cautiously then finally " Where are you moving, you are staying here right"?

"Yes, we are not moving far at all there is a place at Solana Beach we found which is real close".

Michael focused on the " we" and really wanted to understand more as he went right in on that word. " We"? he asked.

"Jack and I"! she returned and then continued before he could speak again. " We have been looking all week and then found a great place called Horizons at Solana Beach down by Del Mar so it is close to home, close to the studio and as much as I could get away from you it is close to you too and we are going furniture shopping today to furnish it".

"Your moving in Jack"? He said in a concerning tone. " How long have you known him"?

"We have been seeing each other for 3 months but it is not the time we have been together it is the time we have spent together". She said not sure if that even made sense in our own mind.

"He gets me, it is like we have known each other for such a long time and his timing, it is like it has been meant to be you know, haven't you ever felt like that"?

Michael was silent for a moment and processing but while he was he was looking at her sitting in the chair and was reminded of the little naïve girl she has always been but she did look happy and it has been a long time since he has seen that side of her which made him smile.

"You really like him don't you"? He asked quieter.

"Of course I do I would not be moving in with him if I didn't, don't you"? She fired back.

"I don't know Amber I don't really know him but have not spent the time with him the way that you have it just seems so fast is all, are you sure"?

"I know that I do want to start my life that does not have mother engrained in every component and us moving into our own place to start a life that is each of ours I do feel sure about"!

They talked more in the empty restaurant just the 2 of them until service staff started to show up to begin doing opening side work to begin their shift and open the restaurant for lunch business. She could always depend on Michael and needed him to support her in her decision and be happy for her they concluded with a hug and she departed for the gallery. Michael watched her leave and in many ways was happy for her for standing up to her mom and having conviction to do this which if it were starting her life he truly supported that but he did have a conversation with Tommy about Jack and needed to get that update before she moved in.

The gallery had patrons milling about with Jayne speaking with 2 of the guest who were looking at the paintings on display but did not let her get far into the gallery without Jayne offering a genuine " Good afternoon Amber, she is in her office". Amber climbed the stairs leading to Lillians office and took in all the energy from space with each step. She loved this place, the energy, the light, the creativity and the people in it. She was fortunate to have found it or it find her.

She knocked on the door until she heard Lillian reply " Come in".

"Oh good day". Lillian said rising to her feet and coming around her desk to greet Amber " Always a good day when I get to see you Amber". She said again as they hugged which made Amber smile and feel completely at ease.

"What brings you here dear, another piece to unveil"? Lillian said returning to her seat.

"Not a piece yet but an update to unveil none the less". She returned

"What might that be, what is new in your world dear"?

"I told my parents I was moving out, Jack and I have found a place down at Solana Beach and we are going furniture shopping today when I leave here. I just had to tell you".

Lillian said nothing for a moment and rocked in her desk chair gently searching her thought for the proper response. " The decision to move out seems to serve you well as you present a light that is different than the light I have seen before, How do you feel"?

"Excited, Nervous, Happy, Ughh How did you feel when you first moved out"? Amber asked.

Lillian laughs, " Oh that was so long ago dear but yes I too felt all of those things the excited, the nervous and the happy". " Are you and your mother okay"?

"No, but she will have to be. My mind is made up and want to do this and it is time to do this you know". She said looking at Lillian.

"You and Jack certainly have a had a whirlwind romance but it is not uncommon for such a romance to move people to quick decisions when in the throws of the moment and the furniture shopping that will be an adventure as will be your first nights away from what has been as you settle into what is and will be". Lillian paused for the moment allowing the sentiment to settle then added " Are you sure Amber that this is what you want to do and whom with"?

Amber takes very little seconds to respond and offers her yes with a smile illuminating more of the light Lillian referred to earlier. " The apartment even has a room for me to paint".

"Well then congratulations are in order for your decision and new chapter so go and do your shopping and begin just know I do wish to be invited over to see it and am anxious to see the next work you produce while on this path and chapter". Lillian said again rising to her feet and coming around her desk to embrace Amber.

"You and Jayne will be over and I will come by when we are all moved in so you both can see it". She said to Lillian and Lillian had each hand in Ambers before they broke and Amber turned towards the door to exit. " Thank you Lillian". She said then departed to meet Jack.

Jack had found a consignment store for furniture where they could meet and go row to row in search of the items they both felt would bring their new apartment to life. The couches, chairs, dining tables and bedroom sets. All the patterns, fabrics and colors they spent hours just sitting in, laying on and laughing the day away enjoying the moment they were in and seeing it come to life, seeing the items in the space that would be their own.

Arrangements for delivery made with the store clerk and a date set based upon their move in but as exhausted as Amber was he reminded her they had more stops to make because we have places to sit and sleep but nothing to cook with or eat it on as she buried her head into her hands making a growling sound and off they went to the mall.

Boxes of colored pans, pattern plates, silverware, glassware, towels, bedding, pillow cases all filled the carts which was loaded into the car and taken to the hotel they were staying in until their move in date which was 48 hours away but the events of the last day have made that move in date more of a reality that they each were anticipating. They needed to coordinate a rental truck for the move of Ambers things she wished to take with her.

They find themselves at Ambers house going through and removing the items to be taken to the apartment. Her father is not there but her mother is and continues to seethe and mourn at the same time weeping in between bouts of anger but trying to show either as they move the things from her room to be loaded onto a truck. Nancy attempts to help but does so in such a slow manner attempting to negate what is happening from happening or slow the process at the very least.

Nancy is in her daughters room going through items and reliving the moments first in her mind then in an effort to remind Amber of the moments they shared as she grew up which Amber did enjoy and her mothers words made her smile also reflecting on each story and memory of each item that was being discussed. Jack remained quiet but enjoyed every moment of the sorrow he felt emanating from Nancy Clevinger and would on occasion offer a sentiment of the reminiscing with " That's beautiful or how sweet".

The truck was loaded with the items from The Clevinger house and her father has now arrived as he wanted to be there to see his daughter off and offered to assist with the move in at the new apartment now that he was home but Jack assured him the furniture company has taken care of the transport and load in of what they have purchased and that he and Amber can handle the rest.

Ambers parents stand at the corner in front of a loaded truck of the items that their daughter once held in her room since she has been with them and the sentiment is hard for each of them to process. Their little girl is leaving and no words they can offer will prevent the truck and its contents from driving away to her new place so they make every effort to offer support for the inevitable and to console one another in the moment. Love you is exchanged and gone she is.

Getting the keys to their place and the loading in of things, boxes, furniture just everywhere was exhilarating for both of them and was something secretly Jack had never experienced either so it was not only a methodical plan that was working but he was enjoying himself in the process. They would spend the next several days putting everything away, decorating and enjoying the moment they were in whether it be eating take out or the attempt from either one to cook a meal that evening which was trial and error for both but it was fun and they were both loving the now.

51

ICHAEL is called by the hostess during their lunch business for a call at the Host podium. He answers to find it is Detective and family friend Tommy Reynolds following up on his promise to Michael regarding his looking into Jack Rodan. Michael asked for him to hold and for the host to transfer the call to the office in 2 minutes which she does so he can speak privately and hear better due to the volume in the restaurant.

"Tommy, thanks for getting back to me what did you find out"? He asked

"Not much kid, there is no criminal background, hell I don't even see a traffic ticket anywhere or even an fine for an overdue book. It looks like his parents moved around a lot you know like military and they passed away about a year ago".

All things that Jack had communicated the first time they had met so why did he still have such an odd felling there was something more. The one thing that bothered him the most was how much he would not look him in the eye that first meeting, it was like at every chance he could he would look somewhere else while talking. He was avoiding something.

"There is something else there Tommy, I know it and I can feel it. I don't know what it is but it is not on paper". Michael finally says back into the phone hearing Tommy ask if he was there.

"What do you want me to do kid, you wanted some background I got you the background and its clean". The seasoned Detective adds.

"How hard would it be to follow him, just a few times to see where he goes and what he does, I can go with you like on a ride along"?

"Wait what, you want to follow him"?

"Something does not feel right and I have always trusted my instincts before which has served me well. You're the Detective if something did not feel right wouldn't you follow it and see where it leads especially if it were family"? Michael asked.

"Okay, I would have to do it on my off time which there is a lot going on so I will have to get back to you as to when but I will schedule some off time to tail him and see where it leads alright Michael"?

"Thank you Tommy, you know how to find me but I do want to go with you no matter what time it is I will make it happen I want to see where he goes and what he does, who he sees to get this out of my system. Amber is moving in with him right now and if there anything there I need to let her know and get her out of there".

———————————

Knight contacts the Prichard estate to speak with Nathanial and sets up for Nathanial to escort the mom there and get a hotel Knight has chosen where they will be notified of further instructions with where to meet and to remind the mom if she speaks to anyone or involves anyone other than who is presently accounted for they will kill her son. Knight calculates for the 2 days of travel and what he anticipates to be the time it will take to find the son and coordinates to meet them in 5 days.

Knight is packing his things for their drive to California. He will not be flying so they pack their weapons and they want to have a vehicle of their own to be able to transport the mom and son wherever they must and they need weapons to control Nathanial. He brings 2 of his enforcers with him and they set out for their trip traveling west.

Taking turns driving and stopping when they must they travel state to state going through the plan to find and detain the son so they have leverage with the mom for the tax they want to impose on the inheritance and insurance money. Once they find the son they will meet with Nathanial and the mom to take another trip to the bank for a final withdraw to conclude their business.

The drive is pleasant and soothing but that could be because of the money Knight is already counting in his head as the largest take he and his crew have done which could even finance a growth in their empire that is west. The further and further they get the sun is different from Texas, the wind is different, the palm trees and it all feels so good. The boy is not big, his mom is not an issue and only wants to protect her son and even the big guy he calls Paso there is nothing in it for him but to turn over the 2 and get some money himself this has got to be the easiest take he thinks congratulating himself for taking the initiative to go after these 2 the moment he got out and reminds himself to thank his old friend Mac for bringing them all together.

Nathanial finds the opportunity to communicate with Camille that they are to travel to California to meet with Knight as discussed so she can make a payment to have her son released and return to their lives for good.

"What I do I tell Nelson"? She asked him

"That your son called and wants you to come visit and since it is your first time there you would like me to come with you as an escort, he will support and agree with that".

"And what if he wants to come with me, he will know I have been keeping something from him".

"This is the perfect time he has clients at the bar conducting business, he has to be here to complete their surgery and he always stays through till the end to ensure the satisfaction".

"You wont be gone long and this will not take long you just want to see your son and see what he has been doing while away. Nelson will agree and even want you to go to get out of the house for a little bit while he finishes his work". He says encouragingly

"Tell him tonight and you can start to schedule the flights and the hotel rooms that Knight said we were to check in at and make sure you let him know that you would feel more comfortable if I was there, I am telling you he will agree".

Camille thinks, processes and agrees with Nathanial that she can speak with Nelson tonight about her traveling to see her son and has become accustomed to the presence of the guards and would appreciate it if Nathanial could accompany her for a few days in California.

The morning light is coming through open blinds in the living room of their apartment. Jack has been up for more than an hour pleased with himself that his plan has worked thus far and contemplates what his next moves should be to conclude his debt to The Amber and her family as he hears her stir in the bedroom then the sounds of her getting up and making her way to him in the living room where he is looking out the balcony window to the landscape below.

She approaches him with a tired sounding voice that barely gets out " Good morning". As she kisses him.

"Good morning to you". He returns and smiles adding " How did you sleep"?

"Sooooo gooood" She announces while stretching her arms out still waking up.

"It feels good here, waking up here, with you". He offers which makes her smile now much more awake.

Jack looks around the apartment where it has been furnished with warm inviting elements and says to her " We have done good, we are in a good place".

"I like it" She returns then adds " For the first time I do feel free and am happier than I have been in a long time". Moving back to him to hug him.

"Thank you for coming into my life". She says while they embrace.

"The pleasure has been all mine, why don't you paint today.

You have not done that here yet". He says to her backing out of the embrace to look her in the eyes.

"I like that idea, not sure what I will paint but I can get in there and see what comes out. What about you"? She asked.

"I have some errands I can run and check back on you when I get back". He answers.

Knight and his team have made it through the rest of Texas, New Mexico, Arizona, Nevada and are approaching their destination of Cardiff. When they do arrive they pull over for some gas and to stretch. The journey has been long but adrenaline has fueled them to achieve locating their target and their money.

Knight thinks out loud to himself but appears he is speaking to the other 2 men. Ok so we know he is in a hotel and if we think logically he is a kid with some money so he will not be staying in a low end place however judging from what we are seeing there is not a lot of low end places nor based on the size of this area there are also not a lot of hotels to begin with.

"Lets get some landmarks and familiar with the area locating as many hotels as we can on this main road then we will backtrack and go office to office asking the clerk if they have seen him". Knight says aloud.

"How do we get the clerk to tell us what room he is in if we do find him"? One of them asked.

"Lets see how many hotels we are talking first and then let me handle that". He says satisfying the question asked.

They drive up the main route or highway leading through Cardiff until it turns into another city then turn around making their back the way they came counting 5 hotels on the main road with varying degrees of how nice they appear on the outside.

"He would not venture off the main road right since he was not sure of where he was going he would stay on the main road to avoid getting lost this way he would always know how to get back to where he was"? Knight says still more speaking to himself then those in the car but one answers " I would".

"Lets start here". Knight says pointing to his right directing the driver to pull over. Knight gets out of the vehicle and heads to the front office where fortunately there is no other guest present only the clerk behind the desk.

"How may I help you"? The woman asked in a cheerful manner.

"I am looking for my son who drove here a few weeks ago but he did not tell me which hotel he was staying in only that he was in Cardiff. He is about 5'10 medium build about 19 and has short hair named Jack Rodan and wanted to know if he was here"?

"That does not sound familiar and I have been here each afternoon".

"Are you sure, I have not heard from him and am worried I really need to find him".

"I am sorry sir" She says again with a look of consolation for not being able to help.

Knight directs his driver to 3 of the 5 remaining hotels where he is met with the same conclusion of the name nor the description matching but at the last one which is nice he does find another female clerk that is just too friendly who did not recognize the name because she hears so many but the description she did because he was the youngest guest they have had in a long time that stayed with them for such a duration. Knight portrayed a scared and worried father trying to locate him.

"It is against our policy to give out guest information so even if he was here I could not tell you the room number but I will say, since you are so concerned, that he has been here".

"Has been here"? He repeated " So he is no longer here"? Asking for clarification then quickly continued. " Did he say where he was going, He is my son and I am worried. He asked me to meet him here that is why I am here".

"I can only say that he had been here, I was not here when he checked out but I know the room he was in is now vacant. I am sorry".

Knight thanked her and left the office confused. He found him, he knew he was in Cardiff and assumed he had been staying in a hotel which he was right, they find the hotel to find he had just checked out shortly before their arrival.

"How could that be"? He mumbles walking towards the car and as he reached for the door handle to open the car door he says " The mother"!

"What happened, did you find him"? one of them asked as he gets into the car and stares out the windshield.

"He was here". Knight said breathing in his nose and out his mouth audibly apparently angry.

He was, where is he now"?

"The mother must have told him we were coming and he checked out".

"So what now, we have already checked all the hotels here and no one has seen him"?

"Paso will be here with the mother in a day, she has to know where he is so we will get rooms in the same hotel I told them to get one and wait for their arrival then follow them or her to him which is fine because that way we get them both at the same time". He said looking at the driver.

"So where to"? The driver asked.

"The Marriot, then we wait because she does not know we don't know where he is. She still thinks we do which is exactly why she is coning and will be here". He said

52

CAMILLE had her conversation with Nelson as planned and said all the things Nathanial had suggested which worked including the escort request preferring Nathanial as the guard. He would miss her but had been working so much he understand her need to get out of the house and of course see her son which she had not since The Caymans. The flight was booked and her bags packed as well as Nathanial. Nelson did insist on driving with her to the airport to see her off.

"I miss you already"! He said to her making her smile and even blush. She did not feel good about not telling him the truth but just did not know what to do about any of this but make the payment the men were seeking and leave them alone so they could move on with their lives. She never had a lot of money herself so it was not a concern to her to part ways with a large sum of it as long as they had what they needed to have a good life together her and her son.

She was not sure what this was or where it was going with Nelson only that it had been such a long time since she had felt so comfortable with someone and she enjoyed that as well as the attention he has paid her.

"I will call when we get there and keep you updated, go commit yourself to work and we will be back before you know it. I just miss and need to see my son".

"Of course you do and next time I will be with you or he will come here if he wants to, he may not want to come back to Texas but I would love a trip to California".

"Nathanial". He says now looking at him " I am trusting you will be with her at her side as well as give her privacy when she wishes"?

"Of course Mr Pritchard" Nathanial replies as Nelson moves in to shake his hand then embrace his Camille one last time before boarding the flight.

The flight there is filled once again with many emotions of trying to understand, forget, move past and to where? She thought to herself in silence. She did not even have a way to reach him right now and has not spoken to him since she warned him they were coming and when she tried him at the hotel it had stated he checked out which she was glad but she did not know where he was yet they did.

She thought only of getting there, seeing him and paying whatever debt there was left to move on. He sounded happy where he was and she was happy where she was again doing whatever it was that her and Nelson were doing. " I need this to be over"! She said looking towards Nathanial.

"It will all be over soon" He responded back reassuring even himself. " Soon "!

Jack while running his errands had made his way to a phone so that he could call the El Paso number his mother had been staying and how he had reached her previous times. Calling he asked to speak to Camille where the person on the other end had responded that she was not there at the moment. Jack inquired when she would be back where he was met with an uncertain response.

"This is her son, is there a way that I can reach her where she is or someone I can speak to that knows where she is"?

"Please hold" The woman replied while Jack waited for some source of information.

"Hello, this is Nelson Pritchard". The man announced taking the phone.

"Nelson, This is Jack Camilles son. May I speak with her"?

"Jack, It is wonderful to hear from you. Of course you can speak with her she will be there with you shortly she left a couple hours ago and should be landing at about 4pm your time. Is everything ok"?

Jack was stunned and mad at himself that he had not called sooner to let her know he was leaving the hotel and would have a new contact number. Why was she coming here he thought? He has been so fixated with the move with Amber and the apartment and setting up his plan he had not thought to communicate with his mom.

"Jack"? Nelson asked.

"Yes Nelson everything is fine I wanted to wish her a safe flight but must have got the time difference mixed up. 4:00pm you said"? He asked

"4:00pm your time, she was so excited to see you and has missed you tremendously but I know you already know that. Is there chances of you taking a trip back this way in the future"?

"There will definitely be a trip in the future just not sure where at the moment and have some things to tie up here before I do anything". He said his mind still reeling that she would be here and what that meant. How would he explain not being at the hotel and where he is staying and that he is staying with someone because Amber thinks his parents are dead? Mom could mess this whole thing up and he cannot let that happen he is so close to pulling this whole thing off and just fucking this family up and wants nothing more at the moment but to see that a reality.

"Nelson I have to go it was great speaking with you and hope to see you soon". He rushed

"Ok Jack have fun with your mom I am sure your time together will be unforgettable"!

"Nelson one last thing I do not have the paper I wrote it all down on, what hotel is she staying at"? Jack asked

"Marriot she said, there in Cardiff". Nelson replied.

Jack thanked him and hung up the phone trying to think of what his next step is.

Michael still could not get Jack out of his mind and even though what Tommy told him had checked out for some reason it all still felt to neat. There was something more and he just did not know what it was only that he needed to figure and find it out. He called Tommy at the precinct to ask when he gets off.

"Unless there is a rash of crime that occurs I will leave here at 4:00 was even thinking of stopping by your place for one of those specials, what you got on for tonight"?

"Forget that Tommy I will get you dinner somewhere else but need your help with that ting I asked you to look into". Michael asked somewhat rattled.

"Kid he checked out, there is nothing there". Tommy replied still thinking about what the special was".

"I want us to follow him, like I asked before. Your off we can do it today I just want to see where he goes and does ... Its important"!

"Will this get you to shut up about it if we do"? Tommy asked

"Yes, I am at the restaurant just come by here and get me when your off and we can go by the apartment and go from there".

"Alright, alright but I need to eat first have my dinner there waiting and we will go tail your friend".

"Done".

Jack returns to the apartment knowing he needs to see Amber and check in then make up something about where he has to go for a few hours when he would normally be home with her as the day gets later. He checks his watch and it is almost 4 so he has some time just need to think about what to tell Amber to explain why I will be gone for a while.

Tommy arrives at the restaurant and as promised his dinner special is ready at the bar where he eats with Michael seated next to him watching him and encouraging him to hurry which is pissing Tommy off but he does finish washing it down with some water and Michael stands from the bar stool in an effort to convince Tommy to do the same saying " You ready"?

Jack greets Amber with a kiss asking how her day has been which she replied with some painting effort and enjoyed the moment doing that for the first time in their new apartment. She inquired to his day which he went on about being at book stores reading on some topics that have inspired him to go to the College Campus and look up registration courses for the summer.

She loved that idea and asked when he was going maybe she could join him so they could go back to school together.

"I would love that" . She said to him hugging him

"I would too but at least for this trip I just want to go see what classes there are how long, how many you know just feel it out. Is it ok if I just go this time and then we go back together once I get a chance to see it"?

"If you really want to, I would rather go with you but if you feel like this is better then I understand". She said smiling at him and liking the concept of them going back to school to take some courses and she knew her parents would love that.

"I will be back later, it is a little bit of a drive and not sure how long I will be there".

"What about dinner, aren't you hungry do you want to eat before you go"? She asked

"No I will get something there. Don't worry I will be back as soon as I can you just relax and enjoy the time to yourself".

"I had that all day but go do what you must and come back to me". She said affectionately

"I will" He ended coming in for one last kiss and hug then exiting the apartment for his car.

Camille and Nathanial arrive at The Marriot and check in but to her dislike she realizes they have only one room so Nathanial can hear if the phone rings and see where she goes.

"Now what"? She asked him.

"We wait". He said turning on the TV " Someone will call and until then we wait".

Knight had been watching the front office for 24 hours waiting for the arrival of the mother and now he has got her and recognized his comrade in this operation Paso. Now he knows they are there as planned and knows their hotel room so all they have to do is be patient and wait as well. His plan since they did not know where the son was and the mom did not know that was to wait for 24 hours and see if he somehow reached out to her and lead them to them both plus he is Paso on the inside helping navigate the operation so he had a man on their door watching and waiting for some sign of the next move.

Michael and Tommy arrive at the apartment complex that Amber had told him they were living and to the building number. Right away Michael recognizes the convertible Jack had been driving and was leaving the complex with the top up and he was alone.

"Turn around". He says to Tommy

"That's him the convertible".

"Alright, alright. I got him".

They make the turn and get behind the convertible following him where he goes which is not that far. He stops in at a gas station to what appears to be to make a call from the payphone.

"He was just at the apartment, why didn't he make the call there"? He asked Tommy.

"I don't know kid, I don't know".

Jack has called the Marriot to ask for the room of Camille Richards which she is registered and the call is transferred to the room bringing a brief sigh of relief to him.

"Hello". She answers

"Mom, what are you doing here"?

"I was told those men from Dallas had you and I was to come and settle one last payment for us to move on with our new lives".

"What, I have not seen them and I know they don't know where I am". He says.

"Jessie I don't know where you are but I need to see you. I am worried, I have not talked to you I need to see my son"!

"I know mom, are you alone"?

"I have one of Nelsons guards with me, I need to see you Jessie"!

"Do you have a pen"? He asked and proceeded to giver the name of the beach access that he and Amber had their 1st walk because it was the only beach area he was truly familiar with and could give instructions from their location knowing the route well.

"I can meet you there in about 30 minutes and you can see the sunset. Its private enough not to be disturbed or seen. Okay"?

"I will be there she said and offered I love to conclude the call".

Michael and Tommy watch Jack get back into his car and proceed on the highway headed back to Cardiff.

"Where is he"? Nathanial asked.

"We are going to meet him in 30 minutes here at this location". She said

They proceeded out the hotel room and the sight of them flew the man watching the door into a rush to return to the room where Knight was.

"They're moving" He says rushing into the door.

Knight jumps off the bed " You stay here in case anyone shows up and continue to watch the door and if the kid shows up get him and get him here quietly"!

"Done" the man responds tapping his gun in his waist

"Lets go"! Knight says to the man that was watching the door and they make their way to their car to get position on the departing vehicle and they follow it to its destination which was not far from the hotel.

The sun is dipping and darkening the sky to a dim orange and the neighborhood is quiet with families arriving home, making dinner, doing dishes and all those things that make up life after work. The mother and Nathanial make their way down to the beach access towards the lifeguard tower while Knight and his muscle tail them much slower not showing themselves on the sand. They instead maneuver through the brush and tall growth at the mouth of the beach access to hide and conceal their presence.

Jack arrives and makes every effort to locate a parking place which at this hour is difficult so he has to walk further than he wanted. Michael and Tommy have the same issue but because Tommy is a

Detective he has the ability to park where he wishes and write off the consequences if any. " Ambers parents live right up the road from here". He said to Tommy getting out of the car.

"Ok". Tommy replies

"Well what is he doing here by himself"?

"I guess were gonna find out". Tommy started towards the direction Jack was going.

Jack walked a full block before deciding to continue he went ahead and went up another pathway leading to the beach and decided to just walk from the sand to the guard tower as Michael and Tommy followed.

Jack could see the tower in a small distance along with 2 shadows in front of it against the dimming and darkening skyline. Tommy motions for Michael to stay back to avoid being seen or creating alarm even though Tommy was not taking the tailing of the boyfriend of his close friend sons cousin seriously he still did not know exactly what to expect.

Jack gets closer and in the darkness can make out his mother and a man he recognized from the space their procedures had been done. She rushes to him and continuously hugs and kisses him so happy to see him. From each distance in opposite vantage points Knight smiles seeing that each target is within his sights and grasp and Michael quizzingly wonders who Jack is seeing that is hugging and kissing him in that manner. Michael urges Tommy to follow him to move closer so he can hear what is being said and even make out the face of the 2 shadows.

"Oh Jessie it is so good to see you, are you okay"?

"Jessie"? Michael says quietly more to himself quizzingly.

"Mom you now I am happy to see you too but why are you here"? Jack asked her

Michael heard that as well and is perplexed first she called him Jessie then she is Mom, he said his parents were dead and as he is processing what he heard and is seeing there are 2 more shadows approaching them that apparently are not seen because the 2 of them are fixed on each other then you hear a voice.

"You really are a spook kid"! Knight announces himself allowing that to settle in.

The voice stuns Jack as he pushes his mom away for a moment to fix on where the voice is coming from as sees the 2 men approaching them closer and closer until the light of the moon reveals the face of the man that has been chasing him and his mother since he got out.

"What the fuck is going on"? Michael whispers to Tommy who are still knelt down in the shadows but in close proximity to hear the conversation but neither understanding what is transpiring so they continue to listen.

"No reason to alarmed, we come in peace and for prosperity Spook".

"Stop calling me that and we paid you"! Jack snaps back

"Yes, yes you did but there is more to be discussed as there is more at stake now than what was a simple hit".

"Hit"? Michael says to Tommy

"Again we paid you for all services you have done, why are you here following us"?

"Our being here is as much of interest to you as it is me and can simply be resolved and concluded shortly where we will then be on our merry way." Knight calmly states.

"What do you want"? The mom finally says.

"Lets me lay it out for you, you paid us 50 for the hit on your father as well as protection while you were inside DOC so were good there but where it gets interesting is that you mom received a large sum of money from the insurance policy which she can attest to would be fraudulent".

"I did not have anything to do with that and did not know that happened"! Camille said with her voice elevated.

"None the less your son did and you it is enough to alarm the insurance company and any investigation they do we will make sure leads back to the man Paso over there got killed in El Paso while you both were getting your identities changed".

The pause there for a moment made Michaels eyes widen as the puzzle pieces were falling into place and he did not want to stop listening to the conversation but he only knew one male Jessie in his life and that is what the mother called him, that same Jessie was sent to Department of corrections in Texas and had heard about the fathers passing from Ambers mother and the identities changed would explain the face but his eyes always looked familiar to him which is also why he came here. He came here for Amber. He turns to Tommy and says

"You gotta stop this that is Jessie the one who raped Amber in Texas"!

"What"? Tommy whispers

"I will explain but it all makes sense now he came back for Amber and whatever is going on there right now has to be illegal on every front you have enough to stop them and bring them in for questioning, he pauses then adds PLEASE"!

"Now we have the sale of the business of course the rust fund Spook there had waiting for him so as I see it to keep you both out of jail and the forfeit of all of the money you pay me 2 million in cash and that would conclude our business and you and I can part company friends". Knight continued.

Camille looks at Jack while Nathanial has stayed quiet the entire time and the silence seems to go on longer than it did but was only broken by the frightening words of 2 men approaching with one of them saying " Freeze, no body move"!

Everyone jumps at the unexpected company but the jolt caused each the man with Knight and Nathanial to both retrieve their weapons and aim towards the approaching figures.

"San Diego PD Get on the fucking ground". Tommy says with his revolver pointed towards the figures he is approaching to identify. " Get on the ground now"!

Everyone freezes Jack and Camille unsure of what to do but the others remained standing until Jack hears " You son of a bitch" Michael is saying standing next to the man holding the gun and when Jack sees him he is in even more shock than the fact there are 4 guns being pointed from every direction.

"Shut up kid" The man with the gun says.

"I knew something was not right about you from the beginning, you came back here for Amber didn't you Jessie"?

"Friend of yours Spook"? Knight asked still holding a gun towards the detective.

"Last time I am telling you, throw your weapons and get down on the ground"!

"Detective". Knight starts. " I have invested in a lot of travel and time to locate these 2 right here in front of me for reasons that are of financial gain which according to your friend over there next to you just got even better now as I see it there is more weapons here pointed at you then there are at us so the wise thing for you is to drop yours so we can conclude this business because I am not letting this go until I get what I came for"!

Tommy fires a shot at Knight which hit him right in the chest causing his muscle to return fire at the detective before he is able to get a second shot off. The bullet hits the officer blowing him back but continues to fire in their direction. Jack pushes his mom down and dives on top of her to prevent her from being hit. Nathanial fires first at the officer but in an instant turns to fire at the direction of Knight on the ground and the man standing still firing and he shoots him but not before also taking fire himself from the exchange.

Jack looks up and sees everyone on the ground but the only sounds he hears is from him Mom and the moans coming from Michael who was moving side to side obviously in pain. He has seconds to get his mom out of here before police are everywhere so he gets up and grabs the gun from knight who was closest to him and walks towards Michael. He sees that no one is breathing but Michael and knows he has no choice but to finish him so there are no loose ends. He stands over him with Michael looking up at him and as Michael says to him " You're not going to get away with this". Jack shoots him several times emptying the clip then returns the gun wiping the prints and re applying back to Knights hand he grabs his mothers hand and says

"We have to go right now, c'mon"!

They take one brief second to see the bodies laid out in the sand and flee as fast as they can.

Jack is running as fast as he can with his mom in tow holding her hand trying to keep up. He runs back up the way he came trying to find the access to lead him back to his car and desperately trying not to be seen and they can hear the sirens approaching so he knows their window is closing to get out of here. Lights are coming on on patios and windows and he can see people peering out of their windows but keeps moving as fast as he can.

They get to the street and stop for a moment to see if he can recall where he parked thinking he has to get the car out of here because if they investigate all registered vehicles in the area it could lead to questioning and if he saw or heard anything or why he was there. Out of breathe and getting his bearings he sees the road and the car.

"c'mon" He says taking his mothers hand and running again. They get to the car, get in, turn the ignition and drive from this place and cautiously yet as fast as they can going back to the area he is familiar with so he can get out of here and not get lost.

"What are we going to do"? His mother asked

"Get out of here first and get you back to the hotel". He said

"They are all dead Jessie, what if someone saw us, what am I going to tell Nelson"?

"Just breathe lets get back to the hotel and we can work it out they may be dead but we are alive so we have to work through this".

They get back to the hotel which takes only 10 minutes but his mom explains she does not want to be here. She was here with Nathanial and if they were followed to the beach they must have been watching my room " What if there is more of them"? she asked.

"Your right, lets get to another one that is safe". He said driving taking multiple looks into the rearview mirror looking for any sign of being followed which he does not see but was glad his mom thought twice about going back to her room because she was right there may have been more there waiting for their return.

Its mid week and out of season so no issue with getting a hotel room but he goes in alone to register and pays in cash this way if anyone did see the 2 of them fleeing there would not be 2 people checking into a room fitting that description. He gets the key and makes his way to the room with his mom.

"Jessie what are we going to do"?

"Fist stop calling me that please lets just focus and think this through". He said calmly.

"Who was that back there and how did he know who you were, what is happening"?

Jack is pacing inside of the room from the front door to the bathroom and back again and again and again. " Let me think"! He said

"Answer my question how did that person know who you are"? Then she starts to cry saying " They're all dead Jessie"!

"Stop calling me that please"! He fired.

"You need to get on a flight back to El Paso tonight"!

"Your coming with me, you cant stay here". She counters.

"Mom I am fine I moved in with someone a few cities away from here and will be fine. I cant just disappear she knows my name and that can lead to what happened tonight if I just don't go back. I need some time to break it off and can then come with you".

"You moved in with someone"?

"I met someone while I was here and we moved in together a few weeks ago, I cant just disappear but you can just go back to Nelson in El Paso tonight"!

"What do I tell him about Nathanial"?

"Tell him the truth he already knows everything. He knows about those guys that have followed us they were at the bar while you were having your procedure and I told him everything. He knows we paid them and he protected us by not telling them anything and now they're gone which took one of his men with them in the process. It's the truth"! He said.

"What about my hotel room and things. I was checked in under my name". She thought aloud and alarmed.

"It is fine your were in your name you were just visiting, what all did you bring with you"?

"Overnight bag and changes of clothes because I was not sure how long I would be here".

"When you get back to El Paso call the hotel and state you forgot your overnight bag and sound embarrassed but then ask for them to send it to El Paso". He replied.

"But Nathanial"?

"What about him"? Jack asked.

"When the police investigate they will somehow link him to El Paso and Nelson what if they find we are won the same plane and what if they link him to the hotel room then me"?

"Ok think, what of his is at the hotel did he check on any luggage"?

"No". She said thinking and trying to remember then added. " He carried on and had only one bag I am not sure what was in it but don't think anything that would identify him".

"So there is no link, you guys were on the same flight but so was about one hundred people he was not registered at the hotel, nothing at the hotel says he was there and you have no address other than the one you had in Italy so nothing to tie you to El Paso other than you boarding a flight from there but nothing that involves Nelson, only the guard." He stated trying to work it out in his own mind as he spoke.

"Get back to El Paso and tell Nelson what happened he is good at these things and it is his business he will know how to handle it, do you have your purse and Id"?

"Yes".

"Get it and lets go to the airport and get you out of here".

Driving there he is trying to think of what to tell Amber when he gets home and trying to keep his mom calm and just get her on that flight but he also thinks he should not be seen with her at the airport to prevent further complicating things so he gets to the departing curb to say good bye. She is visibly shaking and trembling as she gets out of the car and he approaches.

"Mom it's fine and will be fine just get back to Nelson and tell him the truth. I will be in touch with when I am able to join you but I cannot just leave right now it will only raise more unanswered questions that people will want to answer". He says hugging her.

She does not want to let go, she does not want to leave, she wants her son to come with her so they can be together but she agrees with him and just holds him tightly for a long duration.

"You come back to me, do you understand"! She says firmly fighting back her tears and trembling.

"I will, I promise I just have to take care of something here and then I am out of here and will be back with you and we can finally live the new life we both have created".

"You promise"? She asked

"I promise"!

53

S EVERAL police cars have arrived to invade to quiet neighborhood to investigate gun shots fired but to their horror there is multiple bodies on the beach by the guard tower and as they investigate the identification they find that one of them is their own. They fight to secure the crime scene and keep reporters at bay and with what little man power they have they also make the effort to canvas the home in view to understand what they heard or saw.

"4 people with guns one of them being Tommy Reynolds and unarmed kid all shot to death on this quiet beach. What the hell happened"? The lead detective asked his partner.

"I don't know, did Tommy say anything about what he was working on recently, we have to check his case files. Do you recognize any of the others? He asked.

The identification just further baffles them because they have people from Dallas to El Paso then Tommy and this kid Michael Janson both from the immediate area. The house to house canvas produces that they were all occupied with their evening routines but when they heard gun shots they all looked out their windows and that it was dark and hard to see what was happening. All the reports were similar and confirmed multiple shots fired then a pause and final few rounds but inconclusive with how many people were on the beach. Some of them thought they saw others running but were not certain if they were jogging and fled out of fear.

"Lets get these ID's into the system and find out what we can about the men from Texas and see if we can find a link as to why they were here and lets get all of over Tommy's case files and see if there is a link between that and these men". The Detective said to his partner.

Jack makes it back to his apartment and as he gets out he has to check one last time that there is no blood anywhere on him and to settle his rapid heart beat. He steadies his nerves and checks himself then unlocks the door where he finds Amber on the couch watching the news. She jumps up to greet him as he walks in.

"My mom called, there was multiple shootings and people are dead right down the road from my parents house". She says exasperated.

"What"? He says as he is now being led by the hand towards the tv where the news is covering the scene.

> *Multiple shots fired and 5 dead in Cardiff as the terror rips through the small town. Police have not released the identity of the victims but reports at this moment tell us that neighbors heard multiple gun shots and now several people are dead. We now take you to the scene for an update with reporter Sandy Huff.*

Jack is floored and Amber will not let go of his hand and his heart races and attempts to listen to the reporters every word over the volume he can hear of his heartbeat.

"Did they say if they know what happened"? He asked her.

"No or at least not that they are saying just that it happened around 7:30-8:00pm and they believe 5 to be dead". She answered than added " Right down the street from my parents house"!

"That is terrible". He stated still watching and listening to every moment of the broadcast.

The detectives would arrive at Mr. Jansons home later that evening to break the news that his son had been one of the victims in the Cardiff Beach murders. That news has never been nor will it ever be something you gets used to and was simply the hardest part of their roles. Allowing the man to grieve and breakdown they did have to ask him if he had any knowledge of why his son would have been there.

"I have no idea why he was there, he was working. He told me about 5pm that he had to take off but I did not ask where he was going". The man continued to sob trying to understand why his son was not coming home tonight or ever again.

"Do you know who he was with"? The detective asked

"I don't, I know I saw him at the bar with my long time friend Detective Tommy Reynolds right before he left. Tommy came in to eat".

"You know Tommy"?

"Yes, we wen to High School together and stayed friends long after. He has been coming to my place to eat since I bought it and he has known Michael since he was born. Why"?

The Detectives looked at each other knowing the next sentence was going to just add to the mans heartache and they hated that but needed to understand as much as they could about the events leading up to understand what happened so they could solve it for everyone.

"Tommy". The detective paused and gulped to breather before continuing " Tommy was one of the other men murdered at the beach Mr. Janson"!

"Oh my god, my son and my friend. What the hell happened"? He said beginning to cry and burying his head in his hands to get control of himself before standing and now angry but stopping ever few seconds to start to cry again but fighting with himself to gain control but he was having a very hard time. He bent his head down between his knees to breathe and came back up with his hands over his eyes and said " What the fuck happened out there"?

———————

Michaels mother and father would get no sleep that evening and spent the entire evening in silence only broken to console the other who was crying. He did not know what to do about the restaurant since it was mostly he and his son that ran it but he knew he could not go in. He called the Bartender and the Chef who each to his team was probably the longest veterans that he and Michael had worked with and knew how to open and close the place he just had to meet them to bring the keys to open and lock everything.

"I have to meet them at the restaurant to get them the keys". He told his wife " I will be right back I just have to do this".

"Cant you just close it for a few days"? She asked looking into his bloodshot burning eyes.

"People there depend on those hours to feed their families or pay for school and don't want to hurt that. Michael would not want that. Let me just get them the keys and I will be right back".

He left his home for the restaurant to meet the 2 people he would be entrusting for the next couple of days to run it for him till he was able to come back but he needed to be with his wife and there for her.

When he returned his wife was dressed and appeared to be ready to go somewhere so he asked" Are we going somewhere"?

"We have to tell, Nancy, Amber and John about Michael. Michael was Ambers best friend. We have to tell them and I have already called to arrange for them to meet us at Nancy's house". She said very stoic.

The drive over was quiet, silent and somber. Going to hurt family or even share your own devastation was not what he wanted to do but she was right Michael was also a very large part of Ambers family and needed to know. When they arrived they were greeted at the door by Dr Clevinger who invited them in with warm greetings that were immediately felt to be distant. He showed them to the kitchen table where Nancy was standing while Amber and a young man they did not know or recognize was seated. Dr Clevinger introduced Jack to the Jansons and stated this is Michaels mother and father. Jack took his seat returning Ambers hand in his hoping she could not feel the palms sweat or his heartbeat in the palm of his hands.

"Whats going on"? The Dr asked then offered if anyone would care for coffee which was declined. The Jansons took in the room both then proceeded to look at each other then down at the floor with no further eye contact.

"Is everything ok"? Nancy stated feeling the somber atmosphere " What is it"? Now alarmed.

"Michael and my longtime friend Tommy were some of the ones murdered down the street last night". He finally said sending the entire room in tears and emotional crisis.

Amber and Nancy both gasp. Nancy covers her mouth and Amber screams startling Mrs Janson which results in the 3 of them crying simultaneously turning to each of the men in the room to hold and console them. The only audible sounds in the room is crying and finally Michaels father also begin to cry as he holds his crying wife. The scene is horrible and through the tears Amber can be heard saying " Not Michael god why Michael"?

Nancy breaks from her husband and rushed to Amber who is still seated but turned towards Jack who is holding her and she leans down to hold her daughter with her right hand wrapped around her neck and the left rubbing up and down her back. " It's ok baby, I am so sorry" She says wanting to help her daughter not feel the pain she is feeling.

"I am so sorry"! The Dr. says then adds " Do they know anything about what happened"?

Jack is still caught between Nancy and Amber both crying but wants to desperately hear what they know. Tommy is my long time friend from back in High School he is a Detective and Michael has known him since he was born.

"We know Tommy came to the restaurant to eat but he always did that and it was not uncommon for Michael to visit with him which he did that night. That was in fact the last time I saw Michael. He told me he had to leave but did not say where he was going but I did see him at the bar with Tommy then when I checked back they both were gone". He finished.

Amber removed herself from the clasp of hands and arms that Jack and her mother provided to stand and walk towards both of Michaels parents. " I loved your son so much and he was my best friend. I am so terribly sorry"! She began to cry again and she went towards both of them to hug them each at the same time and heard Mrs Janson say through her tears " Amber he loved you too and was always looking out for you he just will be doing it from another place". The tears fell harder and the grasp tighter from all 3 of them.

Jack is just reeling and trying hard to keep his heart rate in check and his thoughts clear. Michael found out who he was but he was not sure if that was before the meeting on the beach or after because he was with a detective. If he did find out before then Amber would have known and she doesn't. If he had the detective with him then he suspected something that would be the only reason he was with the detective and they must have followed him to find out what his suspicions where. He was glad he finished him before he got a chance to talk to anyone because he did figure everything out just before his life ended but he felt certain that what he found out he had taken with him when he died.

"The questions was". He said in his own mind still watching the scene unfold before him was if the detective said anything to anyone about Michaels suspicions before he died and that is a big unanswered question he said to himself still hearing the tears filling the home.

The detectives working the case want to start with making sense of who the 3 men they did not know in the equation were. Speaking with the father they now know that Tommy was friends with the father and his son which somewhat explains why they were together but not why they were together that night and in that location. They take the names of the 3 men to the airport in search of flight records that could tell them a timeline of when they arrived and while that search is under way and awaiting call backs from the security detail and airport management they then canvas the hotels in the area where presumably they might have checked in to stay.

They start with ones closest to the location of the murders and get a hit on the first one where the name Frank Knight matching the

Dallas drivers license at the scene had a room and had been checked in for 3 days prior.

"We need to see that room". He said to the clerk who had notified the Front Desk Manager of the current situation unfolding.

"Is this about those murders on the beach"? The clerk asked.

"We don't know at the moment we are just following up on some leads and need to see that room".

The Front Desk or Hotel Manager arrives and produces the key for the room and escorts them to the location. He opens the door and leaves them to their investigation but stands at the door peering inside curiously. The detectives note the 2 beds but only one had appeared to be slept in and if the 2 men at the beach were there being murdered meant someone else was here but the luggage count is 2 matching the count of the 2 from Dallas beyond that nothing was in the room that was of help it simply was a hotel room. Nothing in the luggage that provided any clues.

The airport would call and notify them that there was no record of flights for the 2 identified Dallas men however they were able to locate a ticket that was checked in for Nathanial from El Paso which when at the hotel they had asked the agent to look his name up for a room but there was no record or match so this left them with a couple of options.

They first scanned the hotel parking lot for a vehicle with Texas plates they could match registered to one of the men from Dallas and that was no luck. They then continued to the remaining hotels in search of a Nathanial registered guest also with no luck but as they made their way back to the crime scene thinking if they drove there the vehicle may still be there they did radio in a records check, W-2's to find out where the 3 men from Texas worked to just try and make sense of why they were here in Cardiff and what they were doing on that beach that just happened to have Tommy and the kid at.

They did locate the car and awaited their search warrant while impounding it and made their way back to the precinct to look through Tommy's desk for anything that could help them but what they were not aware of yet was that in the pocket of Tommy's jacket was that notepad he wrote everything down on was a name that would change everything in their investigation. The name written in there was Jack Rodan which he wrote down when Michael asked him to look into Jack. Only a matter of time before they find that and it leads to Jack and why.

54

CAMILLE exits the plane to be greeted by Nelson who is incredibly happy to see her he does not even notice that Nathanial is not with her but after their embrace and kiss followed by the how much he missed her it finally occurred to him and he asked her. " Where is Nathanial"?

"Can we talk privately in the car"? She asked quietly and without a word but alarmed he motioned for her to begin towards the car and they say nothing until they do reach the car parked on the curb of the arriving flights. Once in the car she begins to tell him the entire story starting with how Nathanial approached her regarding the men from Dallas knowing where Jessie was and were going to kill him unless I met with them to pay more money.

"Wait". He interrupted and apologized but he wanted to clarify that Nathanial had spoken to or been speaking with the men looking for you"?

"He must have been or at least that is what he told me, he told me they were going to kill him if I did not meet with them"!

Nelson had to ponder that and really needed to make sense of how Nathanial even met those men and why he was speaking with them but returned to paying attention to her story of arriving there, checking in and Jessie had called and we agreed to meet on the beach not far from the hotel.

"Ok". He said acknowledging his keeping up and encouraging her to continue.

"We were on the beach waiting for Jessie to arrive and when he did is was in seconds that those men that have been following us appeared on the beach stating they were there for more money because they could tie us to a murder and insurance fraud and he wanted 2 million to let it go which I would have paid just to end this nightmare". She said rushing through the words to get to the point.

"Just breathe". Nelson said placing his hand on her knee.

"Then out of nowhere in the darkness came 2 other people and he had a gun saying he was a detective and for everyone to get on the ground but those men did not and pulled out their guns, Nathanial pulled out his gun. There was a kid there that was Jessies age and he was saying something that I cannot remember but was yelling at him and the detective kept telling everyone to get on the ground. There was a exchange of words from the large man following us and then shots just started going off everywhere.

"Oh God" Nelson said.

"Everyone was shot, everyone is dead except for Jessie and I who ran and I got on the first flight back I could and called you to arrange for you to meet me. I don't know what to do"!

"Ok, let me think. A detective was there and was shot and killed"? He asked

"He said he was a detective and had a gun".

"Did he say why he was there"? He asked.

"No" she had to think then answered again " No he just told everyone to get on the ground".

Nelson knew that it would be a matter of time until they linked Nathanial to working for him and would send people to visit him with an investigation but he also knew that if they did know anything about Camille that could not be tied to him because there is no evidence of her staying with him. He would tell the authorities the truth that Nathanial did security work for him at the bar and some work at his home but beyond that had no knowledge of why he was in California on that beach.

"What am I supposed to do"? She asked him scared.

"Lets get you home and cleaned up then we should get you somewhere safe and not from the men following you but from the authorities because I am sure their investigation will lead Nathanial back to me and at least come to visit and ask what he did for me and if I know why he was in California. If they come here we don't want them seeing you and asking more questions".

"I don't want to be away from you"! She said still scared and uncertain of what to do.

"I know and I don't want to be away from you either, it will only be till we feel their investigation with Nathanial is complete as least in regards to me".

"I am sorry Nelson, I was going to pay them and just wanted this to all be over".

"What about your son, why did he stay there and is he safe"?

"He said that he moved in with someone and that if he disappeared the night of the murders it would lead the investigation to him and it would be better to stay for a while until he was able to break up and would then come back here so we can be together and start over".

Nelson thought about that last sentence " starting over" and pondered that the way he had before with Camille while they were in bed. This life and danger it presents not only to himself but now to someone he cares for and wants a life with. Now there will be an investigation and what if it leads deeper into his bar business front, that could expose everything and lead to charges filed against him and he could go away to prison for the work he has been doing he thought to himself as Camille showered.

"Maybe it is time I started over too, all the way over". He said aloud looking at himself in the mirror and then repeated " Maybe its time I start over too"!

The funeral arrangements had been made and 2 of them planned. The Janson's, The Clevinger Family, Jack the entire community would attend each to mourn the loss of 2 of their own in what still was an unsolved and senseless act in their quiet and beautiful community. The eulogies were touching, heart felt and heart breaking to many including Amber who was now clinging desperately close to Jack in the wake of her loss of her closest friend Michael. She also found herself missing her parents during the times she was at the apartment and found herself calling her mother more and more.

She also returned to her therapy sessions to discuss the grief she was feeling and just not knowing the why of what happened and it almost consumed her to understand how her closest friend who she saw days earlier would be on the beach at night with her father's close friend who is a detective and 3 armed men in the night who all end up shooting each other. " It just did not make sense". She thought and it would become the core of her therapy discussions where the Dr encouraged her to carry Michaels memory close to her heart but heal and continue to move forward with the successful and happy path she had been on.

Jack had been playing the role of the consoler to Amber and helping her through her grief but he knew his window was closing because he just did not know what the detective knew or had said to anyone of if the active investigation can lead to him in any manner and if it does he would not have any way out and if they tie him to being at that beach scene then he goes back to a place worse than the DOC and that was not even an option for him. " Not a chance "! He said to himself.

If he was going to conclude his plan with The Clevinger Family he would have to do it quickly and then get the hell out of here. He could get back to El Paso and arrange for another ID to get him out of the country and this time for good but he had to admit that all the events since beginning this plan had somewhat taken a toll on him. He was happy to see Nancy grieve because she deserved it, she never once heard what he had to say at that trial and it was always just him being convicted, it was always him that was wrong and never Amber so taking her away felt good and payback for he being taken away from his mother.

"Amber has this coming to her" He thought to himself. " She was there that night and knows exactly what happened and she wanted that as badly as I did, she wanted me"! His inner thought elevating in anger and then he thought of Michael who testified at the trial but only to his account of the events which never led to anything other than it was his idea to go to the house and he was in another room the entire time. He was not sure how he felt about killing Michael only that had he not he would not be here right now so he did what he had to do but he was asking himself if what he was doing was worth it or should he just disappear.

He had to decide which one quickly, that he knew for certain. He could just feel it.

The detectives go through Tommy's desk and files with some potential but nothing that is Texas related so they follow up on the records and background search on the 3 men. They find that the 2 men from Dallas area had records for racketeering and some drug charges and had served time and had affiliations with White Supremist Groups and gangs in the area. The other man named Nathanial had no record and resided in El Paso where according to W-2's he had worked at a bar called Heavens Gate.

"Any of this mean anything to you"? One detective said to his partner.

"Nothing that makes sense so far". But called each local police departments in Dallas and El Paso to speak with their detectives in an effort to see if their office had any information that could help them understand more about why they were in Cardiff.

The Dallas region had known of these 2 men from their activities in the Dallas area. He offered they were known to frequent a bar where other Nazis went and they could stop in and question some people to see what they could find out as well as ask some certified informants they have if they knew of anything.

Th El Paso conversation was different. They had nothing on Nathanial but knew the bar commenting it was a popular place that also had some undesirables as the night went on. They too offered to go the bar and see what they could find out about Nathanial and why he may have been in Cardiff. The detectives had done what they could with the out of state leads and now went to investigate the impounded car that they had a search warrant to search. The combed it and dusted it which prints would come back with 3 prints that when run through their base identified the 2 they knew of but there was a 3rd which gave them some hope.

Nothing else was in the vehicle that led to anything. All they had at the moment was that 3rd print and a man that was not in the morgue which as far as they knew could mean that he was alive and knows exactly what happened. They needed to find this man. They pulled up his image from his mugshot and sent out all points bulletin through the California area, the airport, train and bus depots in the effort to locate him but they knew this person had a 4 day lead on them and could possibly have already fled the state back to Dallas so they got that information to their liaisons in The Dallas area that he was only wanted for question in the 5 homicides which included a Detective.

Randy Worthingtons picture was everywhere" *wanted for questioning*" and he was freaking out hiding everywhere he could because he did not want to be in that police station answering questions about his brothers and the possibility one of his brothers was responsible for killing a cop and a kid. He was relying on his brotherhood to hide him and help him get out of the state before the Dallas police found him.

Nelson had made arrangements to fly Camille to a house he had in South Florida where no one else would be aside from Arturo his head of security who escorted her there was told to stay with her until further notice. Sure as he had expected there were 2 detectives from El Paso who visited him at his home asking if they could speak to him about a man who worked for him. He greeted the men who had been let in by the maid and offered a seat in the living area.

Nelson entered the room with a look of uncertainty for the company but offered a " Hello" to the 2 men.

"Are you Nelson Pritchard"? The detective asked

"I am". He replied allowing the 2 detectives to then introduce themselves.

"Were here to ask you a few questions about an employee of yours named Nathanial Serrano, he does work for you correct"?

"Yes, he does security work for me at my bar here in El Paso, is everything alright"? He asked cautiously.

"Heavens Gate, that is your bar correct"?

"Yes".

"When you say security work what exactly is it that he does for you"?

"The Bar serves alcohol obviously and being in a gun friendly state and never knowing who is in your establishment he monitors patrons to ensure that no one is unruly or creates an environment that is frightening to our guest".

"So he is a bouncer of sorts"?

"Security I guess could be referred to as a bouncer but he keeps the place safe. That is his job".

"Do you know why he was in California recently"?

"No, I don't but may I ask if everything is alright, is he ok"? Nelson asked still cautious but appearing alarmed.

"Nathanial was murdered on a beach in Cardiff California along with 4 other men including a Detective and we want to know what he was doing there"! The detective said flatly.

Nelson was silent taking in the comment finally saying " Oh my god"! then silent again until another " Oh my god, he was murdered"!

"Yes, can you tell us anything about why he was there"?

"Let me think". And pauses looking down at the ground then back at each detective one at a time. " He took time off like all of my employees, I honestly have not asked where he went. He did good work, he was always there, on time you know, no one had issues with him and he has worked with me for close to 5 years. I cannot think of anything else that may help". He concluded.

"Do you mind if we ask around the bar to see if he talked with anyone there about his travel plans to California"? One detective asked.

"Of course not, anything we can do to help and please let me know if I can be of further assistance. He was a good man". He added as the detectives stood and made their way to the door to let themselves out.

The detectives get into their vehicle and turn the ignition in silence until one asked " Do you believe him, that he doesn't know anything"?

"I don't know, lets see what we find at the bar but at this moment we have no reason to believe or not believe him we just know the 1 dead guy at the beach worked for him".

They knew of Heavens Gate and knew where it was but had to admit there was not a lot of calls there for acts of violence so the security detail must be good at their job. They make their way in and take in the space which still has some volume for the middle of the afternoon. They know they stick out and that is okay and figure might as well start with the Bartender. They approach the bar and he approaches with the typical " Get you guys something to drink"?

"No". One says showing his badge offering we're with El Paso PD and need to find out what you know about your security guard Nathanial Serrano"?

"I know he works here and keeps people in line making my life easier and safer". He said.

"What do you know about his travel habits when he is not at work"?

"What"? He says making a face that does not understand the question.

"Let me ask it another way, do you know why he was in California recently"?

"I did not even know he was out of the state, I thought he was on his days off".

The conversation with the bartender goes nowhere as does any conversation they attempt to have with any other patrons. Typical they both know but they had to try and see if anyone here or his boss knew why he was in California but where they are is where they started which is nowhere so they call the detectives in California with an update on their minimal findings which were appreciated.

Now they hope and wait to hear something from Dallas that can shed some light.

Amber has clung to Jack significantly almost as a security blanket in the wake of the services that were held for Tommy and then Michael. The news attention has been relentless and the gathering at Michaels parents was morose at best. There were several condolences offered as well as food brought to the home but everyone in the home was in shock. Jack could not help but be riddled with anxiety wondering what if anything all of the officers knew about the scene at the beach, what led to it and if there was knowledge of who he was or being there.

The ride back to their apartment was also silent and empty until Amber finally spoke.

"You know another thing that is just crazy to me is wondering why Michael was there and the fact that the whole thing happened right down the street from my parents' house. You know that that was where we took our first walk and somewhere I have gone to get my head clear since we moved here, that is just crazy to me that it happened right there"!

Jack did not know what to say and could appreciate her curiosity regarding the location which also was alarming that she was pondering that thought.

"Did Michael ever say anything to you about what he might have been doing there or about him being in some trouble"? He asked her to return her attempt at conversation.

"No, I just saw him when I went to see him and tell him about us moving in together". She answered looking out the window at the passing scenery.

"Did he say anything that was odd"? Jack wanted to know because she had never mentioned before about that conversation with Michael and he really wanted to know everything that was discussed.

"No, he said he felt like it was soon for us to be moving in together but he also said that I looked happy and that made him smile, I cannot believe that was the last time I will ever get to see his face or talk to him". She stated and began to cry again which made Jack slow the car to pull over so he could turn to her and let her bury her head into his should to let out the tears she could not contain.

"I am here Amber and I understand what your feeling, I am right here". He said holding her trembling body.

"Thank you Jack, I don't know what I would do without you right now". Her tears subsiding from the comfort of his embrace and words.

"Lets get you home, comfortable and resting". He said looking her in the eyes then proceeding to put the car in drive and return to the highway heading home.

The 2 detectives working the Tommy and Michael case were renewed with motivation for solving following the services because nothing was more motivating than looking all the people that were behind in the eyes and seeing their pain. They had looked at the car, the hotel, did some research in the Texas markets on the 3 men they don't have a lead on the 3rd print yet and they went through Tommys files but still have nothing that is leading them anywhere.

"What have we not thought of"? One asked the other allowing for time to pass in thought to process the question and answer what it is they had in fact not yet thought of.

"Did we every go through his personal effects, like what he had with him that night at the beach"? the response finally came.

"No and as of now we have nothing to lose". He returned getting into the car to head back to the station where his items were bagged as evidence.

They make their way to the evidence locker and greet the clerk who appears to really be enjoying his day. They make their request and await the box which when it arrives is minimal but they both look down and see something that interest them and it is something each one of them carried with them. The little notebook to record notes which is picked up after the moment of each of them pausing to look at one another as a this could be something.

They go through the book studying every page and Tommy did not have the most legible writing but they did find a page that was legible and only had 2 words written on it. Jack Rodan.

"Jack Rodan". One says allowed to the other then adds " Does that ring a bell"?

"Not to me, lets look him up". He responds.

The search does not take long and does not seem to lead anywhere other than the question of why that name was in his little book?

They pull him up which shows no priors but they do have an address and decide to pay him a visit and see what they can find. They arrive at the apartment in which his license has him living and ring the doorbell. Jack opens the door to the 2 men which had looked like the several others he had seen at the funeral he and Amber had attended a day ago.

"Jack Rodan"? One of them asked

"Yes, may I help you"? he responded with his heart rate elevating.

The detectives introduce themselves and ask if they can come inside to ask him some questions at which time Jack is trying desperately to conceal his anxiety and gratitude that Amber had left an hour earlier to go to the gallery because he knew these men knew something

"Jack we are investigating the homicides that took place at the beach last week".

"Alright". He said then added " How can I help"?

"We found your name in the notebook of one of the victims, the Detective to be exact. Do you know why your name was in his notebook"?

Think, think, think he shouted in his own mind and had only seconds he needed to say something.

"I don't know, I had never met that detective mentioned in the papers and news".

"Where were you the night of the murders"? The other detective asked.

"Let me think, I had taken a drive to San Diego State University to look at the campus and look at courses to consider taking because I want to go back to school".

"What time would that have been"?

"I left here at 5pm, the drive up there about an hour and half walking around then the drive back". He said

"Did anyone see you there"?

"Several hundred people but like I said I just walked around to get a feel for the place and look at courses being offered. I even took home some information about the place when I was there so I could think about it, wait". He said standing to go and retrieve the papers he had collected but he had gone a different day and time to make sure he had some evidence that he had been there in the event Amber had asked about it so he was glad he had thought that part through. He offered them some course dates and times with prices as well as information about the College.

"You have never met the Detective Tommy Reynolds"?

"No sir". He said.

"Do you guys have an idea of what happened"? Jack asked as the detective began to hand back the papers Jack had produced.

"That is what we are working on, I am going to leave you my card in the event you can think of anything that may help with our investigation. Anything at all".

Jack accepted the card offering " I will help in any way I can and will call if I think of anything".

The detectives rose to their feet and made their way to the door and left. Jack closing the door behind them and had to exhale a great deal of breath that was almost resulting in a panic attack.

CONCLUSION

55

THE 3rd man with Knight wanted for questioning had made it back to Dallas and then into seclusion and hiding because he did not want any time in a police station answering murder questions or why they were there in California so fled he did knowing that several people in several states were looking for him.

Nathanials investigation came up as not much either and no lead as to why he was there on that beach but there is no other record to be confirmed that anyone else was on that beach because the eyewitness accounts simply stated that it was dark, hard to see and they thoughts they saw people running but were probably residents walking on the beach and ran back to their home when they heard the shots which left Camille safe awaiting updates from Nelson about when she and Arturo could return and what takes place when they do.

The detectives investigating had nothing other than the name of the young man they just visited but were not sure how he fit into the puzzle but wanted to stay with it because again and frankly they had nothing else.

Jack knew his window was closing and his walls were closing in on him but he as much as he knew that he also knew that if they had something or knew more they would have come to arrest him and not question him plus their questions were just here at the house and not somewhere he would not be coming back out of . So as his thoughts raced he was back to his fork or cross road of carrying out his plan to repay Amber or just leave and start all the way over for good now. He truly felt he could do both, he felt that he could leave a start all the way over once he achieved making sure his debt paid was her debt paid so that became his final decision. He would stay just long enough to settle his debt with Amber Clevinger.

That evening Jack awaited for Amber to come home from her day of whatever it was she had done. He had taken the time to cook dinner which he was still in the process of doing as she came in and to her surprise the house smelled wonderful.

"What is that"? She asked coming around the small corner of the apartment that lead towards the dining area and kitchen. As she approached the table was set and flowers were on the table.

"Italian" He announced. " Tonight we feast on Spaghetti and garlic bread love"! He added throwing the towel he was using over his shoulder.

"That smells amazing". She said coming towards him in the kitchen to hug and kiss him.

"And the table, what is all this for"? She asked.

"A feast for us to enjoy celebrating us, who we are.

Who we truly are Amber, you and I"!

She kisses him again and longer until she pulls back to reveal the smile on his face which she returned.

"Why don't you change into something comfortable, this is almost done and then I want to hear about your day". He said to her turning back around to return to completing his masterpiece.

Amber cleans up and changes still taking in the scent of the apartment and anticipating the meal because she was hungry and this gesture was just perfect and what she needed. It has not been the same since Michael was no longer in her life and she had not even painted. She just felt lost with the only good thing being Jack and moments like these. She was falling in love with him and found herself wondering how long it would be before one of them said that to the other followed by who would be the first to say it.

They each take their seats and discuss the events of the day with compliments and gratitude on the wonderful meal Jack had prepared. Concluding the meal now led to Amber starting the dishes and Jack coming up behind her and wrapping both of his arms around her waist pulling tightly yet gently while resting his head on her right shoulder tilted towards her neck where she could feel his breathing. It elevated as he went closer to kiss her neck while his hands still firmly wrapped around her waist.

She loves the moment, it is genuine, passionate and sexy making her stop the dishes she was doing to turn towards him and kiss him hard making his grip on her waist even a little tighter pushing her a step back slightly crashing into the sink counter where she stops kissing him for a moment to exhale but her eyes were closed until they opened again looking into his where he saw that same look he had had several years ago. She wanted him and her eyes closed again moving back to him to continue kissing him passionately.

Jack revels in the moment of what was ultimately their combined desire only his was slightly different, motivated even inspired. He slowly begins to take steps backwards guiding their coordinated steps leading her with him towards the living area. He gets her to the center still kissing her mouth and neck while now beginning to take each button at a time on her loose flannel she was wearing and she went to take his v neck shirt by sliding it up and over his head until removed.

They each begin on the top button of the pants each other were wearing but slowly as they were still lost in the exchange of each other's elevating breath through the kissing that once again had them both captivated. They each slide their pants down until they hit the floor and now much of the clothes fall all around them presenting what looked like their clothes having a party of their own.

He bends at his knees to bring her to the ground with him.

This moment was precisely as it had been years before. It was precise in every manner with the exception of the location and their ages. They lay next to each other laced up with each others limbs tying them closely together. Stopping only for one moment to do one thing.

Jack picks up the remote for the CD player and aims it at the CD player on the entertainment center in the living room.

"Music, great idea"! She says in a low moaning voice.

"I think so". He adds then hit the play button and continues to kiss he again.

The piano introduction,,,,,,, the song is loud in volume. She stops kissing him in the moment of the piano introduction taking only that long to understand what song this is.

"Just a small town girl, living in a lonely world, she took the midnight train going anywhere"!

Jack looks at her while on top of her waiting once again for another click like he had when he was at The Clevinger home and they were announcing they were moving in together. Wait for it, here comes the click.

"Why did you play this song". She asked looking distressed.

Jack smiles at her seeing her distress, drinking her distress and says. " Its our song"!

"This is not our song Jack, I hate this song please stop it"! She said annoyed

"This is our song"! He said again but his smile now menacing and Amber trying to understand what is happening.

"This is Jessie and Ambers song"! Jack proclaimed.

"How the fuck do you know that name and I am not kidding change this song now"!

"The only thing changing Amber is your life right here and right now just like you changed mine 6 years ago"! He said to her looking her right in the eyes.

"You have not figured it out yet". He said making an ahhhh sound after.

"How do you know that name Jessie and why are you playing this song"?

"Because I am Jessie Amber and I am playing our song right

where we were doing right what we were doing and listing to that song before you had my life and families life ruined"!

Amber face freezes, she says nothing but looks into his eyes until she sees them again. Why hadn't she seen them before. She knew those eyes. They were his eyes!

"How"? She says eyes widened. " How is that possible"!

There is it, the click and this one even more priceless than the one with her family he thought looking into her frightened and widened stare.

"You know who I am now, you recognize me now don't you"? His menacing smile present again.

"You,,,,,,,he,,,,,,,,how"? She stumbles through her words as her mind raced and the song still played loud and feeling everything in her world crashing.

"I had some work done when I finished my sentence because I wanted to come for you Amber. I still had work to do and was not going to just let you get away with what you and your family did".

"You raped me Jessie"! Starting to make an effort to free herself of his grip

"No,no,no Amber that is not how I remember it at all but if I had done the time for the crime I might as well complete the act". He said looking down on her below him and watching her start to cry.

"You and your family ripped mine apart and it is only fair that I repay you all for that so being here, meeting you and us moving in was how I would take you away from your mother and father knowing how much that would hurt her was a start but Michael". He said pausing before Ambers crying subsided enough for her to ask him.

"What about Michael"?

"Oh, you still think that was an accident". He said slowly

"What did you do to Michael"?

"Well, lets say that I am not certain how all of those bodies ended up there being shot but I am quite certain of how your dearest friend and relative did"!

Her body tightens from the core of her stomach and her cries are heart wrenching creating a convulsion throughout her body.

"Its alright Amber, my work is almost done here and you will be left with the shattered life you deserve". He said quitter and leaning down to kiss her trembling neck.

The thought of everything that he has said filled her body with compelling fear but hearing that he was the source of Michaels death filled her with a strength she was not aware as the anger was

The thought of everything that he has said filled her body with compelling fear but hearing that he was the source of Michaels death filled her with a strength she was not aware as the anger was beyond her especially as the face of this monster was coming closer to her to do whatever it was he had in his sick mind.

His hands were firmly around her wrist she knew that from a natural reaction to wipe away the tears streaming down her face and each attempt negated by his grip so all she had was her legs which as he began to position them to open she had freed one of them being her right in a flurry he was not expecting and with a strength he too was not aware that she had.

She kicked, kicked and whaled with every part of her lower body until she was successful in connecting one of the kicks to his groin causing him to release his grip enough to where she had a chance at freeing the upper body so she used the one hand she was able to free to scratch deep and hard at the face while he moaned in pain from the groin kick. This allowed her to kick again propelling him back and into the entertainment center which now freed her to stand and run.

As she stood her mind was panicked with each fear but her body had the adrenaline and it confused to run and fight at the same time. She could not find the front door even though she was in the same room as it were located so she grabbed the first hard object that she could from the area she was in which was an end table decorative piece of 3 dolphins that appeared to be jumping out of the water as they swam and the bottom was all wood with jagged pieces and proceeded to hit him repeatedly in the face and head creating divots in the skin that became blood pooled.

She stopped and ran to the kitchen where the phone was to call

911 where she grabbed one of the large knives from the countertop butcher block.

"911 what's your emergency"?

"There is a man in my apartment trying to kill me, his name was Jessie Harrell but is now Jack Rodan". She said holding the phone and the knife looking around the corner at him starting to get to his feet.

"I am at Horizons apartments in Solana Beach in apartment 116". She said throwing the phone onto the counter with the operator still on the line and ran into the living area with the knife to plunge it into the back of Jack as he was beginning to stand bringing him crashing into the sliding patio door and vertical blinds.

911 had dispatched the call out for officers to arrive at the scene for an attempted homicide and gave the names that were provided by phone and the address of the scene.

The detectives covering the homicides heard the call and knew the apartments as they were just there but it was the name that came through that needed to get them to that scene right away.

Amber ran back to the kitchen to retrieve another knife and ran back to the living area where Jack had once again managed to get to his feet now demonstrating the blood from his face running down in multiple areas as well as his face showing pain from the inflicted knife that was still lodged in his back but he with all of this began to laugh.

"hahahahahaha" Then he let out a cough stopping the laughing followed by a grunt then proceeded to laugh some more.

"You will never be the same Amber, you will never forget me all of this and Michael you will have to try much harder to speak with now". He said beginning to laugh again.

Her adrenaline kicked in again at the thought that this individual before her took someone so close to her and screamed as she ran towards him with the knife in an striking position held in her right hand above her shoulder and as it came closer to impact he grabbed her wrist to slow and stop the blow from insertion but the struggle was not over because as she fought to keep control of the knife his strength was greater so she again used her lower body and kneed him again in the groin allowing him to loosen his grip on the knife when he buckled at the knees. Amber plunged the knife into his back but this time pulled it back out and kept holding in front of her taking steps back

The detectives were pulling into the complex and knew the apartment ripping through the area until they and others close behind were heading up to the door. They knew there was only one way out so they rushed to the door with weapons drawn

Jack in pain but also filled with anger stood again upright and as he did simply went towards her forcefully and Amber once again went at him with the knife but this time he still stopped it by grabbing her wrist but spun her around till her back feel into his chest and now the knife was still in her hand but guided by his strength towards her neck as she screamed trying to fight him off.

The door kicks open and one detective with weapon drawn sees the act of an unidentified young woman being held at knifepoint but the same young man he spoke to just a day ago only now his face is bloody. Weapon aimed and his partner right behind him also with weapon right on him all they say is " Drop the knife Jack, there is no way out of here but through us and that is not happening"!

"His name is Jessie Harrell"! She shouts as he is trying to cover her mouth while still holding the knife to her throat but he is losing blood from how fast his heart is pumping and he is getting cold.

"Drop the knife whatever your name is"!

"You said there was only one way out of here but through you and I think your wrong". He said slowly

"What does that mean Jack"? One detective asked while the other whispers " I got him" meaning he had a shot on him and could take him out.

"It means I am going to change my plan and take this one with me where I am going". Jack said holding the knife close.

"NO Jack were not going to let that happen".

"No"? Jack responded back to the detective.

"NO"! and the detective fired a shot so loud it ripped through the apartment and could be heard from a great distance but the bullet hit its intended target right in the forehead first spraying Amber with blood and matter and second immobilizing Jack immediately until his body fell backwards and limp to the ground taking her with him.

Amber starts to scream still in his embrace as both detectives rush forward first to hold the hand of the hand of the weapon removing it as the other picks her up to hold and console her.

56

THE room and apartment is a crime scene so there is minimal people present as they escort Amber downstairs to be looked at by emergency personnel and transported if necessary but they do want some time with her right away to understand what has happened so they stay right with keeping her free of intrusive neighbors and some media vans that have miraculously arrived to interview the witness testimony all of which is being held back by police until Amber is in the ambulance.

"I want to see my parents please". She said sobbing

"Everything is alright and over lets get you to emergency to check on you short ride and we will have you there quickly". The ERT technician said to her.

"Amber were calling your parents now and they will meet you at the hospital". One detective that shot Jack said.

"I am riding with you there so you are safe". Said the one who first entered the apartment and tried to get him to drop the knife.

There in her hospital bed once her vitals had been checked, an iv issued and her parents at her side with both detectives present she began to tell her tale of Jessie Harrell and who the man they shot she believes to be Jessie Harrel but had somehow become Jack Rodan.

She told them everything that transpired in Arlington with some clarification and interruption from her mother but for the first time it was minimal and she perhaps felt that her daughter needed to let this out and she herself even needed to understand what has happened.

She had never heard from him again once he was sentenced and then they moved to California, her therapy, her painting until one day several years later which must have been when he finally got out.

"We have not run his prints yet nor have we determined his identity to be anything other than Jack Rodan but were working on the prints now to solidify that". One detective interrupted to offer.

"Its him" She said then added " I Can't believe I did not recognize him, his voice, his eyes how did I not see that it was him"? She asked everyone in the room frustrated and upset with herself.

"He was the one who found me, he must have been waiting and looking for the right opportunity and then one day at the house I was painting he just showed up and I was dumb enough to fall for it and go walking off with him, moving in with him". Now angry

"He said that he killed Michael on the beach that night". She added almost jumping out of the bed and had to be consoled and massaged back into a comfortable state.

"He said he killed one of the people on that beach, he was there". The detective asked.

"Jessie told me that he killed my cousin and best friend Michael that night, Michael did not like Jack and I moving in so quickly". She said.

"Did Michael know detective Tommy Reynolds as far as either of you know"? He asked everyone in the room. There was silence for the moment as everyone looked at one another until.

"I am sure if you speak with his parents they can confirm if he did but Michael worked with his dad at their family owned restaurant and bar " The Wedge" on the highway and everybody went there". Dr. Clevinger added.

"We know the place and we too have been there even with Tommy who did seem to have plenty of people come to the table to say hi and offer things. The detective responded.

Amber was kept in the hospital with security presence due to the fact there were now 5 deceased and 1 still missing and did not want to take any chances at least until they concluded a few things that would solve and close the case.

The prints did come back as Jessie Harrell and they pulled his file to reveal what he had looked like during his incarceration with DOC in Texas.

"Hell of a plastic surgery job"! one detective said to the other.

"So we now know it was him, we know he was convicted of rape and did his sentence in Texas which is also where the other 3 bodies were from Dallas and El Paso, right"? He questioned.

"Right". His partner answered seeing where it went.

Then there was silence until " What's your point"? was asked.

"He comes back her to do some revenge plot on the girl Amber. He has ties to Texas more so the Arlington area because that is closer to Dallas but we don't know why those men from those areas were on that beach, do we"? He asked his partner.

"We also know that Tommy did know Michaels father and Michael himself and that Michael did not like that Jack Rodan was moving in with his cousin so it is safe to presume that Michael got Tommy to check out Jack leading to his name in the notebook and Tommy found something and brought Michael along with him to check it out leading those 2 to the beach where everyone ends up dead and a confession by the killer to Amber that he killed her cousin, you buying this"?

"What do we know about the parents of the Jessie Harrel kid"? He asked staying with the Texas theme.

"Ah I have that right here. The dad is deceased worked a lot of hours and drove himself of a cliff while the mother sold the business, collected the insurance money and has never been heard from since. How do you like that"? He asked slamming the file onto the desk.

"Was it ever investigated"? He asked looking at the file

"Nope"!

"Get with our Dallas team and tell them everything we know and lets open this back up there seems to be more here with this family that what is on the surface and it may help tie up the murders that took place here that we cannot connect.

The detectives meet with The Clevinger Family back at their home to discuss the current state of the investigation and all that they do know which just is chilling to all 3 of them. The web and deception present that followed them all the way to California just does not feel good at all. They sit on the couch engrossed in the details all holding hands listening to every word.

"We just wanted to update you all on the investigation and let you know you're safe Amber. We will keep patrol cars in the area and you will have someone keeping an eye on you while we connect all the dots beyond what we know". The detective said with sincerity.

"Thank you". They all said almost simultaneously.

The detectives stand and make their way to the exit of The Clevinger home and as they do they offer one more re assurance pointing out to the family the parked car that will be there to keep an eye on the home. They close the door and all embrace in a family hug with the Dr telling them everything is going to be alright. " Its all over"! he adds.

57

CAMILLE is in the living room of the South Florida home of Nathan Prichard and where he had sent her and Arturo to be safe while the police investigate Nathanial just as a pre caution. She has been watching the news religiously looking for any updates she can find on the investigation of the incident that took place on the beach 3,000 miles away. It has been days and because it is not local news there has been nothing until one day on Good Morning America they unfold a story that was chillingly familiar to her.

"A bizarre story with twist and no answers has unfolded in a sleepy Southern California town"

Camille is not certain it is the story she has been looking for but her heart stops and her attention is on nothing but the scene and words before her on the screen as she turns it up.

"A multiple homicide case on the beach of Cardiff California involving a police detective takes another bizarre turn as a survivor of that shoot out is shot by police in an attempted murder of a young woman in the apartment they shared. The story turns even further when that individual who has been identified as first Jack Rodan who admitted to killing one of the victims at that beach murder scene but the strangest twist is that the man identified as

Jack Rodan is actually a convicted rapist who had changed his identity at some point following his release ".

Camille was already not breathing and her heart had felt like it stopped but the voice saying that her son had been shot and killed by police left her as empty as she has ever felt in her life and she began to silently cry until the silence was broken by the overwhelming amount of pain in her heart surfacing bringing her to her knees and screaming as she was crying. Arturo rushes into the room to see her on the ground and shaking terribly while crying incredibly hard.

"What is it"? He asked kneeling next to her and putting his hand on her shoulder.

"Jessie, They killed Jessie my son"! She said to him crying harder and her words were now inaudible but her trembling worsened. Arturo needed to understand more but he knew the only way that he would be able to ask questions would be to calm her down and let her get this out. He was trying to listen to the news story she was watching to understand what they knew and what was happening, but it was all on location in California as a news reporter was speaking to the events of the week that led to the death of a young man that was connected to multiple homicides the week earlier and they then sent it back to the studio.

He held Camille tightly attempting to ask her some questions until he finally settled on that they need to contact Nathan thinking that would help ease her crying but it did not she just kept repeating the same phrase between hard and soft crying.

"My son is gone"! " Oh God my son is gone"!

It had taken an hour but Arturo had gotten Camille from the frantic state to a comatose not even present state so he calls Nelson at his home where he is told that Nelson is at the bar Havens Gate where he then places that call identifying himself and asking to get him immediately.

"Arturo"? Nelson answers the call at Heavens Gate

"Sir, I am terribly sorry to trouble you but there has been some water damage here at the house and feel you should come to inspect for yourself and how you wish to handle". He says not aware if for any reason there is someone listening on the line.

"Understood, I will book a flight as soon as I can. Is there anything I can do now to assist"? He asked Arturo.

"No sir I will handle until your arrival but just wanted you to be aware".

"Thank you Arturo, I will see you shortly". Nelson concluded.

He hangs up and contacts the airport to book a flight but needs to go home first to pack a bag and it will give him a chance to understand if he is being tailed by anyone as a result of that investigation or any other matter he is not aware of but he knew that water damage meant he needed to get to South Florida right away.

He was driven from the bar home with no visible signs of a specific car following him and the same for his route to the airport. He watched everything, every turn and everyone around him all the way till he boarded the flight.

His flight was a little over 2 hours, a direct flight where he then took a cab from the airport to his address also watching as carefully as he could for anyone following him but without looking suspicious. He arrives to be greeted by Arturo as he entered the home.

"What is it"? He asked

"Her son was shot and killed by police in California, I gave her a sedative to help her sleep but she knows you are coming, the police knew about his past and identity change". He answered.

"Where is she"? Nelson asked in a sharp tone.

"In the master".

Nelson proceeded past Arturo without another word and Arturo stayed to allow them privacy.

"Camille". He said softly entering the room and getting closer to the bed to sit on it next to her and leans down to kiss her.

'Im here Camille".

"There is no Camille, I am Kelly and always will be Nelson and now my son and my husband are dead".

He gets on one knee at the foot of the bed to be close to her face as she laid sideways close to the edge. He kisses her again on her forehead and then on her head and says-

"There are no words for the loss of your son and I am here for you, to help you and will help you through this Camille and if they know about your sons past and that he had his identity changed then they will find out that Kelly no longer exist. You need to be Camille now more than ever, I need Camille, Camille I am in love with"!

She started to cry at the thought that in the same day she has lost her son and a man she has been falling in love with tells her that he loves her.

"You tell me you love me today, now"? She says agitated.

"I have been in love with you and today yes because today you are suffering more than anyone I have ever seen and I know your heart and you do not deserve to feel that and I want to take that away from you, help you live again and live life with that love in your heart and your soul and I know I can do that". He says looking right into her watery eyes.

"Nelson my son is dead, he was the last thing of me there was and I do not want to be without my son"!

"You will never be without your son, he will always live within you and your memory and we together will always keep that alive but what he has done and the decisions that he made had led him to that destiny and I do not And will not let that destroy you too"! He said now bringing her close to him and burying her in his embrace and could feel her trembling crying which made him grasp tighter.

"I am not letting go"! He said just allowing her to cry until she could no more.

Nelson would climb into the bed and wrap himself around her and hold her for a couple hours allowing her to drift back off to sleep and then re awaken still in his embrace and grateful he had come, stayed with her and was still with her. She did love this man.

While Nelson laid there with her, holding her and feeling not only her breath but her mournful and exhausted energy of her life he had some revelations of his own life and how their life together could be better than it has been. He was at peace but excited and awaited for her to wake, he did not move at all until she was ready to return to him which would be several hours even watching the sun fade from the shades to a darkness that had now fallen on their room.

The room was still and dark with the only light in the room coming from beneath and around the entrance from the exterior hall where Arturo had turned on the light. Arturo never disturbed them and he too silently awaited their return. Her body stirred and then clinched his unsure of where she was and who was there.

"Its ok". He said. Her head laid back down to its previous location.

"Are you awake"? He asked.

"Yes". Was all she said.

"I have something to share with you and want you to listen to me, can you do that"? He asked still holding her motionless body.

"Yes". Was all she said again.

"I do love you Kelly and my life has been better with you in it than it was without you in it. I have laid here with you this entire time thinking that all of this life that has been my life is over".

"What do you mean"? She interrupted and sitting up to realize the complete darkness that was the room.

"Do you mind if I turn on the light"? He asked with her no longer laying on him.

"No, what do you mean Nelson"?

"Cover your eyes". He said and reached for the end table light to provide some clarity to the moment that would match his thoughts.

"I have done what I do for many years and for people I don't care for and I run a bar again for people I don't care for and all I have is my work which again for a little while now I have not cared for. I don't like the direction my life has taken and where it has led me other than to you".

"What are you saying Nelson"? She interrupted again.

"I am saying I want to give all of this up. I want to give up the bar, my practice, the security detail, the potential of getting caught and going to prison. I want to give up people getting shot and killed and all the pain associated with that and live a life I love again with someone I love"

He was now standing and looking at her in the bed and the confused look on her face that was also still mired with exhaustion and suffering.

"I don't want to see you like this and like this has been part of my business Kelly, I want to sell the bar, sell the homes. I have money put away and with the gross of those 3 properties we would have enough to start over somewhere else just you and I with nothing but us and I don't care if I bag groceries at a local market, I just want to come home to you with no more pain and our love be enough and all that matters"!

She was awake and she understood what he is saying and she did feel the same way.

"Do you mean that Nelson, do you really mean that"? She asked starting to cry again.

"Do you feel the same way"? He asked her.

"Yes"! And he tears started flowing harder and her voice broke.

"Then no more tears, not any more, no more of this and what has been this is going to be about us and what will be and I promise you it will be better than any life you had ever lived". He announced coming to her to hold her tightly and she in turn grabbed him equally as hard.

"What about Jessie"? She asked.

"That is a little complicated and at the moment the only thing linking all us together which is being closely watched because they will start to look for you so you going to attend any funeral is out of the question".

"Nelson, he is my son". She said

"I know that but if they find you they will link you to those beach homicides and even possibly your deceased husband you have to stay all the way gone but I will arrange an anonymous donation for the funeral expenses and stone for your son and give you my word we will find a way to visit that site and every day you can tell me about him all that you wish to keep his soul alive in your heart". He paused and she still said nothing.

"I have a way out of all of this and I mean out of it for a new life together, do you love me"?

"I do Nelson and I do want that life with you. I have wanted that life since I was a little girl and thought that was the case when I married James". She said.

"I am not James Kelly and all I see is that little girl again that will finally get her wish". He said

"You promise"? She asked

James did promise her and he kept his promise. He returned to Texas and immediately started to contact a lot of his powerful friends to set in motion the sale of his business, home in Texas and his home in South Florida. He spoke to his Cayman bank and began to discuss the closing of the account as he will be financing his new life and he even included severance packages for all of the people he employed at his Texas home and the bar.

He was fine with disappearing, he had never been tried or even questioned regarding anything he had done for his clients and as far as he knew the government thought he was a retired plastic surgeon that now owned a successful bar that he has now sold for a sizeable profit and the homes were not far behind. Anyone that came looking for him were more than welcome because he will just be like everybody else living his life financed by great investments from his past.

By the time he got back to South Florida it was only to personally hand Arturo his severance gift, offer his gratitude for his services wishing his friend well and get Camille who will now finally be able to say goodbye to Kelly for good.

"Well I'm here and you here and there is nothing left to do but decide where you want to go" He said greeting her.

"Surprise me"! She returned.

"Well I can bag groceries just about anywhere so we have that going for us". He said kissing her and seeing her smile.

"But we also have about 20 million in the bank too so maybe it can be part time". He added and that not only made her smile but laugh out loud and hard until he stopped her laughing by kissing her and kissing her like she was the greatest thing that ever happened to him.

"One surprise coming up". He said taking her hand and leading her to the car where the 2 of them would wave goodbye to Arturo and South Florida for the last time. Their destination would be their secret and together Nelson continued to keep his promise of fulfilling that little girls Kelly's dream.

58

AMBER returned to living with her parents for the time being but was convinced that she did want to live on her own and set in motion to achieve that goal of standing on her own 2 feet. She also returned to therapy and was seeing the benefit in discussing that as a process of healing the wounds that were there before and now reopened but to a larger degree .

Amber made frequent visits to the cemetery where Michael had been laid to rest to speak to him about all of her goals that she felt were guiding her to a new life, her life. She loved going to see him and for some reason those visits and talks were just as intimate as they always had been even if they were one voice but she knew in her heart he was always there and always listening to her and even perhaps the angel that was guiding the decisions she was making that would lead her to her destiny and new chapters.

Amber also continued to go to The Caufield Studio where her 2 closest friends were always there also as angels to guide, motivate, coach and counsel her on her path towards her new chapters. Her latest chapter or unveiling to her 2 best friends was different than the others. Each painting that Amber had done and shown was so well received and its message personal which is what drew so much attention to her work now that her story had become so notarized on a global sense, but Lillian and Jayne were very taken back and speechless at this intimate portrait that seem to once again captivate the intimacy of senses and say so much with no words.

Amber unveiled a large canvas that was a portrait of innocence and horror. It was a portrait of one half of the face being what Jessie had looked like and the 2nd half of the face was who Jack Rodan had become. Each face and eye looking at its audience with all knowing the sinister events of the face before them.

"What do you think"? Amber asked both of them.

"Is that what or who I think it is"? Lillian asked.

"It is". She said.

"This is the individual who has helped me become who I am, both of them". She said proudly

"I call it Face Value which represents no matter what you see on the outside it can be a contrast of both light and darkness of what is within". She said now almost prophetically looking at both of them one at a time waiting for a response. The room was quiet for what felt like much longer than it had been.

"Well"? Amber finally asked again.

"Not only are you a beautiful girl Amber, not only are you a beautiful soul but you are also a very gifted voice that has the ability to bring that message visually as well as with word or by not saying a thing but you have truly become a talent with the brush"! Lillian finally said moving closer to her leaving Jayne a step behind starting to cry and then rushing forward to catch up with Lillian so the 2 of them could engulf her in a hug.

"I love it"! Jayne shouts while they are still in the embrace.

Ambers parents and the world would come to love the piece as well. Her story gained national attention and of course her paintings were as much a part of the story as they represented healing through tragedy which all on its own took on a life of its own for many people in the world looking to her as a messenger. She would write a book regarding the experience of life in Texas and California and the role that Jessie and Jack would play and even her art would make its way into the book as representatives of those periods and of course her most prominent piece entitled Face Value would be the cover and the title of the book she would write.

Amber had found the better part of herself and was stronger than she had ever been before now truly feeling her own balanced, grounded and peaceful state convicted and passionate about the work she was doing to help others find that same place in themselves through tragedy. She had become a success but more than anything she had become happy again, found love again and lived the life she too had always dreamed of.

THE END ...

Printed in the United States
By Bookmasters